STEAL

THE

NIGHT

Other Books by Lexi Blake

ROMANTIC SUSPENSE

Masters and Mercenaries
The Dom Who Loved Me
The Men With The Golden Cuffs
A Dom is Forever
On Her Master's Secret Service
Sanctum: A Masters and Mercenaries Novella
Love and Let Die
Unconditional: A Masters and Mercenaries Novella
Dungeon Royale
Dungeon Games: A Masters and Mercenaries Novella
A View to a Thrill
Cherished: A Masters and Mercenaries Novella
You Only Love Twice
Luscious: Masters and Mercenaries~Topped
Adored: A Masters and Mercenaries Novella
Master No
Just One Taste: Masters and Mercenaries~Topped 2
From Sanctum with Love
Devoted: A Masters and Mercenaries Novella
Dominance Never Dies
Submission is Not Enough
Master Bits and Mercenary Bites~The Secret Recipes of Topped
Perfectly Paired: Masters and Mercenaries~Topped 3
For His Eyes Only
Arranged: A Masters and Mercenaries Novella
Love Another Day
At Your Service: Masters and Mercenaries~Topped 4
Master Bits and Mercenary Bites~Girls Night
Nobody Does It Better
Close Cover
Protected: A Masters and Mercenaries Novella
Enchanted: A Masters and Mercenaries Novella
Charmed: A Masters and Mercenaries Novella
Taggart Family Values
Treasured: A Masters and Mercenaries Novella
Delighted: A Masters and Mercenaries Novella
Tempted: A Masters and Mercenaries Novella

Masters and Mercenaries: The Forgotten
Lost Hearts (Memento Mori)
Lost and Found
Lost in You
Long Lost
No Love Lost

Masters and Mercenaries: Reloaded
Submission Impossible
The Dom Identity
The Man from Sanctum
No Time to Lie
The Dom Who Came in from the Cold

Masters and Mercenaries: New Recruits
Love the Way You Spy
Live, Love, Spy
Sweet Little Spies
The Bodyguard and the Bombshell: A Masters and Mercenaries New
Recruits Novella
No More Spies
Spy With Me
Love and Let Spy, Coming March 24, 2026

Butterfly Bayou
Butterfly Bayou
Bayou Baby
Bayou Dreaming
Bayou Beauty
Bayou Sweetheart
Bayou Beloved

Park Avenue Promise
Start Us Up
My Royal Showmance
Built to Last

Lawless
Ruthless
Satisfaction
Revenge

STEAL

THE

NIGHT

A THIEVES NOVEL

LEXI BLAKE

NEW YORK TIMES BESTSELLING AUTHOR

Steal the Night
Thieves, Book 5
Lexi Blake

Published by DLZ Entertainment, LLC
Copyright 2014 DLZ Entertainment, LLC
Edited by Chloe Vale and Kasi Alexander
ISBN: 978-1-937608-32-3

This is a work of fiction. Names, places, characters and incidents are the product of the author's imagination and are fictitious. Any resemblance to actual persons, living or dead, events or establishments is solely coincidental.

Acknowledgments

Steal the Night marks the end of a journey for me—and the beginning of a new one. When I finished this book, I realized I had to stop pretending that writing was just a hobby. I had to find the courage to try to make it a career. And it does take courage. It's hard to put our words out there for all to judge, but the ones who find it will also find that there is a beauty and pride that comes from trying to follow your dreams. For all you writers out there—keep trying, keep hoping, keep dreaming.

A deep and special thanks for the people who believed in this series from the beginning, without whom these books might not have come out from under my bed—to my agent, the amazing Merrilee Heifetz, who signed me when she read Steal the Light, to Liz Berry, my friend and champion to authors everywhere, to Kim Guidroz who was there from the moment I had the idea, and to my husband who inspired it.

Thanks to my beta readers, Stormy Pate and Riane Holt, and to the bloggers who have helped get the word out.

This book is dedicated to my daughter whose birth began what I call my second life. This book is for my Zoey.

CHAPTER ONE

Neil howled his pain to the world, the sound chilling my soul. I turned, my weapon in hand. *Too far.* The distance between us was too great. There was no way I would ever be able to get to him in time. I stood on the blood-stained floor, looking at my trusted friend, and there was nothing I could do to save him. He would fall beneath the strange creature, and I would never see him again. It was sad because our adventures felt as though they had just begun.

If only we hadn't gone into the dungeon. We'd been too trusting. We should never have listened to the wizard. He'd promised us great treasure if we only managed to get through the dreaded dungeons of Darkmoore Keep. We ignored all the signs that foretold our doom. The five of us had laughed mightily at the old woman who pleaded with us not to continue on. She warned us, but we were young and arrogant. That treasure could make our reputations and our fortunes would be set. We'd been so sure of our strength. It was going to cost us now.

At least one of us would fall.

The enormous creature screamed his rage and Neil tried valiantly to raise his sword and vanquish the foul beast. Beside me I felt Dev attempt a spell. He called forth his magic and sent it slamming into

1

the huge bear-like creature trying to take our Neil from us. Nim wept at the unfairness of it all. She sent an arrow into the monster's torso, but that only made it angrier. Zack threw a knife and it hit the beast in the leg, but it barely noticed. His odd, beaked face opened and emitted a sound of pleasure as he tore into Neil's flesh and his blood began to spill out upon the floor.

"OMG!" Neil shrieked, pulling me out of my imagination. "I would never be killed by anything called an owlbear. What the hell is that anyway? That's the stupidest thing I ever heard."

"Dude." Daniel's head fell back, his exasperation obvious. It wasn't the first time he'd gone over the rules to the game. "You missed your saving throw. You're dead. You needed a ten and you rolled a seven. You died in the dungeons because the owl bear ate you while protecting its treasure."

Neil frowned and looked down at the offending die. "I don't want to be eaten by a weird thing."

Dev giggled. "After all the crap you eat, it's fitting."

Neil turned on Dev. "You were supposed to use a spell and save me. What kind of mage are you?"

"A drunk-ass one," I posited, which once again sent my husband into a fit of laughter. I attempted to stare him down, but I don't think he cared.

"He can't roll either." Danny seemed to be even more drunk than Dev. "This is the worst campaign I've ever run. Dev sucks. He's not even following the storyline. He just keeps fucking around with his mini."

Dev looked up, his gorgeous green eyes mischievous. He had taken the miniature that represented my character and put it in some very tawdry positions with his own. "I want to know when my character gets to fuck Zoey's character."

"I told you, man. It's not that kind of game," Danny explained like he'd been through this a thousand times. "Seriously, do you think I'd invite Neil and Zack along if we were playing sex games with our wife?"

"Our characters don't have sex?" Nim asked, her lips curving into a naughty little smile. "That is disappointing."

Danny gave the thousands-of-years-old nymph a drunken smile, his dimples on full, heart-stopping display. "Sorry. You know we like to keep those things a little more on the private side."

Dev sighed. "I can't get Dan interested in public sex. There's even a club here in Dallas. He won't let us go."

Dev and Daniel continued arguing about someplace called Sanctum, but my brain was somewhere else. Two months had passed since we left Faery, and every day I worried a little more. We'd come home to Ether and settled back into the penthouse. Dev and Daniel agreed to take two weeks to get our lives back in order before we decided on what to do with the Blood Stone I'd found in Faery. Time runs differently in a *sithein* and though we spent roughly six weeks on Dev's home plane, a full nine months had passed on the Earth plane. Time always moves more slowly there, but sometimes it's a couple of days longer and sometimes whole months can pass. Dev had to dive back into his businesses and Daniel had to make his contacts aware he was back at home.

It was supposed to take two weeks, three tops, they promised me and then we would head to England. Nim had left the Faery plane in order to lead us to Merlin's tomb. It turned out she was the legendary Nimue, who had imprisoned the wizard Merlin. She'd also been known as Vivienne, the Lady of the Lake from Arthurian legend, and she'd decided Daniel was the next warrior worthy of carrying the sword Excalibur.

Nim was sure Merlin could help. We were hoping the old guy would be happy enough to be freed that he would be willing to solve Danny's little problem. The only trouble with that scenario was the fact that Nim was having trouble remembering exactly where she had stashed "the old goat." Apparently the British Isles had changed a little in the past millennium.

The waiting made me anxious. There was a small device on Daniel's heart. It was filled with silver and if Louis Marini wanted to, all he had to do was press a button to kill my vampire. I only knew about the device because Marini was using it to blackmail me into working for him. I'd completed my first assignment. The Blood Stone Marini forced me to steal from the Faery plane was secure in the safe in Dev's office. After numerous Internet searches and questioning everyone I could safely question, I still knew very little about the jewel. I could call Marcus Vorenus, Daniel's patron and a Council member, but he wasn't answering his phone. It was starting to drive me a little crazy.

So we were all in a holding pattern. Daniel was working with his small army of vampires. Dev was bringing in the cash. I was waiting for it all to fall apart.

And now Neil was dead and Daniel's plan to get his friends and family into role-playing games was going very poorly.

Dev smiled. "We could make a better game, Dan. It could be all about sex. We roll the dice and that's how many orgasms we have to give Zoey."

I threw my hands up. "I give up, boys. What's going on with Dev? Who gave the faery hard-core drugs?"

It was the only explanation. Dev could drink all day and never show a single sign of being trashed. Over the course of the last two hours, Dev had downed a single fifth of Scotch in an attempt to help Danny get his drink on. Dev drank, Daniel fed, and a good time was had by all. We'd taken a break about thirty minutes before so Daniel could have his faery snack. When the boys had returned to the game table, they'd both been wasted.

"Don't look at me." Neil sipped his glass of Pinot Grigio. "I didn't help him go all *Trainspotting* on us."

Zack glanced between Dev and Danny and then back to me. "I just smell the Scotch, Zoey. Are we breaking up then?" Poor Zack had put on a brave face, but I knew he was anxious to get back to his apartment two floors down where his girlfriend, Lisa, had just moved in. I was pretty sure Zack couldn't care less about role-playing games, but he would never tell his master that. Zack was nothing if not a good and faithful soldier.

I shot Zack a pleading look. "Don't go yet, please. I don't think I can get either one of them to bed if they pass out."

Dev laughed long and hard. "Oh, my lover, I will always come to bed for you. Just leave a trail of your pretty little underthings and I will follow."

Daniel thought that was hilarious.

"Seriously, I want to know what's going on." I gave them my best "nagging wife" look. "Nim, you didn't smuggle something fun out of Faery, did you?"

Nim's violet eyes narrowed. "Nothing I gave to the boys. Does Devinshea really believe he can perform as plastered as he is?"

Dev pointed at the nymph. His gorgeous face was a mask of outrage. "That is a ridiculous question. I promise you, I can perform. I can perform right now." He looked down and something caught his eye. "Look, Daniel, my little painted character has managed to get Zoey's little painted character into a perfect sixty-nine. Quick, give me yours and I'll work him in."

Daniel laughed as he passed over the little resin figure he used when he played. I snapped my fingers in front of the vampire's face and he turned to me. "Hey, baby. Have I ever told you how hot you look in Hello Kitty PJs? It makes me think of pussy."

"I am serious, Daniel," I said harshly, not pointing out that just about everything made him think of his favorite part of the female anatomy. "What did you do to Dev?"

His blue eyes were sleepy even though it was only two in the morning. He should be at full strength, but Daniel had never been able to handle his liquor. Becoming a vampire hadn't changed that. Dev might be able to perform, but my vampire was going to pass out soon. "It's no big deal, Z. It was just a little experiment."

"Shut up, Donovan," Dev shouted, looking like a five-year-old who was about to be told on. "We're not supposed to tell our wife about that."

Neil looked up from his wine, gasping in anticipation. "Oh, god, Dev and Daniel are experimenting. Someone get a camera. I've waited for this day all my life."

Dev snorted as he laughed. "Not that way. He would always have to be in control. I would always have to catch. He would never let me pitch."

I snapped my fingers. "Focus. What experiment?"

Previous experiments had included shooting Daniel to see how quickly he would heal, Daniel flying Dev into the upper atmosphere to see how fast he passed out from oxygen deprivation, and the infamous "is Daniel really faster than a speeding bullet" incident. I had lost a good set of china to that experiment. I blamed *MythBusters*.

I turned to Zack, who all too often was the guy making notes as

5

Dev and Daniel acted like idiots for their version of science. Zack pressed his lips together in a mulish show of male solidarity.

Shaking my head, I played the brand new card I had against Zack. "I'll just have to ask Lisa. I'm having lunch with her tomorrow. I'm sure we'll have lots to talk about."

Zack's eyebrows formed a perfect *V* in the middle of his brow. "That is so...how am I supposed to respond to that?"

"Don't tell her, Zack," Dev said as he found new ways for minis to fornicate. "Don't give her the upper hand. You'll never get it back."

"Don't tell me, Zack," I repeated with a grim resolve. "I'm sure Lisa would love to hear about all the dangerous stuff you have to do. You know women. We need to vent every now and then. I'm feeling the need to bond with your girlfriend."

Zack's eyes widened in desperation. Yeah, I had him on the ropes. "Zoey, I can't go against my master."

"Your master passed out." Neil pointed to Daniel, who was drooling a little on the table where his head was currently resting. "I don't think he'll even remember tomorrow."

Sighing, Zack stood up and stared down on his vampire master. "It was just a little experiment. Dev can't get drunk and he thinks it looks like fun. So Danny had the brilliant idea to, you know, take a little too much blood when he fed. Danny got more alcohol. Dev got a nice buzz."

"From blood loss!" I was astounded at the idiotic lengths men would go to for a little high.

"I'll build it back up," Dev said nonchalantly, standing up. He swayed a little and Neil got to his feet to catch Dev's six foot five inch, two hundred pound body should he fall—from blood loss. "I think it was a successful experiment. We've proven that you can get buzzed if a vampire takes one pint too much. Make sure you write that down, Zack."

"Zack, carry Danny back to our bedroom, please," I requested as the werewolf lifted Daniel easily over his shoulder. Zack was solidly built, but I doubted he would have been able to handle Danny's powerful two hundred twenty pounds of pure muscle had he not had all that werewolf strength to back him up.

I walked around to my faery. He swung his arm over my shoulders and leaned heavily against me. I peeked back at Nim and Neil. "Why don't you guys have another glass of wine? I'll be back after I get the boys settled down in bed."

"Don't expect her to be back anytime soon," Dev shouted over his shoulder as he shuffled along. "I intend to prove that I can still perform. I'm sure I'm even better like this."

Groaning as Dev stumbled along, I seriously doubted he would be able to waylay me for a little sexy fun. Even if he had enough blood to get hard, he would almost certainly pass out because his brain needed blood, too. "Are you sure I shouldn't call a doctor?"

Dev shoved me up against the wall outside our bedroom door.

Zack walked out of the bedroom. "Do you need a hand with him?"

"No, she doesn't need a hand with me," Dev protested as he crowded me with his inebriated affection.

I sighed and sent Zack on his way. If Dev fell, he could just sleep where he landed. As soon as Zack was out of sight, Dev proved that he actually could function with all his available blood in his penis.

"Baby," he groaned in my ear, grinding that hard part of himself against me. "I want you. I love you so much. You're so fucking gorgeous."

I had to smile. At least he was a sweet drunk. "I love you, too."

"I don't need anyone else." He cupped my face in his hands and stared down at me. "You and Daniel. You're my family. You're the ones who understand me."

"We love you, Dev." My heart ached for him. Our trip to Faery hadn't gone the way Dev had hoped. He'd looked forward to reconnecting with his brother and mother, but it all fell apart when he sacrificed the ascended god inside him to save Daniel.

Bris, the fertility god Dev had bonded with, had made the sacrifice willingly and was still hanging around waiting for the strength to reintegrate, but it hadn't been enough for his brother. Declan had been so angry Dev was willing to risk his people's fertility that the twins hadn't spoken more than two or three words since.

Dev leaned down and kissed me, his tongue playing softly along

7

my lips. "Let's make a baby, Zoey. I want a real family for us. I want a whole bunch of kids. I want little boys who look like me and little girls with red hair and sticky fingers."

I pushed against him and he glanced down, surprised I had stopped the play. "Dev, we talked about this. It isn't the right time."

"I know. I just…" He stopped for a moment but then got his footing back. His lips tugged up in a seductive smile. "Well then, my wife, I'll just slip into something a little uncomfortable and then we'll be safe to practice all we like." He kissed me again, his hand wandering down to cup a breast and rub my nipple until it was a hard little point. "Come on, Zoey. Let's go to bed. I rolled a ten last, so I owe you ten orgasms."

"Okay." I was fairly interested to see if he could pull it off. I could consider it my own little science experiment, though I had no desire to call Zack back with his clipboard. Dev turned and made his way into the bedroom, pulling his shirt over his head while he walked. I followed, hoping he didn't fall down.

The bedroom to our penthouse apartment was a magnificent blend of natural beauty and modern luxury. The back wall of the room was covered in greenery. Shiny green vines, ivies, and ferns dominated the room. It was a fitting domain for a fertility god.

Daniel was already asleep on the enormous bed Dev had ordered when the three of us had committed to being together. It was covered with a huge downy comforter and a whole lot of pillows. I never felt safer than when I snuggled down in that bed between the loves of my life.

Dev threw his big body on the bed, landing beside Daniel. Daniel was still dressed in his T-shirt and sweatpants. Dev smiled up at me, his perfectly cut torso on full display. He looked crazy sexy with his black hair down.

"You want to have wild, drunk sex next to Daniel's unconscious body?"

"He won't care." Dev patted the spot next to him, and his smile promised all manner of dirty pleasures. "If he manages to rouse himself from his stupor, he can just join in, lover."

"All right." I was game for a little pleasure. I would need to get that protection we had talked about earlier, though. I walked into the bathroom and found Dev's stash of condoms. I pulled out a couple to put beside the bed in case he proved to be up for more than one round. I was beginning to get a little excited at the prospect of what drunk Dev might come up with, and there was a smile on my face as I entered the room. "All right, big boy, I'm ready for whatever you can dream up."

My face fell and I laid down the little packets because I wouldn't need them. Dev had fallen asleep with his cheek pressed against Daniel's chest. Before long, Dev would be curled around him because Dev just pressed himself up against whatever was in bed with him. I shook my head. They were awfully cute lying there cuddled up. I pulled Dev's shoes off and tossed them in the closet before covering the boys with a blanket and letting myself out on the balcony.

The spring air was cool on my skin. I could probably use a sweater over my tank top, but I didn't want to bother with it. The lights of Dallas twinkled all around me. It felt so good to be home, but I couldn't ever forget what I'd left behind in Faery. I needed a minute to compose myself before I rejoined the others. Dev had done the one thing guaranteed to get me emotional. He mentioned babies.

I thought about the child I lost all the time. If I hadn't lost the baby, I would have been just about to start my second trimester. How would my body have changed? Would I be getting a curve to my belly? Daniel would be able to hear his heartbeat much more clearly. Dev would have his hand on my belly almost constantly, I was certain of that.

When you combine my miscarriage with the revelation that Daniel and I had a child somewhere on a Faery plane, the subject of children was just a touchy one for the time being. My best girlfriend, Sarah Day, was pregnant with her first baby. She'd recently moved to Seattle with her husband, Felix, who was going to college there. I missed her, but I was self-aware enough to know that watching her glow with happiness might hurt my heart a little.

I didn't begrudge her the joy, but it just seemed so far away for me. I expected resolution to be at hand when we returned from the Faery plane. Daniel was supposed to get that thing off his heart. With the help of the wolves and the Unseelie, we would take down the Council and then the three of us could get around to some serious baby making. It didn't work out that way.

Daniel seemed perfectly happy with the delay. I was beginning to think he didn't really want to go on this little quest. He didn't think there was anything that anyone, even a sorcerer like Merlin, could do. He didn't want to hear that he was screwed. He didn't want to even contemplate that possible reality, so he was hiding away. I knew Daniel well enough to know that he was genuinely happy for the first time in a long time, and he was also waiting for something terrible to happen to destroy his satisfaction.

Dev was still getting over the fact that his people had rejected him again. He was still coming to terms with giving up his post as the Seelie High Priest. He'd been welcomed by the Unseelie, but I knew all those shattered dreams of being able to go home haunted him.

We were all hiding, and I worried the time was rapidly coming when that would no longer be an option.

"Oh no, sister," Neil said as he opened the door to the balcony. He managed the door despite carrying two glasses of wine. "There will be no self-contemplation for you. Thinking never made anybody happy."

He always knew how to pull me out of a mood. I took the glass and enjoyed the fruity taste of the wine. Dev really did buy the best. "I was just getting a breath of fresh air."

"No you weren't, sweetie, but that's okay." Neil put an arm around me and brought our heads together. "I'm sure it seems like it won't happen, but I know it will. You and Dev are going to make the prettiest babies, who are going to turn into the wildest ass kids. Can you imagine Dev's sons as teens? Are you just going to start putting aside a bail fund now?"

I laughed and punched him in the arm gently. "They won't be that bad, Neil. Maybe they'll rebel against their parents and be perfect, law abiding citizens."

Neil shook his head. "I would start that fund if I were you. Daniel won't be any help. He can barely muster up the strength to discipline those vampires of his. Can you imagine how the kids are going to walk all over him?"

I shivered a little and Neil started maneuvering me back into the bedroom. I laughed again when I saw that the boys had been strategically maneuvered around. Daniel had his arms around Dev and Dev was cuddled close to his vampire.

"Neil, they're going to kill you." I chuckled, feeling better than I had all night.

"Not if they don't want the pictures to hit the Internet," Neil replied with a bright smile on his handsome face. "I could start a whole website about their unrequited man love."

I switched off the light, promising myself I would fix them before I went to sleep, and Neil and I returned to the living room.

"Hey, Zoey," Nim said from her comfortable perch on the couch. "I was hoping we could catch up on that model show."

Nim had really taken to reality television. It was her second favorite thing about the Earth plane. The first had been barbecue. Girlfriend was tiny, but she could put away some ribs.

"I'm really hoping that the tall, skinny one will start a fight with the even taller, even skinnier one," Nim explained. The legendary Lady of the Lake liked to watch catfights.

The phone on the table started to ring. "Fine, we can watch some TV, but I get to pick the second show." I was surprised to see it was the phone that rang directly from Ether. I picked it up. "Hello."

"Good evening, Mrs. Quinn," Roman, one of Dev's employees, greeted me. He'd been running Ether while we were on the Faery plane. Dev trusted him implicitly. "Could I please speak to Mr. Quinn?"

I wondered briefly if I could even wake Dev up. I seriously doubted it. Even if I could, there was no way I wanted him handling any kind of business in his current state. "I'm sorry, Roman, Dev is...not available and won't be for the rest of the night. What's the problem?"

A long sigh came over the line. "There's some trouble with the VIP room. I have two parties insisting it is theirs for the evening. My records show that the Hansen party booked the room, but the others are very...persuasive."

"You can't just kick 'em out?" That would be my solution, but then I'm not known for my diplomacy.

"We tried. They said they wanted to talk to the owner."

I found that intriguing. We employed some badass werewolves as bouncers. I wondered what the hell could be down there that the wolves couldn't handle.

"All right. I'll be right there." Dev was a great believer in community property. He liked to share. He got part ownership of my boobs and I'd taken a share of the club. I hung up the phone. "The show's going to have to wait, guys. There's trouble downstairs."

"Okay," Neil said gamely. He helped Nim up. "Let's go check it out."

I pressed the button to the elevator that would take us down to Ether.

"Um, Z…" Neil pointed to the baby blue pajama bottoms that were covered in Hello Kitty faces. Other than that I had on a very nonprofessional white tank top and fuzzy socks.

"Hey, they're pulling me off my comfy couch, they can put up with my style choices," I said as we loaded ourselves on the elevator.

Nim was already bouncing to the music that thudded through Dev's office as we got out of the elevator a moment later. "I really love the club. It's so much better than the bingo parlors Arawn used to take me to."

I shook my head, giving Neil a little look. We were always amused at Nim's tales of her previous life with the Welsh Death Lord.

"Do you want a gun?" Neil gestured to the safe where Dev kept a couple of handguns. The armory was below in the back of the club.

I shook my head. That was a little overkill. "No, I'm just going to tell them to get the hell out. I don't want a major scene."

But as I opened the door that led to the club, I realized a major scene was going to be unavoidable. From the stairs, I could plainly see the VIP room and the group currently occupying it. I thought about shrinking back, locking the door, and heading back up to the penthouse as quietly as possible. But that was a useless dream.

From his place on the elegant leather sofa, Louis Marini was holding court. He was surrounded by vampires, but he only had eyes for one person. Me.

Marini waved me down with an imperious gesture of his hand.

"Shit," Neil said beside me.

Shit was right. My time had just run out.

CHAPTER TWO

"Tell the Hansen party we'll refund their money," I said to Roman, who was waiting for me at the bottom of the stairs.

"Absolutely." He gave me a deferential nod, though I couldn't miss the way he grinned as he took in my choice of wardrobe.

I regretted it now. Every time I'd met with the head of the Council, I'd been in full armor. Designer dresses, stilettos, and full hair and makeup. I felt very vulnerable now, like he was going to see a side of me I would rather keep to myself. "Offer them use of the VIP area for free sometime next week and again on Peter's birthday."

Roman nodded in agreement. He glanced over to the section of the club in dispute. "Is that who I think it is?"

"Oh, yes," I said with a sigh. Roman had managed Dev's club in Las Vegas during the last big vampire meeting there. He hadn't had the misfortune to meet the vampires' leader. "That's Louis Marini, head of the Vampire Council. He's possibly the oldest vampire still walking the earth. I take it they persuaded the wolves to not throw them out."

Roman frowned. "They convinced my best two freaking bouncers to try to take the rest of the night off. They were just going to walk out in the middle of their shifts. It's all right. I caught them.

One of the waitresses is a pretty decent witch. She's clearing them of the influence."

"Just let them know to keep their distance. I doubt Marini will start a scene as long as he gets what he wants. I'll handle it from here." The last thing I wanted was someone getting hurt.

I watched the crowd part as Michael House walked toward us. Michael was a vampire who had risen on the battlefields of World War One. He was Daniel's friend and an ally.

"Zoey," Michael greeted me with a polite inclination of his head. "Mr. Marini requests the pleasure of your company. Won't you please join us?"

I let Roman go back to work and moved close to Michael. The clean-cut vampire leaned forward. He would be intensely formal until he knew he was among friends.

"It's all right, Michael," I said, keeping my voice low. "You know Neil, and Nim is an ally."

"I'm so sorry I couldn't give you a heads up." Michael smiled blandly, nodding his head. He was trying to make everything look merely friendly. Michael lived in the area, so it was natural we would be acquainted. He was supposed to be spying on Daniel for the Council, but Danny had brought him to our side several years ago. "They showed up on my doorstep at sundown and I only had a chance to get a call out to Justin."

I breathed a sigh of relief. That was one problem taken care of. The Council had no idea Daniel had been finding latent vampires and bringing them over by himself. When Daniel wasn't around, Justin had taken a leadership position. He would make sure everyone stayed in tonight. If strange vampires had turned up partying at Ether, it might have given away our game.

My other problem was Michael himself. Michael was blood oathed to Daniel. He'd taken a vow to protect Daniel and everything that belonged to him. Michael took that promise very seriously. He would consider protecting me a big part of that bargain. I'd noticed in the past that Michael had some trouble with his temper. He had no companion and was still considered young for a vampire. If Marini pulled the same shit on me he had in the past, Michael might explode.

I needed to get rid of Michael.

I looked back at Nim and winked. She nodded, letting me know she would go along with anything I had in mind. I didn't think she would have a big problem doing this favor for me.

There was enough distance between us and Marini that I could at least speak somewhat freely. The club was loud so as long as I acted friendly, I could talk to him. "Have you been ordered to stay close to Marini all night?"

"He merely requested that I accompany him to the club and then fetch you," the vampire replied. "I don't know what else he wants from me. Obviously he's not expecting me to act as his security. He brought Ivan and the boys for that."

Michael started to lead us through the club. I could see the big, burly Russian from my vantage point. He was enormous and stuck out like a sore thumb in his dark suit and those ridiculous sunglasses. Someone had been showing Ivan too many movies. Other than Ivan, I counted four vamps, though I didn't recognize them. They were pure muscle from the looks of them. And then I heard Neil gasp slightly as vampire number five gracefully leapt over the sofa and took his place next to Marini.

Chad Thomas looked like a rock star. He was so different from the rest of the clean-cut, conformist vampires. In my experience, vampires tend to be uniform in their appearance and the way they act. There's something about their training that teaches them to follow the crowd. Even Daniel had been a very typical vampire after he'd come home from the Council. I realized now that his conformity had been a part of his defense against the people who tortured him.

Chad looked so different that I worried his individuality was cause for concern.

"He didn't come home," Neil said softly, looking at his lover.

Chad should have been allowed to return to the territory of his choice after his year's training with the Council was finished. When we returned from Faery, the first thing Neil did was go looking for his boyfriend. Chad's house in the country was empty and there'd been no explanation why he was still out of town. I didn't like the fact that our spy seemed so awfully chummy with our worst enemy.

Now I had the added problem of Neil mooning over his lover. Neil is my best friend and the most loyal person I've ever met. He would lay down his life for me, but he doesn't lie well.

I stopped in front of the bar. "Neil, I need you to go back upstairs and wait for me in the penthouse." Neil stared at me like I'd lost my damn mind. "You can't be serious. There's a ton of vamps over there. You can't expect me to let you walk in there alone."

"And you're going to do what?" I wasn't trying to be a bitch, but I needed to point out some weaknesses in our current situation. Neil hadn't had vampire blood in over a year. While he was still strong, he wasn't going to be able to take out one old vamp, much less four or five. "Sweetie, I love you, but you're outnumbered."

Neil glanced back toward the relative safety of Dev's office. "I'll go force Daniel to get up."

I shook my head. "Danny's down for the count and so is Dev. I've got to handle Marini myself, and that's going to be a hell of a lot easier if I don't have to worry about you."

"Why the hell would you worry about me?"

Sighing inwardly, I handled Neil the best way I knew how. I wasn't going to point out how weak he was. That would only make him feel like crap and put him in a place where he might try to prove me wrong. I had one option. "Neil, what happens when Marini starts asking questions? What happens when he asks what we've been up to lately?"

His face fell. He knew he wasn't a good liar. He also knew how dangerous that little imperfection was in our current situation. "God, Z, let me go get Lee."

I shook my head. My personal bodyguard was an even worse risk. He'd wanted to get his hands on Marini for a long time. I doubted Lee would sit back and let me handle the vampire. "Neil, you either trust me or you don't."

"Fine. I'll be in the penthouse. Call me if you need me." Neil turned and stalked off, but I saw him talk to the bouncer at the stairs and knew he was telling security to keep an eye out for me.

One down and two to go. I nodded to Michael that I was ready to continue. He stepped up the stairs that led to the VIP room of the club. It resembled a very plush living room with leather couches, plasma televisions, and a dedicated bar and waitstaff, though I was sure they wouldn't be making much off bottle service this evening.

Marini stood up. The Frenchman was tall and well built. Like most vampires, he was incredibly attractive. He had dark hair that was slicked back and his skin was like fine porcelain, though it didn't make him look even vaguely feminine. There was nothing about the head of the Council that didn't scream dominant male. His eyes were dark, and they heated up with satisfaction as Michael led me to him. His lips quirked up, and he raised an eyebrow at my state of dress. He'd never seen me less than perfect. I could only hope he found casual Zoey unattractive.

"I wasn't expecting company," I said by way of explanation.

Marini held his hand out. Unfortunately, I knew exactly what he wanted. It was a little formal greeting between vampire and companion. Forcing myself to stay calm, I allowed my hand to find its way to his. He towered over me and gracefully flipped my hand over in his palm so the wrist was exposed.

He leaned over and sure enough, I felt the little sting of his fangs. "As always, Mrs. Donovan, it is a pleasure to greet you."

I looked around and saw that the bastard had brought his companion with him. He'd just tasted me in front of her. Most of the companions I'd met were as possessive as the vampires they belonged to. I expected her to look at me with hate, but there was only sympathy in her brown eyes as she watched the scene. Marini's companion reminded me of a little mouse the last time I had seen her. Now she was a little mouse someone tried to dress up. She was wearing a designer gown. Vintage Versace if I was right, and it was meant for a much fuller figure. She was wearing four-and-a-half-inch heels that I would be shocked if she really knew how to walk in. Someone had done her hair and makeup, but she seemed like a little girl playing dress up.

I smiled at her to acknowledge her presence, and she lit up like no one ever noticed her. Then Marini glanced back and her eyes were downcast again.

"You know Rose," Marini said as if it didn't really matter if I did or not.

I didn't. I'd never heard him say her name, but I nodded anyway. I knew how she must feel, the lone female in a room full of predators. "Hello, Rose. It's nice to see you again."

"Hello, Zoey," she replied shyly and I was surprised she had a very British accent. "I like your pants. I like Hello Kitty, too. They look warm and comfy."

"Kevin," Marini barked and one of the vampires moved forward. "Take your mistress home. I no longer need her."

Rose stood up obediently and tottered on her heels. So young. I couldn't imagine she was past twenty-one. She should be in college, figuring out her life, not obediently following her master's wishes. She nodded as she passed with her vampire escort.

Marini obviously forgot about her the instant she walked away. "Why don't you introduce me to your friend, Zoey?"

It was time to get rid of my other two problems. I'd felt Michael tense behind me when Marini had greeted me. Michael hadn't liked it, but as a member of the Council, he had the right. I was more worried about the inevitable time when Marini tried taking rights that didn't belong to him. I would just have to give the man something better to do than watch over me.

Smiling brightly, Nim moved forward. "Hello, I'm Nim." Marini introduced himself but made no move to touch her. She frowned at me. "Is he not going to do that thing with his tongue to me?"

I fought not to smile. Nim was very straightforward. "I think that's a vampire/companion ritual."

"That sucks," Nim protested, looking very disappointed. "When I heard there were a bunch of vampires hanging out, I was hoping I could get one to bite me."

I turned to Marini. I needed to set my plan in motion right away before he offered up one of his own men. A little light flirting was called for. "Louis, I was hoping you could help me with that little problem. You see, Nim is very curious. I was thinking Michael could...well..."

"Bite me," Nim supplied helpfully. "And do all those hot vampire things Daniel does to Zoey. I really think it's sexy when he sits around and licks her neck."

The head of the Council seemed very amused now as he turned to Michael. "Do you have any objections, Mr. House? It seems Mrs. Donovan would like to...I believe the current phrase is 'pimp you out' to her friend."

Michael's jaw dropped in obvious surprise, his fangs already on display. "Does she know all the...stuff involved?"

Nim grinned. "Oh, yes. I've listened in on Daniel and Zoey several times. It sounds like heaven. Of course, she usually has Devinshea as well, but I'll settle for just a vampire."

"You know about the sex?" Michael asked.

"Of course," Nim replied like he was an idiot. "Vampires like sex."

"We certainly do," Michael said in a low, sexy voice. His eyes took in every inch of Nim's form and a slow smile crossed his face. "Hello, Nim, my name is Michael House, and I'll be the one supplying you with multiple orgasms tonight."

"Why don't we go back up to my room and you can rock my world?" Nim led the vampire off toward the front of the club. Dev had given her an apartment in the building. Neil, Nim, and I had spent a fun day at IKEA furnishing it.

I watched the last of my problems leave. Unfortunately, they were also the last of my friends, and I steadied myself as I looked back at Marini. I wouldn't be able to count on Chad. He was in deep cover, and he would let Louis do a lot to keep it. Besides, I wasn't sure Chad could even stop Marini if he wanted to. "I was going to call you tomorrow."

Louis smiled but it was a predatory thing. "That is lie number one, *chère*. I will keep count and mete out punishment when I see fit."

I crossed my arms defensively over my chest. I didn't really like the sound of that, but it didn't seem the time to complain. "I would have called you, eventually. We just got back. It was a hard trip."

"That is lie number two," the vampire said forbiddingly. "Keep this up, Zoey, and the night won't go well for you." My frustration must have shown through because the vampire reached out and took my hand. "Come and sit. Perhaps a drink will allow the truth to flow more freely from your lips." He called over the bartender. "Vodka, I believe."

The bartender nodded. He knew me and what I liked. I gave the shapeshifter a look that tried to convey my comfort with the current situation. If I'd been talking, I was sure Louis would have pointed out lie number three.

"So, Zoey, where are Daniel and Devinshea this evening?" I hated the way he said my name. It was intimate and spoke of a relationship we didn't have and I didn't want. I preferred our previous formality.

I was going for honesty on this one. The last thing I needed was Marini thinking Danny and Dev were out doing something subversive. It was the one time they weren't. "They're indisposed."

I said that last word with a certain emphasis to let Marini know they were doing something naughty.

"Truly?" Marini asked, not hiding his surprise. "They didn't invite you to their little party? I find it hard to believe my *Nex Apparatus* is upstairs fucking his lover while his wife is down here with me."

I shook my head. "I don't think they'll be doing anything like that this evening. Dev finally managed to get drunk enough that he passed out before he got to the good stuff. Danny passed out long before Devinshea."

Marini laughed long and loud. "You sound very much like a harried wife. So Daniel discovered that little vampire secret. It's very hard, you know. The person who donates must have an unusually high capacity for liquor. If, say, I wanted to use your blood to get that sweet high, you would be dead from alcohol poisoning before I could even taste the liquor. Your faery prince must have a legendary tolerance."

"Yeah, well, he doesn't have much tolerance for blood loss," I muttered.

"Your husbands have been very naughty boys," Marini said, and he stopped to gauge my reaction. I opened my mouth to protest but he stopped me. "Think carefully before you react. I wouldn't like another lie to pass those sweet lips of yours."

"Yes," I said finally. "My husbands have been rather obnoxious tonight. I fear it will be even worse tomorrow."

"So your faery prince is not so disengaged as he wanted me to believe." Dev always played the idle, negligent lover around Marini. "I heard of the pagan rites performed at the werewolf gathering last year. Should I offer congratulations? I'm not so sure. You're Vampire property. I don't know how much I like you being tied to Faery. It could cause trouble down the road."

I was very sincere in my response. "I assure you, I married Dev for love. I don't want to be tied to Faery. And Dev and his brother are fighting again, so I wouldn't expect that the Seelies would even care if anything ever happened to us."

It was true. When we left Faery, I was tied to a tribe, but it wasn't the Seelies. King Angus of the Unseelie had allied himself with both Dev and Daniel, but I decided not to mention that little tidbit.

The vampire weighed my words and pinned me with his dark eyes. He finally nodded and sat back, crossing one leg over his knee. "I believe you, *chère*. You're very young and foolish, all three of you, if you believe it will work in the end. The prince should have been kept as a lover and nothing more. Daniel will regret it. Perhaps not. Perhaps he will regret other things."

He let those enigmatic words hang as the bartender brought me an icy cold martini just how I liked it, with two plump olives. I took a long sip as Chad came to sit beside me.

"Mrs. Donovan," he greeted me. "Or is it Quinn now?"

Well, at least I knew who told Marini about my marriage. It would have been nice if he had kept that to himself. "In the vampire world it's easiest to be Mrs. Donovan."

"Of course," Chad said flatly. "Daniel's claim is the one we recognize. You can play house with the faery all you like, but no vampire will recognize his claim on you."

"Though I wonder how being married to the luscious Zoey would change the prince's mind should anything happen to Daniel. In the past, he has been adamantly against belonging to a vampire. I wonder if he would follow his pretty little wife should she require another vampire master," Louis pondered. "He might simply think he could find the nearest *sithein* and hide her from us."

Chad *tsk tsked* that suggestion. "That wouldn't do, master. She's far too sweet to let her rot away in some Faery mound with a man who could never truly appreciate her. Speaking of appreciation— where's that little werewolf who follows you around like a lapdog?"

I was startled at his tone. I turned to see Chad looking perfectly serious. I wanted to slap him and ask him why he would talk about his boyfriend like that. Instead I turned away, for once finding it easier to look at Marini. "He's upstairs."

"Mr. Thomas was very pleased with the hospitality he was shown in Colorado when he brought you the information on that assignment I had for you," Marini explained. "He said the little wolf was very... accommodating."

"I thought they got along pretty well." I would have to keep this conversation to myself if I wanted it to stay that way. Neil wouldn't like to be referred to as a lapdog.

"We got along really well, Mrs. Donovan," Chad drawled with great relish. He set his booted feet on the expensive coffee table. "Mrs. Donovan likes to surround herself with beautiful men. I envy her greatly. Her husband is a paragon of male dominance, but the wolf and the faery are just to die for. I swear that faery is the most beautiful thing I've ever seen, and the wolf isn't far behind."

"Unlike me, Zoey, you will find my friend here is only interested in his own sex," Marini laughed. "It isn't surprising he would love to switch places with one such as you."

The dark-haired vampire was a vision of decadence sitting negligently on the couch and talking about the men he wanted. Chad's dark eyes found mine. He licked his lips, and I could see a hint of fang. "Of course, if Mrs. Donovan here wanted to try me, I wouldn't kick her out. What do you say, sweetheart? Want to see if you can turn me straight? I'd try it just to get a taste."

Marini's hand shot out and suddenly there was blood on Chad's mouth. He didn't react at all to the fact that the Frenchman had slapped the holy hell out of him. He just ran his tongue along his lip, making sure he got that blood back.

"You will not speak that way to her." Marini stood over him, violence in his very stance. "She doesn't belong to you."

"Of course, master," Chad said evenly as he gave me a serious look. "I apologize, Mrs. Donovan. I hope you don't take offense. I meant neither you nor your husband any disrespect."

I wished I could read people better. It seemed like Chad was trying to tell me something. Maybe he'd set up the entire scene to show me that Louis Marini was getting terribly possessive of things that didn't belong to him. It wasn't a good sign. Marini sat back and continued speaking like he hadn't just exploded.

"You will have to excuse our Mr. Thomas," Marini said, looking at Chad with a strange sort of affection. "He's different. His powers of illusion are very rare, and it makes his idiosyncrasies worth putting up with. He's a class of vampire that has gone almost extinct."

"Class?" I'd heard a little something of the different classes, but I'd mostly met warriors.

"It's rare, but some would qualify," Marini explained. "Most vampires are of the warrior class, your husband being a splendid example. Marcus is not a true warrior. His talents lie in persuasion and obviously his ability to walk about during the day. We used to call them academics because they tended toward study and a fascination with specific intellectual pursuits. Mr. Thomas here is what would have been called a magician."

"That's me, full of magic," Chad said with an odd little laugh.

Marini shook his head. "They were not the most stable of vampires. Mr. Thomas is the first to rise in centuries, and he finds himself alone. Most of his class don't survive long. There are other classes who never leave the underground. They are misshapen and deformed, but their brothers care for them anyway."

I decided then and there to never spend much time in the underground.

"To get back to the topic at hand," Marini said, relaxing again, "Mr. Thomas was fascinated by the fertility rites of the prince's people. He said they contained some powerful magic."

Chad's eyes closed like he was experiencing it all over again. "They made me stay far away, but I could still feel it. I was so full. I hear the wolves were happy, too. Many of the couples who were there managed to conceive."

"Yes," Marini murmured, "I'm sure they feel a debt of gratitude toward Daniel. I know they paid him well."

I didn't like where this conversation was heading. I frowned and pouted. Hopefully it was a pretty sight. "They should be grateful to me. I was the one who nearly broke my jaw."

Both the vampires thought that was very amusing. Marini was still smiling when he said, "Perhaps you will perform this little ritual of yours for the Council. We meet next month and we always have certain entertainments to make our political sessions more palatable.

Your husband is already required to be there. I think you and the prince should come as well. I would like to feed from this magic as Mr. Thomas has, as Daniel does every night."

"You'll have to speak to Daniel," I said quietly. Daniel would never agree and it would cause a lot of trouble, but I would have to deal with it later.

Marini stood now and he held out his hand to help me up. "I'll do that. If you will excuse us, Mr. Thomas, Zoey and I have some business to discuss. I assume we can use the office."

My eyes went wide. "You want to go to the office?"

He reached down and hauled me up. "Yes, we shall speak privately. I don't think you have my item in the pocket of your charming little pants, do you?"

This was the moment I'd been dreading. This was the moment I'd been trying to find a way out of for months.

"Or do you want out, companion?" Marini asked, his deep voice silky. "I do have an eject button, if you recall."

And there was no way around that. I took a deep breath and let him start to lead me out of the VIP area. Ivan gave us a look that had me worried.

"Have fun, boss," he said in a thick accent as we walked by.

I glanced back at Chad, but all he did was wink.

CHAPTER THREE

As a person who has actually been escorted to her own execution before, I can safely say that walk with Marini up to Dev's office was the longest of my life. I kept trying to come up with a way to not give him the Blood Stone, but I couldn't think of one that would work. I was going to have to turn it over and then figure out a way to get it back later.

"Zoey?" The bouncer at the bottom of the stairs stared at me with questioning eyes. "Should I come up with you or maybe call Mr. Donovan?"

I tried smiling at the shapeshifter named Erik, but he didn't look very convinced. Neil wasn't the only one having trouble telling a lie tonight. "It's fine. I just have to get Louis something I left in the office. He's an old friend, really."

"Yes," Louis said in that dark seductive voice vampires used when they went into persuasion mode. All vampires had the talent, some more than others. "Allow us to pass. Your mistress is in no distress. We're…good friends, she and I."

Erik smiled suddenly and let us pass. "Good night, Zoey."

I hated the blankness in his eyes. Sometime in the near future he would come out of it and wonder what had happened. He would remember very little.

"Why don't you just do that to me?" I asked as I led the vampire upstairs. In some ways it would be simpler. I wouldn't have to remember that I'd given Marini my prize.

Marini's voice was filled with amusement at the thought. "You really should have spent more time in our society, Zoey. You would know that my talents in persuasion would never work on you. My greatest skills lie in strength and my abilities to kill even other vampires. I would never be able to get past your husband's hold on you. His blood is your protection."

I supposed that made sense. I pulled the keycard out of my pocket, but Marini took it from my hand. He swiped the lock himself and ushered me inside. I shivered as the door closed behind us and we were alone.

"Marcus, on the other hand, could have had you at any time." Marini walked around the office, his eyes taking in everything.

"What do you mean?"

Marini's well-manicured hand ran along the spines of the books on the shelf. This was where I often found Dev sitting in his comfy chair reading. I hated that Marini was getting such a private view of him. "Marcus is probably the most powerful persuasive on the planet. Had he been less of a gentleman, he could have fucked you senseless and you would have been happy to do it. Your husband's blood would be no protection against Marcus. I've often wondered why he did not simply take you when it's so obvious he wants you."

I stood by the desk, putting it between us. "Maybe he's afraid of what Daniel would do to him when he found out, and he would find out." I needed Marini to really think about that. On some level, he feared Daniel.

"Perhaps that's the case." He didn't sound like he believed it. The look on his face softened slightly, and he smiled a little. I think he was trying to be charming. "He would change his mind if he could see you now."

"I doubt it."

"Oh, no, *mon ange*. Don't discount how sweet you look like that," he said quietly. "You look soft and ready for bed. It's a revelation to see you like this. No one dressed you for the occasion. It's what you're comfortable being. You look younger without the makeup. You look vulnerable."

"Your companion is young." I wanted to get him off the subject of me looking like prey.

He shook his head. "I should never have bought her. I should have waited. She was too young. She'll never be a true companion. A true companion used to be a partner. She was a lover and fighter, someone a vampire could be proud to say he owned. When the companion's blood is strong, a vampire will do anything to please her, to make her happy. We used to trust our companions with everything, taking them with us even into battle in some cases. Then they became so rare we simply protected them at all costs, including the sense of contentment that came with the bond."

He seemed sad as he said it, and I wondered if he'd felt that bond before. If he had, it had been so long ago it couldn't mean much. Unlike Marcus, Marini continually kept a companion. When one died, he merely found another, not wanting to go through the withdrawal a vampire felt when he no longer had companion blood in his system. A vampire with a companion had an advantage over the other vampires, but it came at a cost. The vampire was completely addicted to companion blood. One taste was all it took to make the vampire crave it.

"You shine so brightly," Marini whispered. "You should be able to see yourself." He shook his head as though to bring himself out of his haze. "Go on then, Zoey. I've waited long enough. It's time for you to finish the job. You'll note I didn't ask if you were successful. I have complete faith in your abilities. Give me the Blood Stone."

I didn't want his praise. I wanted the man gone, and the only way I was going to accomplish that was to give the bastard what he demanded. He'd sealed off all my exit routes and I was left with no choice. I moved to the wall safe and pushed aside the painting that covered it. I likely wasn't showing him anything he hadn't already seen for himself. Marini had used Chad to spy on Dev, Daniel, and myself one night and I'd been told he'd poked around in Dev's office before they made their way to the penthouse. I dialed the code for the safe and it popped open. I felt Marini step in right behind me, crowding me with his big body as he got a good look at what was in the safe. Luckily, Dev had moved anything even vaguely incriminating to a more secure location. Still, I heard Marini's surprise at the large stash of cash and gleaming guns in the safe.

"Just how wealthy is your new husband?" Marini muttered the question, running his finger along a thick stack of hundred dollar bills. There were several piles of gold coins he had used as currency when we were in Faery as well.

"He does all right." I reached into the back. I wasn't about to give Marini a detailed accounting of Dev's numerous business holdings. His human father had left him a multinational company that produced god knew what. I only knew that it produced cash and Dev took it and turned it into even more cash.

"Yes, I can see that. No wonder Daniel is willing to share. Vampires as young as Daniel usually struggle for money, but he's found a way around that. It seems the prince has more wealth at his disposal than I could have imagined. And all that wealth would come to you, his wife, should anything happen to him," Marini said, finally backing off me as I turned and handed him the small velvet bag that contained the Blood Stone.

Marini quickly had it opened and was holding the red stone up to the light to inspect it carefully. His dark eyes were possessive as he stared at it. I closed and locked the safe while he was distracted with the stone.

"It's been a very long time since I held this stone. I suppose there is only one way to make completely certain."

The vampire held his left palm open and shoved the pointed tip of the stone into it with a violent force. He grunted as he pierced his own skin with the stone and shoved it in even further. I watched as the stone pulsed slightly and seemed to lose just the slightest bit of its luster.

When I looked up at Marini, his eyes were completely black. He dragged a long breath in and steadied himself. It was like he'd taken a nice hit off a particularly good bong. He smiled as he let his head fall back.

"I had forgotten," he said more to himself than to me.

"What is it?" I hoped he would tell me the truth since he seemed a little out of it.

"Just a taste of what your husband feels every day," Marini said enigmatically.

He growled and there was no way to miss what it had done to his fangs. They peeked out from behind his lips. I took a step back. His hand shot out to stop me, and I finally realized just how much danger I was in.

"Yes." Marini licked his lips. "I can hear your heart beating. You're terrified. It'll make your blood even sweeter."

I managed to twist my arm out of Marini's hand. "You forget yourself, Mr. Marini. I belong to Daniel."

I could see plainly that the stone had done something to him. I thought maybe it was bringing out the beast that seemed to reside in every vampire. I could handle Daniel's beast because Daniel loved me. Marini didn't love me. Appealing to vampire laws was the only shot I had.

"Do you know who Daniel belongs to, sweet little Zoey?" His voice was slightly slurred and his accent heavier than before.

I shook my head but took a guess. "Marcus. Marcus is his patron."

"No, companion," Marini said, his face hard. "The *Nex Apparatus* is mine. He made his oath to me. He's my creature."

I knew that ritual well but hated the thought of Daniel being forced to go through it with Marini. Still, I knew what it meant and what had been promised. "If you're truly Daniel's master, then you owe him as much as he owes you. You're supposed to protect him and everything that belongs to him. I belong to Daniel."

He snarled my direction. "Don't seek to tutor me on my duties. You know nothing. I'm the oldest vampire in the world. You're the brightest companion I've ever seen. Why should a seven-year fledgling have you? It rankles, Zoey. Do you know what I was doing seven years after I turned? I was serving my master. I was his creature to do with as he wished. I was his to beat, to ignore, to fuck as he wished. That's where your Mr. Donovan should be, but no, I have to tread carefully. I have to elevate him and treat him with respect. I'm supposed to respect his claims. You should belong to me. Daniel should have given you to me in hopes I would not crush him. He's my vassal and he owes me."

"You're not his king, Marini," I spat and very quickly realized my mistake.

Louis Marini got very still. "Does Daniel believe he can take the crown? Does he seek to take what's mine?"

"What are you talking about?" I had used the exact right word to piss the man off. I had to play as ignorant as possible. My heart thudded in my chest so loudly I wouldn't be surprised if they could hear it thundering downstairs. I wanted out so badly. "You said he was your vassal."

But Marini was already pulling that little box out of his coat. He held it up for me. It was the tiny box that haunted my nightmares. "I'm his god, Zoey. I have the power to kill him in an instant and then perhaps I can simply take what should always have been mine."

"Please," I said breathlessly, praying he wouldn't press down. I knew we were in range. Daniel was completely helpless, and I was the only one with any hope of protecting him. "Please, don't."

"And what do I get for forgetting I can solve my problems with the single push of a button, companion?"

"I gave you the stone," I insisted. "I did the job. I'll do the next one. You promised that you would deal with me fairly."

He shook his head. "I'm not feeling very fair tonight. And there is the problem of your lies. You were supposed to call me the minute you returned from Faery. I think you were trying to find a way out of our deal. That's unacceptable. You will not defy me like that again. Now what is your punishment to be? Should I press the button or can you think of another way to placate me? I think perhaps we should play a little game, you and I." He slipped the box back into his jacket along with the stone, then he took the jacket off and laid it over Dev's desk. He rolled up his shirt sleeves. "I think a little exercise is called for. I would run if I were you."

It was the one time I decided to take the bastard's advice. I ran for the door. If I could get it open, I could scream. Someone would hear me, even over the loud music. Our security guards were all creatures with impossibly good hearing. I just had to make it to the door and I could jump. I would land on the dance floor and it would hurt, but I would heal. Anything was better than being in this room and submitting to whatever Marini had in mind for me.

I didn't even get my hand on the door before he caught me. He wound my ponytail around his hand and forced me to my knees. Pain flared along my scalp and tears pierced my eyes. There would be no reason to scream. Dev had soundproofed the room because the club could be so loud. I was alone and at his mercy, and I was pretty damn sure he had none.

He smiled savagely as he sneered down at me. "Are you going to beg?"

"Would it do me any good?" I knew the answer.

"You're such a smart girl. It's one of the things I admire about you." He got to his knees in front of me, his obsidian eyes on my throat. He wasn't settling for a little taste this time. I felt the force of his will and I fought against it. He tried to pull me in. The last thing I wanted was an ounce of pleasure from him. I used every bit of strength I had to pull back, and he just laughed. He seemed unconcerned with my small struggles. "Have it your way, then. It will taste the same to me."

He struck, the force of his fangs an agony. I heard myself cry out. He drew heavily and held me so tight against his body, I thought I would stop breathing. How do I describe the pain of a brutal feed? There's a quality to it I haven't felt from broken bones or penetrating wounds. No arrow can make you feel like those fangs do. Helpless, hopeless. Like a rabbit in a lion's mouth. The pain that comes from fangs ripping into your throat doesn't even compare to the humiliation of having something as private as your blood drained without permission or care.

I tried desperately to take myself somewhere else, to not think about the vampire and what he was doing to me.

My eyes caught on Dev's desk. So many memories had formed around that desk. It was the first place Dev and I had made love. It was the first place the three of us had sat and talked about our pretend ménage that turned out to be so true. I had so many happy memories of this office, and now I would just remember this one.

I tried to relax and think about the picture Dev kept on his desk. Neil had taken it. We'd gone to a baseball game. It was me and Danny and Dev smiling, our faces pressed together so we could get into the picture. Dev had tried to convince me that hot dogs were good and didn't have anything to do with cats, but I'd had a bad experience with some troll street vendors and wasn't willing to risk it. Daniel managed to catch a fly ball using only a little bit of his superpowers. Sarah and Felix had been with us. It had been right before we left for Faery. It seemed like forever ago.

I was shaking by the time Marini released the vein. The flesh of my neck felt raw and open. I didn't think I was going to need a transfusion, but he'd definitely taken too much. When he released his hold on me, I slumped back, having no strength to remain upright.

"God, I never imagined." He was on his knees over me, looking down. His face was flushed and he swayed slightly, like he was drunk. "I've never had anything like it. Not in all my companions. All these years." His eyes were filled with a mad desire. "Zoey, do you know what we could do together? Don't you understand, if you handled me properly, I would be your slave?"

"Just go." The last thing I wanted to hear were words of devotion. He didn't care about me. He was under the influence of my blood. I've come to accept that Daniel loves me, but even Daniel was so much more affectionate right after a feeding. "You had me, now go."

His fangs made another appearance. I should have remembered that vampires don't handle rejection well. "I haven't even begun yet. You're forgetting there's another thing a vampire wants from a companion."

My stomach churned as he lowered himself on top of me. I didn't have the strength to even push back. My body felt useless, a futile thing.

He used his weight to force my legs apart, and I could feel his lust pressed against me. He was so heavy I couldn't breathe. He leaned over and licked my neck as he started to shove his hand under my shirt. I felt his fingers pinch at my breast when he suddenly groaned and rolled off me.

"*Merde!*" Marini cursed and I scrambled away as he held his head. I saw that a hardback book had somehow hit him.

Marini was on his feet, looking for the threat when the paperweight on Dev's desk flew across the room and hit the vampire squarely on the forehead. I managed to sit up and started to back away. I wasn't sure exactly what was there, but it seemed pretty damn friendly to me.

"Que s'est-il passé?" Marini screamed as another assault began.

I strained, but I couldn't see anyone standing back there. A pen from Dev's desk became a flying weapon, attempting to lodge itself in Marini's neck. He batted it away.

I made some shit up, my mind working when my body wouldn't. "Security measures, Marini. You should go. It's a poltergeist, and it won't stop until you're gone."

Marini snarled, but another book flew his way. He was looking for something to kill but just couldn't find anything. There was no one else in the room. He loomed over me as he grabbed his jacket. "Don't think this is over, Zoey. I would advise you to keep our little affair between the two of us. I would hate for Daniel to become... troublesome. I will contact you soon and Zoey...the next time I'll have you in my territory and on my terms. You should think about what I said before. We do it the easy way or we can do it as hard as you like."

He turned and stalked out the door.

I tried to get to my feet, but I stumbled and fell back down, my cheek hitting the carpet. I needed to get up. I needed to lock the door, push the desk against it, anything to keep him from coming back. I cried, tears making it hard to see. God, I needed to figure out what the hell had saved me, but then I knew. A warmth enveloped me and I knew who my savior was. I cried at the sweetness of it.

Even without a body, Bris had found a way to defend his goddess. I wasn't sure what I'd done to earn such devotion from him, but I was so grateful for it.

"Thank you, My Lord," I whispered as that warm air surrounded me like a blanket. It enveloped me and gave me strength. He couldn't speak, but I thought he was trying to tell me something. He wanted me to get up. He wanted me to get out of here. I was still vulnerable, and Bris had likely used all of his stored energy on his assault. He wouldn't be able to help me again. There was time to cry later. For now I needed a safe haven.

I struggled to my feet and knew just where to go.

CHAPTER FOUR

I knocked on the door to apartment 1021. I glanced behind me every now and then, expecting Marini to show and try to take me away. My heart had settled a bit, but my anxiety was still high. After I'd cleaned myself up a little, I'd snuck into the residential area of the building, praying Marini wouldn't come looking for me. According to Roman, he'd left, but my hands still shook.

I was startled when the door opened abruptly, and Lee appeared with a gun in his hand and a sheet wrapped around his lean waist.

"What the hell is going on, Zoey?" He took a deep whiff of the air and stalked out into the hallway, looking up and down. "Son of a bitch, where is he?"

"Gone." I was pleased that I managed to speak with something of a calm tone. "Can I come in? I need to talk to you."

Lee nodded and stepped back inside. "Sit down. I'll be back in a minute."

I got my first look around Lee's apartment. It was nice, or it would be if anyone gave a damn. Like the other apartments in the upscale building, it had lovely hardwood floors and modern, clean lines. Dev had rehabbed the building when he bought it and it reflected his good taste.

Unfortunately, this particular unit also reflected Lee's tastes. There was an old, well-used recliner and a couch that had seen better days. The only thing new in the entire living area was a large screen TV Dev had delivered and installed as a bonus for the work Lee had done while we were in Faery. Of all the wolves I've known, none of them had Lee's senses. Even with Daniel's blood, Zack couldn't touch Lee's hypersenses. He'd managed to track me across two *sitheins* while riding an eddy wind. If he hadn't, I would have been executed, so the TV was well earned.

I sat down on the couch and heard Lee talking to someone in what I knew had to be his bedroom. I sighed. I'd interrupted something interesting. I stood back up. That hadn't been my intention. "Lee, I'll just go home. It's fine. We can talk in the morning."

"Sit your butt down, Zoey," he yelled out. "I'll be there in a minute."

A woman stumbled out, still buttoning her shirt. I recognized her. She was a local wolf, a friend of Angelina Hernandez's. "Hey, Julie."

She smiled at me and stopped briefly. "Hey, Zoey," she managed before Lee started pushing her toward the door.

"No, ladies. No girl talk," Lee said firmly. "Good night."

Julie frowned at him as he hustled her out the door.

"I'm sure he'll send flowers tomorrow," I said, all the while shaking my head in a negative fashion because that was so not going to happen.

Julie frowned. "If he wasn't so good in bed I would…"

Anything Julie might have said was cut off by the slamming door.

"You're a terrible boyfriend," I said with a sense of awe.

He frowned down at me. He'd put on jeans and a wrinkled green T-shirt. "I'm not her boyfriend, Zoey. We were discussing some security problems she's been having."

"At three a.m.? Naked? Was she having a security problem in her vagina?"

An irritated growl preceded his response. "Well, you seem to have a security problem at three a.m."

He had a point. "I lost the Blood Stone."

"Damn it," Lee cursed. "When did Marini show up? And why the hell do I smell him all over you? Stand up, Zoey."

I knew what he wanted and I didn't want to go through it. I couldn't. "No, Lee. I'll just tell you, okay? He caught me alone and he bit the shit out of me. It wasn't his little greeting this time. It was a full-on feeding, and he gorged himself."

"What else did he do?" The question ground out of his mouth. He went perfectly still, not even blinking.

There was no use in lying to Lee. We'd made a deal a while back. I trusted him and told him everything, and for the most part he followed my orders. I hoped the second part would hold up because I had a big favor to ask of my wolf. "He tried to rape me, Lee."

"Tried?"

Nodding, I sat back down and attempted to get comfortable. "Bris showed up and went through a whole poltergeist impersonation. He threw stuff at Marini until he got off me."

"He's kind of a badass." Lee relaxed slightly. "Are you all right?"

"I think so." I was happy he stayed calm. I needed that from him. "I'm a little weak, but I'll be okay. How's the wound?"

He touched my neck, running his fingers along it and then leaning in to get a whiff. "It's already gone. I can smell it though. He did a number on you. Are his fangs bigger than Donovan's? Those puncture wounds must have been big."

"I wouldn't let him pull me in," I explained.

Lee smiled slightly. "Of course you didn't. So where were the boys while you were getting assaulted?"

This was the part I didn't want to tell Lee. Lee Owens was only ten years older than I was, but he felt like a father figure. He was going to be so pissed. "They were asleep. I didn't want to wake them up."

Lee cursed under his breath. "Tell me they didn't try the thing where Donovan nearly drains the faery to see how drunk they can get."

"Okay. I won't tell you."

"Idiots," he said. "I suppose you have a good reason you didn't call me."

I had to make him understand. "Lee, he was going to corner me.

36

There was no way around it. If you'd been with me, how were you going to take care of five vampires? That fight would have destroyed the club, injured a bunch of people, and probably killed Danny when Marini got pissed enough to push his little eject button. I took care of it. I doubt you would have deterred him tonight. Even if you had, it's just postponing the inevitable."

There was a tightness to his eyes as he stared at me. "You think he'll be back?"

"I know he'll be back." I shivered, thinking of the way he stared at me before Bris had begun his assault. "He thinks he deserves me. He thinks I'm his right or something. God, Lee, the worst part was when he told me how much he wanted me. He sounded like he was talking to his girlfriend. He practically begged me to love him."

"Before or after he had that blood of yours?"

"Right after, of course. He told me he wanted to be my slave. He looked like he loved me."

Lee pulled me around to face him. He knew exactly what bothered me about the whole situation. "That doesn't mean Donovan doesn't love you, Zoey. He feels the same way about you when he doesn't feed. I might not like the son of a bitch sometimes, but I don't doubt for a second that boy is devoted to you. Maybe it's stronger because you're a companion, but he would lay down his life to protect you. That's not about blood."

I felt my eyes start to water as everything really started to hit me. I wished so much I could be one of those people who just shoved their emotions down and moved on, but no matter how much bad crap happened, I still cried. I still wanted the safety of arms around me. "He told me I wouldn't tell Danny and Dev about our little affair. He's not going to stop. He'll come back until he gets what he wants."

Lee seemed to be at a loss for what to do with a crying female on his couch. I realized I was being ridiculous. This wasn't Lee's job. He was my bodyguard. He shouldn't have to listen to me whine. I took a long breath to try to banish the urge to really let loose. I almost had myself under control when he reached out and pulled me into his arms. He seemed uncomfortable at first, but determined.

"You go on, darlin'," he said in a rough western accent. "You cry it out. You deserve it."

Well, then there was no stopping me. I cried and cried, not caring at all that I was getting his shirt wet or that my nose was probably running. I let it all out, the fear, the hurt, the awful feeling of being completely vulnerable. There was nothing I could do against the man. If Bris hadn't managed to use every bit of strength he'd been saving up, I would have been his victim and he would have pretended we were lovers.

In some ways he'd managed his rape. He'd done something to me only Daniel had ever done before. I was sure Daniel would see it as a crime. Feeding was an intimate thing between us. It was something I would probably never do with anyone else if given the option. I hated the fact that he was running around full of my blood. I was sure it played into his demented fantasy that I was meant for him.

After the longest time, I was all cried out. I just let my head rest against Lee's shoulder and felt comfort from him patting my back.

I finally sat up and sent him a self-deprecating smile. "Sorry. I bet you didn't think that was part of your job description."

His chocolate brown eyes were full of some emotion I wasn't sure I could name. "This isn't just a job for me, Zoey. I never told you this, but I think you know I had to raise Zack, right?"

"I know your mom died when Zack was a kid." Lee rarely talked about his past. Hell, Lee rarely talked at all, but I knew he'd had a rough childhood.

Lee nodded. "I was seventeen and Zack was six. Mom was killed one night coming home from work. My dad, he drifted in and out. I think he loved our mother. He wanted her enough to knock her up twice. He would ride through Vegas and Mom would get excited and then he'd be gone again. I know why now. I got the urge to roam when I was thirteen. Mom wouldn't let me and by then Zack had shown up. Anyway, when she died, I had the option of taking care of Zack or sending him to foster care. You have no idea how much I wanted to take that second option. I'm not proud of it but damn, I wanted to be free. I wanted to roam and not be tied to anything."

"Because you're a lone wolf." For the first time, I realized that there was more than just super-senses and strength associated with the condition.

"My instincts make me want to push people away," Lee said

quietly. "I want to be alone. Even when I was a kid and we would run with the pack I would find a way to break away and spend the full moons on my own. I thought about running a thousand times. But I forced myself to stay with Zack and I never regretted it. I looked at that kid and just knew that I would fight my every instinct to make sure he was safe. He was my pack. I only felt that way about one other person my entire life."

"Why me?" I asked, not making him say it.

He shrugged and wiped away my tears with his thumb. "I don't know. I just know that you and Zack…you're like my kids, the only ones I'll ever have because I won't put a kid through this. There was a woman I cared about once. Pretty thing, but she left and I knew I wouldn't try again. I don't want anyone else to feel like I do. I hate it. I push everyone away and I don't always want to. I just do it. It's my instinct. I'll never have a mate. I'll never even have a girlfriend. But I have you and Zack and even Neil. I'm comfortable here, Zoey. I don't feel the need to run like I have in the past. All I know is that I would do anything to protect my little pack."

"Including not telling the only female member of your little pack's husbands what really happened tonight?" I asked.

He shook his head. "Damn it. I knew you were going to do that to me. All right, Zoey, but they're going to find out eventually, and we have to figure out a way to protect you from that asshole."

I nodded. "If you have a plan, I'll follow it."

"All right then," he said, helping me up. "Go take a shower and get that bastard's stink off you. Don't look at me like that. I have soap. I think. Towels, I'm not so sure about."

I let him herd me to the bathroom. When he turned to go, I stuck my head out again. "Lee," I called to him. "I love you."

His normally taciturn face split into a joyous grin. "I know you do, darlin'."

I closed the door and took the longest, hottest shower of my life.

"Why did she need to take a shower?" I heard Dev's voice as I opened the door to the bathroom. I took a deep, settling breath because I was about to have to perform. I couldn't tell Dev what had happened. I couldn't give him that guilt. He would feel bad enough with what I had told him.

"Some asshole spilled vodka all over her," Lee grumbled. "She didn't want to walk around smelling like a bar."

"I'm just a little confused here," Dev was saying.

Lee snorted. "Well, that's what happens when you do stupid shit like letting a vampire drain your ass, Quinn."

"Yeah, that probably wasn't worth it," Dev admitted. "I still feel a little weak and Daniel passed out long before he could really enjoy it. He's going to be very angry with himself in the morning when he finds out Zoey had to face Marini alone."

I walked into the room, drying my hair with the towel Lee had managed to find. My wolf and I needed a quick trip to Target. Now that I knew how he felt about me, I was going to be much more comfortable in the future about helping him out. His apartment needed a feminine touch. It also needed more towels and maybe a nice yellow rug for the bathroom. He would complain outwardly that I was interfering, but I knew deep down he would like me taking care of him.

"I handled it, Dev," I said with as much confidence as I could muster. I was feeling better after my shower and the talk with Lee. I'd taken care of it and no one had gotten hurt. All in all, I was going to have to call it an acceptable loss.

Neil stood with Dev, looking pale and worried. "You didn't come home. I got scared so I slapped Dev awake."

"He did," Dev said, touching his cheek. "It was rather awful. He screamed as well."

"Didn't work on Danny, huh?" I asked.

"He moaned a lot and he tried to kiss Dev," Neil admitted with a delighted smile. "He told Dev he had great boobs."

Dev shrugged at Neil, a frown on his face. "Well, obviously he thought I was Zoey. He played with my hair. I'm afraid he finds my hair confusing since it's gotten as long as our wife's. Somehow he ended up spooning me."

Neil looked around the room innocently.

"He always was an affectionate drunk." I wondered how many pictures Neil had taken and when that website would be going up. I was going to be a big fan.

Dev put his hands on my shoulders. "I'm so sorry, sweetheart. We should never have done that. We should never have left you alone like that."

I sighed, trying to put him at ease. "I wasn't alone, Dev. I had plenty of backup. Marini showed up, he postured a lot, he took the Blood Stone, and he left. I came up here to talk to Lee and he couldn't stand the smell of all that vodka. He's very picky."

"Well, you smelled like a drunk, Zoey." Lee played his part to the hilt. He crossed his arms over his chest stubbornly as he stared down Dev. "She was scared, Quinn. The bastard scared her."

Neil might be a terrible liar, but Lee knew that the best lie had a kernel of truth to it.

Dev's green eyes were filled with concern. "Are you really all right, sweetheart?"

I nodded. "I'm fine. Except for the fact Lee doesn't have any conditioner."

Lee shook his head. "Why would I have conditioner? You should be happy I had shampoo. Normally I just use soap."

"And he doesn't have a hair dryer." I had found one thing in his sparse bathroom that made me giggle. I pulled it out now. "But he does have eyeliner."

Neil gave me a thumbs-up. "I always knew Lee was one of us, Z."

Lee plucked the tube from my fingers. "That's not mine, obviously. This is why I don't have people over."

"Really?" Dev asked. "I thought it was because you were a misanthropic jerk."

"That too," the werewolf admitted. "Now out, all of you, before Zoey starts deciding I need new furniture."

He knew me too well. "You need some rugs too, Lee. I bet your little paws just go all over the place when you run around in here in wolf form."

Hardwood floors would be hard to run on. When he was in wolf form, Neil always did that thing where all four feet went different ways and I had to help him up.

"Out," Lee commanded. "Neil, you stay. Dev can take care of Zoey. Come on in and have a beer with me."

Neil passed me his robe and I put it on over the T-shirt Lee had lent me that hit just above my knees. I was grateful for the robe so I wasn't walking around the building half naked. "Night, Z."

Dev took my hand and walked me down the hall to the elevator. It was a long, weird walk back to our place. The only way back up to the penthouse was to go all the way down to Ether and then up again.

He stopped in the middle of the hall and pulled me into his arms, squeezing me tight. "I'm so sorry, Zoey."

I fought back tears because it felt so good to be close to him. I let my head rest against his chest. "I'm all right."

I said the words as much for myself as for him. I was all right now because I was in his arms again and earlier in the evening, I wasn't sure that would happen. I let him hold me for a long moment, the heat of his body warming me. Finally, I let go and turned my face up to his. "I love you."

His hands cupped my cheeks. "I love you, my goddess. We've been putting off the inevitable, haven't we?"

I nodded, happy that we were at least discussing the subject. "We have to deal with Daniel's heart."

Dev took a long breath and kissed my forehead before letting go and leading me to the elevator. "I'll find a way. I won't let him die on us and I won't allow Marini to use you to steal for him again. I swear I'll kill him first."

"You owe Peter Hansen a couple of nights in the VIP room gratis," I mentioned as Dev hit the complex series of buttons that would take us down to the club.

Dev frowned, obviously putting on his business hat. "Why would I want to do that? Do you know how much a night in the VIP room costs?"

"Nope," I replied tartly. "If you don't want your wife making business decisions for you, maybe you shouldn't party so hard."

"Perhaps I should think more before I pretend I am a teenager again," Dev said. "I will admit I view my actions differently when it costs me money rather than my mother. I will never forget how angry she was to have to pay off the Madrid police force when Declan and I got arrested for public lewdness."

Oh, yes, I might need that bail fund Neil had mentioned.

"I disagreed with them completely," Dev explained. "I thought it was a beautiful act. Apparently there is a law or something…"

I laughed at the thought as Dev led me through Ether. It was quieting down because dawn was coming. The cleaning crew was busy setting everything back to rights. We walked up the stairs and I knew what I needed to do. I wasn't going to let Marini wreck my special places. If he took my good memories of a place, then I would just have to make new ones.

I stopped his hand when he would have pushed the button to take us up to the penthouse. "Can we stay here for a while?"

"You don't want to go upstairs?"

"I want to stay here for a minute or two." An idea played in my brain. A way to burn off the bad memories.

I wanted to be here with him and though he couldn't join us, I wanted to be here with Bris. If Marini had assaulted me in this room, then I had to remember that Bris had saved me. There was a sweetness to that. I could take it back. I could make this place mine again.

Dev turned and there was a slow smile spreading across his face. "You want to be alone with me, my glorious goddess? How may I serve your needs this evening?"

Need was the right way to put what I wanted. I needed him. I needed to shove Marini's face out of my head and I knew just how to do it. "Why don't you sit in that chair for me?"

He studied me for a long moment. I knew what he was thinking. Usually he was the dominant force in our sex life. Dev almost always took the lead. If he sat down in that chair, he would be conceding that power to me. "All right, if that's what you need tonight."

He obediently sat down and rested back in the chair, letting me know he was mine to do with as I pleased. Dev was part fertility god and that meant he instinctively knew what his partner wanted from him. It made him an incredible lover and now it made him rather submissive. I appreciated it and it let me know just how much he trusted me.

"Do you have any condoms down here?" I asked, feeling almost shy.

Dev's lips quirked upward in a sly grin. "I have condoms stashed all over this club, lover. Anywhere you want to throw down, I'm prepared for it. I think about fucking you all the time. Open the top drawer of that desk."

I did and sure enough, there was a box sitting there. I snagged one and shrugged out of Neil's robe, then pulled the T-shirt over my head and wiggled out of my underwear.

"Are you sure I have to sit down?" Dev asked, his voice deep with desire. He'd enjoyed the striptease, and I was sure his clothes were feeling rather confining now. I glanced down and sure enough, his cock was straining against his slacks.

"Yes, Devinshea. I'm going to make it worse for you, baby. Keep your hands to yourself, please."

"Zoey," Dev breathed, dismayed.

I stared down at him, enjoying my foray into the dominant position. It was already getting me hot, the thought of him itching to touch me but forcing himself to be still. I needed to take back a little power, a little control. "If you move, I'll stop what I'm doing. You don't want that, do you?"

"No," he whispered, his hands curling over the arms of the chair. Every muscle in his body stiffened with arousal.

I leaned over and kissed him briefly, letting him feel my tongue running along the edges of his plump, sensual lips. They were practically perfect and wholly masculine. God, I loved kissing him. I could kiss him for hours and not do a damn thing else. Our noses rubbed together, reminding me how sweet intimacy could be. There was no violence to this. There was just love and devotion. I ate at his lips and he let me. I straddled him, and already I could feel the hard ridge of his erection pressing up. The rest of Dev might be willing to play the submissive tonight, but his cock was ready to take over at the first opportunity.

"Give me your tongue," I whispered against his mouth, and he opened underneath me, letting his tongue reach out to caress mine. Dev allowed me full access, letting me delve inside. Our tongues played together, dancing against one another in a perfect sweetness.

Dev's magic started to pulse from his body, a wave that swept away my anxieties and left me with nothing but an easy lust. We kissed and I felt myself getting very soft and very wet. I ground down, loving the way his cock jumped every time I rubbed against it.

"Zoey," he groaned into my mouth. "You're killing me. Let me touch you."

I pulled back and I was sure my grin was mischievous. There was a certain relief that came with being intimate with Dev. I'd worried Marini would be there between us, but this was nothing like Marini. Dev's magic called to me. There wasn't a place for anything but Dev and me here. His magic thrummed through me, relaxing me and reminding me how good it was between us.

"Not yet." I got down on my knees, and he had the arms of the chair in a death grip. I had gotten so wet, the front of his slacks were covered with my arousal. I laughed a little at that. I was glad he didn't have anywhere to go. "Sorry about your pants, baby."

His green eyes gleamed at me. "I'm not. If you humans weren't so sexually repressed, I would be proud to walk around in them and tell everyone exactly how they got that way. It's the one thing I miss about Faery. I liked being able to talk openly about how good it is to fuck you."

It was true. Faeries were big on oversharing when it came to their sex lives. But not all humans were repressed, and I needed to make that clear to my husband. I unbuttoned his slacks and slowly eased the zipper down. My fingers brushed against his taut skin, reveling in the muscles I found there. Dev's body was perfection. Silk covering steel.

"Repressed, huh?" I pulled down the waistband of his blue silk boxers. His cock sprang free and he moaned as I stroked him. I wasn't particularly gentle. He loved it rough. I clenched him in my hand, studying the beauty of his cock. Long and thick, with a gorgeous purple head. There was already a lovely pearly drop pushing from the slit.

"I wasn't talking about you," he said breathlessly, pressing his pelvis up.

"Oh, I think you were." I kissed his cock, just a little peck. I let my tongue lap up the drop of arousal on his cock. Salty. Slightly sweet and wholly Dev. "I might have to prove you wrong, Devinshea."

There is one particular part of my faery prince's cock that I love to run my tongue over. He has a thick vein that runs from the base of his penis almost all the way to the head before disappearing deep into his flesh. I licked all the way up along that vein, feeling it pulse and buck under my tongue.

"Oh, goddess, please, please let me fuck your mouth," he begged, his nails digging into the chair. I knew what he wanted to do. He wanted to wrap his hands in my hair and shove his cock in and out of my mouth until he worked his way to the back so he could press down and come straight down my throat. He liked to stand over me and watch his cock take my mouth over and over again.

I wasn't playing that way tonight. Magic or no magic, this was about me and what I needed. I needed to be in control for a time.

I worshipped his cock with little kisses and licks and let the engorged head disappear briefly into my mouth before starting another assault. Dev was panting, his cock weeping with cream by the time I got around to sucking his balls into my mouth.

"Zoey, I'm gonna come if you don't stop that." There was a desperate edge to his voice.

I wasn't about to stop. I was enjoying myself. "You are not allowed to come until I say so." Turnabout was fair play. I loved the way his balls curled up, ready to shoot off at any minute. Rising up a little, I sucked the cream lubricating the head of his cock like it was a particularly good ice cream cone. "Besides I need to prove I'm not repressed, Dev."

"You're very liberated, my lover," Dev agreed readily. "You might be the most liberated woman I've ever met. Do you know what liberated women like? Penetration."

I laughed against his skin and he moaned at the sensation. "Is that what liberated women want?"

My pussy was about as soaked as it was going to get. I was feeling hot and ready to lower myself onto him. Picking the condom up, I opened it and started to work it down his cock. I had never actually provided this service for Dev. He was an expert and could roll a condom on before I even knew he had one. I was a little less knowledgeable. I tugged and rolled while Dev patiently waited through my ministrations. I finally pronounced it done and heard him sigh.

"Thank the goddess," he breathed out. "If I survive the night it will be a miracle. Between Daniel's bite and your sexual dominance, I think I'm going to die of pleasure."

I straddled him again, positioning my knees on either side of his hips and looking down on his gorgeous face. I ran my fingers through his hair and loved the way he closed his eyes and sighed.

"It would be a fitting way for you to go," I said and remembered what I owed him. I was his dominant this time. It was a little game we enjoyed free from anything heavy, but there were rules. One of the rules was the dominant always let the submissive know how much she enjoyed him. "God, Dev, I love everything about you."

He smiled and I knew he'd been waiting to see if I would remember. Daniel and I tended to be quiet during sex, letting our actions speak for us, but Dev was trying to break us of the habit. He liked to talk. He liked to talk about the sex and the pleasure and what he felt.

"You're so beautiful, my husband." I lowered my pussy onto his stiff cock. He stayed still, letting me work my way down, letting me push him inside me inch by inch. He filled me up and stretched me, every centimeter an exquisite sensation. "I'm never happier than when you're inside me."

And he was. I moved up and down slowly, finding that spot deep inside me that felt like heaven with every stroke. I bit my lip, unable to talk now, focused solely on pushing myself over the edge. My every sense narrowed to the sweet pressure building. I was so selfish in that moment, needing to use him, needing to know he was here and he was mine. The only sounds were our breath and the increasingly urgent slap of flesh against flesh.

"Touch me, Dev." I was so close. I just needed a little bit more.

He didn't play or pretend. He knew exactly what I needed and he gave it to me. I rolled my hips against him as he rubbed my swollen clitoris with his thumb and I came forcefully. I ground myself against him, prolonging the pleasure before finally collapsing onto his chest.

I was drained for the second time that night, but this was sweet. This was heaven.

"My goddess?" Dev was still achingly hard inside me, and he had been a very obedient boy.

"Oh, I'm so sorry, baby," I said, realizing my oversight. "You can come. I'm good now. Take over and do your worst."

He lifted me up, never breaking our connection. He swept his hand across his desk and everything went flying. I was suddenly on my back and he wasted no time. He pounded into me.

"Did you enjoy that, lover?" Dev asked, his voice harsh with need. "I did. You should know that while I found the experience pleasurable, I have no intention of giving up my position permanently. You're my little pleasure slave. You're my sweet little submissive."

"I am." I spread myself farther, denying him nothing.

He pumped away, shoving his cock in as far as it would go only to pull back and start again. "I want you to do that to our vampire, though. I want to see how long he'll last under that sweet mouth of yours when he's not in control. I bet he won't last a minute, wife."

Then he was past the talking stage. He was fully focused on one thing as his head fell forward and his body began to shake. He leaned forward until his pelvic bone hit my clit with every forceful thrust. My hands found that perfectly muscled ass of his, and I urged him on because I was coming again. I held him against me and pushed forward as he groaned and ground himself against me. He pumped out his release and fell on top of me.

After a long soft moment, his head came up. Sleepy eyes stared down at me. "Are you all right now, Zoey?"

His hands stroked my face as he asked, and I knew he realized there was more to my story.

"I feel a hundred percent better, Devinshea," I answered with perfect honesty for the first time in the last hour.

He stood up and disposed of the condom before lifting me into his arms and settling us back on the chair. He cuddled me against his chest and I buried my head in his neck.

"I wish you would tell me what happened." He kissed the top of my head.

"I did." I was back to lying. "I just got scared. It's going to happen soon, isn't it?"

His arms tightened around me. "I'm afraid so. I feel it coming faster than I want. When we started this, I just wanted it to be over and now that this fight is staring me in the face, I want to hide from it. Zoey, I don't know what happens…after our time on this plane is done. I only promise you this; if I go first, I will wait for you. If there is any way, I'll find it and I will wait."

I wrapped myself around him and felt tears threaten again. "I'll wait, too."

"And Daniel will finish what he needs to and he'll follow," Dev said quietly. "If anything happens, I know we'll be together again."

We sat there for the longest time holding on, praying Dev's words would prove true.

CHAPTER FIVE

"Have you tried a locator spell?" Christine's mouth twisted thoughtfully as she regarded Nim.

I was very glad Nim didn't roll her eyes at the question. I'd requested she try politeness with my dad's girlfriend. I found Christine annoying from time to time, but she was good to my father and she'd made great strides in her witchcraft studies. Christine wasn't a latent witch like my friend Sarah. Christine's talents had been earned through study and discipline. They weren't instinctive. I'd discovered that, in some cases, the very fact that Christine had been forced to work so hard caused her to think creatively when it came to a problem.

"I did." The god-only-knew-how-old nymph sat on my father's couch looking young and pretty. Nim was about my height, but of a much slimmer build. She had curly sable-colored hair and the most striking violet eyes. The eyes gave her away. Modern times aided her in passing as human because these days people assumed she was wearing colored contacts. She'd been quiet all afternoon. I expected her to chatter away about her sexual adventures with Michael from the night before, but she merely smiled and said she'd enjoyed herself. I asked if Michael had done anything he shouldn't have and she insisted he'd been sweet.

I think she was missing Arawn, the Welsh death god she'd loved for so long. Michael had been her first foray into sex that didn't include the man she left behind in Faery.

"And?" Christine prompted.

Nim shook her curls. "Maybe I'm out of practice. I've narrowed it down to three different places, but I don't want to clue anybody in to the fact that we're coming. I want to know exactly where I'm going. It would have been easier if I had a piece of the item I'm looking for, but I like to travel light."

"And this…item you lost. What was its origin?" the blonde witch asked.

She couldn't care less what the "item" was. Christine wouldn't care that we were looking for a thousand-plus-year-old wizard, but Nim didn't want witch worship to cloud the issue. Apparently before Merlin had been imprisoned, he'd had his share of groupies. "Was it something you crafted yourself or something you found?"

Nim thought for a moment and then smiled. "No, I didn't have anything to do with that, I'm happy to say. I suppose you could say it's demonic in origin, at least partially."

I smiled as I exchanged a glance with Neil. We'd been doing a lot of research on Merlin. Well, I'd been doing a lot of research. Neil had been listening to the *Spamalot* soundtrack. The legend had it that Merlin was the product of a union between a human female and an incubus—a horny demon who ran around knocking up unsuspecting women who thought they were having a harmless little wet dream until, oh crap, nine months later they had to explain Junior.

"Well, naturally it involves a damn demon," Lee grumbled. Lee sat on the couch in my father's house in far north Dallas. We'd come to see Christine, but I hoped to catch a minute with my dad. He and Christine had been out of town when we returned from Faery, and this was the first chance I'd had to talk to him.

I heard the door open and knew I'd gotten lucky. My father walked in looking dapper in his golf clothes, carrying the clubs I gotten him for his birthday a few years back. He poked his head into the living room and waved to Neil and Lee. I introduced him to Nim, and then he got a very serious look on his face.

"I'm glad to see you, girl," Dad said, his Irish accent heavy.

"Why don't you come up to the office? I want to talk to you."

A little anxiety hit me. He'd asked me to come *up* to his office. My father had two offices in this house. The office on the first floor was the one he used on a daily basis. In the past, he would have taken clients into that office. It was a study in neat professionalism. The office upstairs was where Dad kept the secrets. If he was taking me upstairs, he had something serious to discuss.

I got up, giving Lee a nod. He relaxed and settled in to wait for me. My father's house was secure, so he didn't feel the need to wait outside the door like he normally would if we'd been in public. I followed Dad up the stairs and past the bedrooms that Danny and I had lived in during our high school years. My father and I had settled down once Danny had come to live with us. There wasn't a room in this house that didn't remind me of my vampire husband, my first love.

Dad unlocked the door to his private office and slipped inside. There was nothing vaguely professional about this piece of my father's soul. It was filled with shelf after shelf of books, most of them incredibly old and beyond rare. All of them dealt with the arcane arts. Harry Wharton was a master thief, but he dealt in a very select clientele. He stole for and from supernatural creatures. It made him a very wealthy man.

"Sit down, Zoey," he said in that voice that made me feel like I was eight again and we were about to talk about my report card.

I took the seat opposite the desk, but I didn't relax.

Dad seemed restless as he drummed his fingers on the desktop. "How was Faery, then?"

"All right, I guess." I had to be careful because we'd agreed not to bring my father into our war. "Dev's family was a little weird, but I ended up liking his mom. I was glad to get back to actual technology."

"Did Danny get the alliance he needs to take over the bloody Council?" The words were soft, but there was such accusation in them I was sure the blood drained from my face.

"What?" I asked because as far as Dad knew, Daniel was an ordinary vampire. We worked very hard to keep him in the dark about our political games.

My father sat back in his chair and studied me with hazel eyes that reflected my own. "Did you think I would never ask questions? You were gone awhile. I was worried out of my head, but I figured that was just an old man being anxious. And then I did a job for a friend in New York. I ran into a vampire there. Do you want to know what he called you? Only when we were in private, of course, and only after he found out I was your father, but then he called you his queen, Zoey. His bloody queen. What the hell kind of games are the three of you playing?"

I swallowed and really wished Danny was here being interrogated instead of me. I stalled a little. "Henri Jacobs?" He was the only vampire I knew who lived in New York and was loyal to Daniel.

"I met him and his wife through a mutual acquaintance," Dad acknowledged. "They were eager to be nice to the queen's father. I had to smile and pretend I knew what the hell they were talking about. Tell me I heard wrong. Tell me Danny isn't a king and god, girl, tell me he ain't the fucking *Nex Apparatus*. Do you know what that is?"

"Death Machine." It was the traditional name for the vampire who scared the shit out of the other vampires. "It isn't his fault, Dad. He can't help his DNA."

Dad's fists came down on the table and everything jumped. "No, that ain't his fault, but the rest of it is. He should have told me. I knew something was wrong when they kept him at the Council for so long. He assured me he was fine when he came back. Do you think I would have sat back and let them turn Danny into an assassin? I'm not helpless, girl. I got some serious contacts."

"No amount of money would have worked, Dad," I explained. "I promise you there was nothing any of us could have done. Danny did what he had to do to survive. They knew he was a king. He couldn't hide it. You couldn't have done anything to help him."

"Why did they let him live?" Dad asked, shaking his head and sitting back.

"The head of the Council thought he could have his cake and eat it, too. He kept Daniel at his side for three years, training him to be a good little death machine. When Danny was obedient enough, he was allowed to come home. He's been working for them ever since. Just before Daniel's turn, there was a lot of talk of a revolution. There was a faction of the vampire world that believed the Council had become corrupt. Daniel was a control measure. Once the Council appointed a *Nex Apparatus*, the underground disappeared."

"And what makes the Council believe they can control Danny?"

I explained about Marini's various control measures from threatening me to the device on Daniel's heart. I watched the blood drain from my father's face.

"What's Devinshea's part in all of this?" Dad asked the question like he didn't want to know the answer. He'd never liked Dev. He didn't understand our relationship and would have preferred Dev had never come on the scene.

"Dev is the one who kept Danny from getting himself killed and me sold to the highest bidder." Some good might come from this. I just might be able to get my father to understand just how important Dev was to both myself and to Danny. "Before Dev started advising Danny, he wasn't playing things smart. Now I realize how close we came to everything blowing up in our faces. Dev took over the political aspects of Danny's bid. He got us the wolves and he negotiated the alliance with King Angus of the Unseelie."

"He really is Miria's son, then?"

"For all the good it did him," I said bitterly.

My father was quiet for a while, and I let him contemplate everything I'd said. He ran a hand through his thinning hair and seemed older than usual as he leaned forward. His voice was low as he asked, "What happened? Dev is a Seelie. Why is the alliance with the Unseelie? Don't blow sunshine up my ass, girl. I want to know what happened. You and Danny...you're the best things I ever did. Don't lie and don't block me out because you think I'm an old man."

I shook my head. "It isn't like that, Dad. I never kept it from you because I didn't trust you or I didn't think you could handle it. Danny didn't want you to know because he was afraid of what you would think. It was hard for him to even tell me. Your opinion is so important to him."

"I could never think badly of Danny," he said. "He's like my son."

"Yes he is and he wants you to be proud of him. Some of the things he's done, he isn't proud of."

"He did it to survive," he said, shaking his head like the thought of anything else was insane. "Now what happened to you on the Faery plane?"

I decided I owed my father the full truth and so I told him. I told him about the troubles between the two tribes and how the traitors on each side had worked together to cause a war. I gave him the entire story with the singular exception of my brief foray into sexual servitude. I hesitated to tell him about one part, but decided to go ahead. He was my father. He should know.

"Dad, I need to tell you that I had a miscarriage while I was in Faery," I said calmly. It hadn't really been a true miscarriage. It had been a spell that caused me to lose my baby.

My father went pale, his eyes widening. "You were pregnant? You didn't tell me you were pregnant?"

"I didn't know until we were already there," I explained quickly. "It was over before we came home."

His voice was barely above a whisper as he absorbed that news. "I hadn't...when Danny turned I gave up on the thought of having grandkids. I didn't realize you were planning on having a family like that, Zoey."

I blushed because I was thinking of the night we conceived our son. "It wasn't planned. It happened on the night Dev and I got married."

My father was very firm in his opinions about that. "Those were pagan rites, girl. They won't be recognized on this plane."

"You recognize my marriage to Danny." My wedding to Daniel had been even less recognizable as a wedding than the rites Dev and I had performed. At least the bride's permission was needed in the pagan rites. The vampires did not require my opinion.

"I do," he said. "But you ain't getting pregnant by Daniel. You start bringing kids in and you need to protect them. Are you planning on moving to Faery with the prince?"

Well, that answered one question I had about why my dad didn't like Dev. If my father had been sitting around wondering when the man was going to pack me up and cart me off to another plane, it explained a lot.

"We're not going anywhere. This is our home, Dad." I reached across the desk and covered his hand with mine. "You have to understand. Dev has nothing to go back to. The Seelie nobles refuse to recognize him because he isn't a full Fae. We made the deal with the Unseelie because they wanted a high priest and Dev's fertility powers are useful to them."

"His fertility powers were useful to you, too," he said with a small smile. "So you and Dev want to have babies, then?"

"No," I corrected him because he needed to understand. "Dev, Daniel, and I want to have babies. I know you don't approve of our relationship, but we're happy together. Maybe it isn't normal, but nothing about us is normal. We love each other. We're committed to each other. We're going to have a family together and I want you there, Dad. You're the only grandparent our kids are going to have. Danny doesn't have parents left, Mom couldn't care less, and Miria won't be around."

A long smile crossed my dad's face. "That's a whole new generation'll be needing to learn a profession, the way I see it."

I didn't point out that with Dev's money, our kids wouldn't have to work a day if they didn't want to or that Dev would probably be teaching them how to run his businesses. The truth was Dev would find it amusing that his kids could crack a safe, and Daniel would be teaching them any number of criminal talents. If my dad wanted to pass on his knowledge to his grandbabies, I wouldn't object. He'd been my teacher and a damn good one.

My hand was suddenly caught between both of his as he got deadly serious. "You're my girl. Those boys can do whatever you let them, but you'll always be my girl. Don't shut me out. I want to know what's going on and I want to help."

I had to smile. "You were the one who told me never to mix business and family."

He brought my hand to his chest and placed it over his heart. I could see he was very emotional. "You never learned that, girl. It's the one lesson I taught you that I'm glad didn't stick. And this ain't business. This is war. I want to know everything."

I nodded and sat back. This time when I talked to my father, I told him everything from the very beginning.

Dad's eyes were curious as we walked down the stairs a half an hour later. "So that slip of a girl sitting on my couch really knew King Arthur?"

"Yup," I said. "More importantly, she knew Merlin, who can help Daniel with his little heart problem."

Letting out a deep breath, my father regarded me seriously. "Don't think that wizard is someone to be taken lightly. There's a reason he was called Merlin Satanspawn. He was part demon and that might have been the better part of him. You be careful around him."

There was a brief knock on the door and when it opened, Dev walked in. He was dressed in an immaculate suit and tie. His green eyes lost their light when he saw me with my dad. His mouth turned down and he strode to the stairs, his stance much more arrogant than before. He was ready for a fight.

"Hello, Harry," he said evenly, but there was an undercurrent to his words. He was waiting for the rejection he always got from my dad. "I just finished a meeting and I came to pick up my wife."

"Wife" was said with a nice bit of challenge.

My father shook his head as he stared at Dev. "She ain't your wife. Not by the laws of this plane, and if you're going to knock my girl up, one of you better be marrying her legally. As Danny's death certificate is on file, I'm thinking it's gotta be you, Dev."

The arrogance was gone in an instant, replaced with a look of shock. "You want me to marry Zoey in the human fashion?"

"Well, I ain't talking about a white, frilly wedding, boy. Ten minutes at the courthouse will do. If you're willing to put a baby up in her, then you better be willing to sign a paper that says you're responsible for her."

"I don't need him to be responsible for me, Dad." My father was, for the most part, a modern man, but sometimes he went back to the Middle Ages.

Dev ignored me. He looked like an eager puppy who had just realized he might not get kicked this time. "I am. I mean, I will sign

57

the papers, of course."

"All right, then," my dad said, looking Dev over and coming to a decision. "Come on up then, son. I've got a nice bottle of Irish whiskey that needs opening. I've heard you can handle your liquor. That's a talent I can appreciate. We need to talk about that hair, though. It makes you look like a girl, son. You'll be needing a haircut before we go to the courthouse."

Dev started walking up the stairs, following my dad, who was going on about the joys of a buzz cut. He stopped as he reached the step I was standing on. "Do you think the whiskey is poisoned, my goddess?"

I'm pretty sure he was only half joking.

I shook my head and leaned over for a little kiss. "No, baby, he just realized he's probably getting grandkids out of our arrangement. He really wants some rugrats to corrupt."

"My sexual prowess wins everyone over in the end." He ran after my father, and I only hoped he didn't let Dad cut his hair.

Christine stood at the bottom of the staircase wearing a pink button-down and a pair of khaki shorts that came to her knees. She looked like a suburban housewife about to call everyone down for dinner. The brilliant smile on her face immediately put me on edge.

"Dear god, what does she want to do?" I asked, looking at Neil, who walked up behind her.

He made the universal sign for insanity. "Well, what do you think, Z?"

I knew what her favorite thing to do was. Most women liked shopping or having lunch with friends or going to the spa. Christine liked calling demons. "We have to call up Hell why?"

"It's the only way, Zoey," Christine said with no small amount of glee. "I've given it careful consideration and this is the only thing I can come up with. Tell Dev I'll need that magic of his."

I walked past her and into the living room.

"Tell her no, Zoey," Lee said before I even sat down beside him on the couch.

"I don't really know what I'm saying no to, yet." I wasn't sure what ringing up a demon would do for us.

"You're saying no to inviting a demon to kill us all," Lee supplied helpfully. "That crazy witch is acting like calling up the demon is like looking up movie times on the Internet."

Nim crossed one leg over the other and sat back. "It might work. At least it will be faster than digging up half of England."

Neil threw his body onto the seat next to me. "Christine thinks a demon will be able to locate the old guy a lot faster than a witch. She says demons can sense other demons and should be able to get us pretty close to where the prison is. We could go over to England and hope Nim remembers something or we can call up a demonic GPS and know where the hell we're going. I don't suppose Nim stashed him under Harrods, huh?"

"I doubt it was anywhere so fun, sweetie." I turned my attention to my other wolf, who was already frowning. "Come on, Lee. Do you have a better idea?"

"Yeah, we all just shoot each other," Lee offered sarcastically. "It'll be faster and way more pleasant than the disemboweling we'll all get on the Hell plane when the bugger gets loose. Have you asked yourself something, Zoey? Why would this random demon want to do your bidding?"

"Because he isn't random." I had one and only one option on who to call. He was the only demon whose name I knew and that was a requirement. At least he was a known quantity. "And he owes me a favor. Danny and Dev killed his biggest rival, so maybe he'll be...I was going to say grateful but that doesn't seem right. Maybe he won't do that thing where he rips peoples' throats open."

Neil was already groaning. "I hate Stewart, Zoey. He always comes on to me and then he sics something big on me when I turn him down."

"Unless you know some other Hell lord who owes us big time, I suggest you put on your best manwhore clothes because you're the bait, buddy," I explained, patting him on the shoulder reassuringly.

"I hate being the bait," Neil replied with a pout.

The trouble was he was really good at it.

CHAPTER SIX

"I don't think Daniel is going to be happy with this plan, sweetheart." Dev turned into the parking garage about an hour before the sun went down. He seemed to think Daniel would object to working with Stewart, the demon. It might have had something to do with the fact that the last demon I'd had a working relationship with had killed both me and Dev, and done his damnedest to take out Danny, too.

"Then he can come up with a better one." I wasn't sitting on my ass any longer. If Stewart was our best hope for finding Merlin's prison, then I was willing to take the chance. "I want that thing off his heart. We need Daniel able to fight Marini because he's closing in. Marini wants the two of us in Paris next month."

Dev guided the Audi into his reserved spot. "Why? What are we supposed to do there?"

"There's some sort of meeting. We're supposed to entertain the Council. Marini wants to witness a fertility ritual. He was impressed with what he heard about our wedding ceremony. He'd like an encore, Dev."

"That is a sacred ceremony," Dev said, obviously outraged at the thought. "It is not an entertainment. Why would I perform fertility rites for a group that can never hope to have children?"

"Because they can feed off that magic. Marini wants to feed like Daniel." I tried not to shudder as I remembered how he'd last fed.

"I feed Daniel because he's my partner," Dev said. "I feed Daniel because I care deeply for him. I would never willingly allow another vampire to feed off of what is essentially the passion and love between the two of us. Daniel is a part of that. Marini is insane if he thinks I'll allow a sacred ritual to be perverted for his curiosity."

"It isn't curiosity." I opened the door to the car and got out. I started toward the elevator. At least the club would be quiet at this time in the evening. The only person who might be there was Zack, who went over the security tapes every day. "It's jealousy. He wants whatever Daniel has."

Dev stalked behind me. He was pulling at his tie. "How did Marini even know about our marriage?"

"Chad." I was worried about our spy. He'd seemed…wrong somehow.

The elevator closed and began the descent to Ether. "Why would Chad have said anything about that?"

"I don't know, baby. Have you talked to him since we got back?"

"Daniel's spoken to him," Dev replied. "He didn't seem concerned. Marini is quite taken with his talent. Chad was asked to stay on after his training was done. He thought it was better to not arouse suspicions by denying the request."

"He could have given Neil a call," I muttered.

"I can't tell you why he neglected that. We agreed that he could ask about Neil since they could have met in Colorado, but he had to treat him as an acquaintance would. He didn't ask about him last night?"

I grimaced as I remembered the previous night and how Chad had mentioned Neil. "You guys need to clue me in on this stuff. He did ask about Neil and now I can see where he was coming from. At the time, I just thought he was being a typical vampire asshole."

Dev laughed lightly as he shook his head and gave me a look that told me I was hopeless. "Should he have gently asked about his true love in front of Marini? He needs to protect Neil and the only way he can do that is to treat him as though he doesn't really matter. Neil can be a quick hook-up, but anything more is dangerous. Hey, they didn't actually hook up last night, did they? Shit, I forgot to warn Zack."

"Warn Zack?"

His eyebrows rose suggestively. "Zack runs through the security tapes every afternoon. Sometimes he catches a show like the one we put on in the office last night. I've started trying to warn him so he can skip that part."

That wasn't the only show he was going to see, and there was no way I could intimidate him into keeping my meeting with Marini to himself. If Zack saw that tape, he would take it straight to Daniel.

"Oh, my god," I breathed and I was sure I went pale.

"Sweetheart, it's not a big deal. Zack knows we have sex."

The elevator doors opened and I ran for the security office.

"Zoey!" Dev yelled, running after me.

We both stopped as a table flew past our heads. It knocked into the wall opposite us and smashed to pieces.

Dev pulled me back and I had a moment to survey the damage. If I hadn't known better, I would have said a bomb had gone off. There was smashed furniture everywhere. My eyes followed the track of where the table had come from. Daniel was in a full-on rage. He looked like he'd gotten straight out of bed for his berserker episode. He was still in the T-shirt and sweat pants he'd worn the night before, and his normally shaggy hair hadn't seen a shower yet. The rest of him…didn't even look vaguely human. His eyes had bled to a deep sapphire blue. His fangs were enormous and his claws were out.

The beast was loose.

"He's been at it for fifteen minutes." Zack stood beside me watching the scene calmly. His arms were crossed over his chest.

"What the hell is going on?" Dev asked, his face a mask of confusion as he watched Daniel put his fist through a wall.

"He saw the tape." Zack turned to me and I expected him to be pissed, but his brown eyes were sympathetic. "I couldn't keep it from him, Zoey. I know what you were trying to do and I admire you for it, but you're wrong. I'm sorry. He had to know."

"Know what?" Dev asked. "I thought he knew I fucked our wife. Most of the time, he's there when I'm doing it. Why exactly has this very common occurrence suddenly turned Daniel into a bull in my china shop? Damn it, Dan! Not the bar!"

Dev stepped out into the middle of the room like he wasn't staring down an enraged vampire who he thought was pissed at him. "Stop it this instant, Daniel! If you have a problem with me then fight it out. Do you have any idea how much this is costing us? Contractors are expensive and those freaking shapeshifters are cons, I swear it. They charge exorbitant rates and half the time I find them standing around."

Daniel stopped and stared at Dev. He pointed a long claw at him. "You knew and you let it happen."

"He didn't, Danny." I used my softest voice. I needed to work some serious companion magic to get Daniel to come down from his angry high.

"Well, of course I knew, Zoey," Dev said, still under mistaken impressions. "I was there. I didn't realize I had to ask Daniel for permission to screw our wife."

Daniel was shaking as he spoke. "Was that before or after Marini raped her?"

A dazed air hit Dev as he turned. I started to say something, but he quickly held a hand up to stop me. The strong line of his jaw firmed stubbornly, and I knew he wasn't going to listen to anything I had to say. His eyes found Zack. "Where is this tape?"

The werewolf quietly led his boss into the small security office. The doors opened behind us and the rest of the crew entered, laughing and joking, until they saw the damage.

"What on earth?" Neil's mouth hung open as he set his Starbucks on a miraculously intact table.

"Shit." Lee cursed because he was the only one who knew what had to have happened.

"You!" Daniel yelled, his rage turning to Lee. "Where the hell were you when he was draining her? You're her bodyguard."

"And you're her husband," Lee growled back, shoving Neil and Nim behind him. "You want to know where I was? I was up in my apartment enjoying my night off because I was assured my charge's husbands would take care of her. No one told me they would act like imbeciles, get drunk, pass out and leave her on her own. Marini must have thought he'd died and gone to heaven, Your Highness. She was all alone and vulnerable because the men who say they love her were unconscious."

"Lee, you're not helping." The last thing I needed was for Lee to fan the flames.

"She told you." Daniel managed to make it an accusation.

"Of course she told me. She needed someone to help her after she was brutally assaulted. Maybe she was trying to avoid this little scene," Lee replied.

"Danny, you need to calm down," I said in my most patient voice. "Please, calm down and we can talk about this."

"No, companion," he said, backing away from me. "You will not calm me this time." His blue gaze went back to Lee, who seemed to be the one he wanted to take this out on since his true target was inconveniently absent. "You should have told me, wolf. You owe me the truth. I'm her master."

Lee's hands sprouted long, nasty claws as he confronted Daniel. "I owe you nothing, vampire. I'm Zoey's guard. My oath is to her. I put up with you because she loves you."

"And just what is your relationship with my companion that when she's hurt, she would run to you?" The question was asked with ugly suspicion.

"What are you accusing me of, Daniel?" I crossed my arms over my chest and stared my husband down. "How many lovers did I have last night? Do you honestly believe I went from Marini to Lee to Dev? Damn, Danny, I'm quite the busy bee. I should start charging." I was on a tear now because the last thing I needed was Daniel pulling his vampire jealousy crap on me. "Why do you assume it was rape? I sent Neil up to the penthouse. Maybe I wanted to be alone with Marini. Maybe I'm curious if all vampires are the same or if his bite might be even better than yours."

"Zoey," Lee warned and I could tell he was getting ready to pounce if Daniel took a step toward me.

"He's not going to hurt me, Lee," I said with bitterness. If I couldn't bring him down with patience, I would do it with guilt and shame. I needed my Daniel back. I needed to get rid of the beast before he hurt Lee. "Don't you know? I'm his property. He won't intentionally damage his own property. It might drive my price down."

Daniel roared and picked up the nearest table, hurling it into the wall like it was a discus. The force caused it to lodge into the wall and stick there like a suspended piece of art. Daniel then sat in the middle of the floor and let his head find his hands.

I sank down beside him, my anger expended, too. "I'm sorry, Danny. There wasn't anything you could do."

"You didn't even give me the chance, Z," he said quietly as his claws sank back into his hands. "I'm your husband. You didn't allow me to defend you."

I shook my head, sick to death of this argument. "I didn't let you die and leave me alone. He can kill you. He can do it very quickly, and there's no way for you to survive it."

"You went to Lee," he said hollowly.

"Would you prefer I told no one? What would you have done if I'd gotten you up and told you last night?"

His face was fierce as he thought about it. "I would have tracked him and killed him. I would have made him suffer first."

"Before or after he pressed a button and your chest exploded?"

Daniel growled his frustration.

I just sighed and moved close to him. "If our roles were reversed, what would you have done? Would you have risked my life?"

"It's not the same."

"I love you," I said quietly. "If my suffering will keep us together in the end, then it's worth it. I can handle it, Danny. You have to let me be your partner in this. Are you seriously going to put everything we've worked for at risk because you don't want me to feel a minute's discomfort?"

"Zoey, please." I could hear the heartache in his voice. "You can't ask me to sacrifice you."

"You can't ask me to sacrifice us," I replied simply. "Are you telling me you wouldn't want me anymore if Marini had me?"

He pulled me close and let his head fall against my chest. His ear rested against my breast, and I knew he was listening to my heartbeat. He found the sound soothing. "I don't give a damn what he has. I love you. You're my world. He could have you a thousand times and I would know you're still mine."

I stroked his hair, happy our little crisis had been averted. "Well,

I'm glad you feel that way since you now know about my long-time affair with Lee. I'm glad you know. He's such a kind, gentle lover."

I felt Daniel's chuckle.

Lee rolled his eyes at me as he disappeared behind the bar. "Thank god, he didn't break the damn fridge. I need a beer."

"Is the violence over?" Nim asked curiously.

"I think so." Neil retrieved his Frappuccino and took a long swig.

"We're fine now, Nim," I assured her. "Dev will be infinitely more reasonable than Daniel. We'll sit down and talk it out after Dev is done seeing the tape."

Daniel snorted. "He has you so fooled."

I was about to ask Daniel what he meant when my infinitely more reasonable husband stalked back into the room. He was shoving a semiautomatic pistol into the holster he'd wrapped around his shoulders, but I wondered why he needed it since it looked like he'd already emptied out the armory. He was carrying a P-90 and something I didn't recognize. Zack trailed behind him, carrying a bag that was filled with what I was pretty sure were cakes of C-4.

Daniel sat up and observed his partner with an approving nod. "Nice. You've been wanting to use those flamethrowers ever since we bought them."

Dev acknowledged Danny with a nod, but ignored me. He pointed at Lee. "You will fetch my wife's clothes from last night. I know she left them in your apartment when she sought to hide the crimes against her. You will bring them to me and Zack will use them to track Marini. Daniel, you will stay out of range of that device of his."

"Yes, Devinshea," Daniel said sarcastically. "That will keep me out of the range of the blood splatter that will come when Marini slits your throat."

"Well, I wasn't intending to get close, Daniel. I'm going to blow up whatever building happens to be housing the fucker at the time. If by some chance he escapes the blast, I will get him with the flamethrower. I have to admit, I'm rather hoping for the second scenario. I want to watch him burn."

Dev had forgotten several important truths. "Dev, he travels with an entourage. You're going to kill everyone just to get to Marini?"

He gave me one allowance. "Neil, you may call Chad and warn him he has ten minutes before I blow his ass away."

Neil took a long suck off his straw. "Thanks, Dev. He'll appreciate the heads up."

"How about the humans?" I asked, horrified at the suggestion. There were always humans traveling with vampires. Companions were very rare, so human lovers and slaves would certainly be present.

"Collateral damage, my lover," he said coldly. "They'll be better off in the long run."

I turned to look at Daniel, who didn't seem shocked at Dev's plan of action. He shook his head at my naïveté. "He's as blood thirsty and possessive as I am. He just comes in a softer-looking package."

"Does she expect us to allow this transgression to pass?" Dev's face flushed, his words coming out in a harsh grind. "He held her down. He drank from her. He would have taken her if... What the hell happened? Who else was in that room? I couldn't see anyone."

"It was Bris," I said quietly. "He couldn't say anything, obviously, but I know it was him."

"Remind me to thank him for that once he reintegrates." Daniel motioned for Dev to sit down beside us. "But Z is right. We can't just go around blowing shit up. You can end up on some serious watchlists for stuff like that."

Dev sank down, letting the flamethrower gently find the floor. "Human laws. I find them very confining. Why do humans make all these lovely weapons if they are just going to outlaw their use?"

"It's a mystery," I allowed.

"I have to get this thing off my heart." Daniel's shoulders dropped.

"Yes, you do," Dev said and I heard the relief in his voice.

Daniel nodded Nim's way. "All right, Nim. Tell me what to do."

"Well, first we have to find a demon to help us out," Nim told him.

My vampire turned to me and his face fell when I smiled weakly. Daniel was back to holding his head in his hands. "No. I hate that fucker."

Stewart might not be thrilled with his welcoming committee.

CHAPTER SEVEN

Daniel and I stood outside the small bookstore on Greenville Avenue. It was a quiet little place that was easily missed since it was beside a sex shop with super-bright neon lights that promised every type of condom known to man. An insistent thud of music came from the small clubs all up and down the street. The spring night was slightly cool and pleasant on my skin.

"Where the hell is he?" Daniel glanced down the sidewalk as people moved past.

"I don't know," I replied tartly. "Maybe he had to clean up after someone trashed his club."

"Yeah, Z, he's doing that cleanup himself," Daniel said sarcastically. "He's wielding a broom right now. Dev is so hands-on. You weren't there, baby. You were up talking to Harry, getting us a place to call a demon. He had like twenty maids working less than ten minutes after he made a call. It's like he had a plan in place just in case I went berserk."

I didn't doubt that. Dev was a big planner. He always thought ahead. It wouldn't surprise me if I discovered that Dev kept a playbook in his office for things like Daniel going into a rage and destroying half the club. I chose not to mention that to Daniel. He had felt bad enough when he'd finally gotten his beast under control.

Once we all decided that we were going to deal with Daniel's heart problem, we didn't want to wait to get started. Dev and Zack made our travel arrangements and Christine and Nim were working out the long-distance rates for our little call. Midnight was approaching and we'd divided up the list of things we needed for the ritual. Lee and Zack were at my father's with Christine and Nim, making sure the place was secure while the witches drew the circle. Daniel, Dev, and I were getting the proper herbs and…stuff I wasn't sure I wanted to know what it did. Neil was out getting Stewart a little gift because one doesn't call a demon without having a thoughtful gift on hand. It tended to piss the demon off if he got nothing out of the experience.

So we were in the doorway of the small used bookstore that acted as a front for a creepy weird witchcraft store waiting on Dev, who'd had a mysterious errand he had to run. I let the music from the club across the street flow over me. The Granada was a renovated movie theater and it reminded me of my all-too-brief time in college with Danny. We'd gone to a few clubs to see friends of ours play. We'd been young and in love and he'd been human. Sometimes I felt like that time happened to a different person.

Daniel slung an arm around my shoulders and tugged me close. He kissed my forehead. I glanced up and he was watching the young people walking by. They were chatting and laughing, and many of them were half drunk. They were enjoying their lives.

"You should be doing that, Z." Danny's voice was melancholy as he watched the men and women stroll down the road. "You should be running around on a Saturday night partying with your friends and having a good time. You shouldn't be trying to call a freaking demon so you can go find another one."

I grinned up at my husband. "Danny, how old do you think I am? I'm twenty-eight. Don't get me wrong. It's not exactly retirement home time, but I hardly think I'd be out clubbing every night. If I wasn't getting ready to call a demon, I'd probably be studying for a job."

He shook his head. "I was just thinking of what you and Dev would be doing if I wasn't around."

Wrinkling my nose, I gave the question a little thought. "Well, I would probably be on the run from vampires who want to munch on me or make a quick buck selling me to older vampires who would munch on me. As for Dev, he'd be dead because he was trying to stop the vampires who wanted to munch on me."

"I would be, lover." Dev snuck up behind us. "Daniel and I are the only ones allowed to make a meal of you. I would have proven that point tonight had anyone allowed me to use my flamethrower."

He was incredibly dapper in black slacks and a snowy white dress shirt that was open at the throat. He walked with the supreme confidence of a man who knew he looked damn good and the people he loved were going to approve. I also knew what his errand had been.

"Thank god, you cut your hair," Daniel said with a sigh of relief.

"You cut your hair." I couldn't help but pout a little because I really liked his long, thick hair. I liked getting tangled up in it and brushing it for him. Though I had to admit the current long, sort-of-spiky look suited him perfectly. It was the type of style that seemed messy but actually had taken a lot of work to get just right.

"Harry told me to and since I am now the good son, I chose to honor his request," Dev said with a satisfied smile.

Daniel shook his head. He'd talked to Dad earlier in the evening and seemed relieved that he finally knew what was going on. I never realized how hard it was for Daniel to keep secrets from his father-in-law.

Daniel walked up to Dev and inspected him, walking around to see it from every angle. He reached up and his hand found the back of Dev's head, running his fingers through the thick hair there. He playfully tugged at it. "See. That's perfect. It's just long enough I can pull it and get you in the right position to take a bite."

Dev grinned at me, and I was sure he liked the look on my face. I greatly enjoyed it when the boys teased me. "That was my plan, Dan. I know how important having a firm grip is to you."

I wasn't the only one interested in the boys' little flirtation. The crowd on a Saturday night on Greenville isn't the most conservative group. They were young and decadent and a whole lot of them weren't anything close to straight. Men and women alike watched my husbands with covetous eyes. I couldn't blame them. I often drooled when they walked into a room.

They were two opposite visions of hot masculinity. Daniel was big and broad, with thick golden hair that was perfectly overgrown. His eyes were a deep blue and I loved the way his cheeks dimpled when he smiled. He looked dangerous in jeans, a T-shirt, and a leather jacket. He wasn't a guy you messed with.

Dev was the modern man. He was unashamedly metro and put a great deal of thought into his clothes. His hair was so black, in the right light you could catch a hint of blue. His eyes were emerald green and he had the most beautiful face I'd ever seen on a man. He was slightly taller than Daniel but his build was smaller. He was built more along the lines of a swimmer or a surfer, where Daniel looked like he could take on the Cowboys offensive line and win. What am I saying? He would definitely win.

"Now I won't mistake you for our wife when I'm drunk off my ass." Daniel smiled at his partner.

"Yes, I don't have boobs, Dan," Dev pointed out seriously. Something caught his eye and his face lit up. "Oh my, their condoms have flavors."

"Oh, no." Daniel groaned and put an arm around Dev's waist to drag him away. "Don't let the fertility god into the sex shop, Z. We'll lose him. He'll never come back out."

Dev laughed as he allowed Daniel to playfully drag him away. He put out his arms like he wanted to embrace the store. "But Daniel, they have toys. We need toys to get our wife hot."

No, they didn't. They just needed to do exactly what they were doing because I was getting plenty hot and already wondering how long this whole demonic call was going to take. I was ready to head back to the penthouse and play with my toys.

"She's hot enough as she is." Daniel's voice got low but not so quiet I couldn't hear every word. "I think if I bit you right now, she might let us take her in the alley."

I sighed at the thought.

"Perv," Daniel said affectionately, releasing our fertility god and kissing me firmly.

"Hey, I want in on that." Dev growled and stole a kiss, too.

"You got in on that last night," Danny teased. "I'm not drinking anymore. I miss out on all the fun. And when we get this whole crappy business thing over with, I intend to go home and watch that little sex tape the two of you made last night. It'll get my mind off the other one."

Dev's smile was slow and sexy. "You'll find it amusing. Our wife was very domineering. She was sweet and bossy. We should let her tie you up."

I was suddenly very aware that we were in public. "Guys, people are watching."

"So?" Daniel playfully touched the tip of my nose, letting me know he thought I was being silly. "Let 'em look. They don't know us. How did you think this was going to work, baby? Did you think we'd take turns playing your husband when we're in public? Is the other one supposed to be the third-wheel friend?"

"Not going to happen," Dev assured me, shaking his head. "We have to play enough games. If I want to kiss you, I'm going to. Dan feels the same way. If we receive stares because of it, I'll assume the people staring would love to be in my place. Now kiss me."

Even in my super-cute Dolce and Gabbana booties with four-and-a-half-inch stilettos, I still had to go up on my tiptoes to plant a kiss on his mouth. Sure enough, I heard whispers. I was going to have to get used to it.

Dev turned back to the problem at hand with a longsuffering sigh. "So instead of the very interesting looking sex shop, I get to spend my evening in a smelly old bookstore."

"It doesn't seem fair, does it?" Daniel opened the door and started inside.

Dev and I followed. The owner was not a big fan of proper lighting. The whole place seemed to be in a deep gloom. There was a musty, unused feel to the space, as though it had been sealed off and forgotten. It seemed very small and the stacks of books almost claustrophobically tight. Anxiety started to build in my gut, and I had to take a deep breath. I forced myself to move further inside when all I wanted to do was get back to the street. Even the little bell that rang sounded ominous to me.

"Wards." Daniel pointed at a place high on the wall in front of us.

There were small drawings there. To an outsider, I'm sure they seemed like some arcane form of decoration, but they served another purpose. The whole shop was warded against interlopers. It explained the feeling I had. There was something telling me that this was not a good place. I needed to leave. It was an excellent security system for supernatural stores that didn't want human traffic. The human would never realize anything was weird about the place. They would just have an overwhelming urge to leave.

"It must be for humans only because it's not bothering me at all." Dev stepped up to the small counter with an old-school cash register on top. It wasn't completely in the technological dark ages, however, since I saw a credit card machine behind the register.

There was a shuffling from the back. "I'll be with you in a second," a feminine voice said.

"No hurry," Daniel shouted back as his cell phone rang. He pulled it out of his leather jacket and frowned at it. "It's Marcus, thank god." We'd been trying to get in touch with him for months, ever since we returned to the Earth plane, but he'd been on some sort of retreat. Daniel hit the answer button and placed the phone to his ear. "Hey, Marcus..." He pulled the phone away from his ear as it started to scream at him. "Damn, man, you don't have to yell." I watched as his face turned stubborn. "*Calmatevi! Non parlate cosi,* Marcus."

Dev shot me an amused look. "He always looks so weird speaking foreign languages. I like how his Texas accent makes Italian seem so down home."

Daniel continued his argument, spitting out a litany of Italian. It was one of the things that surprised me about Daniel's Council training. He could now speak Italian, French, and Spanish. Vampires caught on to languages very quickly.

An elderly lady entered the store from the back room. She was small and withered, with steel gray hair that surrounded her head like a football helmet. She was far past the age of a flirty girl, but her eyes still lit up when she caught a look at Dev. "Hello. How may I help you this fine evening, my Fae friend?"

Dev bowed slightly to acknowledge that the lady knew what she was talking about. "You have a keen eye, ma'am."

"I know a *sidhe* when I see one," she said, looking me over. She took the glasses she had hanging around her neck and slipped them over her nose. She moved closer and touched the gold medallion I wore. It was the piece of jewelry that marked me as Dev's wife. "And a High Priest? Seelie or Unseelie?"

"I am Unseelie," Dev replied without hesitating.

"Good, those Seelies tend to be full of themselves," the witch, because that was all she could possibly be, said. "Your goddess is human."

"Mostly," Dev replied enigmatically.

Daniel's Italian curses reached a crescendo and the small witch peeked around Dev. Her eyes widened. "No. Is that a vampire?"

"He's not here to cause trouble." I had to force the words out of my mouth because I really was mostly human and those wards were making me nauseous.

"You'll have to take your friend elsewhere," she said, firmly shaking her head. "I don't allow unattached vampires in my store. They're always looking for a free meal."

Dev laughed at the thought of Daniel prowling dusty bookshops in search of blood. Danny was very particular about his food. "Then feel safe, madam. That particular vampire is very attached. My goddess and I feed him. He has no need to steal a meal."

Her gray eyes narrowed as she looked between the two of us.

"I'm his companion." I held up my left hand showing the gold wedding ring I wore. I then flexed my right hand a couple of times. It had started to shake a little. "We promise we're only here for business."

"What do you need from my humble shop?" She still seemed unsure, but she sighed and nodded. Dev pulled out the list Nim had given him as the shopkeeper spoke. "You'll have to forgive me. I had trouble with some vampires last night."

I frowned and exchanged a look with Dev. Our vampires had stayed in all last night, so she could only be talking about Marini.

"What kind of trouble?" Dev asked, his voice tense.

The old woman took the list out of Dev's hand. "The typical kind when it comes to vampires. I didn't recognize these. They seemed to be from out of town. The big one was speaking a foreign language like yours is, though it sounded more like French."

I wondered if they had come in before or after Marini had played his games with me. "What did they want?"

Her eyes rose from perusing the list. "Pretty much the same as you. They were calling a demon, too. It seems to be the popular thing to do this week."

"Why would Marini be calling a demon?" Dev asked me when the woman turned to fill our order.

"I don't know but I need some fresh air," I said as Daniel made his way toward us. I had started to sweat and I needed to get out of that shop.

"Parlategli voi," Daniel barked into the phone. Irritation flavored his every word as he passed the phone to me. "He wants to talk to you, baby. I warn you. He's in a pissy mood. He better be glad his ass isn't here or I might have to kick it."

I nodded and took the phone. "I'll be just outside. The wards are making me sick. Marini was in here last night. Dev can catch you up."

I made my way back out into the cool night. I heard Dev and Danny start to talk as the door shut, and I felt a hundred percent better. I took a deep breath and then put the phone to my ear. I noticed a young man staring at me, a lit cigarette in his hand. He stood in the doorway of the Granada, and he turned away when he noticed I was watching. I dismissed him as a curious bystander and got to the apparently annoyed vampire on a transatlantic call. "What's up, Marcus?"

"What's up? What is up?" The Italian parroted my greeting. Yup, he was angry. "I will tell you what is up, Zoey. Someone has screwed up a plan I set in motion hundreds of years ago. Someone has managed to take a carefully orchestrated strategy to maintain the balance of power on this plane and blow it all to hell."

"That's awful, Marcus." I sincerely hoped he wasn't talking about what I thought he was probably talking about. I started doing what I always did when I was on the phone. I had a hard time just standing and talking. I paced. And then I stopped again because I'd promised not to go too far. I stared into the window of the sex shop with its neon condom signs.

"Yes, Zoey, it's very serious," he intoned forbiddingly. "Someone has given Marini an object of great power, an object I risked my very life to smuggle off this plane so he couldn't use it."

I grimaced. I didn't point out that he had also risked his virtue since he had an affair with Dev's mother to smuggle the Blood Stone off the plane. Dev was still very disturbed at the thought. "I'm sure someone had a very good reason for doing it. I'm sure whoever did it didn't really have a choice in the matter."

"I'm not an idiot, Zoey," Marcus said and I could just see him shaking his head at me. "I know exactly where I put that stone and with whom. You run off to Faery with your Lancelot, and when you return, Marini has it in his possession again. Do you have any idea what you've done?"

"I saved my husband's life." I hadn't exactly willingly given the fucker the stone. "Marini was going to kill Danny if I didn't give it to him. Then where would your precious plans have been, Marcus? And while we're on the subject, you can't just disappear for months at a time. We needed you. Where the hell have you been?"

There was a tense pause before he continued. "You have some serious explaining to do, Zoey. Daniel says the three of you will be in London in a few days. I'll meet you there, *cara*. I expect a full accounting of how this came about."

The phone clicked off as Marcus hung up. I frowned. The whole "being the uncrowned queen of all Vampire" thing didn't afford me a lot of respect. If I ever got a crown, I was going to do something about that. Now I got to look forward to Marcus yelling at me.

I shoved Danny's phone into my oversized Gucci bag and pulled the silver chain shoulder strap down. I dug around for the keys to the Audi. I decided to go wait in the car because there was no way I was going back into the shop that made me want to barf. I just had to figure out where Dev had parked. I'd let Danny fly me here, but I doubted I could handle the flight back unless my stomach stopped churning. Stupid wards. I held up the keys and tried hitting the alarm button, but no such luck.

I looked up and down the street before deciding to wait it out in front of the sex shop. I could do worse. It was well lit, albeit the lights were red and blue and ribbed for her pleasure. Without Danny and Dev, I kind of blended into the background, just another twenty-something out on a Saturday night. I glanced back at the front of the Granada, but the guy who had been there before had finished his smoke break and gone back inside.

"Hey, lady," a masculine voice said.

I was startled because I hadn't heard anyone walking up beside me. I turned and the man who'd been watching me before was now next to me, and he'd replaced the cigarette with a small pistol. I considered that even more hazardous to my health than the secondhand smoke.

"I need you to come with me," he said in a deep, quiet voice. "Do it quietly and maybe I won't waste the human offal walking up and down the street."

I sighed because I now knew why Marini had called a demon. They were really great kidnappers.

CHAPTER EIGHT

I seriously thought about screaming anyway. Danny would hear me and he would take care of the demon, but there were a few things I was uncertain about. The first was how fast this demon was. It was entirely possible that he might get a half a dozen shots off before Danny smashed his head in. Second, I wasn't sure whether he was the type of demon who could take human form or the type who needed to borrow a body. I would be risking a whole lot of lives for that one or two second scream. Stalling seemed to be the better way to go.

"What do you want?" I asked my would-be kidnapper. I thought about him in this manner because I had no intention of actually being kidnapped. It wasn't on my schedule, and I didn't think I would like where he would take me. It might be one thing if he intended to ransom me back to my husbands. It might make them a little more appreciative of all I do for them, but I doubted there would ever be a ransom request. I would be taken to wherever Marini was hiding out, and I would find myself serving a new master. He'd warned me that the next time we met it would be on his terms. I just hadn't thought it would be quite so quick.

"I want to do my job and get paid for it." The demon's tone was calm and even. He seemed very professional, and I appreciated that about him.

Kidnapping as a profession is an infinitely more difficult criminal venture than, say, thievery. The objects I've stolen—for the most part—don't talk back or fight to get away. Once I've gotten through whatever security my mark has placed around the prize, it was really just a question of running my ass off to get away clean. The kidnapper's job has just started once he gets his quarry in his hands. Then he has to deal with the begging and crying and the occasional petite badass who has no intention of allowing herself to be taken off into the night.

Even Danny's profession of assassin is easier than what this demon was attempting. Danny didn't have to convince the people he killed to allow him to execute them. He simply showed up with a warrant of execution signed by the Council, and whoever's name was typed neatly on the order found themselves without a head. It was quick and no one I knew had ever complained.

This poor guy's job was to get me away from my husbands and manage to deliver me to Marini unharmed. If last night was an indication, I was sure Marini had put in a harsh command that this guy not injure me. He already thought of me as his property, and he was the only one allowed to hurt me.

"Where are you taking me?" I gave him my best helpless, doe-eyed look.

The demon sighed. "No one's going to hurt you if you play along. Look, just come with me and they'll explain everything to you. You're what's called a companion. Vampires are real and they have a thing for chicks like you. It's not scary. They treat their companions really well from what I've heard, and this guy is rich and powerful. Play your cards right, sister, and he'll give you anything you want." He shoved the gun into my side and put his arm around me. To the outside world, we probably seemed like a couple. "Now, get a move on. I need to get you to him so I can get paid and get back home. You have no idea how hard it is to stay in this body."

Well, that answered one question and posed another problem because now I had to deal with the demon's host. I thought about the bag I was carrying. What all had I shoved in it earlier this evening? There was at least one handgun and two knives, and a handy can of mace. The question was could I get to them before the demon wrestled the bag away from me? The silver chain was heavy on my shoulder, and I was suddenly really happy that Dev just bought the most expensive version of anything I liked. Daniel had been disturbed by the actual silver in the long chain. I'd taken it out tonight because he was making me return it to Neiman's for something that wouldn't burn his skin if he happened to brush against it. Now he was going to have to admit that accessorizing was an art form. I would keep that little plan in my back pocket because I always liked to try reason first.

"Is that the line of crap Marini fed you?" I dropped the innocent girl ploy. This guy needed to know exactly what he was up against.

His host's brown eyes opened wide as he started to pull me along with him. He kept his voice low as we pushed past the people on the street. "How did you know his name?"

"Because he's the head of the Vampire Council and I'm a companion. I've met the man many times," I said flatly, letting my stilettos slow us down. "I don't know what he told you, but I'm certainly not shocked to find out vampires are real. I've been sleeping with one for years."

His whole face scrunched up in obvious confusion. "He told me he'd seen you on the streets and I could have half the money you would bring at auction. Your glow is powerful, lady. You could go for a hundred and fifty, easy."

I smiled brightly because that was in millions. "That's so sweet." If one is going to be auctioned off, you should always hope you bring in a damn good price. The last companion I'd seen having her life, her soul, and her dreams sold off had only brought in half that amount. Danny had gotten me for the bargain basement price of absolutely nothing. He was the first vamp to get his fangs in me and he had the strength to back up his claim.

"Well, it's true." He looked up and down the side street before we crossed. "You can't see it, I'm sure, but I can. You light up the night. I'm actually not into the whole blood-drinking thing, but I bet you taste pretty damn sweet."

We turned into an alley. I considered my opponent. "You aren't a full demon, are you?"

"I'm mostly demon. Somewhere in my background, someone liked humans a little too much. I'd love to meet that relative of mine. I'd give them a piece of my mind. The others think I'm weak. We'll see how weak they think I am when I bring in more money than the rest of them put together."

And just like that I knew I was dealing with the demon mob. They were annoying. They were ruthless. They took any job they could get their hands on. They lived mostly on the Earth plane, and many of them had some human in their background. They were also a hell of a lot weaker than a full-blood but just as susceptible to their weaknesses.

"Dude, wake up. Marini isn't paying you," I insisted as he peered around the parking lot for his getaway car.

"Of course he is," the delusional halfling said. I was sure he had visions of everything he could buy with all that lovely money. I wondered if they made diamond grills to go over fangs.

"Ask yourself a couple of questions. First off, let's say I am an uninitiated companion, which I'm not. Why would Marini need to hire someone to bring me in? He's the head of the Council. The man can handle me all on his own. If he was too busy, he could have sent any number of vampire lackeys out to get me."

"Well, maybe he was worried one of them would try to run off with you."

I shook my head. "Those boys with him are very well trained. They've taken blood oaths and they are damned serious about their laws. Well, at least the underlings are. Marini seems to have forgotten them."

"There it is." The demon sighed as he spotted a bright red truck. It probably belonged to the dude he was currently inhabiting. "Look, lady, I don't know what's going on. I only know I got my orders. It's nothing personal. The vamp wants a new chew toy and he picked you."

"Or maybe the vamp wants someone else's chew toy and you're his patsy." I dug my heels in a little, just enough to slow us down. "If you think about it for two seconds, it makes perfect sense. Why wouldn't Marini send in one of his own vamps to bring me in? It would save him a buttload of cash. Do you want to know why he couldn't get a vampire to come after me? Because not a one of them would go up against my husband."

He stopped his quest to drag me to his car. "What did you say your name was?"

I hadn't, but I wasn't going to argue with him. "Zoey Donovan."

He frowned as he quickly found the name. "Is your husband that big, blond guy with blue eyes?"

I smiled and nodded. "That's Daniel, although in the vampire world he goes by another name."

The demon obviously knew it well. His borrowed face went a pasty white. "But he's the fucking *Nex Apparatus*."

"He probably won't kill you if you just let me go," I offered.

The demon didn't let me go but he shook his head and seemed a little dazed. "He hired me to steal the *Nex Apparatus's* companion? Why would he do that?"

"Uh, so Daniel would kill you instead of Louis."

"But we have contracts with the vampires," he argued, looking for a way out of the trap he was in.

Sighing for the naïve demon, I explained a little fact of life to him. "Those contracts are for full-bloods only. Is your boss a full-blood?"

He nodded, obviously stunned at the turn of his circumstances. "Yeah."

I felt a little for the poor guy. "Okay. Let me tell you what happened. Marini got a real taste of me last night and it made him a little crazy. He decided he has to have me. He doesn't want to fight Daniel, so he called up your boss. Your boss decided the best way to handle the situation is to use you as a scapegoat. If you manage to pull it off, Marini will get what he wants and more than likely he has a way to fake my death or something. I'm sure the trail leads back to you so Daniel has someone to take his rage out on. If you fail, Danny just kills your ass and Marini assumes he's so happy I'm safe he doesn't ask questions."

"That's not fair." The demon had managed to turn a lovely shade of pale.

"You're preaching to the choir, buddy," I said with a shake of my head. "I'm a companion. No one asked if I wanted every vampire on the plane chasing after me. One day you're just a normal girl and the next you find out you're the vampire equivalent of Kobe beef."

"What am I going to do?" he asked more to himself than to me but I chose to answer.

"You give me back to Daniel and beg his pardon. And then you should probably run like hell. It won't be hard. Just let this host go and find a new one. You get a new face and a new life."

"My boss can find me," he explained. "He can find me anywhere I go. He won't just accept that I left."

I shrugged, not sure what else to tell him. I wasn't the one who had forced him to join the mob. "Sorry."

He frowned and his face took a turn for the stubborn. "No, I do the job. They think I can't manage this, well, they're wrong. I can certainly handle one small female and then I'll take my money and do exactly what you suggested. I'll take a new host and hide. I'll leave my boss his cut and get the hell out. I can go to a completely different plane with that kind of cash."

He was pulling me along again, and I knew the time for logic had passed us by. It was time to go with plan B.

"Help!" I yelled across the empty parking lot, and he immediately did what I needed him to do. He pulled me against his chest, my back firmly against him. His free hand wrapped around my waist and the gun found my side.

The thing that makes kidnapping so precarious is the inherent need to have the kidnappee comply with your nefarious plans. For the most part, a kidnapping victim assumes that they can be killed at any moment and only their compliance will save them. I was not under that assumption. In this guy's case, it was even worse. He really needed me alive and whole to have any hope of getting out of this job with his head attached to his body. It made it easy to maneuver him into a position where my skills in accessorizing came in handy.

I brought my Italian-made, four-and-a-half-inch stiletto down as hard as I could on the bridge of his foot. He was wearing sneakers that did next to nothing to protect him from that mini sword coming down on his flesh and bones.

He howled his pain and dropped to his knees. I then wrapped the silver chain of my bag right around his neck, which immediately started to smoke. I don't know why silver works on demons and vampires. I only know that it does. He gasped and tried to get his fingers in between the silver chain and his neck, but the silver burned his fingers as well and he begged me to stop.

"Leave this host," I ordered him.

"They'll kill me." He tried to twist away.

"Fine, then I'll kill you first." I put the toe of my bootie into the small of his back. I just needed enough leverage to let the silver do its job. It would eventually slice neatly through his throat, but there would be a lot of pain first.

I felt the instant the demon let his host go. The body I was garroting kind of went limp for a moment and then he started fighting again, but he was so confused about what was happening he didn't know which way to go. His flesh had stopped smoking, and he was able to touch the chain at his neck. I pulled my foot out of his back and in one quick motion had the chain over his head. He fell forward and moaned a whole lot.

"Are you okay?" It was a dumbass question. The poor guy had been the vehicle for a demon. He wasn't okay.

"What happened?" His voice was lighter and younger now that it was back to being his own. His fingers found his neck, and he rubbed the raw places with a wince. He looked down and jumped back when he saw the gun at his knees. "Why the hell do I have a gun?"

"Dude, chalk it up to a really bad trip." It would be easier to live with if he thought it was a dream or a hallucination. If I told him the truth, he would either assume I was crazy or worse, he would believe me and spend the rest of his life praying it never happened to him again.

I hustled back to the lighted street and saw Dev and Daniel standing outside the bookstore. Dev had a bag in his hand. They couldn't have been out there too long because they still looked merely annoyed. They hadn't reached a state of panic, and I was grateful for that. I slowed down and caught my breath.

"Zoey!" Daniel barked as I walked toward him. "Where were you? Why can't you stay put? You said you would be just outside."

Dev frowned down at me. "You went into the sex shop without me, didn't you?"

"No, I did not." I turned to Daniel and patted the lovely leather bag/weapon at my side. "And let me tell you something, buddy, the bag stays."

CHAPTER NINE

"Why would he try to take her now?" Dev asked quietly hours later. "I mean it doesn't make sense to me. Have we been found out?"

"I don't think so." Daniel sat down on the couch beside Dev.

I was lying down on the sofa opposite them in my father's house. From the den, I could hear the hum of Christine preparing the space. Nim busily chopped herbs in the kitchen. The boys had been waylaid by my father the instant we entered the house. He had been standing on the stairs like he'd been waiting for us.

"Upstairs, boys," he'd commanded.

Daniel's face had fallen slightly, like he had been dreading this conversation for a while, but Dev had been up those stairs as fast as his long legs could carry him. Danny had gone up slowly, and when I tried to join them, I was told no girls allowed. This was a boys only talk. I was certain Danny and Dev had told my father all about my recent almost-kidnapping. I'd gone over the entire event with them in complete detail on the car ride over. While the boys filled my dad in, I tried to help out with the witchy stuff, but Christine kicked me out of the kitchen. I'd been relegated to watching Lee drink beer and trying to toss M&Ms into Neil's mouth. Sometime after two, I'd settled down on the sofa and fallen asleep.

I was still drowsy as I listened to my husbands talking softly.

"If we'd been found out, they would be doing a hell of a lot more than sending some idiot demon to try to pick Z up off the street." Daniel sounded confident, but I heard the worry underneath. "He would have come after me. No, I think Marini just got a dose of medicine he wasn't counting on."

"He's tasted her before, Daniel," Dev admitted. "Once at the ball a few years back and then again the night he forced her to become his thief."

There was a low growl. "And you didn't tell me?"

Dev's response was immediate. "Daniel, he had the right. It's a formal greeting between Council members and companions. The other Council members used the informal greeting, but you had no right by law to challenge Marini over it."

"I hate that," Daniel groaned. "I hate all of it."

"I know and we'll change it when we take over. But it doesn't explain Marini's sudden obsession with our wife."

"You don't understand, Devinshea."

"Then explain it to me."

There was a long pause. "You don't know what it's like to crave her. Don't tell me you do, man. I'm not talking about wanting to make love to her or even needing to be with her. I need her like you need to breathe. That little taste Marini got is nothing compared to drinking his fill. Her blood invades your soul. It makes you want to do nothing but protect her. She's the most important thing in the world. Everything narrows down when you get that first taste and then suddenly nothing else matters. As long as she's there, the world is fine."

"And when you can't have her?"

Daniel let out a discontented sigh. "It's fucking awful. I go more than three days and I start to get the shakes. I can't take regular blood for a week because the very taste makes me throw it back up. I'm weak and I just feel lost, like it isn't worth living without her. I never did hard drugs when I was alive, but I can't imagine breaking an addiction is any harder than getting off her blood. The good news is if she's my heroin, you're kind of like methadone. It's not perfect but you keep the shakes away."

"It's good to know I can help," Dev replied with an amused chuckle.

"There's a reason your mom closed the *sithein* to vampires," Daniel said. "I think if we asked your brother he would say I'm the villain of the piece. He thinks you're addicted to my bite."

"I'm addicted to having a family. I'm addicted to belonging somewhere. Besides, we don't have to worry about my brother anymore. He has his wife and son. He no longer needs his perverted brother around to embarrass him."

"Dev," Daniel began but quickly let the matter drop.

There was a long pause before Dev changed the subject. "Have you ever considered that the universe always seems to find a balance? You're a king because of the strength of your blood. It makes you stronger than other vampires. It holds up its influence when pitted against even much, much older blood. Why wouldn't there be an equivalency in companions? As you are a king, perhaps Zoey's blood makes her a queen. Her blood influences vampires when she uses it properly. We have to consider that her blood is stronger than other companions'."

Daniel sighed. "It makes sense. It's hard for me to tell. She's the only companion I've ever had, will ever have. I only know that I find myself fighting my every instinct in order to keep her happy. My instinct tells me to hide her away, to protect her at all costs. You have no idea how hard it was for me to share her with you."

"Was?" Dev asked.

"Yes, I used the past tense. Somewhere along the way, I stopped thinking of it as sharing and it all just became mine. You and Zoey, you're my precious blood. The two of you belong to me. I'm sorry to put it that way, but I'm a possessive man."

"And I accept that about you. I'm possessive as well. I've often found it curious that my particular brand of magic is so dependent on true love and passion and yet I slept with Zoey for a year without it coming back to me. It was the night the three of us came together that brought me into my magic. I was content. I needed you both and I had you and that's where my power lies. Now it works when Zoey and I are alone because I trust that you're there."

"I'm always there, Dev," Daniel said with quiet determination.

There was a long pause and I opened my eyes to watch them. They sat a foot or so apart but they seemed content to merely share the space. It was like they left a place for me between them.

"So you think Marini got all addicted to me?" I asked quietly.

Daniel's mouth tugged up at the corner. "Yeah, baby. You're like the flu, extremely contagious."

I frowned as I sat up. "That's romantic. Will he send someone else to try to take me?"

"I have no doubt if they send someone else you'll handle him with your Chanel sunglasses, my love," Dev replied, grinning at me. "You're much more formidable than Marini believes. He has no idea what you can do with a tube of lip gloss and a well-placed heel."

Returning his smile, I had another thought. What if Marini decided the way to get me to comply was to target my loved ones. "What if they send someone after Daniel?"

"They can send whoever they want, but unless Marini uses his final option, I doubt they can take Dan. Of course if he wanted to bring Daniel in alive for some reason, then his best course of action would be capturing you and using you to lure Dan out," Dev said.

Groaning, Daniel fell back against the couch. "I don't want to think about that."

I leaned forward to let him know I was serious. "If that happens, you have to know that he won't kill me. He would never waste all that blood. You have to bide your time, baby."

Daniel's eyes started to bleed blue, a sure sign that even talking about the subject was making him angry. "Z, you can't expect me to leave you with him. He wouldn't just lock you away somewhere."

"No," I agreed. "And I could handle anything he does to me. You can't risk everything we've worked for. If he takes me, you have to be patient."

"It won't come to that," Dev interjected. "Lee is on full Zoey patrol again. You are not to go anywhere without Lee and Neil if Daniel isn't with you. And no more walking off by yourself. We received a stern lecture from your father tonight on how it is our sacred duty to keep you alive. And I was informed my hair is still too long."

Now that was a serious discussion. "No way, Dev. That is as short as it gets. I swear you cut another inch and I'm cutting mine into that bob I think will look good on me. You know, the one that makes Neil stick his finger down his throat when I mention it."

"Not another centimeter, lover," Dev agreed and Daniel breathed a sigh of relief.

"Is she talking about the bob again?" Neil asked, walking into the room. "Do you understand how curly your hair would be without all that weight? You would look like a poodle. I have personally threatened every decent stylist in the DFW area with death and dismemberment if they listen to your hair choices. Now, Nim and Christine are ready and they need their nine volt."

Dev sighed. "All right. Let's go, guys. If I have to listen to thirty minutes of chanting followed by the smell of brimstone and regret, you at least have to be in the room."

We all got up and followed Neil into the den, passing my father and Lee as they headed into the kitchen for another beer. Neither my father nor Lee was big into witchcraft. It had been a necessary evil my father used on the occasional job, but Lee couldn't stand any of it. Lee would stay close enough to get to me if he had to, but he wasn't about to sit around listening to a bunch of chanting. Zack, on the other hand, sat in a chair beside the door, watching the scene intently.

I shivered as I walked in, though I knew the room was warm. I could feel the power pulsing through it, a cold, dark wave. Nim and Christine stood just outside the circle on the floor on opposite sides from each other. Nim was completely still, though there was something oddly active about her stance. Her shoulders were squared, her hands at her thighs, palms open. Her lips were moving but I heard no sound. She seemed larger than before. I knew her body was still small, but now she seemed to fill the room with her presence.

It was the first time I could truly believe that the funny girl who had bought me as a pleasure slave was actually a powerful, legendary witch.

The entire room was lit with candles and smelled like herbs and incense. The circle itself caught my attention. It was reddish brown and I was assaulted by the smell. Daniel tensed, reacting to that scent.

"You used blood to draw the circle?" I asked.

Nim looked up from her silent meditation. Her face was stark and the charming nymph I knew was gone, replaced with a woman of infinite competence. This was her place of power. "Yes, Zoey. What else would I use?"

"Well, I bought some very nice spray paint just for the occasion," I offered. Nim sometimes didn't understand the world had new technology.

She smiled slightly and I found it reassuring. "I'm sure that works well for you, but I prefer the old ways. I might be out of practice but I assure you, I can handle this. I feel my power tonight and it's good." She turned to Daniel and her eyes narrowed. "There will be more blood, vampire. If you can't handle it, I would advise you to leave. I want nothing to disturb the calling."

She had moved quickly from sweet, silly Nim to a person I was very certain had been called by many names in her long time walking the planes. This was Nimue we dealt with now, and she brooked no disobedience. She turned her violet eyes to my faery prince. "Come, Devinshea. Take your place on the circle."

She indicated a place for him to stand at the tip of the pentagram.

"Tell me something, revered one." Christine regarded Nimue with the greatest respect. "Why do we really need him? I feel the power and magic pouring from you now. You hide it well, but surely we can't need any more than what you have."

Nimue chuckled. "You are young and untried, witch. If I used my own power, I would blow the glass out of all the windows of this home. I doubt our host would be thrilled with that. I need a softer power. The sex god will do, though he seems surprisingly closed off now."

"I don't understand it." Christine studied Dev with a frown. "We did this before. He had magic just pouring off of him."

"I apologize if I am not able to help." But Dev wasn't sorry, not really. He looked almost relieved.

"What was different then?" Nim mused.

Christine thought about it for a minute. "I can still feel the power in him. It just seems more controlled than it was before."

Nimue laughed and for a moment sounded like Nim. "Of course. He found his goddess. Those Fae are serious about their magicks. It flows from his goddess and whatever you would call Daniel. Zoey,

I'm going to need your help. I think I can solve both your husbands' problems if you don't mind donating a little blood."

I shrugged. It wasn't anything I didn't do every day. "You want Danny to bite me?"

She shook her head. "I want the two of you to sit on the couch where Dev can see you and then let the vampire do what comes naturally to him."

Daniel was more than happy about that suggestion. The smell of blood was obviously getting to him. He threw his big body onto the sofa and pulled me down with him. In the past he would have fought to hide this part of himself, but now he just sat me on his lap and let himself do what his instinct insisted he needed to do. He ran his arms over my shoulders and let himself breathe in my scent. I hugged him to me and I felt him start to relax. He buried his face in my neck and I felt the tiny prick of his fangs as he dragged them lightly across my skin and then the warmth of his tongue as he licked up the blood he'd drawn. He sighed, deeply satisfied by our close contact. He would play like this for hours if I let him.

"There it goes," Nim said quietly and I could feel it, too.

The warmth of Dev's unique magic pulsed through the room. His eyes were filled with affection and desire as he watched us. He gave me a stare that let me know he wanted to be there with us. Nim and Christine took their places and they began the ritual.

I closed my eyes and let Daniel's affection wash over me. I settled in because I knew this was a long ritual. Nim asked Dev for his arm and I heard him hiss. Daniel's head came up as he smelled blood and he gave Nimue a pointed look.

"For the ritual I'm performing I need three types of blood," she explained logically. "I'm not hurting him. I'm using my blood, the high priest's, and I need the blood of another. It would work best if it is someone the demon knows, perhaps someone he likes. You said you knew him, Zoey."

Neil growled as he stepped up to the plate. "I'll do it. He has a thing for me. I know it's so typical."

Nim drew a dagger lightly across Neil's forearm. She added the blood to a little pool in a ceramic bowl. Like Dev, the cut on Neil's arm healed almost immediately. Neil's was the result of his werewolf powers but Dev's was all Daniel. Like me, Dev regularly took Daniel's blood, gaining all the positive impacts. Dev and I had stopped aging, and we healed very quickly.

Nimue walked to the center of the pentagram and poured the blood in the middle of the symbol. She sighed and stepped back out of the circle. She, Christine, and Devinshea stood just outside the circle. I've watched this ritual performed before. Sarah had performed it and I'd watched an entire coven call a demon. It always seemed to take forever, with the witches' voices calling and calling to the demon until he had no choice but to come forward. They chanted and intoned for hours.

Nimue said but two words. "Nemcox, come."

There was a loud crack and suddenly the whole world smelled like brimstone. Daniel's arms tightened around me as the smoke cleared. In the center of the circle, a demon stood, looking surprised. He was roughly five foot ten, his skin a deep red. His head appeared almost too large for his body as it was crowned with curved horns. His form was a testament to power. Every muscle was ripped and he stood naked and proud in the circle. His feet were cloven but he was graceful and his pitch-black eyes stared forward ignoring everything but Daniel and myself. He bowed deeply.

"Your Highness, it's a pleasure to see you again," he intoned in his very upper-crust British accent.

"Stewart." Daniel acknowledged him with a regal nod of his head. Daniel sat back, relaxed but powerful. It was a huge change from the first time we met Stewart. Daniel looked like what he was—a king. "I thank you for joining us this evening. I hope we didn't pull you away from anything important."

"Nothing could be more important than reaffirming our alliances, Your Highness." Stewart smiled, a nice show of curved fangs. "It's been a while, but I assure you, I'm still interested in serving you. I see you finally settled things with the companion."

"She's my queen and will be treated as such." Daniel's eyes narrowed, his voice going dark.

"Of course. I honor her as such. I always knew you two crazy kids would make a go of it," Stewart said, his fangs gleaming in the candlelight. "I knew the Fae creature was just a small bump in the road for the two of you."

Dev cleared his throat. Stewart turned and caught sight of him. When he stared back at Daniel, his black eyes were wide with curiosity. "What on earth is he doing here? Have you brought me in for his execution? I've offered on several occasions to perform the duty."

"Devinshea, you've done your duty." Nimue said, with a hint of a smile on her face. "You may leave the circle. My blood will hold him."

Dev gave Stewart a dirty look and walked around the pentagram. He sat down beside Daniel and Daniel's hand found the back of his head. He stroked Dev's neck in a soothing fashion, and I knew Daniel sensed Dev's anxiety. I reached out to him as well, and his hand found mine.

Stewart stared for a moment, his mouth hanging open. "Well, now, that was unexpected. Really? All three of you? The king seemed so...vanilla. Don't get me wrong, companion. I always sensed the delicious potential for perversity in you but I thought the king was all true love and faithfulness."

"You aren't here to judge our sex lives." Stewart annoyed the holy hell out of me.

He gave me a brilliant, fangy smile. "Oh, but it would be so fun. I think I would give you a ten. Could I have a little paddle with numbers on it?"

Neil, who was sitting beside Zack, made the mistake of laughing. Stewart's pitch-black eyes sought him, and his face glazed over with longing. "Hello, puppy," he said, his voice shy.

"Hello, Stewart," Neil returned grudgingly.

When we first met Stewart a few years back, he'd been very taken with Neil. Oh, as Neil had pointed out to me, Stewart had also tried to kill him with a weretiger, but he never let Neil forget just how attractive he thought he was.

As he watched my best friend, the big demon managed to seem almost coy. "I thought you were never going to call. I should be very cross with you for keeping me hanging on so long."

Zack stared up at Neil, a horrified expression on his face. "Dude, seriously?"

Neil thunked Zack in the middle of his forehead. "No, dumbass.

He's a demon. He lies." Neil turned back to Stewart. "Let's make this very clear. I have a boyfriend, Stewart. I'm not looking to replace him."

Stewart thought about that for a moment. Stewart's demonic power was empathy. He might not be able to reach into your head and grab thoughts, but he could gather emotions, and I'd discovered he was excellent at conjecture. He could pull out your deepest fears and use them against you.

"And where is this magical boyfriend?" Stewart proved just how scary he could be. He might not understand exactly why he'd used the word "magical" but Neil did. I watched Neil frown as Stewart pointed directly at Zack. "It certainly isn't the other wolf. You have brotherly feelings for him. As for the king and the Fae creature, well, beyond their talented queen, they only have eyes for each other. So, my lovely puppy, you will have to forgive me if I push my suit. Whoever he is, he'll never love you like I will. I mean that literally. I have detachable parts."

"Could we get down to business?" Daniel interrupted.

"I'm sorry, Your Highness. You have all just changed so much since the last time I was allowed in your glorious presence. I'm taking it all in." Stewart bowed regally to Daniel. "How may I be of service this evening?"

Daniel nodded to Nim. "He's all yours."

Stewart's mouth hung open as he turned to the witch. "Is it really...after so many years? What sort of trick is this, Your Highness?"

"It isn't a trick, Hell Lord," Nim said quietly. "If you do not believe, please, try the blood at your feet. It will tell you all you need to know."

Stewart knelt down and drew a long talon through the little pool. He brought it to his lips and savored it, his eyes closing. I noticed how Daniel sat up a little and watched. Stewart let the blood sit for a moment and began to talk like a connoisseur. "Now, see that's just delicious. Two men, one extraordinarily powerful female. There's not a human in there. I taste werewolf. Oh, my sweet little puppy donated for the cause." He sighed a little. "What is the amazing, savory flavor I'm getting? It tastes almost...angelic."

Dev flushed and I reached over to take his hand. I always got amused at the things that embarrassed Dev. Public sex was fine but a stranger telling him he tasted nice got him blushing. "You knew you tasted good, baby. Hasn't Daniel told you a million times?"

Stewart gave him a wink. "Well, no wonder the king jumped into bed with you. You really are the complete package, aren't you? But the female…" Stewart was almost reverent as he turned to Nim. "Nimue, Queen of the Dark Arts, it is an honor to stand in your presence. Have you taken the king under your wing?"

"I have," Nimue replied.

Stewart practically jumped up and down. "Will he need a mentor as the last one did?"

"Perhaps not a mentor," Nim said, her eyes thoughtful. "But he has need of the old one all the same."

Stewart put a clawed hand to his lips and seemed to take the moment in. He was a very dramatic demon. "Are you asking me to do what I think you're asking me to do?"

"I need your help, Nemcox," Nimue said formally. "Will you aid me in searching for Merlin Satanspawn?"

Stewart bent on one knee and bowed his head. "I would be honored, great one, to aid you in bringing such darkness into the world once more."

CHAPTER TEN

"I don't like the sound of that," I whispered to Daniel.

"It is fine, Z," he assured me. "Nim knows what she's doing. From what I understand, Merlin isn't evil per se."

"Per se? That isn't exactly ramping up my confidence." I didn't want to be the one to unleash darkness on the universe. I'd done that once too often.

Dev squeezed my hand. "What Daniel is trying to say is that Merlin is neither good nor evil. Like most, he's a combination of both. We simply need to be cautious and never underestimate him. He will do what's best for Merlin, and we should never forget that. Stewart is sure of himself because he's been listening to all the demon bedtime stories about Merlin. He's a legend on the Hell plane. They like to claim him as their own."

Stewart looked expectantly at Daniel. "Am I supposed to aid the sorceress from this very small, very confined circle? I'm not complaining, of course. It's a very nice circle. If this is to be my room, then I'm happy for it, though a pillow would be nice."

Daniel rolled his eyes and I found myself being moved into Dev's lap. Dev took immediate advantage, pulling me close and tugging my arms around his shoulders. Daniel winked down at us. "Behave yourself," he said to Dev with a smile. He turned to the demon. "I have no intention of leaving you in the circle, Stewart, but we need to make a few things very clear. If you don't agree to my terms then we'll just send you back to the Hell plane."

Stewart stood up straight and gave Daniel a jaunty salute. "Of course, Your Highness. I'm completely at your beck and call."

Crossing his arms, Daniel stood just outside the circle. "You will remember, at all times, that you are here to do a job. There will be no side projects."

"I promise." The demon was very good at looking sincere. "You have my full attention. Consider my calendar cleared."

"You'll follow my instructions."

"To the letter," Stewart affirmed. "I'm going to be such a good boy."

"In return for helping us out, I'll consider giving you a seat on the new Council," Daniel offered. Daniel's plan was to get rid of the Vampire Council and begin a new government that included all the plane's supernatural creatures. Unfortunately, that included demons as they seemed to be everywhere. Several demons knew about Daniel's bid for the crown. Luckily they'd been told by Lucifer Morningstar to stay out of the battle or we might have been found out.

Stewart gasped a little. "That's a position of considerable power, Your Highness. I'm greatly honored by the offer. I will do my utmost to prove your faith in me is deserved."

Daniel nodded to Nim, who handed him a small package. He turned back to the demon. "We have attempted to follow protocols. This is a gift for you. We know the calling can be…difficult."

Stewart caught the small package. He played with the bow. "Yes, being ripped through time and space can be unnerving. Tell me, Your Highness, did you choose this yourself?"

"No," Daniel replied, a little dour.

Stewart smiled brilliantly and made puppy eyes Neil's way. "I will cherish this forever."

Neil sent me a disgusted stare. I shrugged back at him. I couldn't help it if he had really good taste.

Stewart got even more excited when he got the wrapping paper off and saw the Rolex in the box. "This is so thoughtful. Thank you. I won't ever take it off."

My vampire sighed as Nim indicated the ritual was complete. She and Christine, who was still wide-eyed, stepped back. There was only one thing left to do. Daniel used the heel of his boot to break the circle, and Stewart was gone in an instant. Faster than my eyes could track him, he was out of the circle and flying across the room. The front door opened and slammed shut.

Daniel had been pushed back by the force of the demon's escape. He grimaced as he shook his head, glaring at the door. "Well, that went just as I expected. What the hell are we supposed to do now? Don't tell me to find another demon."

Shaking her sable curls, Nim stared at the path Stewart had taken. "I certainly didn't expect that, Daniel. I thought he was quite reasonable for a demon. I didn't think he would run. I thought he might try to hit on Neil but…"

And then an incredibly attractive young man was walking in the door. He was six foot and lanky, with a killer face and bright blue eyes. He was dressed in a T-shirt and jeans and had probably been carrying a skateboard before Stewart had taken over. The Rolex on his wrist looked odd since the rest of the young man's accessories were chains.

"I'm ready to go, Your Highness." Stewart's accent seemed lighter, his voice younger in his borrowed body. "Sorry about the quick change. I needed a body to go with my lovely new watch."

I got off Dev's lap and stood with Daniel. It was always startling to realize the demon could just switch bodies like that. "Stewart, you can't bring civilians into this."

Daniel and Dev were both looking at me, staring like I'd said something really dumb.

"Baby," Daniel started, holding his hands up in the universal sign for "what the fuck." He shook his head at me. "Were you expecting to run around England with a big red demon? We might have to answer some questions when we try to get him through security at the airport. How would we explain the horns?"

"Don't feel bad, companion. This one is an awful person," Stewart offered with a bright smile. "He's a bully and tells girls he's going to call and then he doesn't, but only after he has used them sexually." He turned to Neil again. "I know what it feels like to be rejected so I try to be a very conscientious lover. I always call the very next day."

I shook my head. I hated compromising but we had to find Merlin and Danny was right. We really couldn't go anywhere with Stewart if he wasn't nicely hidden inside a host body.

Dev ran his hands soothingly up and down my arms. "If it helps, I'll set up a monetary fund for his mental health care after Stewart's done with him."

Stewart laughed at that. "Oh, how silly, Fae creature. He won't need mental health care. I seriously doubt he'll survive the experience." He showed off his new body to Neil. "So do you like my suit? I thought he would look good with you. Our eyes match now. I'll have to get a haircut and certainly some new clothes. He's dressed atrociously, and I believe I reek of marijuana. Really, I prefer something designer. Calvin Klein's Obsession will do."

Neil rolled his eyes and walked out of the room.

Stewart looked over at me. "Was it something I said?"

"Is it over then?" My father strode into the room. His eyes found Christine. "Are you happy now, dear?"

She smiled brilliantly. "Yes, it was wonderful, Harry."

"It will be even more wonderful when we get the blood up off the hardwoods," he said, inspecting the circle on his walnut floors. "Those grandkids better be worth it, my darlin' daughter. I've had to replace those floors twice now because you like to play around with demons."

Lee followed my father. He took one look at the new guy and growled, his senses telling him exactly who he was.

"Why are all wolves so unfriendly?" Stewart asked, pouting. He regarded Lee seriously. "Well, you can't help it, can you? Poor loner. Always so alone. You're rather happy right now, but you're waiting for it to all fall apart."

"What's he talking about?" Lee asked.

"He's an empath," Nim explained with a wave of her hand. She was already putting things to rights. "He can't help it. Let him get it out of his system."

Stewart moved in on Zack. "What's wrong with this wolf?"

We all turned and looked toward Zack, who seemed a little confused. "I think I'm fine," the werewolf said.

"I'm getting nothing off him." Stewart walked around the chair

Zack sat in, contemplating the wolf. "He's completely content. Oh, there's a worry. What did you just think, wolf?"

"I was just worried that Lee ate the last of the ham I saw in the fridge earlier. I was thinking about making a sandwich," Zack answered. "I'm hungry."

"It was pretty good," Lee answered and Zack's stomach grumbled.

Stewart shook his head. "The rest of you are filled with worries and small miseries. This idiot is completely content."

Zack shrugged. "I have a nice place and a hot girl who always buys my favorite beer. My master is awesome and I trust him completely. My brother's with me. What do I have to be worried about? I'm upset about that sandwich, though."

Stewart shuddered. "It's just wrong." He turned and sighed contentedly as he caught sight of Dev. "Thank you, Fae creature. I feel so much better now. He just sent out the most delicious wave of hurt. Zack's brother cares for him but you can't please yours, can you? He can't stand the sight of you. You're never going to have that family you want. You'll never be able to pull it off." He brightened and turned toward Daniel. "Yes, yes. You worry that when those two kids with the fully functional sex organs start popping out babies there won't be any place for a vampire in their suburban paradise. Why would anyone want a death machine around their precious little ones? He'll win in the end because you can never give her those children. And you, companion, are terrified you're going to be the reason they both die. You're probably right, you know."

My father walked straight up to Stewart and smacked him upside the head.

"Well, that was rude." Stewart rubbed the back of his borrowed head.

"Shut yer trap, demon," Dad said forcefully. "You leave my kids alone or I'll forcibly evict you from that body yer riding and you won't like how I do it. I don't believe in exorcisms. They're for pussies and priests. I'd rather just beat that body until you can't take the pain no more and you leave. And I don't give a damn what happens to the host. Do we understand each other?"

Stewart held a hand up and managed to look halfway apologetic.

"I believe you. Sorry. I got carried away. I really am pulling for the three of you, you know. I love a romance, especially when it involves a good old-fashioned double play. I think the vampire king will look awfully cute with one of those baby carriers strapped on his chest, and obviously two fathers will be required to keep the Fae creature's spawn in check."

"How soon can we leave?" Daniel asked Dev, a pained expression on his face.

I was with Danny on this one. The sooner we left, the sooner Stewart did his job, the sooner we got to give him the boot.

"We leave two days from now, Dan," Dev said with a shake of his head. "I couldn't get the jet until then and don't think you're going to go ahead and fly out before us. You aren't leaving me with him."

I could see the thought had crossed Daniel's mind. "No way, mister. You are grounded until the rest of us can go with you."

"Fine," he said.

"Then we have a few days," Stewart interjected. "Who wants to go to Six Flags?"

Daniel ignored him. "Where the hell are you planning on putting him for two days, Dev?"

Holding up one hand, Stewart interjected, "I have a suggestion…"

"Not happening," Neil screamed from another room.

Stewart winked at me. "He's playing hard to get."

Nim walked up and put a hand on Stewart's shoulder. "I'll take him, Daniel. It's the least I can do. Consider it partial payment for my boyfriend almost killing you a couple of months back."

"Thanks, Nim." Daniel breathed a sigh of relief.

The door from the kitchen opened suddenly, and Neil walked out, carrying his cell phone. He walked straight up to Lee. "Could you take me back to Ether now?"

Neil's face was blank when he asked the question, and I could see plainly he was trying to reign in his emotions. Unfortunately, Stewart could see it, too.

"What's wrong, puppy?" Stewart was really good at sounding like he gave a damn. "You've completely shut yourself down. You don't have to do that. I'm a good listener. And if that boyfriend of yours has done something he shouldn't, I am also an excellent evis-cerator."

Neil ignored the demon, looking up at Lee.

"Sure," Lee said. "I just need to get some stuff together and get everyone ready to go."

"I need to go now," Neil said firmly.

"I'll take you," Dev said. "I'm ready to go home."

It didn't take long to say good-bye to my father and Christine, and then we were pulling out of the driveway. I sat in the back with Neil, letting Danny ride shotgun. I peered across the darkness at my best friend whose face was still closed off. He silently passed me his phone and I read the last text. It was from Chad, asking Neil to meet him at Ether. I felt Neil relax as we got farther away from the empath. The last thing we needed was for Stewart to figure out we had a spy in Marini's camp. I certainly didn't trust him that far. Daniel was offering him power in exchange for his help, but I didn't think we should give him anything else to use against us.

Neil knew exactly what I was worried about. "It's all right, Z," he said. "I might not be the best liar in the world but, trust me, I'm damn good at making my mind blank. He feeds on emotions. He doesn't read minds."

"It seemed like he was reading mine," Dev said bitterly.

"You can't let him get to you," Daniel replied, but I sensed that he was upset about what had happened as well.

"Do you really view this as a contest between us, Daniel?" Dev asked, his voice short.

"No, I don't," Daniel responded just as tersely.

"I thought we had settled everything but we haven't, have we?" Dev's fingers tightened on the steering wheel.

Daniel ran a frustrated hand through his hair. "My hang-ups are my own, Dev. I'm allowed to be worried about things. Damn it, you're really going to let that fucker do this to us?"

"Dev, if you were in Danny's place, you would be worried, too." I wasn't able to stay out of it. I understood what Daniel was worried about. It was hard for him to think about Dev and I having children. I knew he wanted them, but it was difficult knowing he could never get me pregnant.

Dev was quiet for a while, simply driving on autopilot. "I don't understand why he would be worried. It makes me think he doesn't trust me. I'm not trying to take you away."

"I know, baby." I put a hand on his shoulder.

"I know that, too," Daniel interjected quietly. "But when Harry said he wanted you to marry Z…I can't help being jealous."

"He only wants me to do it because I have the proper papers," Dev explained. "You died on this plane. It would be difficult for Zoey to marry a dead man. He only wants any children we have to be protected."

"Tell me you weren't happy about it, Dev," Daniel challenged.

"I can't. I've wanted Harry's approval for years." Dev's voice was tired. "If, however, it means giving up yours, then I'll tell him I refuse his request."

Daniel kicked the floorboard, making the whole car shake. "Damn it, I didn't ask you to do that. Can I not have a freaking emotion? Do I have to immediately be okay with everything that happens? Look," he turned to include me and Neil in the discussion. "I'm not going anywhere. I'm not running or trying to break us up. I just…need some time. See, this is why we don't have demons on the crew. They fuck up everything. If Stewart hadn't been around I could have kept my freaking thoughts to myself and not have to talk about…feelings and shit. I hate this touchy-feely crap."

Dev parked the car and suddenly Daniel was interested in something other than his manly distaste for relationship discussions.

"You have a gun, Dev?" he asked, his every muscle tense and ready to pounce.

Dev pulled out the SIG Sauer. "Always. Demon?"

"Vampire," Daniel replied.

Neil was already out of the car and Daniel followed suit.

I scrambled out even as Dev was trying to pull me behind him. "Danny, it's Chad."

But he could already see that because Neil was throwing his arms around the vampire who'd been clinging to the shadows. I saw a great wave of relief fall over Chad's handsome features as he pressed his face into his boyfriend's neck. He nuzzled but controlled himself. They spoke quietly for a moment. Even Daniel backed off and came back to stand with Dev and myself.

"Is he all right?" I couldn't help but think about Chad's odd behavior from the previous night.

"Neil's fine, Z," Daniel said. "Chad's apologizing." Even from this distance and with the couple speaking in hushed tones, Daniel could easily hear their conversation. "He says he couldn't get away until tonight. He didn't want to call because Marini keeps him under close watch. Now he's...well, that's a little more private than we should go into."

"Prude," Dev accused softly. "You always stop before you get to the good parts."

Daniel laughed and I felt a little of the tension between them leave. Chad kissed Neil one last time before catching sight of us. He nodded and, after taking his boyfriend's hand, led him to where we stood.

"My king," Chad said, bowing his head slightly.

"It's good to see you, Chad," Daniel said with a sincere smile. "Are you still okay?"

Chad's eyes were cloudy with something...doubt, maybe. "I'm coping. I have to admit to you, I've begun having memory lapses. I meant to call earlier tonight to warn you that Marini was sending agents to bring in the queen. He's obsessed with her after last night. I...I forgot."

Neil's light blue eyes were beyond concerned. "What's wrong with him, Daniel?"

Daniel put his hands on the vampire's face, studying him closely. "From what I understand, it's an unfortunate side effect of his powers. His powers of illusion are very rare. Marcus explained that Chad could have some trouble with his memory and certain impulses. His mind works very differently from other vampires. It's what makes him an excellent spy. Marini can't read him."

Chad laughed and I found the sound worrisome. "He calls me his little jester. I can say whatever I want and get away with it because he thinks I'm hopelessly insane." He shut down, his hands fisting at his sides. "I'm not insane, damn it. I just have to concentrate."

"And your master's blood should help." Daniel slipped out of his jacket and offered Chad his wrist.

The vampire fell to his knees in his haste to get that blood into his mouth. Daniel didn't react as Chad's enormous fangs penetrated his flesh and he began to drink. This part I understood. Daniel had been the vampire to take Chad through his turn. A vampire rises with very little impulse control. He dies thinking he's human and the vampire part of his DNA reanimates him, but the newly risen vampire is a killing machine until the Council has trained him. One of the first rituals for a newbie is the taking of a mentor's blood. The mentor is then the vampire's master. A vampire's first blood is very potent. His master's blood would help Chad with any problems his odd nature was causing. If Chad was around Daniel on a regular basis, he might be perfectly normal.

Neil's hand sought out mine as we watched. I squeezed his fingers and I could feel his worry for the man he loved. Daniel let Chad drink his fill and it was a long time before Chad finally sat back on his heels and released his master's arm.

"Is that any better?" Daniel asked.

Chad's eyes were dark, but there was such relief in them. "You have no idea, my master. It's like my mind is clear for the first time in months."

"Does that mean Marini will be able to read him?" Dev asked.

Daniel shook his head. "No, my blood is some protection."

"I doubt he'll even try, Dev." Chad sounded like the lawyer I'd met so long ago. "I've found Louis only tries that crap when he really needs to. It doesn't come naturally to him and it takes a lot of energy." He turned to me. "I apologize for my lapse, Zoey. I can only be glad that the demon hadn't tried to abduct you before I could correct my mistake."

"Oh, he tried," I acknowledged. "I kicked his ass back to the Hell plane."

Chad chuckled but his smile was tight on his face. "I thought he was underestimating you, but he needed to keep it all very quiet. He doesn't want Daniel to come after him. Zoey, you have to be careful. I don't know what happened last night…"

"He raped her," Dev said, his voice cold and hard.

"He bit me," I corrected. "He took a chunk out of me, that's all." I wanted to keep everyone calm.

Chad shook his head. "We consider that rape, Zoey. You're Daniel's companion. He had no right. Daniel can challenge him legally over that. This is what Marini is afraid of. He's afraid of being discovered. You understand who the academics are, Zoey?"

"Marcus is one. I think Henri Jacobs is as well," I replied.

"No Council head has ever held his seat without the academics. They're a small subset, but they run our legal system. It's why Marini must be very careful when dealing with Daniel. If Daniel wants to take Louis to court, it's likely Louis could lose no matter how much he's damaged Daniel's reputation."

"If we could prove it." Dev shook his head. "We could show the video, but he could twist it. I don't think a legal case is going to go in our favor. It would be our word against Marini's. Daniel's not well thought of and our lifestyle doesn't help us in this case."

"What do you mean?" I didn't like the way that sounded.

"He means that because we're a threesome, I'm a bit of an outcast, Z," Daniel said, his lips a flat line as he considered the problem. "The others don't approve of me sharing my companion."

"If they weren't so afraid of Daniel, some might challenge him over what happened in Colorado," Chad said. "It's my fault they even know about it. I don't know why I told him. As Daniel said, I have impulse control issues. That magic of Dev's was on my mind and it just sort of popped out. I told Marini that Daniel had made money from the ritual. I'm afraid certain members of the Council likened that to treating you like a prostitute."

My head was swimming with the depth of their hypocrisy. These were men who stole women off the street and sold them to the highest bidder. How dare they question my lifestyle choices? "Are you telling me they want to save me from Danny?"

"Marini has painted Daniel as a terrible villain," Chad replied. "Those who know Daniel aren't swayed but the others…They've only heard stories of how he kills for sport and mistreats his beautiful companion. They think even less of Dev."

"Well, naturally," Dev said with a frown.

"Don't think that will protect you. Marini will take you in if he can, Dev," Chad warned him. "He would love nothing better than having Zoey and the prince under his control."

Daniel's eyes were dark, and he was trying to keep his temper in check. I went to his side and slid his hand in mine. "Does Marini know his first attempt failed?"

"No," Chad replied, wrapping his arm around Neil's shoulder. He held his boyfriend close. "He gave the demon three days. We're staying close so he can take Zoey with us when we return to Paris. He's gathering evidence against Daniel for his own court case. He's been doing it for a while. The academics won't have a choice but to break with Daniel. He intends to use the Council meeting next month to declare you an outlaw and marry Zoey himself."

"He's insane," I nearly yelled.

"He's obsessed," Chad corrected. "It all makes sense now that I know he got a real taste of you. My master, you're going to have to kill him. He won't give up. I don't know what he was talking about, but he seems to think he can defeat you in battle. He wants to force you into a challenge that he believes you will lose. He'll use Zoey and Dev if he can."

"I'm working on it," Daniel replied, but I could see he wasn't satisfied with his answer.

"That demon isn't going to go back to Marini and tell him I got away," I interjected. "We have a couple of days before he realizes this particular plot failed."

"We'll be gone before then." Dev pulled his phone out of his pocket and hit a single number. "Albert, I need you to get my traveling bags ready. Yes, that's what I mean. The cleaning staff will be in tomorrow along with the exterminators. I don't think it will take more than a few weeks. Roman will handle everything. Yes, I promise. I will see you soon, my friend."

"What was that about?" Chad asked.

"It's better you don't know." Dev went to the trunk of the Audi. He unlocked it and pulled out the false bottom. It was a weapons cache, among other things. Dev glanced back up at Chad and Neil. "The two of you should go. I assume Marini thinks you're hooking up with Neil."

"Yes," the vampire replied, looking a little sheepish. "I'm also supposed to pump him for information on how your household works."

"Hell, give him the keys to the penthouse," Dev said arrogantly. "We won't be there. Now, we have things to do. I would rather Chad is able to say he has no idea where we went and mean it. We'll be in contact. Neil, call in the morning and we'll send a car to get you."

I hugged Neil and then he reached for his boyfriend's hand as they walked slowly to Chad's Mercedes. When they were gone, Dev was back on the phone. "Lee, I need you to go to ground. Take Nim and Stewart and stash them somewhere, then meet us. I'll have the two of them on a flight to London in the morning, and we'll follow when the jet is ready. I'm sure between you and Zack, you can find us." Dev shut the phone off, grimacing. "He doesn't like this plan."

"What is this plan?" Daniel asked.

"We go to ground until we can leave for England. If Marini can't find us, he can't even attempt to take Zoey. I have new identification and credit cards for all of us." Dev passed out the new cards. "I have several others for each of us if we need to change identities again. Albert is bringing down several bags with necessary items. Guns, knives, cash."

"I need my swords," Daniel said quickly.

"Albert will bring them."

"So Albert is going to call Justin tomorrow?" Daniel asked.

"What's Justin supposed to do?" I wondered aloud.

"Angelina and the girls will come in during the day dressed as a cleaning crew," Dev explained. "They'll clean out the armory and move it to the safe house along with anything even vaguely incriminating. Justin and Jean-Marc will follow tomorrow night and they'll wipe all the hard drives on the computers. If Marini breaks in, at least he won't find anything to use against us."

"We're not going home." My heart seized a little at the thought.

Daniel reached out, pulling me close. "Not for a while, baby. We'll stay with an ally while we're in London. Marcus is making sure the place is safe. We're going to take care of you. He won't get anywhere close."

"Where are we going to stay until we leave?" I asked, thinking of all the nice hotels in town.

"I'm taking you to the safest place I know," Daniel said, nodding at Dev.

Chapter Eleven

"This might be the safest place, Dan, but it's also the most uncomfortable," Dev complained quietly. He kept his voice low because he didn't wish to insult our hosts.

Daniel nodded at Ingrid and Halle as they lay down to sleep for the night. We were under a bridge on the outskirts of the city. It was one of those places that people had forgotten. The world had moved away from this bridge and the road over it. It was a small bridge but I found it comfortable. We had a little makeshift bed and blankets. The incline we were on actually seemed comforting to me. Danny and I had slept like this many times in the past. I could trace the summers of our teen years by how close we'd slept. When we'd been thirteen, we kept several yards apart, and we'd gradually gotten closer until our eighteenth year when Danny had given up hiding anything and I started sleeping in his arms.

"Wimp," Daniel shot back quietly. "Z and I lived like this every summer of our lives for years. It's not even hot, dude. I think it's funny that we're way more Fae than you are in this instance."

"I'm not a troll, Daniel." Dev squirmed as he tried to find a comfortable position. He bumped against me as he rested his head in one hand. "I'm a royal *sidhe*. We don't sleep under bridges. We sleep in big, comfy beds with our warm wives and many, many servants to take care of our needs."

"Danny's right." I shook my head as I looked up at Dev. "You're a wimp. You wouldn't have lasted a summer with us."

"I most certainly would have," Dev replied, a little offended. "Believe me. If I had met you when we were seventeen or so, I would have walked after you and never once complained."

"So your seventeen-year-old self was way tougher than you at twenty-nine?" I asked, breathing in the late spring air.

"No, darling. I would have followed you without complaint because I would be trying to sleep with you." Dev's voice was smooth and silky in the darkness. "I would have gone through an enormous amount of discomfort to have gotten into your teenage pants. Daniel speaks of those days fondly."

"Daniel speaks of those days in confidence," Danny said, half laughing and smacking Dev on the forehead. My vampire smiled in the dark. He seemed to be feeling better now that we had found our godparents and settled in. He was comfortable in this world. "I loved those summers, Z. I couldn't wait for school to let out so we could find Halle and Ingrid and just walk the bridges all summer long. Do you think our kids will do that?"

"Not if Devinshea has anything to do with it," I joked.

Even in the dark, I could see Dev frown. "I would never stop our children from walking the bridges in the heat without any proper comforts if that is what they truly want to do. You should just be prepared that our children will be much like me."

"Spoiled rotten?" Daniel's voice was amused.

"Well, yes," Dev replied. "And that will not be entirely my fault. I don't know if you've noticed but Daniel isn't exactly a hardass when his emotions are engaged. He might seem tough, but when it comes to his loved ones he's very mushy."

Dev seemed to have found a comfy spot on the pallet we had rolled out. He snuggled up to me, which pushed me into Daniel. I was sort of smooshed in between the boys, using Daniel's chest for a pillow.

"Hey," I said quietly as I felt a hand trying to find a way into my undies. I had shucked my jeans and bra and was trying to sleep in

Danny's T-shirt and my cotton underwear. Now I felt another hand working its way up to a breast. I slapped at both of them. "None of that, people."

"What?" They managed to say it at the same time and with the same innocent tone.

"Go to sleep," I ordered, settling in between them.

"Do you see how uncomfortable it is, Daniel?" Dev asked.

"Yes, I'm beginning to." Daniel's head came up and he listened intently for a moment. "Lee's here."

I saw the shadow of a huge wolf on the opposite wall of the bridge as my bodyguard prowled in. Zack followed him, carrying a backpack. Lee took one look at the three of us and growled low in the back of his throat.

"He wants to know why we're sleeping under a goddamn bridge," Zack translated and he sounded an awful lot like his brother in that moment.

Daniel sat up, regarding the wolf seriously. "We're hiding out from Marini. He's after Zoey, remember?"

Lee growled again and once more Zack spoke for his older brother. "And you hate motels why?"

Dev fielded that one. He was very serious about his answer. "There are many reasons for that, Lee. They don't have a mini bar, for one. And the beds there are not very large. The mattresses are of an inferior quality…"

Zack didn't have to translate for Lee this time.

"Well, you don't have to be rude," Dev said, turning to me. "He's your wolf, Zoey. Handle him."

"Lee, this really is the best place." I used my most reasonable voice. "No one will think to look for us here. We can get to the airport easily, and Marini won't even know we left. Also Ingrid is really good with glamours. She's going to help me and Dev since Danny will be flying on his own."

"I hate airplanes," Danny explained. "They give me the creeps. It's not natural."

I shook my head. "Because flying on your own at thirty thousand feet is completely normal."

"I would take you with me, baby, but Dev passed out at twenty thousand feet and then Zack had to give him CPR. It wasn't a successful experiment." Daniel yawned. It would be dawn soon and we hadn't fed him from Dev's magic. He would be out all day.

"I never, ever want to know what the two of you do when you're alone," I said, horrified, and then turned back to the werewolf. "It's just tonight and tomorrow night, then we'll get in a comfy jet. The good news is we have beef jerky."

Albert had included it in our traveling bags. It was Lee's favorite.

The wolf barked once and then lay down, his head on his enormous paws. He sighed and his eyes closed.

"He says the beef jerky better be good and he's staying in wolf form because it's more comfortable," Zack interpreted. He saw all three of us looking at him and shrugged. "He mostly just growled throughout my childhood. I learned to translate. It was a survival skill."

Zack smiled and tossed his pack down before setting himself on the ground without a complaint.

Dev wrapped himself around me from behind and I lay my head on Daniel's chest. I snuggled down, loving the feel of them around me. Then a hand started caressing my ass.

"Dev," I hissed.

"Go to sleep, Dev," Daniel commanded with a chuckle. "She's not playing with us tonight."

"I am very uncomfortable, Daniel," Dev pouted back, though he settled his arm around my waist. "I pick the next hideout."

"Deal," Daniel agreed as he drifted off to sleep.

Two days later, I looked curiously at my husband. "You're staring again."

I'd been trying to sleep. The seat on the private jet was surprisingly comfortable, and I'd had some anxiety dreams the last couple of days. I was weary and the flight was really long. I thought I'd take a nap, but I kept feeling Dev's eyes on me.

"I'm trying to get used to you as a blonde," he admitted.

Touching the small amulet that hung around my neck, I had to admit I understood the feeling. Ingrid had worked up glamours for Dev and myself over the two days we spent with the trolls. It was odd to look at the stranger staring at me when I caught my reflection, but Daniel had been serious about taking every precaution while we were still in the same city Marini was in.

"I think the eyes bother me more," Dev said, looking me over thoughtfully. Though he'd sent Nim and Stewart across the pond on a commercial jet, he preferred to travel in his company's Boeing. No muss, no fuss, and absolutely no security to worry about. Regular airport security might have had problems with some of our luggage. "I'm used to your hazel eyes. Brown doesn't suit you. And the breasts bug the crap out of me. Why did she have to make them so small?"

"I'm supposed to be incognito." It wasn't any easier for me to look at him. At first I thought it might be kind of fun, but I didn't like the way the glamour dulled Dev's natural shine. I realized how much comfort we took from the familiar.

"I thought I would enjoy this," Dev frowned. "I thought we could slip away and enjoy joining the mile high club, but it feels like cheating. Maybe we could take off the amulets while we're…."

"No." This wasn't a thing we could just take off and put back on. There was a magical incantation to make the amulet work, and while Dev might be able to get his back on, I would never get it right. I'm crap when it comes to magic. "We're almost there, baby. Once we get to Hugo's place in London, we can just be ourselves again. You know Danny is worried that Marini will have men watching for us at the airports now that he knows his little plan to kidnap me failed. Even the private ones."

Chad had sent Neil a text letting us know that Marini was aware I'd slipped out of his grasp and he wasn't happy about the situation. There was no going back now. Our only sanctuary was with Daniel's supporters.

Hugo Wells was a vampire who lived in London. He'd been deeply involved in the rebellion plans Daniel's rising had crushed. He was now a strong supporter of Daniel's bid to take over the Council. He'd offered us safe haven while we were in England.

Neil turned in his seat. "I'm with Dev on this one, Z. You look weird."

"I look weird?" I asked my BFF. "You're a ginger. You look like Conan O'Brien."

Neil, or rather ginger Neil, huffed a little. "Hey, I rock this glamour. Lee is the one who looks really freaky. He looks like he's twelve, and who decided Zack should be an old man?"

"I lost at Rock, Paper, Scissors," Zack explained as the plane began its descent.

"He always picks rock," Lee grumbled.

"Next time, I'll pick paper," Zack vowed.

Neil was shaking his head as he frowned. "He won't. He'll think that we'll think he's picking paper and go with scissors, so he'll go with rock. He does it every time. It's kind of sad."

"Well, I don't get the difference." Lee never actually opened his eyes. He'd slept almost the entire time we'd been in the air. The only time my wolf managed to rouse himself was for the excellent lunch we'd been served. "You all still smell the same to me."

I took a deep breath because while I didn't mind the flight, I wasn't real fond of the taking off and landing process. I just wanted to get to the ground. Dev reached over to take my hand. Even though he stared at me from brown eyes, I knew that smile.

"I'll be glad to get back to being me," I said.

"I'll be glad to get back to doing you," Dev whispered, but it didn't matter because both Neil and Zack laughed. Dev didn't care. "I can't believe you made me go without for days. How did you and Daniel go without sex for entire summers at a time?"

"We didn't," I replied with a self-deprecating grimace. "We were a lot younger, Dev. We were much less discriminating."

Dev's eyes lit with amusement. "Ah, you made do with quickies under a convenient bush."

I laughed at the memory. "It wasn't comfortable. I was often stuck between a rock and a hard place. I mean that literally. There were rocks and Danny was a hard place."

Dev brought my hand to his lips. "Well, I promise, my lovely wife, that I will provide you with a nice comfy bed. I gave Hugo a list of the things we'll need. Your every comfort will be seen to. I'm back in charge now."

The sad thing was I bet Danny was happy about it, too. Dev had spoiled us both. We were used to living in his world. I sighed at that thought because we weren't going to be in Dev's world anymore. The minute we entered Hugo Wells's home, we would be in Vampire society and have to deal with everything that went with it.

"What's wrong, lover?" Dev asked.

"I suppose this Hugo Wells is an older vampire."

Dev's smile was weak. He knew where I was going. "Yes, my love. He is old, but he's also an academic. I will have to be circumspect, but he will likely prove tolerant. He knows we sleep together but we can't rub his face in the fact that we're together even when Daniel isn't around. He won't understand. But, Zoey, in the privacy of our bedroom, there will be nothing to stop us. Daniel will join us this evening, and I'm sure after his long flight he'll need some comforting."

I nodded, not mentioning how much I hated playing these games. Dev knew. The plane was in steep descent and I could see the city. London was huge and I got excited for the first time.

"Cool," Neil said, looking out his window.

"I see Big Ben, Lee." Zack tried to point out the enormous clock to his brother.

Lee shifted in his seat but resumed his light snoring as we passed over the city proper and into the suburbs where the small private airport was located. We would be driven back into the city where Hugo's home was.

Neil's strange eyes were excited as he grinned back at me. "We have to do that thing where we try to get the guards with the fuzzy hats to smile."

"When all of this is done, I think we should do some traveling," Dev said as we touched down in the private airfield. "I would like to go on a vacation that doesn't end in gunplay or me getting stabbed in the gut. Perhaps someplace tropical. Daniel could use a tan."

Knowing Dev, that meant he would probably buy us an island. It would be worth it to just lie around in a bikini and drink fruity drinks and not worry about who was going to try to kill us next.

Dev helped me up as the door to the plane was being opened. We would depart right on the tarmac, and I could see the limo Dev had ordered already pulling up. I saw the driver from the window. He was a tall, strong-looking man who might be able to double as muscle. He stood beside the limo that waited to take us into the city.

Lee stretched as he woke up. He took a deep breath and then he was on his feet, his eyes wide and his hand going for his gun.

"Close that door!" he yelled at Zack, who was just starting to head out.

"What?" I asked as Dev started to push me down. He wanted me on my knees, safely out of the range of the windows and whatever bullets might pass through them.

"We're surrounded," Lee said.

Dev looked out the window, shaking his head. "I only see the driver."

"There's at least ten of them," Lee said as Zack pulled the door closed.

"Shit," Dev cursed.

I peered over a chair out the window. Sure enough, Lee was right. Two men carrying rifles came out of the limo. Two more flanked the plane, and I watched as three came up from hiding spots in the long grass by the airfield.

"Who the hell sent them?" Neil asked, crouching down beside me.

"Louis." Tears filled my eyes because I was about to be taken in. How would I keep Marini from killing my wolves? My heart thundered in my chest. He would keep Dev alive, but he would try to kill my wolves. I couldn't take that. I couldn't imagine a world without Neil and Lee and Zack. They were my family.

"If you're referring to the head of the Vampire Council, I assure you he has nothing to do with my Order," the pilot said, opening the cockpit door. He stood there with a Glock in his hand. "Get that door open," he ordered Zack. "These bullets are silver. I'm not sure just how many of you they will work on, but I know if you take me out, the others will simply blow up the plane and that should work."

"What do you want?" Dev asked tightly.

"For starters, we want your kind to stop attempting to bring about the apocalypse," the pilot said in a crisp British accent he hadn't had before. "You will not be allowed to wake the wizard."

"So much for keeping things quiet," Lee said, crossing his arms defensively.

I heard three thuds against the side of the plane as soldiers slapped C-4 against the side. Guess they were serious about blowing us up.

"I'm going to kill Stewart if I see him again," Dev promised.

"I'll help you," I offered as Dev helped me up.

"My wife is human and has nothing whatsoever to do with this little plot of mine," Dev lied. "If you would allow her to go, I would be more than happy to answer any questions you have. We're seeking out Merlin for peaceful reasons, I assure you. We can explain everything."

"I doubt she's innocent, Mr. Quinn," the pilot said. "And if you want to live, your explanations had better be excellent. Now get that door open or I'll give them the signal to blow the plane sky high. Do not doubt my resolve. I joined the Order at sixteen and have devoted my life to our cause. A death in the line of duty is one of my greatest ambitions."

Dev nodded, and Zack pushed the door open again.

Lee glared at the pilot. "If we're going to die, I would rather take you with me."

"I have no intention of killing anyone if you follow orders," the pilot explained. "We have questions we want answered. We would prefer to talk to you first. We're not animals. Now move if you want to keep your heads on your bodies."

Dev squeezed my hand as we passed the pilot. I studied our welcome party. There were ten of them, each with a high-powered rifle in his hands.

Looked like gunplay was definitely on the itinerary for this vacation.

CHAPTER TWELVE

"Hands up, all of you!" a masculine voice shouted as every soldier-of-fortune-looking guy kept us in their sights. Zack went down first.

"Zachary, obey them," Dev ordered. "Do you understand?"

Zack nodded his old-man head as he walked down the steps to the tarmac with more bounce to his step than a man his "age" should. Neil went next, obediently holding his hands over his head.

"Lee, stay calm," I ordered my personal guard. He wasn't known for dealing well with authority.

"I'll try." It was so weird to hear Lee's growl coming out of a lanky teenaged boy.

"Stay close to me," Dev said, worry in his eyes. I knew what he was thinking. We had hours until Daniel would make it here. He had to wait until dark, when his powers were at their peak, before he would even start the flight. We had to stay alive until Daniel could come for us.

I followed Lee down the steps, wishing I could hold onto the handrail. It was fine for the boys because they were all in comfy sneakers or loafers, but I was in four-inch Ferragamos. Dev followed after me with the pilot and his gun close behind. I looked out over the private airfield. It was completely deserted except for our small party and the group taking us hostage. It could only mean one thing. This group had power and a plan. They had completely isolated us in a place where that would be hard to do.

They had us line up and lock our hands behind our heads. Then, one by one, they had us toss our guns their way.

"I don't have one." Neil never carried. In the entire time I've known him, I've only seen him with a gun once. "Search me if you like."

"Don't touch him," the pilot ordered. "We have no idea what these beings are yet. Follow standard protocols until we have confirmation of their species."

The rest of us gave up our guns. Well, we all gave up one. If they were afraid to touch us, then we could use that to our advantage. They didn't know how many we were wearing. I knew Dev was practically an armory on his own. They would have to get him naked to find everything he had on him. When they had the guns, the pilot nodded to the limo driver, who opened the car door.

Two men stepped out. One was dressed in a T-shirt and jeans. I would have guessed he was nineteen or twenty. His face had the softness of youth that hadn't reached its masculine potential yet. The other man was older and dressed in an immaculate suit and tie. His hair was dark, matched by his dark goatee. He was obviously the big guy. Everyone treated him with the utmost respect.

"Who do we have here?" the older man asked. His voice was strong and sure and his dark hair was just beginning to show lines of silver. He asked the question as though we'd been invited to tea and simply hadn't been properly introduced yet. He focused on the younger man, who was a good half a foot shorter. "Jacob?"

The young man named Jacob walked up and down the line, staring at each of us in turn. He stopped and studied me, his youthful face lighting up a little bit. "Who did your glamour?"

I wasn't sure how he knew I had a glamour, but there was no point arguing with him. His voice was soft and curious, with a very cultured British accent. I answered him quietly. "A friend."

He watched me for a moment. "You're so much prettier in your natural form. Your hair is truly beautiful. Like the finest mahogany."

So he wasn't human if he could see through Ingrid's magic.

"Are you going to hit on my wife all afternoon?" Dev asked, annoyed with the kid. "I thought we had an interrogation to get to."

The boy blushed and stared at his shoes for a moment. "Sorry. She's just very pretty on the inside as well as her outside. She's tough and practical, but she's also quite loving." He turned to Dev. "It's obvious you love her very much."

Dev had that look on his face he got when he was playing poker and trying to get an opponent to muck the best hand. He kept his voice solid, but I knew he was appealing to the boy's better nature. "I do. I would do just about anything so these men don't shoot her. She isn't a threat. Please let her go."

"I am sorry, Mr. Quinn. I cannot authorize that. We have questions that must be answered," Jacob said sadly. His face changed and became very professional. His hand encompassed our guards. "Those three are werewolves."

The man in the suit nodded and just like that Neil, Lee, and Zack were hit with gunfire. I screamed and tried to get to them but Dev held me back. I could feel his hands shake with anger and fear, but he knew there wasn't a lot we could do about it. Zack and Neil fell almost immediately. Lee went to his knees, and his eyes watched me bitterly as he finally fell forward.

"They didn't do anything to you," I yelled at the asshole in the suit. "They were doing what you asked."

The suit waved off my anger. "They're wolves. They will inevitably attempt to protect their masters. Calm yourself, woman. I only knocked them out. They were tranquilizer darts. Please, see for yourself."

I looked down at Neil and sure enough, there was a dart sticking out of his thigh. I just had to hope it wasn't too much.

"Mr. Quinn, please don't," Jacob said softly. His look was sympathetic but firm. "It won't work. They'll just shoot you and then your wife will be left alone to answer their questions."

Shiny green vines crept across the asphalt, working their way toward us. Now all those guns pointed straight at my faery prince's head. His hands relaxed and the vines curled back up, finding the field once more.

"Well, I don't need Jacob to tell me what you are," Pin Stripe

Suit said. "You don't look like Devinshea Quinn. Is he wearing a glamour? He doesn't look like the photos we have of him."

Jacob walked up to Dev and shrugged apologetically before pulling the amulet he was wearing off his neck. Dev was immediately Dev again, his natural glory back in full measure.

"Yes, that's him." The suit nodded, satisfied. His voice took on an academic nature, like he was lecturing. "Gentlemen, this is Devinshea Quinn. I hope you've all read the file on him. Be careful around him. He looks like an idiot male model but, by all reports, he's quite dangerous. He's considered a fertility god by the Fae. You're in the presence of actual royalty. Mr. Quinn is what we call a *sidhe*. His mother is the Queen of the Seelie. He's chosen to come to our plane and become a notorious gangster."

Dev laughed at the thought. "I'm hardly a gangster. I'm a legitimate business owner."

The suit shook his head, not buying Dev's claim. "We've tracked several arms shipments that went directly to those clubs of yours. You buy weapons, explosives. You deal with smugglers. If someone wants something illegal in the supernatural world, they go to your clubs to obtain it. Two of your clubs are strip clubs catering to some of the more predatory creatures on this plane. There are rumors you run illegal gambling rings."

"I don't consider them illegal," Dev said with a jaunty smile.

"And the kickbacks you give to certain members of the mafia?"

Dev sighed as though the man was very naïve. "Are merely one of the costs of doing business."

"Who's the girl? Is she one of his strippers?" the man asked Jacob.

I reached up, sparing Jacob the trouble of ripping my necklace off. I pulled the amulet off myself and was shocked when everyone took a step back. All those men with the guns seemed terrified of me. "Do I really look that bad, baby?"

"Find the vampire!" the suit yelled and half the troops ran back toward the plane, looking for evidence of Daniel's presence. Whoever this Order was, it was obvious they had a file on me.

"He isn't in there," I said.

The leader looked down on me, his displeasure obvious. "You

expect me to believe a vampire allows his companion to fly halfway around the world on her own? I think I know a thing or two about vampires, Mrs. Donovan. Let me ask you something. Are the rumors about your master true? Is he really a *Nex Apparatus*?"

"He isn't my master." I didn't like the term. "He's my husband, well, one of them, and I'm not answering any of your questions until you tell me who the hell you are."

The men were coming back now.

"Donovan isn't on the plane," one of the men said. "We didn't find anything that even vaguely resembled a coffin, though there were a lot of weapons. He's got some wild shit in there. I don't recognize some of that stuff."

"I'm wondering if Mr. Quinn isn't an arms dealer himself," the suit said, shaking his head. "Let's move this back to base. If the vampire is somewhere close, he won't come after us until dark. We can get ready for him by then." He gave a wave of his hand and everyone was suddenly in motion.

A Jeep pulled up and more men got out and began loading the wolves into the back.

"Where are you taking them?" I watched as they hauled my bodyguards away. Would I see them again? I couldn't help the little sob that came out of my mouth.

Jacob put a warm hand on my shoulder. "They won't harm the wolves. They'll be placed in a holding pen while we question you. I promise no one is going to hurt you."

The man in the suit seemed deeply disturbed by Jacob's promise. "Are you serious, Jacob? She's a companion. Do you understand what that means?"

Jacob stared at the other man. "I understand it more than you can. I like her. We shouldn't hurt her. She is to be treated with respect. Trust me, Ronald. Have I steered you wrong in the past?"

"No, Oracle, you have not," the man named Ronald answered with a deferential bow of his head. "I apologize for questioning you."

Maybe I would have to rethink who was the boss around here.

"And perhaps we should talk to Mr. Donovan before we attempt to kill him," Jacob offered. "I'm beginning to see an interesting pattern emerging. I must think on it for a while. I'll meet you back at the base. I like this field. It's peaceful."

As he started to move off toward the field, I saw his eyes roll back and they were replaced with a glassy white I found somewhat disturbing.

"Of course," Ronald said. He gestured to the others. "Let's move, lads. Take the wolves to the holding pens. I'll ride with our guests."

"Come along, darling." Dev put his hand in mine and led me to the limo. His head was high, as though the limo really was there to pick us up. He nodded to the driver as he held the door open.

Ronald sat across from us and we were flanked by two gun-toting guards. Dev sat back, crossing one leg over his knee and inhabiting the seat as though he owned it. I wasn't feeling a tenth of his confidence. I wished the kid in the jeans was with us.

"Hey," Dev said, catching my attention as the limo began moving. I was trying to watch to see where that Jeep was going. He ran a hand gently across my cheek. "It's going to be fine, Zoey."

"Are you on the run from the vampire?" Ronald watched our intimacy intently.

"I thought the vampire was Quinn's partner," the blond man with an enormous scar on his face said. He sat next to Dev and watched us like we were a particularly good TV show and he wanted to know what happened next. There was no mistaking that accent. Pure Sydney. I half expected him to say crikey at any moment. But that might just prove I haven't traveled much.

The soldier on my side was even scarier looking, but he remained silent. He was dark to the Aussie's light.

Ronald sat back, looking at us in a new light. "It wouldn't be the first time a woman screwed up a profitable partnership. Terry, you've read the file on Quinn, right?"

"Many times, boss," the Aussie replied. "He's a favorite of mine."

"And what did it tell you?"

"That he's a moneymaking bastard who'll fuck anything that moves," Terry said with a laugh. He regarded Devinshea with an amused sort of fascination. "The bloke likes guns and women and booze. And there's hell to pay if you think about crossing him. I know he took out an entire band of Nagas who tried to steal from him. They said there wasn't much left of those snakes when he was done with them."

I remembered the incident well. I'd been the one to catch the scam on the very night Dev and I met. I didn't know anything about him seeking revenge. "Are they serious, Devinshea?"

Dev's smile was predatory. "They can't prove anything, my lover. They're fishing. Why don't you cut to the chase? What exactly do you want from me? What is this secret Order of yours?"

"My name is Ronald James. I represent the Order of Galahad," Ronald explained. I could see from the light in his eyes that he was a true believer. "We're a force of knights set up more than a thousand years ago to ensure that Merlin stays put. He was a demon who influenced our kings."

"Obviously that isn't your only job." I settled in close to my husband and I could feel the SIG Sauer in his arm holster. He'd given up the handgun in his pocket. I leaned in such a way as to obscure the outline of the gun. "Otherwise why would you have files on us? Unless you're some sort of supernatural vice squad, I can't see why you care what we do."

"Zoey Wharton Donovan," Ronald said, proving my point. "Daughter of the infamous thief Harry Wharton. He did a few jobs for us over the years. Of course, he had no idea who we were, but we found him helpful in obtaining dangerous antiquities and getting them away from those who might misuse them. We actually thought about approaching you for membership at one time. We're sadly lacking in female agents and you fit the profile. But then you became Daniel Donovan's companion after his turn, though by all accounts you lived apart for many years. The Order doesn't police the supernatural world, though we intervene from time to time when human lives are at stake. We keep a close watch on your world. You have a curious relationship with the rumored assassin. Did you finally give in only to find how cruel a vampire master can be?"

"I love my husband," I said even as Dev's hand went possessively to my knee. I smiled because it was the only indication I had that any of this was bothering him. I didn't want this man thinking he might do Daniel a favor by killing his rival. "I love both of my husbands. Your file is sadly lacking. I married Devinshea last year with full Seelie rites. The queen sent witnesses and Daniel was there. We're not on the run from Daniel. He merely prefers another mode of travel. We're meeting Daniel here and we won't have separate quarters, if you get my meaning." They should know right off the bat that they couldn't get us to turn on one another.

Ronald's very cultured eyebrow went up in surprise. "Well, we heard that rumor but I discounted it. I assumed Donovan and Quinn were strictly business partners. I thought Quinn ran the businesses, legal and otherwise, and Donovan scared the living shit out of anyone who dared to take a look at Quinn's territory."

"You thought Danny was Dev's muscle?" I asked, shocked at the thought.

Dev couldn't stop his short laugh. "Seriously, Ronald whatever-your-name-is, if you wish to keep your head on your neck, don't ever let Daniel read that file. The Council may use my partner as a mindless killing machine. He is anything but. And if you think a few hours will prepare you for him, then you've never dealt with a vampire king."

Ronald's very British arrogance faltered. He paled a bit. "He isn't a king. That's a rumor the two of you put out to enhance your reputations. Donovan is a common criminal. He ran small-time jobs with a two-bit crew until he met you. He may be a death machine, and that in and of itself is something that concerns us, but he's nothing more. If he really was a king, he wouldn't be the Council's executioner. He would have killed the Council and taken over the way the last king did."

"Of course, because they're all the same aren't they?" I replied, hating the prejudice. "Wolves are all the same. Vampires are just blood suckers. Companions are victims. Mostly I agree with you on the last point, but the rest is just ignorance. It makes me wonder why you don't just kill us all and make this a human plane."

Now the soldier on my side sneered at Dev and me, the hatred plain in his eyes. "Many of us would like that," he said in a thick Russian accent. "We find the Order's dictates confining."

"Yuri, we're not hunters," Ronald replied in a voice that told me it wasn't the first time they'd had this argument. "These creatures were born on this plane. They have as much right as humans to be here. We merely attempt to keep the demonic influence in check."

The burly Russian ignored his commanding officer. I didn't like the look in Yuri's eyes as he regarded my husband. "He isn't keeping the balance. The werewolves were dying out as they should have. Did you think we wouldn't hear about what you've been doing, *sidhe*? You and your human whore? Do you know that your blasphemous ritual caused fifty new wolves to be born?"

"Fifty-four, I believe. Really, it was a good night for me," Dev replied with a humorless smile. He leaned forward and spoke directly to the Russian. "And when we're alone, Yuri, and I assure you I'll find a way to get you alone, we're going to have a discussion about calling my wife names. Have you seen the pictures of what happened to those poor Nagas? That was just money, my friend. While I take my wealth seriously, it doesn't begin to compare to the way I feel about my wife."

But Yuri was just getting warmed up. He moved to the other side of the limo so he could look Dev in the eyes. "You're not from this plane, *sidhe*. Yet you come here and act like our world is your personal playground. You think you can do whatever you like and never have to deal with the consequences."

"Yuri!" Ronald barked at the soldier.

"Calm down, mate," the Aussie said, looking like this was a situation that could get fucked up really quickly. "I know this guy. I've studied him for the last two years. He ain't dangerous unless you push him. He's just a bloke trying to make his way. His father was born on this plane. His father was human, for god's sake, so he has some rights. And there ain't no reason to talk to the woman like that."

Yuri wasn't listening to reason. "He makes his way in the world by performing fertility rituals on creatures who should be allowed to die out. You should have stayed in Faeryland, *sidhe*."

Yuri pulled his gun and aimed it straight at Dev's head as all hell broke loose in the limo.

I did the only thing I could. I put myself between the bullet and my husband.

CHAPTER THIRTEEN

I fell forward into Dev's lap as the bullet tunneled into my shoulder. I felt that horrible burn and then the agony of the metal lodging itself in my left shoulder blade. I would have screamed, but I was too busy watching Dev pull the SIG Sauer from its hiding place and without a second's remorse, aiming and firing, the report loud in the confines of the limo.

Terry was screaming now for Dev to stand down. Ronald suddenly had a pistol in his hand. I was sure both men were aiming for Dev's head. I shook as I managed to force myself back into my seat. The first thing to catch my eye was the corpse of the man who had shot me. I saw the neat little hole in the Russian's forehead and the gray matter on the back of his seat. He died a fanatic's death, and I sincerely hoped it brought him some form of peace. Dev had his gun aimed at Ronald's head while both the Brit and the Aussie had their semiautomatics ready to splash Dev's brains all over the car. I was just thinking about the fact that we were lucky Dev hadn't hit the driver, too.

"Dev, I'm fine," I said calmly, trying not to let him know just how fucking much that hurt. I could feel the wound already closing and I grimaced at the thought that Dev was going to have to cut the bullet out. My left arm hung limply at my side because any sort of movement brought a fresh round of mortifying pain.

Ronald touched his ear piece. "Keep driving. We need to get to HQ as soon as possible. We'll try to keep the gunfire to a minimum."

"We should try to keep the gunfire to none." Besides being painful, it was also really loud.

"He shot you." Dev's jaw clenched in righteous anger as he stared at Ronald.

"He was trying to kill you, baby," I pointed out reasonably.

"I take offense to that, too."

"Look here, Quinn," Terry started. He took a deep breath and I could see he really wanted to bring down the adrenaline level. He looked to his boss. "You mind if I take this?"

Ronald's voice was tense as he stared between me and Dev. "You're the expert. Be careful though. If we have to take him out, make it a head shot only. The female is obviously on vampire blood. We have to assume that Quinn is as well."

"Well I, for one, am damned happy the girl is on the juice," the Aussie said with a half smile. "I'm going to put my gun down now, Quinn." The soldier settled the gun back in his holster and showed us his hands. I wasn't satisfied. Only half the threat was gone. "I got assigned to this mission because Ronald is right. I'm the group's expert on you. I've studied you ever since you came on the Order's radar four years ago when you opened your third club. I don't have any problems with you, mate. My plan was to meet you at the airport myself, take you to the nearest pub, and ask what you want with that bastard Merlin."

"That plan would probably have worked better than shooting my employees and trying to kill my wife," Dev acknowledged. I noticed his previously pristine white dress shirt had a fine spray of blood on it. It was my blood.

"They didn't listen to me, mate. They thought you were too dangerous to handle casually. You and Donovan are considered to be two of the most dangerous men on this plane. We have to be careful. Yuri obviously had another agenda. He wasn't following orders. You were well within your rights to blow his arse away."

"Thank you for giving me the right to defend my own wife," Dev sneered. "Look, I don't give a shit what you want. You lost me when your boy there forced my goddess to take a bullet meant for me. Here are your options, Terry. I can shoot your boss and then you, your boss can shoot me, take my wife into custody and wait for our vampire to kill you, or you can let us out, let our wolves go, and we walk away."

"We can't allow that to happen, Mr. Quinn." Ronald's hand started to shake just a bit. I would bet it had been a while since he'd been in the field. "It's too important to keep the very destructive force that Merlin represents under control."

"The only destructive force I've seen here is Yuri over there." Dev's hand was steady. Unlike Ronald, he was always in the field. Dev never had the option of letting his guard down.

"I didn't want to bring him along," Ronald said quickly. "Jacob insisted. Our oracle plays a deep game at times. For some reason he wanted this to happen. Terry is correct in that there will be no reprisals for Yuri's death. He brought that on himself. Our only problem with you is your plan to awaken the wizard."

"We don't have a choice." Pain flared every time my arm moved. I couldn't actually move it myself. It didn't work in any way except to hurt like fucking hell.

"Zoey, they don't need to know a damn thing, sweetheart," Dev said. "Let me handle this. I'll get you out of here."

"Yes." I agreed that he probably would. "But how much of a body count are we going to have when you're done, baby? I'm going to start listening to Daniel. You have some anger issues, Devinshea. We need to work through them."

Terry suddenly knew who to talk to. "Mrs. Quinn, please, we fucked this up. Let us take you to a nice pub, just me and Ronald here, and we'll talk this out."

Ronald sighed. "I can't risk it, Terry." He pulled out a small walkie-talkie and pressed a button. "We're going to need backup. We have one down and an injured female."

Terry groaned his displeasure. "They never listen to me. Any minute now we're going to be surrounded. Please lower your weapon, and I'll do what I can to take care of your wife. I promise. I'll take her straight to the medics and we'll get that bullet out of her. Ronald can question you but we'll keep her out of it, okay, mate? You got my word on that."

"And mine, Mr. Quinn," Ronald affirmed. "We'll treat Mrs. Quinn as a guest."

"I don't think we'll need to do that," Dev said with a smile. "Zoey, my lover, do you see that Jeep anywhere?"

I glanced out the back window and sure enough, the Jeep that had taken our wolves away was speeding up the road behind us. "Yes. Are they bringing our guards back to us?"

Ronald immediately got on his little radio. "Peters, you have been given a direct order. Take those werewolves to the holding pens."

Dev had a shit-eating grin on his face. "I don't think Peters is driving that particular car anymore, Ronnie boy."

Cringing from the pain, I forced myself to look back again. I saw Zack had gotten rid of his glamour and was driving the Jeep full tilt. Lee, also back to being himself, was standing on the passenger seat, his whole torso hanging out of the car. He had a purloined rifle in his hand.

"Blimey," Terry said, his mouth hanging open.

"Not all wolves are alike," Dev explained. "I knew I only had to keep you talking for roughly nine minutes and thirty-four seconds. That's how long it takes Lee to metabolize a standard dose of ketamine. You see, lover, our experiments have been helpful."

"Lee let you experiment on him?" I asked, shocked because Lee always thought the boys were idiots when they played around like that.

Our limo driver had apparently figured out he was being followed because now he picked up the pace. He was a sad underdog compared to the lighter, faster Jeep.

"Sometimes science is best served when you take the subject by surprise," Dev admitted. "He was pissed when he woke up, though. Zack has been letting me shoot him for several months to up his tolerance. He's only a little behind his brother now."

"This won't work, Quinn," Ronald snarled, getting really pissed off that his plans were going awry. "I already called in for backup, and all your little ploy will do is cause us to kill those wolves this time around."

The limo swerved almost the same time I heard the gunfire. Lee had blown out one of the tires and Ronald lost his hold on the pistol he had been aiming at Dev. My faery took immediate advantage. He shot Ronald in the shoulder and then, for good measure, brought the SIG Sauer down on his head. The Brit slumped to the side and fell into the dead Russian's lap. Dev immediately turned and focused on the last man left standing. Terry held his hands up, proving he wanted to stay alive.

"Now that your boss is taking a nap, we can talk," Dev said darkly. "Don't think I've gone soft because I didn't kill him. If we were alone, he'd be as dead as Yuri over there and you would be next."

"Dev!" I said forbiddingly because there wasn't any reason to kill now. We had the upper hand.

Dev ignored me, focusing his will on the soldier. "The two of you are alive because she can yell really loud and she holds a mean grudge. She might cut me off and I've already gone without for days. I'm a Green Man. I need sex to survive. I'm in a shitty mood, Terry. You're alive because I'm horny and she really will insist I go into therapy for my so-called 'anger issues.' I don't like therapy."

"Hey, mate, I think your anger is entirely reasonable," Terry said quickly. "Women don't understand that sometimes nothing works like a fist fight. I appreciate your restraint. Now, how about I call up to the driver and we find that pub?"

Just for a minute, I thought Dev might give in to the Aussie's reasonable attitude, mostly because I suspected he could use a beer. It might have worked had the limo not swerved out of control as it was hit forcefully in the side. I groaned as my shoulder hit the door. Dev flew straight into me as the car started to roll. My world went upside down, and I felt the SIG Sauer hit me straight in the forehead when Dev lost his hold on the gun. The big car seemed to roll forever, but it was really only twice before we ended up with me pinned down by Dev's big body. I was up against the ceiling when I heard a mighty groan and then the car was righted. I managed to stay conscious as the door next to me was ripped off its hinges.

Lee's shadow blocked out the sun. "You all right?"

"No, I'm not all right, Lee," I complained as he hauled me out of the wreckage. I screamed as he pulled me out. "I have a freaking bullet in my shoulder that someone's going to have to cut out. Just as I get used to that horrible pain, some asshole hits the car I'm in and I took a gun to the head." I pointed to my bruised forehead with my good hand. "And I touched a dead guy."

"Only one?" Lee asked, surprised.

"I showed remarkable restraint," Dev pointed out as he crawled out of the wreckage.

"You always do, sir," Zack said with a grin. Zack gave me a wink. "I'll be more than happy to cut that bullet out for you, Zoey."

"Don't you even think about it, Zack Owens," I shot back as Dev was reaching back into the car. There was no way I was letting Zachary anywhere near me with a knife. He would enjoy his work far too much.

"And Zoey, that's one more in my column," Zack pointed out as he slid back into the driver's seat of the Jeep.

He was talking about the fact that he'd saved my ass on several occasions but I hadn't managed to return the favor. Zack liked to point it out at every given opportunity.

"One of these days," I grumbled to myself as Lee helped me into the Jeep. Except for some weapons, the Jeep was empty. "Where's Neil?"

"I stashed him after we took care of the soldiers," Zack explained. "He'll be out for hours. I'll go back and get him when we're safe."

"But what if those soldiers wake up first?" They might take out their anger on Neil.

"Uh, Zoey…" Zack began.

"They'll sleep for a while, Zoey," Lee interrupted, giving Zack a pointed look. "Neil is way stronger. He'll wake up first. Trust me. We would never leave him in danger."

I guessed it made sense. Even without Daniel's blood, Neil was still a wolf.

Dev pulled an unconscious Terry out of the wreckage. He patted the Aussie down and got rid of his weapons. He would never make the same mistake the soldiers had with us.

"Hostage?" Lee picked up the heavy soldier with absolutely no trouble. He tossed him in the back of the Jeep.

"I have a few questions," Dev admitted. "And I'm sure Daniel would like to have a word with him."

"Hey, guys, we have incoming." Zack pointed to a place behind us.

I heard the heavy thud of a helicopter and several cars rushing toward us.

Dev hopped into the front seat of the Jeep and hit the side twice to let Zack know he could take off. Dev reached a hand out to Lee. "Give me the rifle."

"And I'm supposed to?" Lee asked, gamely passing the rifle to Dev.

"Take any bullet that comes her way." Dev stood up and started to fire at the helicopter.

Unfortunately, it fired back and I found myself thoroughly covered by Lee. I tried not to complain about the pain in my shoulder. It wouldn't do me any good. Dev would try his damnedest to make me comfortable even in a situation like this. Lee would tell me to suck it up and take the best defensive position he could find. It was probably why Dev had given the assignment to Lee. My faery was a man who was willing to admit his flaws. Lee wouldn't give a damn about my comfort. He only cared that I was alive at the end of the road.

Zack swerved mightily and we were lucky we were on a deserted road. From my vantage it looked like we were still in the country, but we were headed toward some sort of civilization. In the distance, I could vaguely see buildings, but for now we had very little cover and the only thing keeping us from getting hit was Zack's crazy-ass driving.

Though Lee covered my body, I could see that Dev stood up in the passenger seat and he was facing backward. He must have been a huge target, and it terrified me. I hunched down and prayed to whoever listened to such things that Zack continued to dodge those bullets meant for Dev.

Dev fired again and then there was the terrible sound of metal screeching. It filled the air and sounded like an enormous monster roaring its rage to the world. There was the sound of rushing air and then a loud crash. Heat splashed against my skin.

Lee looked up, unable to ignore the fury going on around us, and then there was a righteous boom and I felt the heat from an explosion.

"Motherfucker," Lee breathed in awe.

"My brother is not the only one with good aim," Dev said and I knew he was satisfied with the destruction.

My faery prince had a preoccupation with explosions. He ducked suddenly as a large piece of the helicopter's blades flew overhead. Dev had to hold on for dear life as it landed in front of us and Zack narrowly avoided it.

"Are we good?" Zack yelled the question.

"Not yet," Dev responded, getting back into position. "I count four Humvees. I think we've managed to piss them off, Zack."

"You always do, sir," Zack yelled and I heard the laughter in his voice. I was glad Zack and Dev were getting off on our near-death experience. "It's a special talent of yours. Hold on, sir. I'm heading into town. Maybe it will make them think twice."

"It seems to be," Dev replied. "They're pulling back."

I felt the car turn and then heard Zack yell. "Shit!"

He slammed the brakes on, and I groaned as my shoulder hit the back of the driver's seat. I felt Zack slam the Jeep into reverse.

"It's no use, man," Dev said and I heard something heavy hit the ground. "Lee, come up carefully and show them your empty hands."

The Jeep stopped moving entirely. We were still. My heart fell. I could only pray the fact that we hadn't killed Ronald and Terry would help. I would have to talk damn fast to keep Lee and Zack alive. "How many did they send this time?"

"It's not the Order, sweetheart," Dev said carefully. "It's much worse."

"Hands up!" I heard someone scream through a bullhorn. "We have you covered! One wrong move and we will open fire."

Lee got up and out of the Jeep. I felt the weight shift as everyone got out. I sat up and saw the long line of flashing lights covering the road, making it impossible for anyone to get by. Dev was right. It was way worse than the soldiers.

It was cops.

As I managed to get up, all the boys were already on the road on their knees, hands locked behind their heads. We knew the drill. I held my hands up as the police sent their first line toward us. Each carried a high-powered rifle and seemed damn serious about their jobs.

"On the ground!" I heard someone scream.

I knelt down beside Dev. I laced my hands and put them behind my head even though the pain was excruciating. I started to see little stars as the pain threatened to overwhelm me, but I took a deep breath and vowed to stay conscious.

"Daniel's gonna kill me," Dev whispered as the cops shoved him roughly to the ground.

Chapter Fourteen

New Scotland Yard was a model of neat efficiency, but even for a metropolitan police force dealing with a helicopter crash, a limo crash, and several homicide victims in the course of one afternoon caused a bit of stress. They were working overtime to keep the press at bay. So far everything had been fairly quiet. We'd been in a surprisingly isolated part of town and the local papers hadn't picked up the story yet. They would before too long. We had to try to keep our faces out of the papers.

"Bugger had fourteen different weapons strapped to his body," a burly officer complained as he brought my husband back. Dev's hands were cuffed behind his back. "Ain't never seen the like."

He shoved Dev into the seat across from me and quickly cuffed him to the chair before turning his attention on Zack. "How many am I gonna find on you?"

Zack thought for a moment. "Four—no, five. If I just give you the weapons can we forego the strip search?"

"Not on your life. Let's go," the officer said, leading Zack away. He glanced back at me. "We're getting a female officer for you. Don't worry. You'll have your turn, miss."

Dev was a nice shade of pale and he shook his head as he gazed at me. "I am never joking with you about body cavity searches again. I have been violated on a level I never expected to be by the hairiest man I've ever seen."

"It's after dark, damn it." Lee was getting antsy because his time was coming. "Where the hell is Donovan?"

"Probably somewhere over the Atlantic, I'd guess." I bit back a cry as some jerk hit the chair I was cuffed to as he walked by. The cops didn't believe I had a bullet in my shoulder. They couldn't explain why my shirt had a hole in it, but the smooth skin of my upper body hid the injury. If I stayed very still, the pain was manageable.

"He needs to get his ass moving," Lee grumbled. "Shouldn't Neil be awake? He should be here making bail for us."

"They're not going to let us out on bail, Lee," I said, shaking my head gently. "We blew up a helicopter. We caused an accident and they found gunpowder residue on your, Dev's, and Zack's hands. We're being accused of multiple homicides, and I heard them talk about holding us for MI5."

"Shit," Dev said, his head hanging forward. "They think we're terrorists."

I nodded. If MI5 was getting involved, that's exactly what they thought. This was serious. This wasn't some Podunk police department in the middle of the country with two cops on staff. This was London's finest and their counterterrorism unit. I had a hard time seeing how Danny was going to get us out of this. We were going to need a damn good lawyer.

"Well, all I can say is thanks so much for taking me with you," Terry said from across the aisle. He'd been taken in the same time we had. They hadn't cared he was unconscious and they didn't believe his protestations of innocence. He just didn't look like an innocent man. "You couldn't just leave me behind? You couldn't just shoot me?"

"I explained my reasons for not killing you," Dev replied, his stare stony.

"Yeah, you're scared of your wife," the Aussie grumbled. "Next time, just shoot me and take your bloody medicine."

Dev stared at me across the aisle and his eyes softened. "Are you all right, my goddess?"

I sighed and told him what I was really afraid of. "It won't be hard for Marini to get to me, Dev. Even locked up, I'm worried he can get me out. They're already talking about moving me to a women's facility. I don't want to be separated."

Dev shook his head. "It won't come to that. I realize that this is nothing like the last time we got arrested. Daniel won't be able to walk in and convince these people to let us go, but he will get you out. No matter what. The rest of us will make do. He knows I don't mind rotting in jail if it means you're all right."

"Well, I do mind," Terry grumbled.

Dev turned back to the Aussie. "Shouldn't your Order be storming in to get you back?"

"No, mate. I'm under strict orders to commit suicide if I get taken in. You didn't give me a chance. By the time I woke up, those pommy bastards had taken my guns. Not that I actually would have. It seems a bit extreme to me."

I kind of agreed with him on the whole suicide thing, but I didn't have a chance to delve further. Zack was being brought back in. Zack had turned a nice shade of green and there was no way to miss how he winced as he sat down.

Poor Zack.

"Shit." Lee cursed as the officer came back for him.

The officer frowned and started to haul Lee up. Then he stopped, his mouth dropping open. "What the hell?"

I turned to try to see what he was talking about.

Every eye in the building focused on a dark-haired man in an immaculate three-piece suit. He wasn't the tallest man in the room, but there was no doubt he was the most powerful. His face was handsome, with a strong jaw and a Roman nose. He came by the nose honestly. He'd been born in Rome sometime after Christ.

Marcus Vorenus walked into the police station like he owned it. His dark eyes sought me out and he immediately made his way toward me. What happened next was like something out of a horror movie. There's that moment when the heroine is standing in a hall and one by one the lights start to go off. She runs, but the darkness just chases her. Marcus was the darkness in this scenario. As Marcus made his way down the aisles of detectives' desks, every human in the room fell where they were standing. They were like puppets that had their strings cut.

"Fuck me," Terry said, his eyes wide. "That's a vampire."

"He's on our side," Dev said quietly. He watched Marcus move toward us.

A couple of the officers brought out guns and began to shout for Marcus to stop. Yeah, they went down, too. Marcus turned those dark eyes on them and they slumped to the floor, guns clattering.

Marcus wasn't the strongest vampire in the world, but his mental powers were something to witness.

"Stop right..." I was sure the officer was going to complete his sentence with "there" but Marcus turned dark eyes at him and he crumpled like a rag doll. I noticed Terry had passed out in his seat.

"Hello, *cara*," Marcus said, his deep voice intimate. There was a small smile on his face as he stood before me. "You've caused trouble."

"I got shot if it makes you feel any better," I offered lamely.

He frowned. "It does not, *cara*. Are you all right?"

Even as he asked the question, a group of people were walking up behind him. I heard them speaking to each other in rapid-fire Italian. There were two men and two women. They quickly found the keys to our handcuffs and began letting us out.

"I'm not looking forward to pulling the damn bullet out, but I'm alive and apparently I'm not going to be shoved in jail." I winced as my hands came out of the cuffs.

The minute Dev was let out, he knelt down beside me. "I need to get you to a doctor."

"We need to get everyone out of here first." Though I wanted desperately to get the damn bullet out of my shoulder, I needed to make sure Lee and Zack were safe. They'd done their duty. I could handle a little pain if it meant doing mine.

"Let's go. Hugo is waiting outside with the car. We must hurry. He's keeping people out of the building, but that will only work for so long. My servants will erase any trace of your arrest from the system." Marcus began barking orders to his assistants in Italian.

I stood up with Dev's help. "What did you do to them, Marcus?"

"I told them to sleep and they did," Marcus replied simply.

"Is there any sign of Daniel yet?" Dev asked. I could tell from the sound of his voice that he wasn't sure which answer he wanted to hear. I wasn't either. Daniel wasn't going to be happy.

Marcus's dark eyes narrowed. "The king has been informed as to what his royal consorts have been doing in his absence. I managed to contact him when he stopped in New York earlier. I preferred he not hear of your…adventures from the press. I've had to work very hard to keep this story quiet."

Marcus was really good at making me feel like a naughty teenager.

"They started it," I grumbled because I was really good at sounding like a grumpy teenager.

"Do you have any idea the trouble you have caused your husband, Zoey?" Marcus asked, his voice rising. "You are not on the continent for ten minutes before I have to assemble a cleaning crew. What would have happened if someone had taken pictures? Or video? Do you ever think?"

"Hey," Dev said and I could see he was ready to take out a little of his previous anger over his not-sexy strip search on Marcus. "You don't talk to her like that."

Marcus turned to my husband. "I won't even go into my displeasure with you, Devinshea. You were tasked with one goal—to get your queen safely to London. You couldn't even accomplish that. It's your fault that she was injured and you will be held accountable. Unfortunately I must leave your punishment to Daniel."

"Punishment?" I asked, my voice filled with amused disbelief. The thought of Danny punishing Dev was amusing…and a little hot.

Dev didn't see it that way. "You think he's my fucking master, Marcus? You think he tells me what to do?"

"I don't claim to have any understanding when it comes to your relationship with the king," Marcus said. "Why he has allowed you to live I have no idea, but perhaps this incident will cause him to rethink the situation."

I watched Dev's face get red with rage and knew it was time for the queen to take over. I was done playing the victim here. I'm not used to having any real power and I sometimes let it get away from me. Now was not one of those times. I knew exactly how to handle the Italian. Marcus liked a firm hand.

"Marcus, you will hold your tongue if you can't think of anything kind to say to my consort." I placed careful emphasis on the word "my." I stared down the Italian. "As you said, the king will handle us as he sees fit. It isn't your place to chastise me or mine. Or do you claim rights over me, vampire?"

Marcus bowed his head slightly, a show of deference to his monarch. "I do not, *mia regina*. It's my pleasure to do you this service."

"Then do me the service of getting me to a place where I might deal with my injuries," I requested in my best "I am queen" voice.

If my time in Faery had taught me anything, I had to act the part of a hardass royal to get any sort of respect. Even our vampire allies tended to think of me as Daniel's lover rather than his partner. I didn't like to think about how they regarded Devinshea. Daniel wanted to keep the peace, but he didn't have to deal with constant disdain like Dev or perpetual misogyny like me. I was tired of being thought of as a sweet piece of ass the king got to bang. Daniel was asking us to live in this world, never understanding how marginalized we were.

"Of course." Marcus politely gestured toward the door. "I think you will find all is in readiness for you. I've taken care of your requests personally."

I held my hand out for my escort. This was for a dual purpose. In vampire society, a companion was almost always escorted. I also needed someone to lean on because I was getting weak from dealing with the shooting pains in my shoulder. Marcus moved in to lend his hand but I held back. As the highest-ranking vampire in the room, he should be my proper escort, but I was done doing things properly. "You are not my consort, Marcus."

Dev walked up and took my arm, not able to resist flashing the vampire a little smirk. He looked down at me and I knew this was an important moment for us. "We're not going to be circumspect are we, my lover?"

I shook my head, sure in my path now. "We are not. I'm either their queen or I'm nothing. I won't play games any longer. They'll accept me or not."

I heard Marcus sigh but he spoke quietly to his people as we prepared to leave.

"Zack, would you be so kind as to bring along our Australian friend? I still have questions for him." Dev's face was a picture of calm now that he was sure of his status, at least in my eyes.

Zack hoisted Terry over his shoulder and we started out the doors toward the waiting limo. Even as we walked out the door I heard Lee as he approached Marcus.

"Uh, Marcus, Zoey there might be a little pissed at you, but I just wanted to say thanks." It was the most sincerity I'd ever heard coming out of Lee's mouth. "Your timing was impeccable, man."

"Not for me, it wasn't," Zack grumbled. "You couldn't get here ten minutes earlier?"

I laughed a little as Dev led me outside. I was surprised at the calmness of the London night. I could see people walking up and down the street, but they seemed to not notice the large black stretch limo or the people walking out of the police station. They didn't even bat an eye at Zack, who was carrying an unconscious man dressed in fatigues over his shoulder. Now that I really paid attention, I noticed everyone seemed to walk around the station house, giving the place a wide berth without ever realizing why.

Hugo Wells was shielding us from their eyes. I thought about what I knew of the man. He was an academic, like Marcus and Henri Jacobs. His mental powers were the bulk of his strength.

"My god, Marcus," a cultured British accent said as I stepped up to the limo. His cerulean eyes were locked on me. "You said she was bright but…" I knew that look. If he were a younger vampire, this would be the part where Dev would have to defend me, but Hugo Wells was at least five hundred years old. He had control of his instincts. "No wonder Marini is obsessed with her. I could get obsessed with that." He said that last bit with such longing, I heard Dev curse beside me.

I felt Dev reach into the back of my skirt where I kept a small pistol in a holster. They hadn't taken my guns and Dev knew just where to look. Lee, who had also avoided the strip search, pulled his hidden gun as well. Hugo Wells suddenly had long fangs. He took exception to being considered a threat.

"Mr. Wells," I said, meeting the vampire's eyes. "I'm sure you'll discover my guard will lower their weapons if you would kindly stop looking at me like I'm a particularly juicy steak."

The vampire had the good sense to look slightly embarrassed. Marcus chuckled. He was unconcerned with the amount of guns being pointed all around. "You have another conquest, *cara*. Don't worry about it. We all have that reaction, Hugo. Don't beat yourself up over it."

"No, Hugo," Dev drawled. "Allow me to beat you up over it."

Hugo Wells was roughly the same height as Marcus, so he stood about five inches over me but was certainly shorter than Dev. He was solidly built, with a barrel chest and what appeared to be an incredibly strong body. His face was smooth and white, but he was the first vampire I'd seen who sported a beard. From what I knew about the vampire, he'd been born during Elizabeth's reign and, like all academics, was considered extremely intelligent. He was used to a red-haired queen, and that was a good thing.

"If we might get to more comfortable accommodations, Mr. Wells, I would appreciate it," I said evenly. He was blocking the way into the limo. "I believe I've had enough of Scotland Yard's hospitality."

The vampire graciously moved to allow us in. "I can only hope my hospitality proves more pleasant, Your Highness. I'm a great admirer of the king. I think you will find I'm one of Daniel's strongest supporters. I've believed in his cause for many years now. I've written several papers supporting Daniel's legal claim to the throne."

Dev got in first and I smiled as I saw Neil was waiting in the limo. He looked surprisingly well for someone who'd been shot and knocked out mere hours ago. Now I knew who to thank for getting Marcus so quickly.

"Hey, Z," Neil said. "I woke up surrounded by corpses. How about you?"

I turned to Lee because that wasn't the story I'd heard.

He shook his head and managed to make his face completely blank. "I have no idea what he's talking about. The streets just aren't safe these days."

I sighed and let Dev help me into the limo. After we had Terry safely stashed in the trunk, we proceeded to move toward Hugo's enormous townhouse in a fashionable section of London. Since I'd taken Dev's leash off, he did what came naturally to him. He'd been through a harrowing afternoon and he was still anxious about how mad Daniel was going to be. He needed comfort and for a Fae, comfort came with close contact. Carefully avoiding my injured arm, he stroked my hair and let his head rest against mine. I looked across the seat at Hugo, who was staring.

"Does your master know about your guard's affections?" Hugo asked.

Marcus said something under his breath in Italian, but I ignored him. "He isn't my guard and you know that, Mr. Wells. He's my husband—my consort, if you prefer. If you have a problem with the way he's behaving, you should take it up with me. Daniel has more important things to worry about than a vampire's preoccupation with a female who doesn't belong to him."

"It's not proper in our society, Your Highness," Hugo argued.

"I don't give a shit," I admitted flatly. "And who are you to tell me how to behave? What was it your Shakespeare said? I am a queen. I am the maker of manners. Has it been so very long since you had a queen, Mr. Wells, that you've forgotten how to show one proper respect?"

"Not at all, ma'am," he responded quietly, and I caught the hint of a smile he quickly covered.

Marcus exchanged a look with him. "I told you. She is not a proper companion but she might be an excellent queen."

"Then why do you always push me, Marcus?" I asked, irritation flavoring my voice.

The Italian's smile was smooth. "Ah, *cara*, it is because you always look so beautiful when you're angry."

Dev groaned. "Is every man in the world going to hit on my wife today? First it was that oracle boy, and now I get to listen to Marcus fawn all over you."

Hugo's hand went to a switch in the ceiling. "Stop the car immediately."

The car was expertly pulled over and Hugo jumped out, shoving Zack aside in the process.

"What was that about?" I watched out the window as the trunk was opened.

Marcus frowned my way, obviously irritated again. "Why did you not mention it was the Order of Galahad you had trouble with?"

"You didn't give her a chance," Lee growled. "You just started yelling at her the minute you walked in."

Marcus gave the wolf a look that told him he didn't need to speak.

"What he said," I replied because Lee had been succinct and to the point, as always.

"Did you think I blew up a helicopter because it was fun?" Dev frowned at Marcus.

I gave Dev a look and he grinned slowly.

"All right. It was fun," he admitted. "But they were also trying to shoot us down at the time. One of their soldiers tried to kill me and ended up shooting my goddess instead. I was very irritated."

I heard a shout and then the car shook briefly. When Hugo got back in the car, he was holding something in his hands and there was just a tiny spot of blood on his fingers.

"Got it," he said, handing the small dot to Marcus.

Dev sat up because he was a technology junkie. "Is that a locator device?"

"Yes." Marcus tossed it out the window as the car picked up speed again. "The Order surgically implants these in all their knights so they can always track them. I'm surprised we got to the station before the Order could. They're very quick to retrieve their knights. I suspect they hoped we would take the knight with us and he would lead the others straight to you."

So Terry had lied. I couldn't really get pissed off at him. He was just doing his job, but I needed to find out just what that job was.

"Does anyone want to explain what this group is and why they think Dev is a gangster?" It was getting really hard to ignore the pain in my arm. I shifted uncomfortably.

"The Order has been around longer than I have," Hugo explained. "They're a sort of watch group. They're primarily concerned with demonic influence on our plane. They attempt to keep the demon groups at bay. They only step in outside of demonic activity during the direst of circumstances or when a group directly requests their aid. They take the whole knight ideal very seriously. They can be extremely aggressive when they believe the balance is at risk. As for why they believe the faery is a gangster…well....”

There was a certain amusement in Marcus's eyes as he took over. “What Hugo is trying to say is the Order keeps very detailed files on the plane's more interesting citizens. I read my own file about a hundred years ago when I did some work with the oracle you spoke of. I found it surprisingly correct. They have excellent intelligence. If the Order has determined Mr. Quinn here is a gangster, then it's because he's a gangster. Did they discover the brothel you started last year?”

My mouth opened and my head turned. Dev attempted to look very innocent. “I was only an investor, lover. Some of my Vegas girls thought it would be a good idea, and might I point out that brothels are entirely legal in Nevada. My partner and I thought it was a good investment. Have you ever seen a shapeshifter at work? Those girls can make a ton of money.”

I'd only gotten one pertinent piece of information out of that lecture. “You brought Daniel into your venture into pimpdom?”

“I wouldn't call it a venture,” Dev said seriously. “I would call it a subsidiary. Daniel is the one who had the idea. We're expanding. We bought a small production studio in Los Angeles as well. The supernatural world has needs, too. Who better to meet those needs than a fertility god? Really, sweetheart, Daniel and I view it as bringing a little more joy into the world.”

Zack laughed. “That's funny because one of the hookers' names is Joy.”

The car turned and I wasn't ready for it. I slammed against Dev and heard myself scream just before the lights blissfully went dark.

CHAPTER FIFTEEN

I woke to the smell of the ocean and the sweet heat of the sun on my skin. Blinking, I opened my eyes and saw fluffy white clouds and a perfect blue sky. Whatever I was reclining on swayed softly, the motion a comfort.

"Are you feeling better, *cara*?" a deep voice asked.

I turned slightly and tried to focus on Marcus. "Where am I?" Even as I asked the question, I realized the answer. I was in one of the most recognizable cities on the planet. The canals kind of gave it away. "How did I get to Venice?"

The last thing I remembered was being with Dev in Hugo Wells's limousine.

The Italian chuckled and motioned to the gondolier behind us. He lifted his pole and suddenly we were moving. I touched my clothes, which had strangely morphed from a Marc Jacobs skirt and blouse to a sumptuous silk gown like something out of a historical film. It was a rich emerald green. Dev often selected this color when he picked a dress for me. Marcus was in rich-looking silk and velvet. I touched my waist and felt the hard bones that lined the corset. It made my waist very small and shoved my boobs up. I glanced around and noted that Marcus and I were not the only ones dressed in historical garb.

All around us people walked and worked on the cobblestone streets. Vendors squawked their offerings. Mothers tugged children behind them as they did their shopping. Men spoke to each other as they trudged along.

Marcus lounged negligently against the cushions of the flat-bottomed boat, his sensual lips curling into a lopsided smile. "You, gorgeous girl, are obviously having a delicious dream."

I was having a stunningly vivid dream. It was like dreaming in HD. I was hyper aware of everything. The gondola skimmed the surface of the lagoon gracefully, swaying as we passed other boats. The heavy velvet of the cushions was a welcome softness against my skin as I let myself rest back against it.

"You know, you can do whatever you like in your dreams," Marcus said with a gleam in his dark eyes. "A dream is the perfect place to live out a fantasy."

"I suppose so." I murmured, though my brain was working overtime. If this was my dream, why was I in sixteenth century Italy? I usually ended up on a beach with a fruity drink in my hands and someone rubbing my feet.

Even through my heavy skirts, I felt Marcus place his hand on my knee. His voice was seductive and smooth. "Perhaps there is a man you have always wanted but have been afraid to try. In a dream, you can do what you wish. You can take that man you've wanted from the first time you laid eyes on him and do as you wish without fear of your husband finding out. It isn't cheating in a dream, *cara*. It's merely wish fulfillment." His hand squeezed my knee as he turned toward me. His other hand gently tilted my head up as his thumb brushed across my lips. "Haven't we waited long enough?"

Uh-huh, I thought. There might be some wish fulfillment going on, but it wasn't my wish that was going to get fulfilled if that horny Italian had his way. Marcus leaned in but just as his lips were about to touch mine, I shoved a hand between us and pushed his "trying to get me to cheat" lips back.

"So this is one of your powers?"

Marcus's nearly black eyes narrowed, but he laughed anyway. "You can't blame a vampire for trying, *cara*. Here we are in the most romantic city on earth and the day is beautiful. Can you think of a more pleasant way to spend the afternoon? I can taste you here and not risk the addiction. After you've fed me, I would be more than happy to lift your skirts and allow you to ride me for as long as it takes, *il mio tesoro*. You haven't lived until you've made love in a gondola on the Grand Canal."

I rolled my eyes. He never gave up. "I'll be sure to bring that up when Danny, Dev, and I discuss our next vacation. Now, want to explain why I'm here?"

Marcus sighed. "I thought it was better than you having to deal with Devinshea and that wolf of yours pulling the bullet out of your shoulder. You passed out in the limo. In reality, you're on a table in Hugo's kitchens with Devinshea carving up your shoulder. I'm sorry, but we felt it best to stay away from hospitals."

Grimacing, I took a deep breath. "Okay, I'll go along with that. So this is your version of anesthesia?"

"It's taking you away from the pain," the vampire allowed.

"Is this the same as the stuff Chad can do?" Chad was good with illusions.

"Not at all," he explained. "This is not an illusion in the strict sense of the word. I joined with you on a mental level. Chad can make people see things that aren't there. I've merely drawn you into my memory."

"Vulcan mind meld. Nice," I said with a grin.

Marcus laughed. "You and Daniel. You're incorrigible—what is the word now?—geeks." He leaned his head back and seemed to enjoy the sun. "This is my favorite place in the world. I thought I would share it with you."

"And the people in costumes?"

"They aren't costumes, Zoey," he explained. "This is what we wore in 1593. You look lovely in a corset, by the way. The people on the street are all looking at you and wondering if a new courtesan has come to Venice. They're thinking that Don Vorenus has always found the most beautiful of courtesans to keep him company."

I looked up and sure enough, people were staring and talking behind their hands. "You have a vivid imagination, Marcus."

"I need no imagination to come to this place." The vampire smiled as he took in the bridges and streets and houses that made up his home city. "I merely need to close my eyes and the memory is ingrained on my brain. This city has been my great love. I was born in Rome, but I am a son of Venice. I helped to build her. I watched her stand up to tyranny and fight off invaders. I saw the plague take a third of our citizens in a three-year period and still she rose again. This is my heart and my home, Zoey."

"It's beautiful, Marcus." I was touched by his passion for his home. "How did you manage to live here for so long without being detected?"

"Venetians are incredibly practical and tolerant. For a long time, the ruling class knew exactly what I was. I caused no trouble and actually helped make them money. I've always been good at knowing how to make money. At one point in time, the Inquisition came for me and the people of Venice hid me and my companion at the time. For months we hid, being moved from house to house and treated like honored guests in each home."

"You must have been good to those people," I commented as I enjoyed the sights. It was a marvel to think the city was built before modern technology.

"I was good to them and they were good to me. There are still many people in Venice who know exactly what I am and they would never betray me. Look up ahead, *cara*."

We were turning down a narrow canal and suddenly we were in shadows. Marcus pointed to an ancient house. It was marked with a small engraved plate.

"This was the home of Marco Polo," Marcus said. "He was a good friend of mine."

Marcus was the ultimate name dropper. He enjoyed talking about the interesting people he'd met over his very long life. "He was the explorer, right?"

I could have mentioned he was also the inventor of the great swimming pool game, but Marcus would have given me that look he always gave me when I said something stupid.

"Oh, yes, it's been my privilege to meet many important people over the years. It's another of my talents."

"How is meeting people a talent?"

"My talent isn't in meeting them," Marcus explained. "It's in knowing who will be important and who will not. You see, most vampires' skills lay in their strength..."

"You're talking about warriors," I interrupted, wanting to understand more about the different classes. I sure as hell wouldn't be calling up Marini to fill me in. "Like Daniel."

Marcus laughed at the thought. "Daniel is a warrior and so much more, *cara*. There is only one word for Daniel and that is king. Daniel takes all the good traits of each class and blends them to make a vampire of immense strength. Louis is a warrior. Most of the members of the Council are warriors. They are the most prevalent of the classes."

"You're an academic, right?"

"Yes, I am. It is the category they use for vampires whose talents are almost entirely mental. I'm stronger than a human, but I could never battle Daniel or Louis. My talents lie in persuasion and the ability to draw another person into my mind. I can usually tell when a person is lying to me, and I always know what a human is feeling. It makes it incredibly easy to find a meal and go undetected. I know who's attracted to me and I can use that."

I could see how that would be very helpful to a vampire. He could have his dinner and leave the victim alive after persuading the person nothing had happened. "So how do you know who'll be important and who won't?"

Marcus thought about this for a moment, obviously trying to find the best way to make me understand. "I see patterns. Some people would call it seeing the future, but it's nothing so interesting. I see the needs of the world and somehow I manage to find the person who can fill those needs."

"Like Daniel?"

The vampire's smile was rueful. "I knew Daniel was important the moment I laid eyes on him. It's why I fought to become his mentor. I knew he would need me if he was to become what the supernatural world needed. I've found that when a true need arises, somehow, some way, the right tools show up."

I turned to my host. It was long past time to get some answers. If he wanted to use Daniel, I needed to know what happened the last time he had met a king. "If Daniel is supposed to stop the threat

Marini poses, then what was the last king supposed to do?"

The gondola glided gracefully across the water as Marcus turned to me. "What you have to understand, Zoey, is that Louis has not always been as he is today. I've counted him as my friend for almost two thousand years. When I rose, it was Louis who turned me. He gave me my first blood. He became my master."

"Then I'm sorry for you, Marcus. He told me he hates the fact that he cannot treat Daniel as a master should," I said bitterly.

Marcus shook his head. "But, Zoey, he was a kind master. His own master had been terrible to him, and he vowed to never treat another vampire in such a manner. This is what I'm trying to explain to you. Time weighs on him. Immortality changes you. You see so much, watch everything change so quickly, that it all seems temporary. If everything around you becomes temporary then nothing is meaningful. It happens to many vampires. It has happened to Louis. He believes he's the only thing on the planet worthy of ruling because he's the oldest of us. That is why the last king rose."

I nodded because I understood what he was trying to tell me. "So inevitably the Council becomes corrupt."

"Yes. It was about a thousand years ago. The Council was made up of ancients, true ancients. These were beings that had walked the earth as humans were evolving. It was the Dark Ages and we were being hunted. The Council made a deal with the demons to build great armies to subjugate the human threat. We still needed human blood to survive, so the plan was to kill the strong and make slaves of the weak. There was no mass media in those days, so it was easy to take over a territory and never have the neighboring villages know what was coming for them."

"And the last king put a stop to this?" I didn't quite understand why they needed to execute him. He sounded like he'd done something good.

Marcus shook his head. "He was not Daniel, Zoey. He was a hard man. He was power hungry. When he rose, he killed the Council members without a thought to the fact that the act plunged us into civil war. Without a strong Council to guide us, the vampires sought out their own territories and the bloodshed was…I've never seen the like. The demons took advantage and joined the king in trying to force the remaining vampires to do his bidding, which included giving their own companions to the king as tribute."

"Louis and the old king have a lot in common," I muttered, thinking about the conversation we'd had about Daniel owing him. Marini believed he deserved whatever companion he wanted because he was the head of the Council.

"More than you know, *cara*," Marcus replied enigmatically. "Niles, Elof, and I were relatively young vampires. Niko was older and more on the same level as Louis, but we banded together. We were sick of the war and thought we could do better. Niko talked about the ancient Greeks and their views on government. My own Roman upbringing had me believe that people should have rights. It wasn't democracy as you know today, but it formed the roots of it. The king was a bit more feudal. Might made right in his eyes. We had to stop him."

"How did you do it?"

"We did the only thing we could. He was stronger than all of us combined so we relied on being smarter than him."

"You came up with a plan." It had to be Marcus.

His eyes were grave as he nodded. "I did." He was silent for a while and when he began speaking again, I could hear the many years in his voice. "I'm not particularly proud of what I did, but there was no other way. I didn't have a companion at the time but Louis did. She was a beautiful, strong woman from Brittany. The king had decided to take her. She loved Louis and came to me asking how she could kill the king and save her master because she worried Louis would attempt to defend her. I knew an alchemist. He was an intensely talented man. He could liquefy silver in such a way that it was ingestible."

"Like colloidal silver?"

"No, Zoey," Marcus said, his teeth biting out the words. "Colloidal silver doesn't kill in small doses. Marie had but hours to live when she went to the king and let him feed from her."

"Oh my god," I breathed, thinking about the woman's sacrifice. "She must have loved him."

"It was a different time and Louis was a different person. In the end, it did not kill the king." Marcus's voice turned academic now. "It did, however, weaken him to the point that we were able to get him into a prison."

A prison for a vampire king consisted of yards of silver chains and a coffin. I had seen Daniel in one. The sight still haunted my nightmares. "Is he still alive?"

The thought that he was still hanging around, desiccated and forever hungry in his prison horrified me.

"In a sense," the vampire said. "Louis was devastated by the loss of Marie. He wanted to kill me and the alchemist. The other members of our new Council made Louis see reason when it came to me, though it took many years to repair our friendship. The alchemist had another way to repay Louis."

My blood went cold as I realized what he was talking about. "The Blood Stone."

"Yes. The alchemist made the Blood Stone from the living body of the vampire king. Of course, when the alchemist was done, the king was no longer alive in any way that we would recognize."

The ramifications of what the Blood Stone was hit me like a tidal wave. I felt my stomach clench and nausea swept over me. "Oh god, Marcus, what have I done?" I barely heard my own words. I remembered the words Marini had said to me that night. I asked what the Blood Stone was and he told me it was merely what my husband felt every day. Marini had found a way to take the essence of the last king into his body. For a brief time, he was a king with all the strengths of one. "He can fight Daniel."

Marcus turned my face toward him. "Yes, *cara*, I fear that he can. It would be better for Louis if he kills Daniel in a duel. It would be legal in a way and there would be nothing we could do. The effect doesn't last for long, but he merely needs to get Daniel into a position where he loses a properly witnessed duel. After that, if he can, he will likely try to create another Blood Stone from Daniel."

I was confused. "He's had Daniel at his mercy before. Why wait until now?"

"Until now Daniel has been exactly what Louis needs," Marcus explained. "Before Daniel rose, we were dangerously close to another civil war and Louis had lost the Blood Stone. He needed another king to keep everyone in line. He thought by keeping Daniel ignorant and properly training him that he could make Daniel his assassin, his executioner. I believed Daniel was worth more to him alive than dead. Now that he has the Blood Stone, that balance has tipped. He needs to kill Daniel while keeping the Council and the academics on his side. Louis has bigger plans, you see. The Council has become corrupt again. Louis wants to subjugate the supernatural world and once he has them, he'll go after the humans. He has promised us the world if we follow him."

"What did he promise you, Marcus?" What did Louis think could tempt Marcus into betraying his own strong beliefs?

Marcus laughed softly and brought my hand to his lips. "My dear, he promised me you. I'm to be your master once I help Louis trap Daniel. I've been promised that I will be allowed to take you to Venice and we'll be left alone for the rest of your natural life. My city and my companion will be left untouched by any war that follows."

"He is lying, Marcus." I had to make him believe.

"I know, *cara*, and even if he wasn't, I could not betray Daniel." Marcus sat back, a sad look on his face. "I've waited too long for him to rise to throw it all away because I want a woman who can never love me."

I didn't want to go into that. It seemed cruel to agree with him. "Why has everyone else been corrupted but you remain true?"

"I believe it's merely a part of who I am. Academics view the world differently. We study those around us. We've watched humanity grow up. We respect and even admire the works of man," Marcus said. "Niko is also an academic. Daniel has two strong supporters on the Council, but we would be outvoted by the warriors if it came to that. The warriors...in the end they want war. Daniel is different. Daniel has you and, as much as I hate to admit it, he has Devinshea."

"You obviously care for Daniel," I said. "Why do you have to be so awful to Dev? He's sacrificed a lot for this war of yours. If we win, it will be due in large part to him."

"I know," Marcus admitted. "Let me tell you another story that might help you understand. It involves the boy...I call him a boy, but god only knows how old he is. It involves the boy you met earlier today. The one called the oracle. He's the one who sought me out many years ago and requested I get the Blood Stone off the plane. He introduced me to Miria. It was the first of several requests the oracle had of me, but there was one that is meaningful to our discussion. About a hundred years ago, the oracle came to me in Venice. He told me there was a young girl in Ireland who needed protection. I was to ensure that no vampire ever found her. When I made my way to a village in County Galway called Ballymoe, I found the girl and made sure she was protected. I became her family's anonymous patron. The girl became a woman and married and later her grandson made his way to America."

My eyes narrowed. "My father was born in Galway."

"Yes, *cara*, it was your great grandmother I was supposed to protect. Even as a child she lit up the night. It was very difficult for me to watch her from afar, but I did it because I was promised my heart's desire should I manage to keep the girl safe."

"What did the oracle promise you?" It must have been impressive to keep a vampire from a truly brilliant companion. I had to wonder at that particular twist of fate. Had a vampire found my grandmother, she almost surely wouldn't have had children. I wouldn't exist without Marcus's protection.

Marcus turned from me. His eyes watched the houses as we floated by. I wondered if he was going to ignore my question when he spoke again. "I was promised that this woman would give birth to a line that would produce the one woman who I would love so much, when she died I would go with her."

"Oh, Marcus, I'm so sorry." Tears pricked my eyes because I could practically feel his pain. It had been a cruel deception on the boy's part. "I am sorry but…"

"You were meant for Daniel," he said solidly. "I know that. You love Daniel and Devinshea and I can see how necessary you are. I told you that the day after we met. Without you, Daniel is merely a death machine. With you, he is a true and proper king. The oracle lied because he needed me. He knew if I found the girl on my own, I would have protected her until she became a woman, and then I would have taken her as my companion. I would have taken her before she had a husband, before she could bear children. Your line would have died with her."

"I can see why he did it, but it still seems cruel. You really want the transference thing? It scares me."

The condition Marcus was talking about was called sympathetic transference. It occurred when a vampire bonded so strongly with a companion that his own body gave up its strength to keep hers alive. In the end, a companion is not immortal and she took the vampire with her when she died. It didn't work in sudden situations, only in long-term chronic illnesses. We'd discovered Daniel had the condition while we were in Faery. I'd tried to figure out how to cure it but Daniel had been thrilled.

Apparently immortality isn't everything it's cracked up to be.

Marcus's brows rose. "How do you know? Of course. Daniel already has it. How did you diagnose his condition?"

It was my turn to admit something. Marcus had been so open with me I felt compelled to be honest. "A couple of months ago, Sarah discovered the condition along with a Fae healer. Daniel was weak. We found out his body was bolstering mine when I was weak."

"Were you sick, *cara*?"

"I was pregnant," I admitted. "I had a miscarriage."

Marcus turned away. "I'm sorry to hear it. I'm rather surprised Daniel allowed Devinshea to impregnate you."

"It was an accident but we're used to the idea now. We're going to try again after…all of this is over. Daniel wants a family. Dev can give that to him. Dev is more than willing to share his children."

Marcus thought about it for a moment. "Please forgive me. I'll attempt to be better about the prince. I was bitter toward him because I believed he could never love you as I could have, but now I see what he can give to the both of you. He is loyal, your Lancelot. He's loyal to you both."

"We're his family, Marcus," I said, hoping the vampire would make good on his promise.

Marcus laughed at something I couldn't see. "And he's getting impatient. Your little surgery is over and he wants his wife back. Know this, Zoey, you are my queen and I will never betray you. I will be your faithful servant to the end." He kissed my hand and I was suddenly lying in a soft bed with Dev shaking me gently.

"Hey, baby," I said softly, glorying in the fact that I could move my arm. "Sorry about the passing out thing."

He leaned over and kissed me. "I'm sorry about the bullet in your arm, my wife. It's out now. Lee held you down while I had to cut you open. It was horrible. Next time, just allow them to blow my head off, won't you? It will be easier on me in the end."

I shook my head and noticed that we weren't alone in the room. All three wolves were there, and Marcus stood in the background watching me. I sat up and smiled at him. "Thank you, Marcus. That was much more pleasant than Lee having to knock me out with his fist."

"I wouldn't do that," Lee grumbled.

"I would," Zack offered, smiling.

Dev frowned, looking between me and the vampire. "Just how pleasant was this little interlude?"

"I merely took my queen on a tour of my home city," Marcus said with a deferential bow of his head.

"That better be all you did," Dev muttered under his breath.

"Is all to your liking, Devinshea?" Marcus asked with no malice in his voice. "I've stocked the kitchens with her favorite foods and her clothes have been properly placed in the closets. I hope the bedding is to your specifications."

Dev watched him warily. "Yes, it seems to be. I appreciate that."

Marcus nodded and then listened intently. I noticed the wolves perked up, too.

"Daniel is here," Marcus said with a frown. "I doubt he will be in a good mood."

I glanced up at Dev, who grimaced. He looked like a man waiting for his own trial. I held his hand and waited to see if Daniel was going to judge us all.

CHAPTER SIXTEEN

There was a brisk knock on the door and when Marcus opened it, a woman walked in the room. I'd been informed on the jet that Hugo Wells had an assistant, a human female who also served as his lover. I wasn't expecting the pretty woman who walked in. She was roughly forty, perhaps a wee bit older, and solidly built. She was attractive but no great beauty. Her blonde hair was streaked with gray and she wore a comfortable skirt and button-down shirt. She pressed her stylish glasses up as she gave me a quick once over.

"Your Highness." She greeted me with a formal curtsey and a nod of her head. "I'm Diana Spelling, Mr. Wells's assistant. It's a great pleasure to meet you. I hope everything is to your liking."

"Oh, yes," I replied while Dev found a robe for me. "Everything after the attempted kidnapping went very well, once we were retrieved from the police, that is."

"Sorry about the mix up, ma'am." Diana nodded to Neil. "Lucky for you, the little wolf there knew where to go. He came straight into the kitchens and demanded that Hugo save his mistress. As you are our mistress as well, we got right on it. It's been a very exciting day."

"I got to have tea while they were getting everything ready," Neil said with a smile. "And some little cookies. They were good. It's a whole other meal here, Z. They have four instead of three. I think I should have been born British. Also, even the straight guys are gay."

"He's very amusing," Diana said with a smile on her face. "The king has arrived and craves your attention in the parlor. He's discussing the events of the day with my master, but he would like to hear from you and Mr. Quinn."

"Please call me Zoey, Diana," I said, indicating I was ready to get into my robe. Everyone but Marcus and Neil turned around. Dev sent Marcus a dirty look and with a shrug he finally gave me a tiny bit of privacy. Neil wouldn't bother. He'd seen everything there was to see. "I'm afraid I'm not big on formality."

"I heard that about you," Diana said and I could hear the approval in her voice. "Well then, Zoey, please let me lead you and that glorious slab of male beside you to your husband."

Dev smiled as I belted the robe. He was used to positive female attention and turned to the woman. I heard him talking as I made my way into the bathroom where someone had thoughtfully placed a pair of jeans and a soft green sweater. "Please call me Dev. Diana, you've done a marvelous job making us feel comfortable."

They spoke while I dressed, discussing the way the household was run and who was expected to arrive when. I dressed quickly and rejoined them.

"Have our guards' rooms been prepared?" Dev asked. "If Daniel has not instructed they be present, then perhaps they could retire? It's been a long day."

"Yes, sir," Diana replied as I reentered the room properly dressed. "Their rooms are on the first floor, by the kitchens. Neil, if you would lead the lads there, you will find I've had a buffet set out for you."

I heard Lee sigh in anticipation of his long-neglected meal time and he and Zack hurried along after Neil. Dev, Marcus, and I made our way down the stairs at a more sedate pace. I got my first glimpse at Hugo's home. It was enormous by London standards and had to be worth millions. The steps were marble, as was the entryway we crossed to get to the formal parlor. There was artwork on the walls I'd only seen in books before. The carpet in the entryway was lush with rich colors. Everything about the townhouse was in impeccable taste.

Daniel was speaking quietly with the Elizabethan vampire. He frowned our way as we entered the room, and my heart clenched because he looked so tired and so very disappointed. I felt Dev stiffen beside me.

"I can't believe you did that, Devinshea," Daniel said, shaking his head.

"I told you he was upset." Marcus slipped past us and sat down beside Hugo on the couch. Diana had bowed and left the room, leaving us behind with three disapproving vampires.

"I'm not sure what you would have me do, Daniel," Dev said tightly.

"Daniel, they were coming after us. Dev didn't have a choice." I wanted to avoid a Daniel/Dev smackdown. It had been a while since they got into a knock-down, drag-out fight, but they were legendary. They tended to throw heavy objects at one another, and I didn't want them destroying this magnificent mansion.

"You blew up a helicopter, Dev." Daniel stood up to regard us with his heavy stare.

"It was trying to kill us," Dev shot back.

"You shot it down with a rifle from the back of a moving Jeep," Daniel said, his voice strong and rising. He stared at Dev for a long moment before his lips split into a brilliant smile. "That must have been fucking awesome, man. I'm so pissed off I wasn't there."

I heard Dev's sigh of relief, and his head dropped slightly.

Daniel moved in, his body close to Dev's. He put his hand on the back of Dev's neck and brought his face up. "What's that look on your face, Devinshea? You looked like I was going to beat the crap out of you. You can't possibly believe I would be angry you brilliantly defended our wife."

"I got her shot, Dan." They stared into each other's eyes, saying more than words could.

Daniel nodded and let his forehead find Dev's, both his hands holding Dev's neck. "No, you didn't. I know you and I know Z. She was trying to protect you. She's fierce. You got her out and that's what counts. That is all that counts to me, Devinshea. She's safe and so are you."

Dev nodded, his hands on Daniel's waist, and I just wanted to scream at them to hug each other already and maybe exchange some saliva. I moved in because they seemed stuck. The minute I was close, both their arms were around me and they seemed to relax.

"Was the explosion really cool?" Daniel asked with an easy smile.

"Yeah. It was something to see." Dev sat down on the couch, leaving plenty of space for Daniel and me.

Daniel leaned over, kissing me senseless. "Are you all right, baby? Did Dev get the bullet out okay?"

Dev went a little green at the thought. "You will not leave us alone again, Daniel. I didn't enjoy playing the field medic."

Daniel grinned. "I won't leave you alone again because you do all the fun stuff when I'm not around."

"Well, if you had been around, I would never have gotten the chance." Dev said, relaxed as we sat beside him. "You would have flown up and grabbed the thing with one hand and sent it into the ground."

Daniel's eyes lit up, and he gave Dev a big eager smile.

"I'll tell Zack to make a note," Dev agreed and I could already see how that experiment was going to go. Bell Helicopter might be getting a strange order in the near future.

"Daniel, that crash was huge," Marcus argued, obviously shocked at Daniel's attitude. "We did what we could, but I can't guarantee that there wasn't video or photos taken. This could be a real problem."

"Marcus told Dev you were pissed off," I explained to Daniel.

His blue eyes heated up with anger. "I was. I still am, but certainly not at Dev. I'm pissed off at this Order thing. They shot you."

"They were trying to kill Dev. It was a head shot for him, but I just took it in the shoulder instead."

Daniel shook his head. "You're going to kill me someday, baby." He turned to Dev. "Tell me you got some of the fuckers."

"Many of them," Dev admitted. "I also kept one alive for you. I thought you'd like to have a word."

Hugo nodded. "The soldier is being held by my employees in the basement. He'll be quite unconscious for a while yet, Your Highness."

"Tomorrow is soon enough to deal with him." Daniel sighed and held me tightly. His voice was low and weary. "Hugo explained to me about the Blood Stone."

"Danny, I'm so sorry," I whispered.

"What?" Dev asked, his face worried. He'd been left out of this particular loop, and Marcus took the time to fill him in. He told Dev about how the Blood Stone worked and I watched my faery's face fall. "And we gave it to him."

"I gave it to him." Guilt gnawed at my insides.

Daniel shook his head. "We gave it to him, Z. This isn't your fault. We all went after that stone and we left you alone to deal with Marini when he showed up."

"It gets worse," Hugo said in his clipped accent. "I got a call from your butler earlier this evening, Mr. Quinn. He says Marini attempted to raid the club. He has declared Daniel an outlaw and claims rights to the queen. At this point, he's only claiming that you belong to the Council, but that won't last for long."

We couldn't go home. I felt my heart start to race at the thought. He was backing us into a corner. He was really going to go through with it. He was going to try to kill Daniel and take Dev and me as his playthings.

"Calm down, Z," Devinshea said soothingly. "We knew this would happen eventually."

"He called the entire Council tonight for a vote on your status," Marcus concurred. "Niko and I were forced to agree with him. We're outnumbered, Your Highness."

Daniel waved off that worry. "Of course, Marcus. You do what you need to do to escape detection for now. Tell Niko I understand." Daniel was a practical man. It did us no good for our allies on the Council to out themselves, but I could see he was upset by the turn of events.

"Was Albert all right?" I didn't want to think about the ramifications of what Daniel's status meant for all of us.

Hugo chuckled slightly. "Apparently there was a plan in place. I was told the club is in something called lockdown mode and that the local werewolf alpha has brought the Dallas pack in to defend the place. Marini wasn't ready for such a vigorous defense."

Dev nodded. "The new alpha's wife recently had twins, thanks to my goddess and me. When I asked him to watch after things, he was more than willing to help out. Of course, I didn't expect him to have to handle a siege, but he was Special Forces trained. Marini will have his hands full with him."

Marcus shook his head. "Marini has already figured out you fled. He's returning to Paris this evening until he can discern where you have gone. We all must be very careful. We'll be closely watched. As soon as your mission here in England is done, you'll be moved to New York where you'll stay with Henri Jacobs while we gather our forces and decide our next move. If needs be, I'll hide you on Poveglia. It's an island off Venice. It's very isolated and closed to tourists. I have a small villa on the island that you can stay in."

It struck me that we were really on the run now. I took a deep breath because I didn't want to cry in front of Marcus and Hugo. I needed to keep it together for Daniel's sake. He was already looking far too serious.

"Your Highness, do not worry." Hugo interrupted my thoughts. "This isn't the first time a king has been forced into hiding. This is the way the game is played. It's not even the first time Henri and I have aided a king on the run. We both hid Charles II before we managed to smuggle him out of the country and into France."

Daniel looked over my head at the vampire. "I appreciate everything you have done, Hugo. Please pass on my thanks to Henri. You'll have to forgive me, though. It is the first time I have lost my wife's home. I find the feeling unsettling."

"Daniel, we knew this could happen," Dev said reassuringly. "Everything is in place for us. We have a network of supporters willing to help us. We planned for this."

"I lost your home, too, Devinshea," Daniel said bitterly. "Shouldn't you be more pissed off?"

"I'm not angry," Dev said quietly, trying to get Daniel to look at him.

I stood up. This was rapidly turning into a discussion that was not for public consumption. "Gentlemen, I thank you for everything you've done for us tonight, but the king is tired and needs to rest. We'll retire for the evening and see you tomorrow."

Daniel allowed me to take his hand and lead him out of the room. It was time to discuss this privately. More importantly, it was time to comfort my husband. He'd had several shocks tonight. Daniel didn't handle change well. Dev said his good nights and followed us back up to the guest suite assigned to us.

Daniel was silent as he sat down on the bed. I looked back at Dev, who seemed as concerned as I was about Daniel. I didn't like the hollow look in his blue eyes or the way he quietly let me slip his jacket off and then pull his T-shirt over his head. Dev walked into the bathroom, and I heard the shower running.

"Baby, I need to get your pants off if I'm going to get you in the shower," I said, trying to pull him up.

He ran a hand through his hair. It was a gesture he always used when he was frustrated, and I knew what was coming. "No. I'm really tired, Z. I'm going to have Diana set me up in one of the smaller rooms so I can get some sleep and not disturb you and Dev."

I looked up and saw that Dev was back in the room, and his face had flushed with anger. This was what Danny did when he felt guilty. He ran. He might not be running very far, but I wasn't about to let him get away with even a short jog away from us. We had moved past that and he needed to be reminded. Forcefully, if necessary. I wasn't above manipulating him to get my point across.

"Let me get this straight, Danny." I looked down on him. "Dev and I went through hell today. I got shot. Dev got searched in places he was really sure no one would ever search. We're on the run and without a home and you want to sleep by yourself?"

Danny was suddenly deeply interested in the floor. "I'm just tired. You and Dev will sleep better by yourselves anyway."

"I won't," Dev said and I saw that he was itching for a fight. I knew what he was thinking. Danny didn't respond to sympathy. He needed a swift kick in the ass from time to time. "I don't know about Zoey, but I feel vulnerable sleeping in a strange vampire's home. But really, Daniel, we wouldn't want to disturb you with the possibility of us needing you. Feel free to sleep wherever you wish. I'll take care of our wife as I always do."

Now Danny's blue eyes were heating up. "Do you think I like being at other people's mercy any more than you do, Dev?"

"I'm not the one pulling away, Daniel," Dev pointed out. His voice went low. "I'm not the one who has stayed away. I'm not the one who won't talk about it."

I went completely still because I was suddenly fairly certain that they weren't talking about what had gone on today. Something had happened between them while we'd been in Faery. It happened when they went off by themselves right before my miscarriage. When they returned to me, there had been a distance between them. Even after we were back together, I would still catch them at odd times, staring at each other when they thought no one was looking. Something was sitting in between them, and I had been very patiently waiting to find out what it was.

I had a suspicion and it made my heart ache.

"Don't you dare bring that up here and now," Daniel said, his eyes drifting away.

Dev growled his frustration and began to pace. "Of course not, Your Highness. Fine. It doesn't matter and it never did. Let's talk about what does matter. Let's talk about our wife. Let's talk about the fact that you're leaving me alone to take care of her yet again. Why do I have a partner in the first place?"

And just like that I got really frustrated. Daniel stood up and got into Dev's space. I was tired of the posturing and that shower sounded really good to me. While they faced off, I got out of my clothes. I let them fall wherever and didn't care that they would get wrinkled.

"I'm not pulling away," Daniel snarled. "I'm a little fucked up because we're on the run and it's my fault. Z got shot and it's my fault. The club is under lockdown and it's my fault. Forgive me if I want to give y'all a little time to get over being pissed at me."

"There's only one problem with that scenario, Daniel," Dev said, his voice rising. "I wasn't pissed at you until you pulled this shit."

I sighed as they started to yell at each other in earnest. I was tired. I was worried. I was needy and not a little bit scared. We were on a path and there was no way off of it now. Maybe there had never been a way out since the instant Daniel died in that car accident all those years ago, but it was settling in on me now and I could use a little comfort. I needed their arms around me, telling me we would stick together, but the boys had opted for another form of stress release. I was on my own. I thought I might point that out to the boys. They had told me not to go off by myself, and I didn't want to make them worry.

"Don't be an asshole, Dan," Dev yelled and I was pretty sure the whole house could hear us. So much for keeping it private.

I put a hand on both their arms, gaining their attentions. "I'm going to go take a shower, okay? That hot water is going to waste and I'm tired and spent way too much time in a police station to feel clean."

There was a long pause as they both stared down at me.

"You're naked," Daniel said, proving he was good with the obvious.

"That's usually how one takes a shower, Danny," I replied. "Dev, you said you brought along all sorts of necessary items, right?"

Dev's eyes were on my breasts, the prior fight seemingly forgotten. It was nice to know that after all the times I had slept with these men, I could still stop them in their tracks by taking my clothes off. "Yeah, I brought along everything we could need. Marcus sent some of his people out to get our luggage. Luckily the Order left our clothes and personal items behind. They took my weapons cache though. Fuckers."

"Good," I replied evenly. "If you wouldn't mind finding something that would aid in the masturbation I intend to do in the shower, that would be great. You know, whenever you and Danny get through with your fight would be fine. I'll make do with a couple of fingers until then."

I gave them both an innocent smile and walked off to the gorgeous shower I had spied earlier. I wasn't surprised by the silence in the room as I left.

The shower was luxurious, like the rest of the house. It was bigger than most bathrooms, with natural-looking tile and a rainfall shower head. The hot water felt like bliss against my skin, and I thought about how nice it would be to be made love to and then crawl under those crisp, clean sheets and sleep between the two men I loved more than life. I could close my eyes and for a while nothing would matter because I was with them. I sighed and let my hand slip between my thighs. I smiled when I felt a warm hand covering mine.

"Did you find something to help me with my problem, Dev?" I asked, knowing exactly who was behind me.

His erection was already firm against my backside, and I leaned into it as his strong hand gently started to rub my clitoris. His voice was soft and warm against my head. "You don't need anything but me to help you with that particular problem, lover."

I frowned. "Did Danny leave then?"

"No," Daniel said and I turned, following the sound of his voice. He stood in the door of the shower, still in his jeans. He'd ditched his shoes and my mouth watered at the sight of his cut chest and perfect abs. His jeans hung low, and I could see he was extremely interested in the proceedings, but he made no move to join us. He was so hot, with the singular exception of the sadness in his eyes. "I'm still here, Z. Dev just gets his clothes off faster than anyone I've ever seen. It's his superpower."

"She was naked, Daniel," Dev explained, his hands molding my breasts now. He delicately rubbed my nipples, getting them very stiff. "It's rude to leave her alone like that. Don't act like I'm the crazy person in this scenario. We haven't gotten even an inch inside her for days. Tell me why you're not naked and trying to find a way in?"

"I don't switch gears the way you do, Dev," Danny said, his eyes getting hot as he watched us. He might not switch as fast as Dev, but he was getting there. "I'm still a little upset about losing our home."

"We haven't lost it." I tried to keep my voice even but Dev was playing around with his tongue in my ear and that always got me hot for some reason. I tried to focus on the problem at hand. I had two ears and only one of them was being playfully nipped. I had gotten used to a certain amount of symmetry when it came to lovemaking. "It's still there. We just can't go back for a while."

"What if we can never go back, Z? What if we get this thing off my heart, but I can't beat Marini because he's full of the old king's blood?" Daniel asked seriously. "What if I die while some thousands-of-years-old wizard is playing around with my heart? What if I lose one of you?"

Dev stopped what he was doing and his arms went around my shoulders. He hugged me tightly against him. "Daniel, we can't know any of those things is going to happen. If we can't go back then we'll make a new home. If we seriously believe you can't beat Marini, then we make a run for Scotland and the Unseelie *sithein*. We can live there for the rest of our lives quite happily. If you die under the wizard's hands, and I intend to make sure you do not, then I will haul Zoey off kicking and screaming to the same place. As for losing one of us, if that happens then you have to go on. If I die, then you have to take care of our wife."

"And if we lose her?" I could see the unshed tears in Daniel's blue eyes. It was his worst fear, and I knew right now it seemed so close.

Dev's hands tightened further around me. "Then we will have some work to do, my friend. But none of these scenarios is aided by any of the three of us sleeping alone. We don't need time apart to think, Daniel. We need time together."

Daniel's sadness changed to great longing, and he walked into the shower not bothering with his jeans. He walked up to me and took my face in his hands and kissed me for all he was worth. He wasn't subtle or seductive. He shoved his tongue in my mouth and didn't try to hide his fangs. His fingers wound in my wet hair, holding me in place for his mouth. I let my hands roam across that muscled chest of his. I heard him moan when I let my tongue graze on his fangs just enough to draw blood.

"God, Z," Daniel groaned when he let me up for air. "You're everything to me. I live off your blood. I fill my every sense with you, your scent, your taste, the sound of your laugh. I can close my eyes and see every inch of you. You can't blame me for being worried about losing you."

It was the way Marcus had talked about Venice, his city, his home. I was Daniel's home and he hadn't lost me. The club was just a place, and while I might miss it, I was home as long as I had Danny and Dev. "I love you, Danny," I said against his lips as I stretched up to kiss him. "As long as we're together, everything is going to be all right. We stick together, baby. That's all we have any control over."

"It was the whole reason we came together in the first place," Dev said from behind me. "We're stronger together than we are apart."

Daniel's smile was wistful as he remembered that night they told me we were going to be a threesome. "I thought we did it because we both wanted to fuck Z, and it was either do it together or we could kill each other."

Dev laughed. "Well, you have to admit that the one left standing would have to deal with a very angry Zoey."

"I'm a very confused Zoey," I admitted.

"Confused about what, my lover?" Dev asked, nipping my ear.

"I want to know what happened between the two of you in Faery. I want to know why you won't talk about it," I explained quietly. "Do you think I'll be angry? Do you think I'll accuse you of cheating on me?"

There was really only one reason for the tension between them. Only one I could think of.

Daniel shook his head. "It didn't go that far."

"Only because we were interrupted with news of your miscarriage," Dev said. He backed away, and I missed his hands on me. "That's right, my goddess. You were losing our child and Daniel and I were drunk and playing around."

"I told you it wasn't our fault, Dev. We didn't cause it." Danny kept his distance, but I could hear in his voice that this was an argument they'd had more than once.

"Not everyone thinks that way. Fate has a way of punishing hubris, Daniel." Dev leaned back against the stone of the shower.

I wasn't about to allow him to pull away from me, too. Especially not over something utterly foolish. I left the warm stream of water and did what we should have done months ago. I placed my body against his, went skin to skin so there wasn't any distance between us. I let my hands stroke along his skin, trying to ease him. I couldn't stand the fact that he'd held this inside.

"Please tell me Declan wasn't the one who found you." I could only imagine that he would have made it so much worse. It would explain his intense hatred for Daniel. It had become even worse after my miscarriage. Now I knew why.

"He practically relished telling us the news," Daniel admitted.

"He simply pointed out that if we'd been with Zoey, it might not have happened." Dev's hands finally started to move on me. He dropped his head to mine, and I could feel his whole body sigh as though he was deeply relieved.

Had they really thought I would be angry?

"You couldn't have stopped it. If they hadn't gotten to me with the cursed tea, they would have found another way. You were doing your job and being with your partner. It's your right, Devinshea. It's Daniel's right. You should take pleasure and comfort from each other."

Daniel stayed on his side of the shower. "Zoey, we made a mistake that night."

I kissed Dev's chest and turned to stare down my husband. I was done with this argument. "Yeah, you really did. You didn't finish. You would have felt a shit ton better if you had, and maybe you wouldn't have gotten so angry with each other. Damn it. How many times do I have to tell you? I want us all together. You and Dev talk about how you feel safe because if something happens to either of you, you know the other one will love me. I want that, too. I want to know that the men who love me love each other, too." I wouldn't have said the words if I didn't believe they were already true. If Daniel and Dev hadn't been attracted to each other, I would have been content, but there was an electricity in the room when they got close. It was unmistakable. Undeniable. I couldn't see how it was wrong.

Daniel took a deep breath, and I watched as he made a decision. He unhooked the fly of his jeans and pushed them off his hips, tossing them to the side before closing the space between us. The minute he stepped close, Dev moved beside me again as though Daniel making his choice had broken the tension.

"I do love him," Daniel said achingly as he dropped his mouth to mine. "I love you both. But I've loved you as long as I can remember. I never thought I would love anyone else."

"I love you, Daniel. Nothing else ever has to come of it. It's enough," Dev said, emotion thickening his tone. "What we have is more than enough for me."

It wasn't enough for me, but I thought arguing that I wanted to see them get down and dirty when I finally had them admitting they loved each other would be a little tacky.

Even though I really, really wanted to see it.

Dev covered my back, his hands coming around to skim down

my torso. He moved me closer to Daniel, forcing our bodies together. They had me trapped, and I couldn't think of a single place I wanted to be more than in between them.

Daniel's hands started roaming restlessly across my skin, and he was leaving his guilt behind as his desire took over. "It might be enough for you, Devinshea, but I think our wife needs more than words tonight."

"What do you want, our sweet, hot little wife?" Dev asked, making the simple question seem so deliciously dirty. He slid a finger over my clitoris because he knew exactly what I wanted. "Are we going to give her what she wants, Dan?"

"I think I can handle that." Daniel dropped to his knees and suddenly I could feel the warmth of his mouth right over my pussy. Heat suffused me, making me shiver, but Dev wouldn't let me move.

He held me tight, his arms a sweet cage. "Let him do what he wants. I think our vampire wants a taste and he's going to get it. You've got the sweetest little pussy either one of us has ever tasted, my goddess. You will be still and let us have our way tonight."

Daniel's tongue came out, licking at my clit while his fingers foraged inside. Dev's hands moved to my breasts, plucking and playing with my nipples.

I let my head drift back against Dev's chest, reveling in the fact that we were all together. I had them both close and had no intention of ever letting them go again.

Daniel was back on his feet after a few paltry minutes of play. Frustration ran through me, but then I saw the look in Daniel's eyes as he peered over my shoulder at Dev.

"She has the best pussy ever. Do you want a taste?" Daniel asked, his voice low.

Dev groaned a little and moved to my side, but Daniel didn't cede his place. He stood right in front of Dev, his shoulders squared, everything about him—from the look in his eyes to the way he held himself—screamed challenge.

Dev wasn't one to back down. He got into Daniel's space. "I can't taste her if you won't move, Dan."

"Yes, you can."

I thought my heart would stop right then and there because I was all over Daniel's lips and mouth and tongue.

Daniel's hand went to the nape of Dev's neck. Despite the fact that Dev had a few inches of height on him, there was no question who was the dominant player in this little skirmish. Daniel easily handled Dev, moving him into the position he wanted. Dev's hands went to Daniel's chest as Danny brought their mouths close.

"She's right here on my lips. You know you want a taste and I want to share her with you."

Dev leaned down and drew his tongue across Daniel's plump bottom lip in a slow, ridiculously sexy movement that threatened to send my blood pressure right to the moon. They didn't have to touch me again. The sight of Dev licking my arousal off Daniel's lips had me hot and ready to go right that second.

"I lied, Daniel. I do want more," Dev said against Danny's lips.

"And you know I try to give my precious blood what they want." Danny tightened his hold and suddenly their mouths fused, their tongues making a brief appearance before disappearing inside for an intimate dance.

I watched with love and lust as my men kissed because this went beyond putting on a show for me. How much guilt had they gone through? I hated to think about it because I didn't blame them for what happened. Not for a second.

Daniel finally broke the kiss, his eyes sliding my way while Dev caught his breath. "Join us, Zoey. Don't think for a second we're doing all the work while you watch. Get on your knees, baby. We need you."

I didn't hesitate for a second. Watching was lovely. Participating was something I lived for. I let Daniel help me down to the tiled floor of the shower, the water's warmth at my back.

Daniel's hand stroked my hair. "Baby, you know you're going to have to work a little to get what you want, right? You need to get us both really hard so we can fuck you."

Dev had an arm around Daniel as though he didn't quite want to let go yet. He chuckled a little. "I've been hard since I realized she was naked."

Daniel looked at his partner like he'd lost his mind, and I could see their relationship could handle the back and forth between lovers and friends. "Dude, do you want a blow job or not?"

Dev's face went from arrogant to innocent in the blink of an eye. "I do seem to be having some trouble. I might require help."

I giggled because he didn't and neither did Daniel. They were both ridiculously hard and ready, but I was willing to play their games. I sighed as I licked the tip of Daniel's head and tasted his salty sweetness.

"Fuck, baby, that feels so good." Daniel's hips moved, shoving his cock against my mouth, trying to get inside. "Take me in. Suck me in, baby."

I sucked the head of his cock into my mouth and let my tongue swirl around it, teasing and playing. I let my hand drift up to cup his balls. They were heavy in my hand, tight against his body. I let my free hand drift over to stroke Dev. His cock was thick in my palm, responding immediately to my firm grasp.

They'd never let me play this way before. Sex had always been about the two of them pleasing me. This was more. This was the three of us pleasing each other. This was what I'd dreamed of. I stroked Dev while I sucked Daniel. When I let my eyes drift up, they were kissing again, though it was softer this time. Both men had a hand on me. Connected. Together.

Another long pass of my mouth and I was surprised when Daniel pulled his cock out.

"It's not going to be that easy, baby," Daniel declared. "Not tonight. Now suck Dev. Suck him hard, Z, not that playful shit you just gave me. You suck him deep, but don't you let him come."

"When did I lose control?" Dev asked with the sweetest smile on his face. It didn't stop him from offering me his cock. "I always knew you would be bossy, Daniel. You should do what he says, my wife. He is the king."

I chose to follow Daniel's instruction and ate up Dev's dick in one long swallow.

"Fuck that's good." Dev didn't play around. He took what he wanted. He loved to fuck my mouth and that's exactly what he did. He shoved his hands in my hair and pushed himself in and out of my mouth. I fought him, sucking as hard as I could, trying to keep every inch in as he pulled out. I decided to make it a little harder for him by reaching up and rolling his tight balls in my hand.

"How serious are you about me not coming?" Dev asked, his voice hard as he shoved his cock to the back of my throat. "Because I could be ready again really fast. I could come straight down her throat and be ready for that pussy of hers faster than you can imagine."

"Don't Dev," Daniel ordered. I glanced over and he was stroking himself with one big hand as he watched us. "We go together tonight."

Dev made a kind of strangled sound and pulled himself out. "Seriously?"

I felt strangely empty. "We're together every night, Daniel," I pointed out, not seeing what the big deal was. We needed to hurry because that water wasn't going to stay hot forever.

Daniel reached a hand down to help me up. He settled me under the nearest showerhead, pulling my back to his front. His hands closed over my breasts and he licked my neck in a long pass. "We're going to take you together, Z. You wanted us together, you better be willing to take the consequences. We won't accept anything less tonight. Bring that soap over here, Dev. We need to clean our queen up before we get her seriously dirty. Can you handle her hygienic needs while I take care of a little problem I'm having?"

Dev frowned. "So I get to clean her while you fuck? How is that going together?"

"No, Devinshea. I had a long flight. No one thought to give me peanuts. I'm hungry and I want dinner." I felt his tongue lick where his fangs would pierce, and I relaxed against him because his magic filled the room, pulling me in and making me even wetter than I was before.

Dev decided he didn't need the soap. He dropped to his knees and looked up at Daniel. "This newfound belief you've adopted on delayed gratification doesn't apply to her, does it?"

I felt Daniel's chuckle on my flesh. He dragged his fangs over my skin, sending a shiver of pleasure through me. "No, man. Make her come. The more orgasms she gets, the better."

With perfect timing, Daniel struck just as Dev's mouth closed over my pussy and he started to eat me like I was a particularly sweet treat. He parted my labia and went straight for the throbbing pink pearl hidden inside. He sucked it between his lips in perfect time with Daniel drawing from my neck. Pure pleasure crashed through my system. I couldn't draw in the breath to scream, so I had to settle for a low moan as I came hard between them and sort of let Daniel be responsible for keeping me on my feet. I was boneless and didn't care if I fell to the tile or not.

Dev pulled at my clit again, his fingers spreading me wide, and a second wave smashed into me, even stronger than the first. Dev's magic made an appearance, so much more powerful than I'd felt it since we lost Bris. It rolled over me and I let my eyes close.

When I felt like opening my eyes again, Dev was settling me on the bed.

"Come here," I heard Daniel growl.

I smiled because he wasn't talking to me.

"Bossy." But I heard Dev moving.

I opened my eyes and sighed. Daniel was hungry again. He had Dev on his knees on the bed, his head to one side as he offered our vampire his body, his blood, his everything. I watched as Daniel's fangs pierced far more savagely than he ever did with me. I heard his low growl and Dev's whole body shook, his head falling back against Daniel's shoulder.

When Daniel released the vein, his eyes immediately found mine. He licked his fangs as he held Dev up. "Devinshea, our wife is in need of attention."

Two sets of gorgeous, predatory eyes turned my way, and I knew what it meant to be the absolute sweetest of prey.

Dev moved my way, climbing onto the bed. "Hello, sweetheart."

His mouth covered mine, his tongue going deep.

Daniel joined us, lying down beside me and then reaching out to roll us together. I found myself chest to chest with Daniel, who had that same gleam in his eyes. "Welcome back, princess. Dev and I were hoping we hadn't killed you back there."

"You don't seem too concerned," I pointed out because Daniel's hands were on my hips and I felt his erection seeking entry. I pushed myself up and reached in between us, my hand finding his cock and giving him the help he needed. Daniel sighed as I sank onto him. He shoved his hips up and grunted as he pressed into me, filling me up.

He was big, so hot inside me.

"Hey, wait for me, please," Dev complained and I felt him at my back.

Daniel tried to still his hips. "Sorry. She's just so fucking tight, man. She feels so good."

"Not half as good and tight as she's going to feel in a minute," Dev promised and somewhere in the back of my head a little alarm bell went off. Was he planning on…?

I felt something cold against my rear as Dev parted the cheeks of my ass and inserted something really foreign.

"Hey!" I protested.

"It's just a little lubricant," Dev explained, as if squirting cold lube against someone's ass was an everyday occurrence.

Danny couldn't help his laugh. "I told you we should warn her."

Dev's thumb rimmed my ass, spreading the lubricant where he wanted it to go. I moaned as he gently worked his thumb in. "Where exactly did you think our little ménage was going, lover? We want to fuck you and we want to do it together. Why did you think I've been stretching you with my fingers back here?"

He'd been playing around for months. If I had thought about it, I should have known this was what he wanted. I gave him my honest answer, which came out giggly and breathy because I was getting really aroused again. "I just thought you were a pervert, baby."

Dev shoved in another finger, and I had to take a really deep breath because I was getting full and he was bigger than his fingers. "I won't disagree with you, but I was preparing you for this. Daniel and I agreed this was the best way to proceed."

"Did you two have a meeting or something?" I breathed over my shoulder, squirming to get used to the feeling. I was wondering where I had thought this whole threesome thing was going. It wasn't like Dev hadn't talked about doing this before. I just had thought that it was something we'd get to later.

In the very distant future. We'd experimented a whole lot already.

Daniel was terribly amused by the entire situation. He shot a grin my way, those fangs on full display. "It mostly consisted of Dev talking about it incessantly. It's his fantasy. We gotta indulge him.

Besides, it feels really good and he hasn't even gotten his dick in yet."

But he was trying now. I felt the broad head of his now seemingly endless cock at the edge of my anus. I bit my lip as he started to push his way in. Danny held me tight. I was caught in between them. "Damn it, Dev. This has to be your fantasy?"

"Give it a minute," he ground out and I heard the effort it was taking for him to go slowly.

It burned as he moved in another inch. "When was the last time someone shoved something big up your ass, Devinshea?"

I felt his laugh deep inside me. I had to admit, it was a hell of an intimate feeling. "Oh, my lover, it was about three hours ago, and I assure you the officer wasn't as gentle with me as I'm being with you. He was quite rough, actually."

Danny's chest moved under me with the force of his glee. He seemed so young and carefree in that moment that I vowed to get through this with minimal complaining. I leaned over and kissed him.

"I want this. I want us both inside you. I want all three of us together. Do you want this, Z?" Daniel asked, the smile still lighting up his face.

I nodded. I wanted it all. I wanted to explore everything. We could try anything, do anything, as long as we were together. "I want it, Danny. I want it more than anything."

Daniel's eyes became serious and suddenly the room was flooded with his magic. I sighed and let myself sink into the soft lust that flooded the room when Daniel pulled me in. I felt him running his hands along my curves, brushing against Dev's from time to time.

"Push back against me, my goddess," Dev ordered, his voice hoarse, and now his magic was shoving Daniel's aside. When Dev got his lust on, Daniel's magic couldn't compete. When Dev got going, I would do anything he wanted sexually and I would enjoy it. Dev's magic made pain feel like exquisite pleasure. He pushed himself carefully against me as I thrust my ass back, making sure not to lose Daniel. I moaned because I was so full I could barely breathe.

"Oh, goddess, I'm never going to last." Dev groaned behind me.

"You'll last as long as you need to, Dev," Daniel warned even as he started to move. "We need to make her like this. I'm already a fucking addict."

"You should try it," Dev complained as he worked his way out only to tunnel back in. "She's so damn tight back here. She's like a vise on my dick."

"I'm going to try it," Daniel agreed, pleasure drugging his eyes.

"Can you...?" I was unsure how to phrase the question, but I so wanted to know the answer. "You know, what can you feel?"

Daniel seemed to know what I meant. "Are you asking if I can feel him? Yeah, we can feel each other. I feel him sliding against me and it feels fucking amazing."

"It's so good," Dev agreed. "It's what I wanted. The three of us together, sharing this."

They were still moving very cautiously, allowing me to get used to the feeling. I was used to it and now I wanted more.

I bit my lip because I was so full of emotion, of lust, of them. "I'm dying here, guys. Please, please fuck me."

Daniel's eyes were dark and I couldn't see Dev, but I heard him grunt as he got damn serious about what he was doing. Danny held my hips and pushed up while Dev ground into me, shoving me harder onto Daniel's cock. I just held on for dear life, surrendering everything to the men who rode my body. I threw back my head as Dev hit someplace I had never known existed and I exploded.

I felt a wild magic hit me, and I came again, crying out as a wave of heat rolled over me.

"What the hell is that?" Danny asked, his eyes wide with wonder. I could tell he was feeding off the lust magic, and it was doing amazing things to him. His body was flushed and his skin had a sweet sheen of sweat.

"I think we have a visitor, Danny." A great joy overtook me because I recognized that magic. I'd felt it on the night I married my faery prince.

"He's here," Dev said as he pounded himself in, holding nothing back. He knew nothing hurt when that magic was riding me. He could fuck me as hard as he wanted to and I would just beg him for more. The fertility god, Bris, had reintegrated, and Dev was an ascended god once more. It had happened far faster than anyone in Faery could have imagined, but Bris fed off emotion and love, and we were full of both. "He's weak, but he's with me again. It feels so good to have him back. I'm going to come. Goddess, I'm going to come hard. I can't hold it back. Bite her now."

I felt the first hot wash of Dev's release and Daniel bit down. I was penetrated by Dev's cock and Danny's cock and fangs and I screamed as I came, my sight surrendering to little starbursts in my eyes. I shook and tried to figure out which way to shove myself so I could get more, but any way I went was a new high. I bucked and convulsed with pleasure, and just when I thought I couldn't handle another second, Daniel shoved his hand between us and pinched my clit and I couldn't think anymore.

Daniel released the vein in my neck as his hips jerked up, and I felt him lose that control of his as he groaned and fucked me as hard as he could. He bucked up, pulling my hips down even as I felt Dev collapse against my back, shoving me closer to my husband. Daniel swelled inside me and came as his lips found mine. He moaned against my mouth as his hips ground out the last of his semen.

I rested my head on Daniel's chest and felt Dev softly kissing my shoulders. I should have felt suffocated and sore, but I was jubilant. I felt victorious. Dev rolled off my back and pulled me with him. I landed in the safe cage of his arms.

"Hello, my goddess," I heard a soft voice say.

"Hello, My Lord," I replied, looking into eyes that didn't belong to Dev. These eyes were emerald with not a hint of white. The Irish fertility god looked tired but so pleased to be with us once more. It was difficult to believe I'd been afraid of him the first time we had met. Now I was thrilled to see the being willing to give up his corporeal life to save my vampire. He'd defended me on several occasions and proven himself a great asset for my faery prince. He occupied Dev's body, strengthening and refining the magic they both shared. I reached up and touched that face I knew so well. "It's a pleasure to see you again."

He leaned over and kissed me and I let his languid, addictive magic flow over me. It was weaker than it had been the first time, but I enjoyed the feeling all the same. He deepened the kiss and let his tongue dance lazily around mine while his hands moved across my skin. "Did the vampire hurt you again? I was unable to do anything but stay close to my host until this evening."

"He didn't get his hands on her again, thanks to you," Daniel said and I saw the gratitude on his face. He knew how much this would mean to Dev. Daniel knew how much Dev would enjoy rubbing this in Declan's face. "We're on the run, though. You have impeccable timing because Devinshea will need your strength. You know what we're going into."

"I do, Daniel, and I'm glad to see you have recovered from the Death Lord's use of you," Bris said. "But tonight is not for politics. My host is very insistent on that. He loves you both. He cannot imagine his life without you. His passion for his goddess and his need for Daniel, they are what brought me back. I'm eager to get this war of yours over with. My goddess and I have rituals we owe the Unseelie. As for the Seelie, they can...I believe the term Devinshea is urging me to use is suck it. I'm not sure I understand."

Daniel laughed and rolled me onto my back. I was comfortable between the two of them. My body was happy and well used. "I'll explain urban lingo to you later, Bris. How about you lend me some of your mojo? I'm not ready to be done with our goddess or your host yet."

Bris grinned and I felt a warm pulse from his body. I sighed as it hit me, and I felt myself warming up all over again. "My host and I are in perfect agreement with you, Daniel. She has not passed out yet. We must work harder."

"Agreed," Daniel said to his partner with a decadent smile on his face. "But this time we change positions."

Yep, I would be sleeping in tomorrow.

CHAPTER SEVENTEEN

A hand snaked under the covers and I felt my ankles, first one and then the other, trapped by strong hands as the intruder began to pull me out of my soft, warm cocoon. Dev shifted in his sleep and I felt Danny move as I was being pulled away from them. I was halfway down the big bed before I thought to fight against whoever was idiotic enough to try to kidnap me from in between my husbands—who should really be way more defensive about me being taken away from them. They seemed more concerned with not having their sleep disturbed.

I clawed at the sheets as my kidnapper pulled. I was lying on my stomach and tried to kick out, but he had me firmly in his hands. "Danny, help me."

"No, Z," Daniel replied, his voice sleepy as he pushed my hands away. "That one is your responsibility."

Dev groaned, and I felt him sort of half sit up so he could get a look at whoever was invading our room. He glanced at the clock and then rolled over. "Neil, it's only one. It's hours and hours until we need to be up. What are you doing?"

Neil didn't stop pulling me inexorably toward the end of the bed. "Need to talk to Z. You two feel free to sleep away the afternoon."

"No," I whined because it wasn't fair. They'd kept me up forever. "Sleep."

"No more sleep for you," Neil vowed. "Lee sent me. He wants to talk to you. Naturally after the events of last night, he knew you would be all naked and stuff, so he sent me, who is not at all disturbed by nakedness. I was looking forward to it because it meant the boys would be naked, too."

Daniel's blue eyes opened as he realized I was clutching the covers and it was uncovering him. He frowned at me and snagged the sheet from my hand, which sent me a good foot in Neil's direction.

"Your wolves, Z." Daniel was immovable on the subject. "We offered to find you more amenable guards but no, you had to have hard-case Lee, who sends Neil in to drag your ass out of bed."

Dev pulled a pillow over his head to shut out the noise. Neither was going to be any help. It was just like a man. They would defend you to the death before the sex but after they just wanted to sleep.

"Come on, Z," Neil was saying as my ankles left the warm confines of the bed. Ankles were followed by legs and I gave up the fight. "Lee says the coffee is really good."

"Coffee?" I asked, though I was sure my voice was muffled because my head was still under the covers.

"I have a mug waiting in the bathroom," Neil promised. "You can drink it while we scrub you down with really hot water. You need it, Z. This place smells like a brothel."

I forcefully shoved the covers back and tried to climb out of bed more gracefully than Neil's plan for my exit. I scrambled over Daniel, not caring that he got an elbow to the stomach.

"Damn it, Z," he cursed, reaching down to pull the covers back up. "Dev, roll over or you're going to be cold."

Dev moved his body, bringing himself closer to Daniel. He rested his head down, just barely touching Daniel's shoulder. He closed his eyes again, and they looked so gorgeous there together.

I stood up and saw Neil staring at them, his eyes wide.

"They're just cold," I replied, walking into the bathroom even as I heard Dev start to snore lightly. Neil was my best friend, but I was holding last night close to my heart for a while.

"I doubt that, Z, but we have other things to talk about. Less fun things. Less superhot dudes getting it on things, and that makes me sad."

The shower was already on, and Neil had pulled out clothes for me. I opened the door to the shower after a long gulp of some really good coffee. "What's with all the help?"

Neil shrugged. "That Diana woman asked if I was your Lad in Waiting. I thought it sounded like fun. She explained it was like a body servant."

"These Brits take the whole queen business very seriously," I commented as I washed away last night's overindulgences. "Bris is back."

"Yeah, we got that. All the houseplants grew like three feet and then there was that lust magic that never seems to stay contained in your little room. I'm getting a T-shirt, Z. *Secondhand lust can be hazardous to your health.*"

I cringed a little. That magic really could be hazardous. If you weren't ready for it, there could be some serious morning-after regret the next day. "How pissed off is Lee?"

"We went pub crawling when he realized what was happening," Neil explained. "He drank a lot of beer and charged it all to Dev. I think he's okay with it."

I breathed a sigh of relief. Lee would have been super pissed if he'd found himself in bed with some stranger because he got caught up in Dev's lust magic. "So if Lee isn't pissed off, why did he feel the need to drag me out of bed?"

Neil lit up a little. "We thought you might like a chance to ask our Aussie friend some questions before Daniel gets a hold of him and all he can do is cry and pee himself. Zack's out running errands, so the timing is perfect."

I took the towel he offered me and smiled brightly. No one ever let me ask questions. "That is a brilliant idea."

"Lee has noted in the past that you get left completely out of interrogations even though it's usually your butt on the line," Neil explained as I started getting dressed. "Who would have guessed he would be a champion of women's rights?"

"Or he just wants to piss off Daniel and Dev because he got his ass shot again yesterday."

"He doesn't like that," Neil agreed. "Either way, I think it'll be fun."

I concurred and proceeded to get ready for my stint as badass interrogator.

I peered into the small room in the basement and wondered exactly what Hugo Wells was into. The basement of the townhouse contained three small rooms, each with steel reinforced doors and small bars over the little windows in the doors. On the wall opposite the rooms was an arsenal. Guns covered the stone siding along with long lengths of silver chains. Off in a corner was a coffin, and I knew what it was reinforced with. Silver was the only way to go when one wanted to keep a vampire under control.

Diana walked down the stairs, carrying the keys to the containment room. The British woman appeared younger and very energetic this morning. I was sure she and Hugo had a raucous good time last night. She had the look of a woman who had been well loved.

"Here we are, Your Highness." She nodded to Lee and Neil as she moved past them. "It would be safest if I locked the three of you in with the prisoner."

"Don't worry, darlin'," Lee said. "Neil and I can ensure your safety."

"I wasn't worried." I trusted him implicitly. He would never allow me to get hurt.

I shot Diana an anxious look as she moved toward the door. "Was everyone...all right after last night? Did anyone warn you about...?" I left the question hanging out there because I wasn't sure exactly how to ask if she had known orgies kind of followed my faery prince around.

Her small, satisfied smile told me she didn't consider it a burden. "The gardener is going to have a fit. The back garden is dreadfully overgrown and the houseplants look like they exploded. Marcus explained what was happening just before he retired with the females of his household. Does that happen every time you..?" It was her turn to be a little evasive.

"No," I said, not sure how much to share. "It's not usually that strong, but we were a little emotional last night."

"Hugo said the magic was amazing." Diana's hand went to her throat, which was smooth. I was surprised at that. I assumed vampires only shared their blood with companions. Hugo must truly care for the human. "I couldn't feel it the way he did, but he looked like he'd gorged himself on companion blood. He looked almost human last night and his skin was so warm."

"It's a little like that," I agreed. Vampires fed off of sexual energy, and Dev's was unique. He was part Green Man and with Bris inside, he had the powers of an ascended god. It wasn't the sex energy vampires got on a daily basis.

"The rumors are wrong about the three of you, aren't they?"

"I don't spend much time in vampire society." I knew a little bit concerning the rumors about us but found myself very curious as to what Diana would say. "I don't know what they say." The assistant seemed wary about pressing on, but I wouldn't let her back down now. "Please, I would rather know than wonder."

She nodded briefly. "The rumor is that the king prefers the company of the faery to that of his companion."

Lee belly laughed. "They think Donovan's gay?"

Neil slapped at Lee's arm. "There's nothing wrong with being gay."

"In vampire society, there is something wrong with preferring anyone to your companion," Diana explained. "It's why vampires who prefer men to women tend to never take a companion. Companions are rare and treasured. It upsets a vampire when he thinks a companion isn't being treated well by her master."

"I don't think Marini treats his companion very well," I pointed out, remembering Rose's sad face.

"No one questions the head of the Council. It's a sad fact of our lives. He can do what he likes and then turn around and accuse Daniel of the very crimes he commits. It's obvious to anyone who has spent more than a few moments with you that both the king and the faery prince are enamored of the queen," Diana said. "They both seemed very much in love."

"We love each other. That's all that matters, and no one else's opinion should come into it. How much trouble are we going to have once Daniel takes the throne?"

"It won't be easy," the more knowledgeable woman admitted. "You'll have to get to know the influential vampires. You'll have to do some work to bring them into line. There will always be some who won't approve."

I supposed that wasn't going to change any time soon. I didn't like to contemplate the fact that Dev and I caused Daniel trouble, but we made up for it. Daniel wouldn't be anywhere close to happy without us. He wouldn't have nights like the one we just had if we weren't around. I had to believe we were worth it.

"And just what are you up to, *cara*?" I heard from the stairs.

I frowned. "Do you ever sleep?"

Marcus entered, looking immaculately casual in slacks and a royal blue polo. "I slept very well last night. I was well fed and my body was exhausted from all the pleasure. That magic is more intense than the last time I felt it."

He was referring to the time he, Marini, and Chad had snuck up on us. Chad was an illusionist. He could make you see things that weren't there. When he wanted, he could make you look right through what was standing in front of you. Dev hadn't integrated with Bris at the time, and though his magic had fed the vampires, it hadn't rocked their world the way he could now.

"He's better at it now, I guess," I replied.

Marcus shook his head. "Or perhaps the fertility god, Bris, managed to reintegrate with his host last night." I must have looked surprised because Marcus sighed. "Daniel trusts me, Zoey. He tells me almost everything. He could have warned me just how powerful that lust magic was going to get. I would have brought along more females."

"How many did you have?" Neil was always curious and never let little things like tact get in his way.

The Italian seemed to count in his head. "Four, no, I'm forgetting that little blonde, so five. With so few to see to my needs, I was forced to send the men in my retinue away."

"You had five women and you couldn't share?" I asked, a little shocked.

Marcus waved away the thought. "That is a perverse impulse of Daniel's." His lips turned up in a naughty smile, and I was actually happy that Marcus hadn't let our deep talk from yesterday affect our weird flirtation. I would have missed it. "Of course, *cara*, I would put aside my distaste for sharing if it means getting my fangs into you."

I put a hand on my hip. "I'll let you know the next time I'm accepting applications."

"You do that," Marcus replied, invading my space a little. Vampires liked to do that. "Now, you will explain to me why you are down here when you should be upstairs doing your hair or taking tea."

He got the full force of my index finger poking right into those rock-hard pecs of his, that I was pretty sure he'd done nothing to earn. "You see, Vorenus, every time I start to like you, you just have to turn into a caveman. I'm not taking tea while we're in the middle of a war. And my hair looks fine."

"Actually," Neil piped up, "it could use a flat iron." I moved that pointy finger in his direction and he quickly backtracked. "Or we could go wavy. Whatever you like, Z."

Diana looked from Marcus to me, and I could see she was confused as to which one of us had the real power here. She'd been more than amenable when I had asked her to let me in to speak to the prisoner, but now I could see she was faltering. Marcus was a Council member. Women in vampire society didn't have a ton of power. I needed to establish dominance and I needed to do it quickly.

"Diana, please open the door," I ordered, my voice a flat monotone that brooked no disobedience.

Marcus's mouth was a stubborn line of disapproval. "Diana, you will leave the prisoner for the king. The queen has not been trained in methods of interrogation. She will not interfere."

"Do you think she can't form a question, Vorenus?" Lee asked, rolling his chocolate eyes.

"I'm sure she would come up with brilliant questions," Marcus replied sarcastically. "But I have no intention of allowing my queen in the room with a soldier who tried to kill her. You should be fired for standing by and almost allowing her to go through with this insane plan, wolf."

"Oh, he's not just standing by," I commented. "It was his plan in the first place."

"And I didn't try to kill her," a voice pointed out from behind us. "That was Yuri, the wanker, and the faery already blew his brains to hell and back." Terry stared through the bars of his little prison. He was calm and collected and seemed to be entertained by the show we were putting on.

"We don't need anything from you," Marcus snarled in his direction.

"Seems like you do, mate," the soldier replied casually. "If it helps anyone make a decision, I'll talk to Mrs. Quinn there."

"Donovan, she is Mrs. Donovan," Marcus insisted.

"How about you just call me Zoey." I wanted to avoid my unfortunate last name problems. I'd come up with the perfectly reasonable plan of keeping my own last name to avoid confusion, but no one would use it.

"Right, Zoey," the Aussie said. "What kind of questions have you got for me?"

"Diana, if you would please." I gestured toward the door. She hesitated. "What were your instructions regarding me? I'm not trying to be a bitch, but I assume you were told to obey me, not to only obey me if Marcus says it's all right."

Marcus cursed as Diana slipped the key in the door. He seemed to understand I wasn't budging, so he did what he could. "You will step back, prisoner. Take a seat at the table and keep your hands where we can see them. You will not lay a hand on Her Highness or I will rip your throat out. Is that understood?"

Terry's eyes were solemn as he backed off with his hands in the air. He sat down in the chair Marcus indicated but kept his hands carefully within our sight. Diana opened the door and Marcus shoved me back, demanding to go in first. I heard Lee say something about vampire drama queens and then he escorted me inside.

Marcus stood over the prisoner, intimidation oozing from his pores. "Soldier, I am..."

"Marcus Vorenus, a venerable member of the Vampire Council, third in line to head, Louis Marini after Niko Rallis and Elof

Magnussen. You're Daniel Donovan's patron," Terry started reciting from a file he had probably memorized. "You were born in Rome in fifty AD to parents who were some of the first followers of a prophet named Jesus Christ..."

"Yes, we can see you're well informed," Marcus interrupted Terry's interesting lecture. I could tell he was a little disconcerted. It had probably been a long time since he thought about his parents.

"Not well enough, it seems," Terry murmured, looking at me in a different light. He bowed his head slightly. "Your Highness, I apologize for my earlier casualness. The Order didn't believe Mr. Donovan was really a king. It's been a long time since the vampires had a king and even longer since they had a queen."

I sat down and sent Marcus a dirty look. "Yes, well, I wasn't going to mention that since I have no idea what your ties to Vampire are. You could be a spy for Marini for all we know."

"I'm not," Terry said quickly. "The Order tries not to take an official stance on these kinds of things, but I can tell you we've been watching the Council very closely for the last hundred years. They're slowly moving toward something we don't like."

"If you're referring to their plans to subjugate the supernatural world, then I would have to agree with you." Marcus crossed his arms over his chest and a little of his prior stubbornness seemed to flee. "If we can get the Order on our side, it will do nothing but help us, *mia regina*. Will the Order acknowledge Daniel as the King of all Vampire?"

"I believe they will," Terry said. "If there isn't a bloody civil war we have to quell."

"We're trying to avoid that," I explained earnestly. "We're also trying to ensure that the Council never again has the power to subjugate the races. Daniel wants to change the Council, to bring the other races in and form a new government that includes them."

Terry's eyes got very wide. "Are you serious?"

"As a heart attack. Don't you think it's time our world caught up with the rest of the planet?"

"You're telling me this Donovan fellow is willing to give up absolute power over the strongest, most well-organized race of supernaturals, to give werewolves and Fae creatures a seat at the table?"

"He's a modern man, our king," Marcus replied. "While I find the situation a bit uncomfortable, I can see that rationally it's the proper time to make this move. Civilizations that don't change with the times tend to burn out. Our small society is reaching a breaking point. I believe if we follow the path Louis would set for us, we will be eradicated by war."

"That's been our assessment, as well," the soldier replied, warming to his subject. "We've been running several scenarios involving all-out war between the vampires and the other supernaturals since we started tracking the loss of several alphas in the large werewolf packs across Europe. Someone's been trying to make sure the wolf packs are fractured."

"Yes." That had been Marini's plan. "But you will note that the North American packs recently chose to make their allegiance to an alpha named John McKenzie. There will be no fractures in our wolves. Daniel has made great strides with the various wereanimals and shapeshifters, as well. We also have an ironclad alliance in place with the Unseelie."

The soldier thought about this for a long moment. "How did we miss this? Our assessment of Donovan was completely wrong. We have him as a two-bit criminal who might, and let me emphasize might, be a death machine. Nothing in our files indicates Donovan is capable of doing anything like this. How could we have been so wrong?"

"I felt it best that Mr. Donovan be allowed to develop on his own," a soft voice with a lilting British accent said from the supposed to be closed and locked doorway.

We all turned quickly and Lee pointed his semiautomatic straight at the newcomer. The oracle stood in the doorway wearing a T-shirt, well-worn jeans, and Converse sneakers. Jacob focused his attention on Terry. "If the Order had known what His Highness was planning, there would have been pressure to push him one way or another. We're at a crossroads, Terry. I didn't join the Order to watch it manipulate things to its own liking. Our mandate is to watch and only step in when we absolutely have to. Had some members of the Order known the importance of the Donovans, they would almost certainly have either tried to influence the royals or tried to assassinate them."

I laughed outright. "I'd like to see them try to take out Danny."

Jacob's eyes were very grave as he regarded me. "Daniel Donovan is not the only royal of import. In fact, it would be much deadlier for the creatures of this plane had someone managed to assassinate you."

"You can put the gun down, Mr. Owens," Marcus said warily. "It won't do any good. The oracle is unlike anything you've encountered before."

"He doesn't smell human." Lee kept the gun trained on the young man.

"He isn't," the vampire replied. "I'm not sure he ever was."

"But the host is human, right?" I thought perhaps we were dealing with either a demon or something that took human form.

Jacob smiled softly. "Do you believe I'm a demon, child?"

"Or an ascended god," I admitted.

His brows rose over those endlessly dark eyes. "What do you know of ascended gods?"

"My goddess knows much of them," Bris said from behind Jacob. He'd crept up quietly and held Dev's SIG Sauer in his hands. He seemed to have dressed hurriedly and wore only a pair of jeans. Dev's gorgeous body was on full display, but his eyes were not his own.

Jacob's face broke into a full show of joy. "I truly love it when I'm surprised."

"Explain why you're here and what you want with my goddess, Apollo," Bris demanded.

Neil sat back, just enjoying the show. "But he said his name is Jacob."

"I've taken many names over the years and had many faces." Jacob didn't seem to care that two guns were aimed at his head. "Awhile back, I called myself Apollo and there were some kind people who chose to worship me. At the time, it was advantageous to me, so I allowed it. I prefer to take on no followers now, though I enjoy the company of humans as do you, Bris. As for what I want with your goddess, I must confess, I didn't realize she was your goddess."

"I'm surprised that escaped you." Bris brought the gun down. He nodded to Lee, who lowered his weapon as well. Bris gestured that he wanted me to come to him. I stood and joined him. "My goddess, this is a prophet. He's walked the Earth plane since…well, long before I came into being. He's a creature of great wisdom, though for the most part he uses his wisdom for his own betterment."

Jacob's eyes narrowed as he shot Bris a perturbed stare. "I haven't seen you in thousands of years, Bris. While you slept and waited for your perfect host, I've been here with the humans, watching them and guiding them. Allow that thousands of years' congress with these beings may have changed me."

Bris's hand slid to my wrist, like he was waiting to pull me or push me out of danger. "I'll believe it when I see it. Now, I'll ask again, why are you here?"

"Your goddess took one of my men prisoner," Jacob replied.

"You came to spring me?" Terry sat up a little straighter and a grin lit his face.

"Despite what that fertility god will tell you, I don't leave my men behind," Jacob replied. "I admit that I also wanted to speak to the female again. I meet so few true nexus points."

"The *bean si* called me that," I said quietly as Marcus said something under his breath in Italian.

"Is this true, Oracle?" Marcus asked, his mouth a tense line.

"It is," Bris replied for Jacob, who was staring at me. "I've found it terribly amusing that everyone is so concerned with the vampire when the truly important one was standing right in front of them."

"What's that supposed to mean?" I asked the god in my husband's body. I was getting the same panicked feeling I'd gotten when the washer women had called me that. I hadn't understood it all at the time. I had my mind on other things that night.

Lee crossed his arms. He didn't like the mystical crap. "The washer women said something about her having no fate."

"She is fate," Jacob said with a small laugh. "Everything on this plane rests on her small shoulders. If she succeeds, we all get to live another day. If she fails, this plane will run red with blood."

Bris sent Jacob a dark look. He felt my panic. He took my hands in his and rubbed them briskly because I was suddenly very cold. "A nexus point is like a blank space in the fabric of history, my goddess. It merely means that you have no particular fate written for you."

193

"And because of that you change the fates of those close to you," Jacob continued. "Someone with the power of prophecy can see the way a person's life will most likely go. Nothing is for certain, but we tend to be correct most of the time. I can look at the British woman upstairs and tell you that in forty years' time, she will die in a plane crash. Her vampire lover will miss her terribly, but he'll take a companion ten years later and be very happy with her. I can look at the faery Bris currently inhabits and know that he should be dead many times over. He entered this plane with a death wish. He's impulsive and prone to rages that should have gotten him killed on at least seven different occasions, but he got close to the nexus point and now his fate is tied to yours."

"And Daniel would have lived if he hadn't been involved with me," I said, repeating what the *bean si* had told me.

Jacob nodded. "Yes. Donovan would have lived a nice, simple life as a boring IT guy who would have been far too old to be effective when he turned. Daniel Donovan needed to turn in the prime of his life."

We were all looking at the prophet now. There was something about the way he said the words that made me wary. This Jacob had been watching us for a very long time. He'd been the one to send Marcus to protect my grandmother. Just how much of a hand had he had in our lives?

"Did you kill Daniel?" Neil asked because he never prevaricated.

Jacob held his hands out, trying to bring the intensity level down. "I did not. I merely see patterns and play the odds. I knew that it was likely Donovan would die young if he had a companion in place. You'll find latent vampires tend to die young when a companion is right there, ripe for the taking. Something deep inside tells them to end their human life and begin to walk the night. I didn't have to kill Donovan. I've only made three moves in this little chess game."

"You sent me to protect Zoey's grandmother." Marcus offered one of the moves.

"Yes," the boy agreed. "And I introduced Harry Wharton to his best friend, George Donovan. I also chose to keep Donovan off the Order's radar. I feared if the Order knew about Donovan, they would figure out what Zoey was and then all hell could break loose."

"Are you telling me you joined the Order seven hundred years ago so you could protect one girl from people trying to influence her?" Terry asked, awe in his voice.

"It was a long game." Jacob sighed with satisfaction. "And now it's almost over. I'm very interested in seeing how it all turns out, but alas, I must watch the play from the cheap seats, as the Americans would say."

Bris's eyes were wary. "You mean to leave her alone now?"

"I do. I fear if I stay, the temptation to interfere will be too great, and I have promised to allow things to play out as they will from this point on," Jacob insisted. "I merely came back to retrieve my Australian friend. It's time for me to travel again. The Order is well established. They will act as a check on the demonic influences on the plane and, if Zoey succeeds, they'll represent humans on the new Council."

"And if she doesn't succeed?" Lee asked, his mouth tight with worry.

Jacob shrugged. "Then nothing will matter, will it?" He turned to Terry. "What do you say, Terry? Would you like to play Sancho to my Don Quixote?"

The Australian seemed confused. "I got no idea what you mean, mate."

"Not a big reader then," Jacob mused. He hit on the right phrasing. "I'm going walkabout. Want to come with?"

Terry nodded over at the prophet who had once been a Greek god. "Count me in. I want to get as far away from this war as possible."

"Not so fast," I said. "I still have questions."

"I'm sure you do, Your Highness," Jacob replied. "But they'll have to wait for another time. As for you, Vorenus, I see the way you look at me. You think I lied to gain your cooperation, but I assure you this is not the case. You'll have your death, vampire, and sooner than you think."

"Wait," I insisted as Jacob went to stand by Terry.

"I can't," he replied with an enigmatic smile. "And you have a phone call to answer. Tell Donovan he'll need the sword if he wants to wake the wizard, but remember a demon is always a demon no matter how helpful he seems."

He put his hand on Terry's shoulder and then they winked out of existence. One minute they were there and the next they were gone.

Just then Lee's cell phone rang. He flipped it open and answered it before holding it out to me.

"It's Nim," he said. "She found Merlin."

CHAPTER EIGHTEEN

"And these people speak English?" Neil asked as we passed the sign for the ferry to Ynys Ennli.

We'd stopped for directions since the ones Nim had given weren't the clearest. We were on the coast of Wales, and it had become very clear to me that the Welsh did not, in fact, speak any type of English I understood. Everything that came out of their mouths sounded like it had been stuck at the back of their throats for a while.

"It's all right, Neil," Daniel reassured the werewolf. "I've listened to it for long enough now. I can translate."

Dev drove the Mercedes along the lonely road. We'd been driving most of the night and dawn was close now. I was glad that vamps picked up on languages quickly because when the Welshman had opened his mouth to tell us what road to drive on and where to turn, I'd just stared openly, trying to figure out what the heck the dude was saying. Our vampire, however, made a nifty universal translator. It made travel so much easier when all I had to do was wait for Danny to soak up enough local speak that he could order another beer for me without having to refer to a handy basic phrase book.

Daniel sat in the front seat with Dev. I looked out the back and saw that Zack and Lee were keeping up nicely in their car. There had been almost no traffic at this time of night. We left Hugo's home at dusk and spent the night on the road. It would have been faster to let Daniel fly, but I put the kibosh on that idea. We needed to stick together from here on out. I didn't want Daniel facing things on his own while Marini had the Blood Stone.

During the day, while I sat waiting for all our travel plans to come together, I had been struck by one of my awful, terrible, shouldn't-even-consider-it plans. Jacob had made it very plain to me that this was my show. Danny might be the king and Dev might be the man with the plan, but they weren't a nexus point. I was. If the fate of the entire Earth plane was up to me, then that could only mean one thing. Someone, somewhere needed a thief.

If I was going to save us, I would have to steal that damn Blood Stone back. I didn't think either one of my husbands would like how I was going to have to do it, though.

The plan was simple, as almost all good plans were. I had to get close to Marini. That might have been hard if it wasn't a state he had devoutly pledged to attain one way or another. I would just have to make his little fantasy come true. I would surrender myself and play into his demented delusions that I was unhappy with Daniel. It would get me close to the Blood Stone and my blood would do the rest. I would need a way out or a way to tell Daniel once I had the stone, but this little plan in my head was a work in progress and I hadn't shared it with anyone but Neil yet. His pale blue eyes had widened, and I could tell he had wanted to talk me out of it but couldn't think of another way.

"You called ahead?" Daniel asked Dev for the thirtieth time.

Dev's voice was calm and patient. It made me wonder about the changes being with me and Daniel had wrought in Devinshea. If the prophet was right about Dev's past death wish, then the changes were phenomenal. "Yes, Dan. The boat will be there to pick us up. Nim and Stewart are waiting at the inn."

Daniel's fingers drummed against the dashboard of the rented Benz. I could feel his leg bouncing, too, a sure sign of his nervousness. I reached up and placed a hand on his shoulder. He covered my hand with his palm and gave me a little half smile. "You all right back there, Z?"

"It's not how I planned our first trip out of the country." I'd been to Faery and the Hell plane, but this was my first Earth plane foreign country.

Dev's hands tightened on the steering wheel. "I know, sweetheart. I promise, once all of this shakes down, you, Daniel, and I will have that honeymoon we've talked about. We'll go to Hawaii and drink and have sex and just relax."

"I'm holding you to that." We could make babies, too.

"It'll be good, Z," Danny promised, but I didn't like the sound of his voice. It was the tone we use when we want something to be true but don't think we'll actually get there. I use the same tone every time I promise myself I'll lose the ten pounds that would put me in a size six.

Danny sounded like a man who didn't think he had a future.

We drove the rest of the way in near silence, each of us caught in our own fears. Mine played out over and over again in my head. I was going to lose them both, and it would be my fault. I would fail at whatever I was supposed to do. All my friends and family would suffer because some idiot at the Fate Office made a terrible clerical error when they assigned this shit to me. I didn't want to be a nexus point. I didn't want to play with fate or have some grand-ass destiny. I wanted to go to Hawaii with my two hot guys and make babies and be as ordinary as we could possibly be.

I felt Neil's hand slip into mine, and he squeezed it reassuringly. I leaned into my BFF and rested my head on his shoulder. I had to give whoever had chosen me as this nexus point some props, though. If I had to face all of this crap, at least I had the best friends a girl could ever want surrounding me.

"Whatever happens, Z," he vowed, "I'll be there with you."

The miles passed silently and I knew that I couldn't ask for more than that.

"Wake up, baby," Daniel said from the front seat.

I opened my eyes just as the sun was coming up. I stretched as Neil sat up beside me.

"Are we there?" Neil yawned behind his hand.

Daniel nodded shortly. "We're at the docks. Dev is making sure the captain he hired has everything ready for us. Lee's trying to get you some breakfast."

"How far away is this island?" I asked as I got out of the car and caught sight of the coastline. It was stark and from here I could see the island we were trying to get to. Even though it was spring, there was no doubt these waters were cold and the morning air left me chilled. I pulled the sweater I wore tightly around my shoulders. There was a mist on the water and it wasn't hard for me to believe that island in the fog held some serious secrets.

"It's only two miles." Daniel adjusted the sword he was carrying. We wouldn't be seeing many people from here on out, so Daniel put Excalibur in a sheath along his back. He shrugged into a leather jacket, but he could easily pull the sword with one hand if he needed to. "We're in someplace called Porth Meudwy. We'll travel by boat across St. George's Channel to Bardsey."

"I thought it was Ynys Ennli." Neil got out of the car, joining us.

"That's the original Welsh name." Daniel repeated the information Dev had told them. I'd heard them talking about it while Neil and I tried to sleep. "Long ago Christians renamed it Bardsey. It means the Island of the Bards."

"Why didn't you say so?" Neil asked, irritated as he watched Lee and Zack approach. "That's so much easier to say than the other way."

"He's gotta show off those vamp talents and that brain of his." Lee passed out the coffee and little packages of pastries. "Sorry, this is all I could find. What I wouldn't give for a 7-11 right about now. Come on. Dev says the boat's ready for us."

I wished I hadn't downed that coffee fifteen minutes later as the small ferry started across the channel. The boat listing in the heavy waves. It was not doing great things for my digestion.

"Come here, my goddess," I heard Dev say and he gestured me over to where he and Daniel stood. They didn't look as green as I felt.

Daniel grinned as he pulled me into the circle of his arms.

"You've gotta see this, Z."

I stared down into the waves where Daniel was pointing. I took many a deep breath before I finally realized what those shapes moving through the waves were. They followed the boat and I counted twelve just on this side alone. At first I thought they were dolphins and I grinned, but then one turned. She rolled her body over and I was shocked by the human face solemnly looking up at me.

"That's a real, live mermaid." I'd never seen one before. I thought they were extinct or pure myth.

"Yes, it is," Bris said, taking over suddenly. He leaned his tall body over the bow of the ship, and I had a heart-stopping moment as he placed his hand close to the water. He let his fingers graze the surface and the mermaid smiled a watery smile and allowed her long fingers to brush his before turning back over to swim with the school.

Lee, Zack, and Neil had come over and were staring into the water.

"You can't eat them," I growled at Neil because I knew that look in his eyes.

He pouted. "But I like seafood."

Bris was amused at our exchange. "I wouldn't try it, little wolf. They look lovely and docile, but they've plagued these waters since men first thought to take to the sea. Can you hear their song?"

I listened closely and discovered that the sound I thought was merely waves against the side of the ship had a rhythm and lilt that nothing natural could produce. Once I knew to listen, I could hear the mermaids' song. It was haunting but also warm and welcoming.

"Are they dangerous?" Lee was always looking for a threat.

"Usually, I would say yes." Bris pointed to the edges of the school. "The selkies are here as well."

Sure enough, I saw the seal-like creatures swimming along with the mermaids and mermen. Their seal-brown pelts were shiny in the water and they moved so gracefully I caught my breath. They were in full seal form, not a hint of the human-like creature they could become when they removed their skins.

Daniel had a concerned look on his face as he turned to the fertility god. "What do you mean by usually?"

Bris smiled down at the creatures following us. He seemed

wholly content with the situation, his free hand on my waist. "Normally when a group of mermaids or selkies show up it is to cause trouble. These have announced their intentions with their songs. Daniel, listen for a moment and tell me what you hear."

Daniel listened intently, trying to see if he could make sense of the lilting song of the seafolk. After a moment, his face broke into a cautious smile. "They're welcoming…their king?"

"And their queen," Bris completed with a pleased look.

"How do they know Daniel and Zoey?" Neil asked. "We've never met a mermaid before or a seal thing."

"They don't know them, Neil," Bris explained. "Not in any way you would understand. They do, however, know that sword on Daniel's back."

"Excalibur?" Daniel's hand went to the sword. Ever since we'd returned from Faery where Nimue had told Daniel the sword was his, Daniel hadn't like to be parted from the gorgeous weapon. He'd spent hours and hours practicing with Dev until the sword worked like an extension of his arm.

"Yes, Daniel," Bris said teasingly. "Did you think it was just a trinket the Lady of the Lake gives out as a party favor?"

Daniel's face was blank for a moment. "I guess I thought she gave it to me so we could find Merlin."

"Myrddin, please," Bris corrected, now in full-on "I know more than you do" mode. "Merlin seems to be the modern version, but his original name is Myrddin Emrys. I'm certain Excalibur will do wonders in waking the wizard from his sleep, but when you accepted Nimue's gift, you took your place in a line of kings. The mermaids and selkies recognize their king and their queen, and they will aid you in any way they can. Excalibur is only needed in times of great danger. They're throwing their lot in with you, Daniel. It's a great honor."

Daniel frowned. "How do I…I don't know, thank them?"

Bris gestured down at the water. "Do you see the shining one?"

Daniel nodded. There was one who shone above the rest, her hair glimmering in the water, and she stared straight at me. She held her hand up to the surface. I leaned over with Bris's strong hands around my waist as he lowered me to the water so our fingertips touched. We smiled at each other before the moment was broken and Bris pulled me back in.

He nodded at me approvingly. "Very good, my goddess. Daniel, your greeting is different. You're a king but you're also a vampire."

"Of course," he said with a self-deprecating grin. "It always comes back to the blood, doesn't it?"

"Blood is the true language of all creatures," Bris explained sagely. "Humans simply neglect that truth because it's unsavory to them."

Daniel rolled up his sleeve and his fangs popped out. The creatures following us got very excited. The water swirled around them and bubbled into a froth as they got ready for their king's gift. Daniel winked at me as he bit sharply into his wrist and poured the blood over the water. The merfolk and the selkies came to the surface for that velvety blood, and Daniel opened his wrist three times before Bris said it was enough. The boat sped toward the island as we left the creatures behind. I could still see the foamy churn of the water as they lapped up that unique blood and their song reached a grateful crescendo.

"You did well, Your Highness," Bris said.

"Please," Daniel returned with a sigh.

"Daniel," Bris corrected himself. He looked down at me and brought his lips sweetly to mine. "I'm tired, sweet goddess. It will be many days before I'm at my full strength, but if you have need of me, you have only to say my name and I'll find the strength."

He kissed me again and then Dev was back. I knew the instant my husband regained control because the kiss became deep and domineering. Bris enjoyed a certain sweetness to his sex that Dev just didn't have the time for. Devinshea liked it down and dirty, and it showed in his kiss.

He came up for air and stared back to the spot where we'd left the seafolk. "Mermaids. Cool."

I saw a look pass between Dev and Daniel. It was over my head, but I knew that look. Daniel's blue eyes widened and his lips quirked up on one side and then Dev replied with a sure, satisfied smile and slight nod of his head. I rolled my eyes because I could read that conversation.

"So you slept with a mermaid once."

My husbands stared at each other, the same slightly startled expression on their handsome faces as the boat slowed and we pulled into the dock. The island was small, barely two miles across, but there were some signs of civilization. A few houses. A dock.

"We're going to have to get new signals, Daniel," Dev said, flustered that I understood their silent boy speak. They sometimes held entire conversations without saying a word when I was listening in.

"Yup." Daniel laughed as he jumped off the boat onto the dock and turned to help me. "She's got us translated."

"Where are we supposed to meet Nim and Stewart?" Lee asked, leaping to the pier behind his brother.

Neil pointed in the distance. "There they are."

There, past the small village, stood Nim and Stewart. They didn't move, just stood there waiting. The fog from the channel made them look like ghosts peeking in and out of the early morning light.

"Shit," I heard Lee curse as he looked back and the boat suddenly pulled away. He had a hand on my arm, and I could tell he was thinking about making a jump for the boat, but it was too far away now. "We're not alone."

"How many?" Dev pulled his gun, his eyes looking for the threat.

Zack was at Daniel's back, and Neil and Lee stuck close to me.

Lee opened his senses. "Too many."

"Very good, Mr. Owens," a familiar voice said as he walked from behind a small building. There weren't many buildings on this island, but the roofs were suddenly full of men with high-caliber rifles. Snipers. Ronald walked out in his flak jacket. He wasn't taking chances this time. I had to give the old guy some credit. It was less than twenty-four hours since Dev shot him and he was standing tall. "It's true. There are far too many of us. Surrender, Mr. Quinn, if you want to live to see the inside of our prison cells."

CHAPTER NINETEEN

"This is the same group we dealt with earlier with the exception of a male of unknown species," Ronald said into his headset. The Order of Galahad was very up-to-date, technology-wise. They each had a small Bluetooth device in their ears. "The faery is in charge and should be considered very dangerous. The three males in the back are werewolves and the female is a companion. Assume they're all on vampire blood. Head shots only for a kill."

Daniel had snorted when the leader of the Order said Dev was in charge. "He thinks you're the dangerous one, Devinshea."

Dev lifted one shoulder negligently. "I did shoot him. You haven't shot him yet. Besides, I don't think he has any idea who you are."

My husbands stood together, presenting a united front against the Order. Dev handled his gun like it was an old friend, but Danny's hands were still empty because he didn't need anything yet. Daniel was in his day clothes. After feeding off the magic of Bris's reintegration, Daniel probably didn't need the mirrored aviators to protect his eyes or the hoodie under his leather jacket to protect his head. He wore them out of habit. He was dressed in head to toe black with the exception of his favorite pair of Levi's. While the clothes

Daniel wore protected his skin from the sunlight, they had the added bonus of concealing his identity.

Lee held my arm with his non-gun-toting hand. He never took his eyes off the men on the rooftops. "You obey me, Zoey. This is one of those times, you understand? When Donovan and Quinn pull whatever crazy-ass stunt they're gonna pull, you obey me."

Lee and I had an understanding. We'd made an agreement the day he became my formal bodyguard. He let me go crazy most of the time. He'd followed me into some wild shit, including several illegal ventures. But when he decided the situation was too hot, he put his foot down and I let him do what he did best—keep me alive. I nodded, letting him know I wasn't going to fight him.

"Should I change?" Neil asked because he followed Lee's lead. Zack had moved to stand by his master, who was his primary responsibility. Zack stood at Daniel's side, ready to obey his command or take a bullet for Devinshea if he had to.

"Not yet," Lee said out of the side of his mouth. His eyes darted around, looking for a potential escape route. Unfortunately the Order had blocked us off. They surrounded us on four sides and I didn't think we would be swimming in that cold channel any time soon. We were well and truly stuck. "I think it might start them shooting, and I want to put that off as long as possible."

I looked into the distance and saw what had been hidden before. A group of soldiers had been hiding in the background, but they were on their feet now and had started slowly escorting Nim and Stewart toward us. I wondered how they managed to catch the two powerful creatures unaware.

Ronald walked down the small road with his escort of five well-armed men. The lanky Brit was more like his soldiers today. Gone was the expensive suit. He was dressed in fatigues and combat boots. "So, Mr. Quinn, I underestimated you the first time. I think you will find I have not made the same mistake twice."

Dev looked around at the troops, and his eyes showed that he wasn't particularly impressed. Dev had some major issues with authority figures. "Is that a fact, Ronnie? I think you'll find you've fucked up again. Once we've mopped the floor with your ass, I'll explain some realities of our world to you."

Ronald's eyes narrowed. "Mr. Quinn, I suggest you have your men relinquish their firearms. I'm offering your werewolves the chance to live if they submit. If they do not, I'll order my men to kill them on the spot. Our bullets are silver and these men are highly trained. They won't miss."

"Tell me, Ronald," Daniel said, his voice commanding attention. "How many of your men are you willing to lose?"

Ronald turned his attention to the newcomer. Though Dev held his gun and the wolves were known quantities, I saw the minute Ronald decided that whoever this dark man was, he was potentially deadly. "I intend to lose no more men this day. I've lost enough to a common criminal."

That last bit was said straight to Dev. "I take offense to that, Ronald. I'm anything but common."

"Tell me, Quinn, you bottom-feeder," Ronald spat out. "How did you kill Terry? He was twenty-three years old, you know. His father is one of the men on the rooftops, and he's itching to pull that trigger. I promised him a little alone time with you, if you understand my meaning."

"We didn't kill Terry." I moved a half inch forward before Lee's hand had me in a vise grip.

"Zoey, stay back," Dev growled. He gave Lee a pointed look that told him to control me.

"You'll forgive me if I suspect your husband keeps you in the dark, Mrs. Quinn," Ronald responded with a hint of sympathy in his voice. "As you discovered yesterday, he has been damn good at hiding his crimes from you. He lies to you, Mrs. Quinn. He's a stone-cold killer."

I shook my head because Ronald was just flat out wrong on this one. "I was there. I interrogated Terry myself, although it wasn't so much a Q&A as a lecture once Jacob showed up."

Ronald stilled. "The oracle found you?"

I nodded. I had found the discussion with the oracle both illuminating and intensely disturbing. I didn't know what to think about the fact that he'd spent an enormous amount of time maneuvering Daniel and me into position. "Apparently he's known where I was most of my life. He explained a lot to me. Look, I know you guys think that Merlin is the enemy, but we need him. What will happen if we don't get Merlin to help is all-out war. We're not going to let that happen, so you should just get out of our way and let us do what we need to do. We'll help you deal with the ramifications of anything that goes wrong. The oracle thinks we're on the right path. He's gone, by the way. He said he was done with this particular mission and he took Terry with him."

"I don't believe you. The oracle has been a part of the Order for seven hundred years," Ronald explained. "He wouldn't walk away as the biggest threat to our mission is standing in the doorway of the wizard's prison."

I looked straight into Ronald's eyes. "He said the king will handle everything from now on."

Ronald's head whipped back around to Daniel, and his jaw dropped open. "No, I don't believe it. The oracle would have warned us."

"I think you're the one who's been lied to, Ronald." I felt some sympathy for him. He'd dedicated himself to his cause, to a creature he believed was as dedicated as he was only to find out he'd been manipulated for reasons he couldn't fathom. "My husband is the king the oracle has been waiting for. He waited seven hundred years for the King of all Vampire to rise."

"Daniel," Dev said quietly. "I don't think he's going to believe it until he sees it for himself."

Daniel reached up and pulled down his hood, revealing his face. He pulled his sunglasses off and when he smiled at Ronald, he made sure everyone got a good look at his fangs.

Ronald's reaction was to take a step back. "But it's daylight."

"Daylight doesn't affect the King of all Vampire." Dev didn't mention that it was because of him that Daniel could walk in the light but after what the oracle had said, I had to believe that Dev coming into our lives wasn't a coincidence either. We needed Dev and he'd been given to us.

"And my queen will be referred to as Her Highness," Daniel said seriously. "I'm told the Order should be well informed of our traditions. Traditionally, it's not considered proper to greet a monarch with bullets and a show of force. I'll allow that you didn't know who

Devinshea and my queen were the first time you met them, but you know now. I will take any threat to my partner or my wife very seriously."

Ronald was talking on his Bluetooth again. "The newcomer is a vampire. I want every operative trained on the female."

"Down!" Lee yelled and I found myself eating dirt as Lee covered my body with his. Neil added his own body and I just tried to keep breathing.

"Keep her head covered," Lee ordered, but Neil was already doing his job.

"Mr. Donovan, stand down," Ronald said, his voice shaky. "We have all our weapons aimed on your companion. Please inform your guard that our weapons are of a high enough caliber that they should merely pass through their bodies on the way to hers. What they're doing, while noble, won't solve your problem."

"We'll take that chance." I heard Daniel say. "You'll have to kill us all to get anywhere near her."

"This time I kill you," Dev vowed.

"And then my men will simply shoot until your wife is dead," Ronald replied, sounding more sensible now. He was a professional at heart and he was getting himself under control again. "I'm sorry, but I really have no other choice. I don't like to use a woman in this fashion. It goes against all of my teachings, but we cannot fight a death machine. If I attempted to fight honorably, I would merely watch my men die one by one at your hands, Mr. Donovan. She's the only way we have to counter the threat you pose. We can only hope your feelings for your companion will lead you to rethink this mission."

"I'm rethinking a lot of things right this moment, Ronald," I heard Daniel say. His voice was a low growl. "I don't think you'll like a thing that's going through my brain right now."

"Mr. Donovan, I just sent a text to bring in the vampire containment unit. The helicopter should be here in fifteen minutes. Mr. Quinn will hand over his weapon and any others he has hidden on his person. The wolves will kneel and submit to silver chains while we wait on the silver rope and coffin. Once you're all properly contained, we'll go back to HQ and sort through everything. If you behave, your companion will be treated as a guest. She's no threat to us, so we can treat her gently if you allow us to do so."

Daniel's laugh boomed through the morning air. "That just shows me what a dumbass you are if you think my Z is no threat to you. Z can be a threat to the whole planet when she wants to be. Devinshea, protect our wife."

I felt Lee tense above me as he waited for the bullets, but before anyone could fire, the ground around me rumbled and I shrank back as thick green vines sprang from the ground and shot into the air. It made a little cocoon around me, Lee, and Neil. Those woody vines made it hard to see exactly where I was and would be effective in stopping even high-caliber bullets. I heard Lee sigh above me and he backed off the slightest bit so I could breathe.

"I hope there's no poison ivy," Neil said, looking a little claustrophobic. The small space wasn't tiny. We could move around but Neil, despite being a freaking werewolf, was really more of a city boy.

I peered through an opening in the green canopy and watched as Daniel flew straight up and Zack pulled Dev back. They ran for us and Dev flicked his hands, suddenly opening the canopy to allow them in. I heard the sharp report of gunfire and Zack picked up his boss and tossed him in as he leapt for safety. He and Zack were inside our green cave and it closed behind us again. It was a tight fit, but Dev pulled me close and made it work. He put his back to the front of the small protective barrier, and I knew he was trying to make sure any bullet that made it through got to him first.

"Everyone all right?" he asked.

The wolves all nodded that they hadn't been hit.

"What's Donovan's plan?" Lee asked.

Dev shook his head. "You won't like it."

Ronald's voice rang out over the fields. "Very impressive, Mr. Quinn. You truly are a Green Man. Unfortunately, you're trapped and that vampire of yours has taken off. I am afraid he doesn't quite live up to what I would have expected from a *Nex Apparatus*, much less an actual king. He left his own companion behind to deal with this. Truly remarkable. I thought a companion was like a vampire's gold. You learn something new each day. Gentlemen, take the prisoners.

Shoot the wolves if they give you any trouble at all and for god's sake, if Quinn mouths off, please fill him full of silver. He's only half Fae. It should kill him. Go!"

There was a strange whining sound coming from somewhere high above us, and I felt Dev tense. It seemed to be getting closer with each passing second as the sound grew louder.

"Oh, shit," Lee cursed. "He's going to hit the ground at that speed? Does he know what that's going to do to us?"

"No choice. Cover your ears," Dev said, shoving me under his body.

I did as he asked and felt his hands come over mine. I tried to glimpse the world outside and saw Ronald look suddenly up at the sky. He pointed his warning and then there was a whole lot of shouting and screaming and running to get away. Then I couldn't see anything because Dev was flattening his body against mine until he covered every inch of me.

When Daniel hit the ground, it was like an earthquake. The ground under me shook and rattled. Even through the dual barrier of my and Dev's hands, I heard the strange, unnatural thud followed by the shattering of glass and the moaning of the soldiers who'd been hit by the concussive wave following Daniel's impact.

Dev moved into a sitting position, allowing me to get up. Lee and Zack were bleeding from both ears but they'd covered Neil, who was shaking his head as if trying to find his equilibrium. I was so thankful to the wolves right then as Neil stuck his pinky finger in his not completely shattered ear. Neil was the only one of us not on vampire blood or just super-freaky powerful like Lee. The wolves' ears were far more sensitive than anything else out here. It stood to reason that they would most be affected by the boom Danny's body bomb had set off, but Lee and Zack would heal quickly where Neil would struggle with the pain for a lot longer. Zack and Lee had done their duty and protected the weakest member of their pack.

Dev helped me up and I could see his more sensitive Fae ears hadn't gotten out unharmed. He'd been too busy protecting me, and there was a thin line of blood running from both his ears. I reached up and wiped it off with my fingers before going on my toes to gently kiss the ears that had taken the pain meant for me. I'd heard him say it

211

before, but it hit me that he meant what he'd told me. He would die for me. I hugged him and vowed to not let that happen. He turned to the front of the canopy and the protective barrier melted away at a wave of his hands.

"Stay close," he said in a too-loud voice.

Daniel was just crawling from the small but substantial crater his body had created. I watched as one clawed hand dug into the earth and then a black boot came over the edge. Daniel swung himself up and appeared none the worse for the wear. He brushed dirt off his leather jacket and his eyes immediately sought us out.

Dev gave Daniel a thumbs-up as he held my hand and led me around the bodies of the soldiers on the ground. The humans hadn't been prepared for Daniel's play. They were alive, but some were unconscious and the ones closest to the impact had their eardrums completely shattered. Dev had his SIG Sauer out ready to shoot anything that started to move toward us. He wasn't in a good mood, and I got the feeling he was more than willing to use that gun in his hand at the first sign of a threat. I felt Lee at my back and his gun was out as well.

There was shattered glass all over the place, and I could see that one of the buildings had slightly caved in on itself. The soldiers who had previously been targeting me from the roof were lying in the grass.

Daniel walked through the wreckage, seeking his target. He used the toe of his boot to turn over the soldiers on the ground, but didn't see the face he was looking for. Some of the soldiers were starting to stumble to their feet, but they were still disoriented and not at all ready to fight it out.

Daniel finally located Ronald, who was struggling to get to his feet. The thud of a helicopter filled the world. The helicopter moved quickly and it didn't wait to land. The men began to come off the chopper, dropping to the ground from ropes secured to the aircraft. They hit the ground and ignored the devastation around them. They were professionals and immediately locked onto us.

"Drop your weapons!" they yelled, walking aggressively toward us.

Daniel hauled Ronald up by the nape of his flak jacket. He'd been far enough from the epicenter that his eardrums seemed intact, but he was dazed as the vampire pulled him to his feet.

"Get back," Daniel warned in a growl as he used the Order's leader as a human shield. He moved toward us and shoved Ronald's body at Dev. "Take off his head if they shoot at us."

"With pleasure," Dev replied, his voice sounding more normal. The vampire blood in his system was already working to heal the wounded tissue in his ears. He held Ronald close to his body, an arm under his neck, and pressed that SIG Sauer into his temple with a certain amount of malicious glee. "How do you like being used as a human shield, Ronald? Did you think for a minute we would let you get away with pointing a fucking gun at our wife's head?"

"Dev, we'll gut him later, man. For now, we need him alive." Daniel turned out to be the unlikely voice of reason.

I was stuck between Lee and Neil as we watched the soldiers from the helicopter advance on us. Daniel moved to the front of the party and I got nauseous at the thought of what could happen. He was making himself an enormous target, and they really did have silver bullets.

"You can't win," Ronald said. "They've already sent for more reinforcements. We'll have you surrounded and this time we'll have air support. The minute the vampire takes off, we'll see if he can handle a surface-to-air missile. There's nowhere to run, Mr. Donovan."

"We'll come up with something," Dev swore.

Daniel didn't look so sure. Ronald was taking advantage of his obvious discomfort.

"You'll probably survive, vampire, but your companion will likely not," Ronald said reasonably. "I can assure you that Mr. Quinn won't survive. He'll go down in a hail of bullets. Do you want to be responsible for the deaths of the two people you supposedly love, Mr. Donovan?"

The whole time he was talking, more and more guns were trained on us. More and more soldiers surrounded us.

"Shut up, Ronald," Dev said, his voice a harsh grind. He pushed the gun in tight against the man's skull. "Daniel will get us out of this and there's nothing you can do about it."

"I will get us out of this, Devinshea," Danny promised. He

looked over at me, his face grave. He stared for a moment and then turned his blue eyes back to Ronald. "You will allow Devinshea to leave with my companion and there will be no reprisals. He'll take her to a *sithein*."

"Daniel." Dev shook his head.

"No," I shouted. I was pretty sure he wasn't going with us, and I wasn't leaving him behind.

Daniel didn't look at me. He focused every ounce of his will on Dev. "Dev, you promised me. You promised me you would take her kicking and screaming if you had to. Ronald is right. I might be able to get away, but I could never live with the cost. Fighting Marini was dependent on getting what we needed from Merlin. That's not going to happen. The time has come to cut and run."

Dev cursed but his shoulders slumped in defeat.

I stepped forward even as we were completely surrounded. They formed a circle around us. "Do I get a say in any of this?"

"No, baby," Daniel said sadly. "None of us gets a say. Will you think about it, please? If you stay and fight, Dev and I will die to protect you and so will Lee and Neil and Zack. If you go to the *sithein*, then they live."

I squeezed my eyes shut at the unfairness of it all. Daniel knew where to stick the knife in.

"You'll allow my companion and partner to go? I'll submit to the chains and the coffin and I'll submit to whatever punishment the Order has for them, but I will be the only one punished," Daniel offered.

"Mr. Quinn isn't allowed to come back to this plane." Ronald gave his own amendment. "If we get the slightest hint that he's returned, all of our bets are off and we will hunt your companion down."

Daniel nodded. "They'll live in exile."

"I agree then." Ronald made his deal. "To show I'm a fair man, I'll allow the wolves to go as well."

Zack laid his gun down, bringing his hands up. "I'm staying with my master."

"Zack, you will go," Daniel commanded.

For the first time since he became Daniel's servant, Zack shook his head at him. "In this, I cannot obey you, master."

Daniel nodded and my love for Zack shot straight through the roof. Daniel held his hands in the air. "Devinshea, let him go. It's time."

"Damn it," Dev cursed as he let Ronald go. When he turned to me, I could see the raw emotion on his face. He hated what he was doing. He wanted to stand and fight, but he'd made a solemn vow and would never break his word to Daniel. He walked back and took my hand. His face was set. "Come along, my goddess."

I tried to pull away, panic starting to take over. "We can't leave him here, Dev."

Dev shook his head. His face was pale, his eyes older than before. "We have to. I meant what I said, wife. Kicking and screaming if necessary. Lee? Neil?"

"I'll come with you," my wolf vowed and I couldn't imagine how hard it would be leaving his brother behind.

"I'll go for now," Neil said, but he had commitments to his lover, too.

I was shaking as I looked back at Daniel. His face in the morning light was so beautiful as he stared at me. "I love you, Z. Always have, always will. You and Dev go make those babies."

I started to cry as Dev led me away. I turned as Ronald demanded Daniel disarm. There were two men walking forward with long, thick strings of silver rope that would hold my husband and burn into his flesh.

"Mr. Donovan," Ronald's voice was all business again. "I see the sword on your back. Carefully take it out and set it on the ground."

Dev cursed again and I heard him sigh because I wasn't complying. I wanted to get to Daniel. Dev swept me up into his arms and started to walk away. I couldn't stand it. We would get on a boat that would take us to Scotland and I wouldn't see Danny again. I wouldn't see my home plane again. I might have those babies, but they would never know their other father who would have loved them so much. I struggled in Dev's arms to try to get one last look at Danny as his hand pulled Excalibur from its sheath and the sword glittered in the morning light.

"Oh my god," I heard Ronald swear.

Everything seemed to still as Daniel held that sword and then one by one every soldier in the area dropped to one knee, head down, right fist over their hearts.

"Dev, stop. You have to stop." I practically screamed at him because something was happening. Something amazing.

"You should stop, Quinn." Lee had turned, his eyes taking in the scene. Neil stood beside him.

"What?" Dev asked, turning to take in the scene. He set me to my feet as we heard Ronald's reverent voice.

"My liege, the Order of Galahad is yours to command."

CHAPTER TWENTY

"**I**s the coffee to your liking, Your Highness?" the soldier asked. "I could try to find some cream if you like or perhaps some sugar?"

It was surreal. One minute Dev was hauling my ass to another plane because we'd worn out our welcome on this one, the next minute we were being given the freaking keys to the kingdom. It had been an hour since that dramatic scene had played out and our whole world had changed.

"Black is fine, thank you." I was lucky they'd been able to find coffee at all. "If you wouldn't mind seeing to the needs of my guards?"

"It would be my honor, ma'am." He scurried off to look through the rations the soldiers had been carrying.

I sat back, taking in everything that had happened. Daniel stared intently at all the action moving around him. After Excalibur had been drawn, everything moved very quickly. The soldiers had lain down their weapons and sworn fealty to the very surprised new head of the Order of Galahad. We'd been escorted into one of the buildings that had survived Daniel's crash down and the highly efficient soldiers quickly set up a command post and did their best to make the king feel comfortable. I reached across the table we were sitting at and placed my hand over his. He glanced up and a brief smile touched his lips.

"You should be thrilled," I said quietly.

He sighed. "Baby, there was a part of me that was relieved when I thought it was over. You and Dev would have been safe."

I frowned at him. "Well, suck it up, Your Highness. Fate isn't letting you out of this so easily."

He shook his head and refused to let go of my hand. "Don't be pissed at me. I'm adjusting."

The door opened and Dev walked in, looking nothing like the reckless man who had wanted to take on everyone on the island not so long ago. He'd cleaned up and was polished and in control once more. "I found someone with proper skills. He believes he can make a fairly decent Eggs Benedict from what he found in the rations and got from some of the locals. There's a shower in a small room on the second floor some of the ferry captains use when they get stuck on the island. It's worse than a motel but it will have to do."

"I'm sure we'll survive, Devinshea," Daniel murmured, slightly amused at Dev's distaste. "We've slept in worse places."

Dev agreed. "The soldiers are bringing in Nim and the other one, but the giant ass who tried to kill our wife wants a word with you before I execute him."

Daniel laughed outright at that one. "Please send him in, Dev. I would hate to refuse the final request of a condemned man."

Dev walked back out to bring Ronald James in and I turned on my husband. "You are not going to execute that man."

Daniel grinned, sitting back in his chair, looking every bit the king. "I'm not, baby. Dev is going to. Really, you should take it up with him."

"Oh, I will."

Dev hauled Ronald in, dragging the poor man by the front of his flak jacket. "Say whatever you need to say to the king, Ronald, and then get ready to kiss your ass good-bye."

I stood and Dev got a stubborn expression on his face. "You aren't killing him, Dev."

"Oh, yes I am, my goddess." He walked around the table to go toe to toe with me. Though he towered over me, I felt not a bit intimidated. "You aren't talking me out of it this time. He almost got you killed and he felt no remorse about potentially blowing you away."

"Yes, I did," Ronald interjected. "I believe I said at the time I regretted the need."

"You shut up," Dev spat before looking back at me. He traced the line of my jaw with his thumb and I felt a hint of warm magic pulse along my skin. "Besides, I have Bris back. I don't think you'll be cutting us off any time soon and if you try, I'll persuade you otherwise."

I took a step back. "I promise you, Dev, if I decide to cut you off nothing you or Bris do will sway me, and you're forgetting something very important in all of this. We need him."

"Give me one reason we need this asshole."

Daniel took that one. "How about the fact that we just acquired an army located on the very continent where we have to fight Marini and a good portion of the Council? Did it occur to you that a show of force against Marini might get us out of this war with minimal bloodshed? It would make us look less like barbarians to our new army if we don't immediately execute their leader."

Dev huffed and shook his head before dropping my hand and taking his place at Daniel's left-hand side. He sank into his chair, a sullen pout on his lips.

"And don't you think about going behind my back," I warned husband number two as I sat at Daniel's right. "You will not be arranging a handy accident, is that understood?"

"Well, my lover, I've found I have to kill people behind your back," he shot my way. "You so rarely allow me to kill them in front of your…front."

Daniel laughed out loud as he gestured Ronald forward. "I'm so glad we had this little adventure. I like that our wife finally has to confront your savage nature. You hide it so well, but now she'll force you into therapy just like me. We'll do group therapy and make Lee join us."

"As long as she doesn't make me read self-help books," Dev muttered.

"She made me watch old *Oprah* episodes, Dev," Daniel confessed. "She found copies of all the Dr. Phil episodes."

Dev shuddered and I sent him a look that let him know I would do it to him, too.

"I think you're safe, Mr. James," Daniel assured the Brit.

Ronald James looked very serious as Daniel nodded for him to take a seat. "I'm willing to accept whatever Your Highness thinks is correct."

"You were doing your job," Daniel said. "You'll have to excuse my partner. He often lets his anger get the best of him. He has the luxury. It's not one I can afford any longer. Now it would be helpful if you would explain what just happened out there, Ronald."

"Of course." The Brit sat very upright in his chair. "I didn't understand who you were. We only knew that the wizard's prison was being threatened. It's our highest directive to protect the crystal prison of Myrddin Emrys until such time as the King of the Sword returns."

"I'm not Arthur," Daniel said firmly. "If you're waiting for the reincarnation of King Arthur then we should go with the first plan and send my queen into exile."

Ronald stared pointedly at the three of us, and I could see his brain working. "You'll have to forgive me if I see some similarities, but you don't understand. It doesn't matter that you can't remember some mystical past life. That isn't what Excalibur is about. Over the years there have been several to carry the sword. No one is exactly sure where the sword was created but many believe it was forged on the Heaven plane by those who fought the demons in the early days of creation. Since then, when this plane was in danger of falling into darkness, a king has risen and the sword taken up. An order of supernatural females was formed to protect the sword and make the decision when the time was right."

"Nimue," I said.

"Yes," Ronald agreed. "She's the latest and has been at her work for the longest time. Arthur was hers. He's merely the most famous of the Sword Kings, but by no means the first. You, Your Highness, are this era's champion and the first vampire to hold the sword."

"Yes, I believe I mentioned that to you after I woke up from that grenade thing you used on me," Nim complained as she walked in the door.

Daniel's eyes widened and Ronald explained. "It was a flashbang. We've found them effective on almost all supernatural creatures."

Nim's mouth was a flat line as she stared at the Order's head. "They're also very good with wards and binding magic as well. They aren't so good with believing the truth when it stares them in the face."

Ronald stood and gave her a deep bow. "I apologize, Lady. We've had trouble in the past with witches who believed they were the Lady of the Lake. Some were simply insane and some tried to use the Order for their own designs."

The door opened and a nervous-looking soldier stuck his head in. "King Daniel, there is a…there is a thing out here that claims to be your servant. I think it's a demon."

"Never heard of him," Daniel said with a smirk. "You should exorcise him ASAP."

"Daniel," Nim said, sighing. "We still need him. I need him to wake the wizard."

There was a long pause. "Fine. Let him in."

Stewart walked in with a radiant smile on his borrowed face. Gone was the skate punk clothing and in its place an immaculately made pair of trousers, dress shirt, and sport coat. His shoes were polished even out here in the isolation of the island. He had cut the young man's hair into a trendy, fashionable style.

"He made us stop for a manicure, too," Nim admitted, noting my surprise.

"Oh, you liked it, you little minx. Don't lie," Stewart said with a wink.

Nim shrugged. "I certainly like the rubbing my feet part."

Stewart made a great show of bowing deeply to Daniel. "Your Highness, it is my greatest pleasure to find myself once again in your glorious presence. We have located the place you seek."

"So I heard," Daniel said shortly. "Are we close?"

"Very close, but it will be more easily accessed at an in-between time," Stewart said. "I thought dusk would be perfect."

That got Daniel's attention. "Does this have something to do with the veil between worlds?"

I heard the slight hitch in his voice as he asked the question. It was important to him. We'd been searching for someone who knew how to navigate the veils as the Tuatha Dé Danann, the oldest of faeries, did. The ancient Fae had left the plane and the faery worlds attached to it long ago. The only way to access those pieces of Faery was to open the veil, but the magic was old and for the most part had passed from our plane. We'd met a group of Fae who knew how to navigate in such a fashion, but they were long gone. The only trouble was they'd taken my and Danny's daughter with them. Daniel had been seeking a way to get her back ever since the revelation that the magical child had truly been a combination of us.

"Very good, Your Highness," Stewart said obsequiously. "It's very much like that. Nimue created the pocket world that contains the crystal palace and hid it from this world in such a fashion."

"I did the same thing with Avalon," Nim replied, sympathy creeping into her voice. "But Daniel, this isn't what you need to know. I can create a pocket world, but I don't know how the ancient Fae travel. I came into existence long after they were gone. I will research it further. I won't give up."

Daniel's face remained passive though I knew he ached inside. It was a private hurt, and he wouldn't dwell on it in public.

"The thought makes the king very sad," Stewart said, looking seriously at Daniel.

"Drop it," I warned.

Stewart's eyes shifted to me. "It's a private ache between the two of you. It doesn't include the Fae creature, though he worries about it. On the one hand, the Fae creature wants the two of you happy, but he worries if you and the king resolve the trouble you will no longer have a need for him. Is it a child?"

"She said drop it," Dev growled as he stood.

Stewart held his hands up innocently. "I apologize. You're a very strong transmitter. So easy to read, unlike the king. He has to ache with the pain before I can see an image from him. But you, Fae creature, you're just one big ball of ache. Deep inside you're still the little boy everyone loved one day and wanted to toss out with the garbage the next. You would fade if these two abandoned you. I can see it clearly. You would lie down and fade from existence. It would take a while, but time would mean nothing to you because you would be dead the minute they discarded you. Everyone discards you. You're useful for short periods of time, but you always prove unworthy in the end. When the king has his crown and a child with his queen, he won't need you anymore."

"Shut up," I yelled at the demon as I crossed to Dev. His face was pale and his hands trembled slightly. Stewart must be diving deep in his head to make him shake.

"Stewart, if you don't get out of his head, I'm going to have my soldiers cut off yours," Daniel explained.

It was kind of cool to see six men step forward ready to do Daniel's will. Stewart actually backed off.

"Devinshea," Daniel said quietly, looking up at his friend. "Those are your worries, not my feelings."

Dev nodded shortly. "I understand."

"Trust me, the last thing I would want if we found Summer would be to leave you. I have no intention of having the women outnumber me." Daniel tried to smile at Dev, but he seemed to avoid his eyes.

"Why do we need Stewart?" I asked Nim.

"Because he'll be able to see the veil better than I will," Nim admitted. "And I need his blood along with the sword to wake Myrddin. The wizard is the child of an incubus and a devout woman. I need something from each plane to call to him. Excalibur is a gift from the angels and Stewart here…"

"Came straight from Hell," I finished for her.

"Our prophecies have all pointed to the next king being the one to free the wizard from the prison," Ronald interjected after a short silence. "The question becomes what is the Order to do if the wizard is supposed to walk free? It has been our quest to ensure it didn't happen."

"Until such time as he was truly needed," Nim corrected. "That time is now. The Order is still necessary. The Order was comprised of the Knights of the Round Table who survived Arthur's final battle. The Order's main objective has been to guard the wizard's sleeping place, but its true mission is and always has been to support the King of the Sword. You are his knights, an honor passed down through the generations. The time has come again and the Order will stand behind

Excalibur."

Ronald put a hand over his heart and bowed his head. "We will do anything the King needs."

Daniel chuckled, but there was no real humor in it. "Don't offer the impossible, Sir Ronald. My little war isn't going well. I've been declared an outlaw by the Council. I'm on the run and unable to go home. Even now, my vampires are going into hiding."

"Hugo is making arrangements for Justin, Jean-Marc, and the others to meet us in New York. We need to regroup." Dev seemed calmer now.

"But Your Highness, there's no place more secure than our headquarters," Ronald replied. "We have no affiliations with any vampire and we're heavily fortified. If your intention is to raid the Council's home base, then you need to be close to Paris. We have everything you need."

"Except our allies," Dev pointed out. "We need to bring the wolves and the Fae with us if this is going to work. We need a united front."

"Agreed, but perhaps the Order is more capable of handling our exile than an endless procession of borrowed homes until we're finally ready," Daniel mused. "Louis wouldn't think to look there and it would keep our vampire allies' hands clean until the battle."

"I can have everything ready for you," Ronald promised. "I'll begin working on it immediately. As I said, your knights stand ready to provide you with anything you need."

"Do you know what I need right now? I drove all night and if I can't meet with the wizard until nightfall, then I would like to rest," Daniel said pointedly. He stood and took my hand. "Devinshea, can I trust you to not kill the head of our knights?"

Dev frowned. "I suppose so."

"Good," Danny said shortly. "Then do what you do best and organize our exile. I'm very hungry. You'll join us when you're done?"

"It's a small bed, Daniel," Dev pointed out.

"Then we'll have to cuddle. We will not have separate rooms. Not here and not at the headquarters. We stay together. Always," Daniel said over his shoulder as he led me away. "And Stewart, leave

Dev alone. Go find Neil and bug him."

"Absolutely, Your Highness," Stewart said with a grin. He was out the door in a flash.

"That was mean," I complained as I followed Daniel up the narrow stairs.

"Neil still couldn't hear the last time I saw him," Daniel pointed out. "Deafness will make Stewart infinitely more tolerable."

Daniel pulled me up the last two stairs, and before I knew what was happening, his mouth was on mine, devouring me. His tongue plunged in, dominating mine. I let my hands sink into his hair, loving the silky feel of it. I'd almost lost him. I'd thought I had. I'd almost lost him and I let that wash over me because he was still here and still in my arms. Pure emotion drove me as I held him close, every cell in my body responding to him. He was my husband, my first love. I couldn't remember a time when I didn't love Danny.

I kissed him with everything I had. I didn't care that there was an army downstairs. There was only me and Daniel.

He pulled my legs up and around his waist and then my back was up against the wall. He pressed his body against me, grinding his erection on my pelvis. I lit up, pleasure flaring along my skin.

"God, I need to be inside you, Z," Daniel groaned against my mouth. "I don't want any of this. I didn't want to be the freaking king, much less this. I just wanted to be your husband. That's all I ever wanted."

I wound myself around him, holding him tight. "I know you don't want it, baby, but we need you. You're the only one who can do this."

He was the only one who could save us all, the only one who could bring everyone together.

Daniel opened the door to the tiny bedroom. He walked us inside, seeming to not feel my weight at all. We fell against the double bed together.

"And I need you," Daniel said, his eyes dark. "Take off your clothes for me. Don't be a queen. Don't be a nexus point. Don't be a companion. Just Daniel and Zoey, okay? Just for a little while."

He stood up, staring down at me.

I didn't hesitate at all. My hands were already on the hem of my

T-shirt, pulling it over my head. I tossed it aside and started on my jeans even as Daniel was shoving his off his hips, looking like he would die if he didn't get what he wanted and soon. I unhooked my bra as he completed his task and got down on his knees. He reached up and pulled me toward him by my ankles. I was trapped by his strong arms parting my legs, spreading my naked flesh.

"I know you think I love you for the way your blood tastes," Daniel said, his voice deep. "But god, Z, that wasn't the first taste I got of you. I was an addict even then."

He brought his mouth reverently down on my pussy, kissing me gently. He let go of my legs, sure that I would hold myself open for him now. He breathed in my scent, the happiness in his eyes letting me know how much he loved it.

"Fuck, baby, you're already wet." He parted me with his fingers and let his tongue run the length of my pussy, gathering cream as he went.

I took a deep breath because I needed the oxygen. His tongue speared me, fucking deep and making me squirm. "I always am when you're around, Danny."

I curled my fingers around the bedspread, trying to let Daniel have his way. He loved to play with me. He would spend what seemed like hours licking, sucking, and loving his favorite part of me.

"All I thought about for five years was getting back inside you. I was so fucking alone without you. Don't you leave me, Z. Don't you ever leave me. You take me with you wherever you go."

Even through the pleasure he was giving me, I felt the ache at what had almost happened. I almost lost him. I almost had to walk away from my first love. I wouldn't have known what happened to him.

"Baby, don't." But I could see he was emotional, too. "Don't think about it. It didn't happen. I won't ever let it happen. I would have come for you. You understand. I'll tell them whatever I need to say, but I'll come for you and Dev."

"I love you, Danny." I couldn't imagine a world without him.

His tongue found my clit and he worked his fingers inside. I let myself go, fucking his fingers and loving the firm tongue pressed against me. My hands found his hair and held him where I wanted him. I cried out as he curved his fingers inside me and found my sweet spot. One long lick against my clit sent me flying. I came against his tongue, and he held himself close even as I shivered in the aftermath.

He let me settle before covering my body with his, the weight of him pressing me into the mattress and making me feel so safe. We weren't a king and queen in that moment when he made a place for himself between my legs and connected us with one sure thrust of his body. We were seventeen again, just starting out with the whole world ahead of us and unknown. We were kids who had just found the greatest feeling in the world in each other's bodies. We were Danny and Zoey, kids who loved each other, who never thought about a world without the other one in it.

He looked down as he held himself tight inside me, savoring the connection between us, and he said the same thing he had said to me that first night we made love. "You are everything to me."

"You're my world." I gave him back my words.

He lay on top of me, giving me all of his weight, his cheek pressed so close to mine I could feel the tears that left his eyes. I wrapped my legs around his waist and forgot everything but the magnificent feeling of him inside me. I pushed back, and it didn't take long for his pace to pick up and his silence to turn to long groans. He lifted his body up, and suddenly he was rubbing against my clit with every thrust, sending me over the edge again. I looked up and his fangs were out. He quickly closed his mouth.

"Don't, baby," I said because the truth was we weren't seventeen anymore and I wouldn't go back. I wanted this Daniel and he was a vampire. He was my husband. "Please, take me. Take what only I can give you."

Daniel, my vampire, groaned and his eyes flashed. He never lost the rhythm of his lower body as he struck and my blood flowed into his mouth, making his heart pump, his lungs work, giving his soul a body to stay in. I closed my eyes and gave myself over to the now, where Daniel loved me fully and wholly.

The future might be uncertain but the now was perfect.

"What is it?" I asked, roused from my light sleep by Daniel's movement.

He was up on one elbow, his eyes looking toward the door. "It's Dev. He's been out there for half an hour, Z. Why doesn't he come in? It isn't like him. He knows we're naked. He should be clawing his way in."

"Stewart got to him." I knew exactly what the problem was. I shoved Daniel's T-shirt over my head and opened the door.

Dev sat on the floor opposite our borrowed room. There was a tiredness to the set of his shoulders. A general air of the forlorn hung on him, his hair drooping and his clothes dusty. He had a bottle of whiskey in one hand. Only my faery prince could find a bottle on this isolated island.

"Is it helping?" I crossed my arms over my chest and cursed Stewart's existence. The afternoon should have been relaxed. So many of our problems had been solved, but the damn demon had to bring up all of Dev's insecurities.

"Nope," he replied, taking a swig anyway.

"Are you coming to bed? We only have a few hours before dusk."

Dev just stared up at me. "I am not a good man, Zoey."

I sighed. He was going to play the drama out to its fullest. "And yet I still love you."

Daniel walked up behind me wearing only his boxers. "Get in bed, man. You have got to stop letting that prick get to you. I'm not going to dump your ass if we manage to find Summer. I would expect you to accept her, Dev."

Dev looked up, his face very serious. "I already accept her, Daniel. I've been very intent on finding the information we need. I would love her as my own daughter."

"I know that," I said and then I got to the heart of the problem. "Now stop thinking Daniel is anything like Declan. He isn't. He knows every shitty thing you've done, probably so much more than I do, and he hasn't used any of it against you." I turned to husband number one. "And yes, I know all about the brothel."

"Shit," Danny cursed.

"He could have brought up any of that stuff the Order knew to try to wrestle me away from you," I explained flatly. "There are probably things he knows that would have worked, but he didn't try to fight you. He became your freaking partner in crime and tried to hide the fact that the two of you want to become the Hugh Hefners of the supernatural world. He's committed to this family and that means something to Daniel. He won't toss you out. He loves you. He wants you. He'll accept you for all your lying, illegal arms dealing, gambling, pornographic, and pimping ways."

"I am not a pimp." Dev refuted only that statement. "I'm an investor."

"Fine." I gave him that much. "Then get your gangster ass into our bed. If we can all fit."

Dev got up, leaving the bottle behind. "Are you sure? You didn't seem to be in a sharing mood earlier."

Daniel grinned, his dimples on full display. "I told you. I don't share. It's all mine, man." He kissed him swiftly, a brushing of lips that was so much more intimate for how brief and casual it was. "Now come on. I learned something today. I can't go back and I don't want to. What Z and I had was beautiful and damn near perfect, and nothing compared to what we have now. I love what we have so fucking much…I want to die when I think about losing it."

Dev nodded but didn't speak, emotion choking him up. He walked into my arms and let me shut the door behind us.

"We love you, Devinshea," I said as his arms tightened around me. "We will never leave you. Now come to bed and make love to me. Daniel can watch."

"I like to watch," Danny allowed. "I might even join in. We do have a few hours."

Daniel sank back on the bed and pulled me down with him. He settled me between his legs. My back was to his chest. He stripped the shirt off me and glanced back at our faery prince. "Do you have a condom, Dev?"

"I'm always ready to go," Dev assured him with a smile.

"Then toss it out," came Daniel's reply.

We all stopped. Dev stood there for a moment. "Daniel, I have Bris back."

Danny's arms tightened around me. "Yes, and I can't think of a better way to welcome him. I want our family. I want us to find Summer, but I want our family, Dev. You're the only one who can give it to us."

We had a long road ahead. We had to wake the wizard, but after that we would spend a lot of time in the Order's headquarters. I would never see the war zone. I would be coddled and surrounded by guards. I could do that while I was pregnant. The idea brought tears to my eyes. I could have our babies. I could have the sons Oliver Day had promised me. He'd told me if I did my job, I could have my twins, my boys.

Maybe I wasn't thinking at the time. Maybe I was throwing fate a big old finger, but in that moment I wanted nothing more than to know we had a future.

Dev stared at me. "I don't know. I'm worried that the time isn't right."

I shook my head. I might not be going into a war zone, but I doubted anything would keep Dev out of it. I didn't like to think about it, but if anything happened to Dev, I wanted something of him, something to keep. I wanted our children. I wouldn't say it. Neither would Daniel, but I was sure we were both thinking about it. We were going into something dangerous. It might be one of our last chances to try. "The time is never going to be right for this. After we take over the Council, we'll want to wait until things settle down and then something else will come up. Screw that. Nothing is more important than this. I want to have our babies. Do you want that, too?"

Dev's smile was radiant, and I felt it in my soul. "I want it more than anything I've ever wanted in my life, my goddess."

"Then come on, Dev," Daniel said solemnly. "Let's make a family together, the three of us."

I know I should have worried. I was a nexus point. I had a job to do, but I let all of it go. I didn't want to be important. I didn't want power. I just wanted to be a wife and a mother. I wanted a family with the men I loved.

Daniel held me, whispering his love for me as Dev was gentler than I could ever remember him being. His magic flowed across us, feeding Daniel and making my body sing. His magic felt like love and lust and hope, wrapping us up, sheltering us and preparing us for anything that might come along.

Dev leaned down to kiss me when he gasped, holding himself against me, letting his fertility flow from him into me. It was perfect. We were together and as I settled down to sleep between them, I hoped it had worked but I wouldn't mind more trying if we had to.

Dev's hand came over my belly as he pressed himself against me. He held his hand there like he could feel what was happening. Daniel's hand found its way there too and Dev moved to give him room. We slept like that, the three of us connected waiting, hoping for what we all wanted.

CHAPTER TWENTY-ONE

"And you are sure this is the way to go, Your Highness?" Sir Ronald asked as the helicopter thudded.

The sun was starting to set in the background. It was hours later and the time had come to make our way to the crystal prison of Myrddin Emrys.

"We have no idea how long this will take," Daniel replied. "I think an entire army encamped on a small island off the coast of Wales will garner some media attention. The locals seem to be in on all of this, but someone is going to call a reporter eventually. I worry some vampire might catch a little CNN and mention it to Marini. We'll be fine. Once we're back on the mainland, I'll call and you can come pick us up."

"We'll be waiting on the call," Sir Ronald said.

Dev stepped up, treating Ronald with far more respect than he had before. "Until then, you should ensure that our vampires are comfortable. They'll be bringing their girlfriends with them. Most of the girls are either wolves or shapeshifters, so the vampire's dietary needs will be taken care of, but we expect them to be protected. These are vampires who were turned by the king himself. They're of his bloodline and have never lived in vampire society. You'll find them very different from other vampires."

"I look forward to meeting a non-Council vampire. I think I will find the experience refreshing. We're already renovating the basement complex for them," Ronald shouted over the hard thud of the chopper. "And we've spoken to Henri Jacobs. He's coming as well. He wants his companion under full Order protection while this war is going on. I also spoke to your butler. He's a very bossy man and plans to come with the vampires."

Dev laughed. "Ronald, you have no idea. Albert will be running things before you can blink."

"Was the butler serious about closet space?" Ronald asked and he looked like he wanted to be let in on the joke.

Dev never joked about closet space. His face was very serious as he replied. "Absolutely. Proper closet space is what sets us apart from the animals, Ronald. You can't expect us to be improperly dressed for a war. Her shoes alone will require a room of their own."

Daniel's head was in his hand as Ronald looked to the king for confirmation. Daniel sighed, obviously embarrassed, but it didn't bother Dev at all. Daniel could bitch all he liked. Dev wouldn't budge on the issue of wardrobe. "I assure you he's serious. Apparently it's a Fae thing. He'll have her dressed to the nines and in five-inch heels for the entire war if he has his way."

I didn't mention it, but I intended to be pregnant and in PJs with an éclair in my hand and far away from any battle. I would deeply prefer to bomb Marini from afar. As for my previous plans to steal the Blood Stone, it looked like I wouldn't have to. We had an entire army at our disposal. Maybe everyone had been wrong about all the nexus point stuff. I certainly preferred to think that way.

"I'll make sure all is ready, Your Highness." Ronald turned and walked to the last chopper. He hopped on and gave his king a serious salute. "We will await your orders."

We watched as the helicopter flew away and then the island was quiet again. It was almost too quiet, and I shivered a little in the late afternoon chill.

Daniel looked at Dev, still shaking his head. "Closet space? We're on the run and you're worried about closet space?"

Dev shook his head. "It's very important, Daniel. It could be a while before we gather our allies. We'll need to entertain them. Appearances are very important. You must look the part, even in exile. Did you intend to meet with your people dressed…well, like that?" He gestured up and down, encompassing Daniel's T-shirt and jeans ensemble.

Daniel rolled his eyes as we started back to meet with Nim, Stewart, and the wolves. "See, this is why I prefer to just kill things. When you kill someone they don't give a crap that you're wearing jeans and boots. I hate those freaking dress shoes you make me wear."

I whipped my head around. "And the five-inch heels are just heaven on my toes, Danny, but guess who won't let me take them off even when I get in bed."

"They're hot, baby," Daniel admitted with a grin. "I like the way they poke into the small of my back when you wrap your legs really tight around me just before you come."

"I enjoy them propped up on my shoulders as I drive into her," Dev offered with a sigh. "Sneakers just don't do the same thing for me."

I hid my smile. "So nobody gets to complain about loafers or the next time we go for some sexy fun, I'll be wearing my old combat boots. You know, the ones I bought at the thrift store."

Both men shuddered at the idea, and I knew they would be toeing the line.

"Do we have everything we need?" Daniel asked Nim as we rejoined our friends.

The nymph nodded, her brown hair bobbing. "We're as ready as we're going to be."

Zack and Lee checked their weapons, and Zack handed Daniel a gun after he inspected it. We were going in fully armed. My new Ruger was settled into the holster at the small of my back. The Order had been very happy to replace some of the weapons we lost to Scotland Yard. I found I had one small question before we left.

"So I'm glad this whole Order of Galahad thing worked out for us, but one has to wonder. I know I didn't call them up and request they meet us on the tarmac. Who put in that little heads up?"

Stewart blinked as seven pairs of eyes suddenly turned on him. "Well, you couldn't expect me to just drop everything without a little call to home."

Yep. That was what I'd thought. When everything goes to hell, look to the demon.

"Yes, I could, asshole," Daniel said.

"I merely told a friend." Stewart pouted prettily. "He probably told a friend or two and so on and so on. We're demons, you know. We have a little trouble with gossip, but like you said, it all worked out in the end so I should think you would actually thank me."

"Don't count on it," Daniel ground out. He turned. "Lead the way, Nimue."

Nim began walking across the vast green carpet that makes up so much of Wales. We marched along, Daniel at the front and Lee and Zack protecting our six. Dev walked just behind Daniel, his gun in hand. Neil was beside me and then, just like a dog you probably shouldn't have ever fed in the first place, Stewart was on my heels.

"The Fae creature seems different," Stewart said conversationally. "Whatever you did while you, the king, and he were 'napping' seems to have done the trick."

I couldn't help it. It just came out. "How so?"

Stewart's blue eyes lit up because I'd fallen into the horrible trap of actually responding to him. "Well, he seems much less troubled. In fact, he seems downright content today. Something happened to make him feel worthy. He's just bursting with self-esteem. Normally, there's a well of sorrow just below his surface no matter how happy he seems. He's always waiting for the worst to befall him. That's what happens when your entire world gets ripped out from under you at a very young age."

"Is he talking about the fact that the nobles turned on him when they discovered he was mortal?" Neil wasn't able to resist either. It was part of why Stewart was so dangerous. He sucked you in.

"Yes," Stewart said. "That one incident has colored his world ever since. Much like the time your father attempted to get you to bed a female and you couldn't do it and he…oh, you poor puppy."

"Get out of my head, Stewart," Neil growled, his icy blue eyes flashing.

Stewart gave Neil a shy smile, not at all perturbed by his show of temper. "You're very good at that, you know. Of all the people I've met, you can toss me out of your mind faster than any of them. Your emotional control is incredible. It's one of the things I find most attractive about you. I find it interesting that you and the Fae creature had very similar upbringings, but your reactions are different. You were both tossed out by your families, considered perverse and freakish by your people, yet he walks about an aching ball of pain, naked to my eye, and you're completely closed down."

"Just to you, Stewart," Neil said, getting himself under control. "I'm not closed off to the people I love. I think it just bothers you that Dev and I can go through some terrible shit and still be perfectly capable of loving those around us and allowing ourselves to be loved."

Stewart considered that. "I suppose it confuses me. I understand the Fae creature. His mother still loved him. His brother still loved him. He was considered lesser, but the core of the bond was still functional. It sent him off on a quest to find a family who truly needed him. Your family always knew there was something wrong with you. They despised you for it."

"I probably gave it away when I wanted Madonna to sing at my tenth birthday party," Neil admitted.

"Silly little puppy. They never gave you a party," Stewart said solemnly. "They knew you were wrong the minute you were born. Your father would have tossed you out, but your mother wouldn't have it. She died far too young, if you ask me."

"If I just tell you what you want to know, will you be silent for the rest of the walk?" Neil asked, slightly exasperated.

"Neil, you don't have to tell him anything," I swore. "I can have Lee gag him."

"Oh, please don't," Stewart said, his voice sounding charming. "I really am interested, Neil. I know you don't believe me, but I do greatly admire you. You have such strength where I worry I would not."

Neil still didn't look completely convinced, but he plunged on ahead anyway. "It was Daniel who brought me back. I made my oath to him and through his blood, I was able to feel his connection to Z."

"The obsession a vampire feels for a companion must be very strong," Stewart commented.

"It wasn't obsession." Neil didn't seem to care if Stewart believed him, but it was the truth so he was going to put it out there. "It was love and it was the first time I'd really felt it. I liked it. I liked loving someone but then I realized somewhere along the line that Z loved me and I liked that, too. Being on that crew with Z and Danny and Sarah was the first real family I could ever remember, and I was safe for the first time."

Stewart's eyes never left Neil. "But you're not on the vampire's blood anymore. Did he not offer it to you when you returned from your sojourn?"

I was silent because I'd wondered about that as well. For the longest time after we got Neil back, he and Daniel had danced around each other until they'd finally come to an understanding while we were in Faery. Daniel could handle more than one servant, but he and Neil had not renewed their oaths.

"I don't need it anymore," Neil replied. "Daniel offered, but I had to say no. I need to be me now. I'm strong enough. I can love and I can accept love without anyone else's blood influencing me. I know I'm weak, but I'm Neil. I'm finally just me."

I reached out and squeezed his hand because he should know that was more than enough for me.

Stewart's eyes had softened. "Little puppy, that…"

"You promised," Neil reminded him and Stewart fell silent. We walked along for a moment, our fingers tangled together. "See, that was totally worth it."

Nim held her hand up. We stood in the middle of a flat, emerald green plain. There was nothing at all to see but grass, yet Nim stopped like she didn't want to hit something. She motioned for Stewart to come forward. I stood there not sensing anything at all in the cool of dusk. The sun was just beginning to set on the horizon, and I could see the Irish Sea. This island was so small. It seemed impossible that it held some sort of prison and no one had ever discovered it.

"Do you sense anything?" I asked Neil, who shook his head, just as lost as I was.

"I can't describe it, but I know something's wrong," Lee said, coming up behind us. Zack had gone to stand with Daniel. "It's like I can sense that something should be here, but it isn't."

Stewart scented the air. Perhaps in his normal body the gesture would seem natural, but it was odd in the human body he was riding. He walked around and the movements seemed jerky, like he couldn't get the limbs to do exactly what he wanted and was forced to compromise.

After a long while, he went still and turned to us, and a long, satisfied smile crossed his face. "It's here, Your Highness."

Nimue went to stand next to the demon and gestured for Daniel to stand beside her. "We need the sword now." She took it in her hand when Daniel passed it to her and frowned, looking the slightest bit nervous. "Now we find out if I did my job properly."

"What do you mean?" Danny asked.

She tugged at her bottom lip with her teeth. "Well, there's always a test with things like this."

"Like the sword in the stone?" I remembered my Arthurian lore, or at least the Disney movie.

Nim nodded. "Yes, that was the test for the boy. I set up the test for this king a very long time ago. I didn't know exactly why I chose this method because at the time it seemed odd, but something told me this was the proper challenge."

"Why a test?" Neil asked. "You're the Lady of the Lake. Don't you just know who to give the sword to?"

"Think of it as a fail-safe," the nymph replied. "Excalibur in the hands of the wrong person could prove very bad for us all."

"But Daniel already has the sword," Dev pointed out.

Stewart chirped up to answer that question. "Oh, he won't for long if he doesn't pass this test. If he fails, we all die. Well, all of you die. I just go back to the Hell plane and resume my former life. But I would mourn you all terribly."

"What's the test, Nim?" Daniel asked.

Nim smiled a secret little smile. "It's simple, Daniel. I thought at the time it was too simple, but now it's very fitting. I'm sure it will all work out. The world needed Arthur's strength, so his test was one that proved it. The world needs something different from you."

Daniel sighed. It always came back to that. "Where am I supposed to bleed this time?"

"Stand right here where the veil is the thinnest and the door can open." Nim watched him, holding the sword easily.

Daniel did as instructed and the minute he was in place, Nim's hand came back and she sent Excalibur straight into Daniel's gut with a horrible twist.

All hell broke loose. Zack leapt forward, his semi pointed straight at the nymph's head. Lee pulled me back even as I tried to run toward Daniel. Dev made it to our vampire first. Daniel had fallen to his knees, his blood spilling all over the green grass, but before Dev could reach down to haul him up, he put an arm out to stop him.

"I'm fine," I heard Daniel growl, clutching his middle.

"She gutted you," Dev yelled as he turned his face accusingly to Nim. His gun was on full display. "Give me one good reason I don't put a bullet in your skull, Nimue or Vivienne or whatever the hell your name is."

"If you're going to shoot me, you should step back to do it, Devinshea," Nim announced even as I felt a wave of energy flicker across my skin. Lee cursed softly and I knew he felt it, too.

"The veil is opening," Stewart said. "Someone should get the king back unless he wants to be ripped in two."

Dev put his arm under Daniel's shoulder on one side and Zack took the other. They started to hurry him away from the site.

"Didn't I just get ripped in two? Sure as hell felt like it," Daniel muttered as they made their way to me.

Lee let me go and I went down on my knees even as Daniel hit the ground.

I knelt beside him, feeling for the already healing wound. I expected it to be deep and still bleeding, but it was already closing. In moments there wouldn't even be a scar. "Do you need blood?"

He nodded. "Not you, baby. I already took my share from you."

Dev didn't hesitate. His sleeve was already rolled up, as though he anticipated the need, and he came in behind Daniel, offering his wrist. He didn't hiss at the pain as fangs pierced his skin. There was only a slight tightening around his eyes to show he felt anything at all as Daniel began to draw from him. I didn't even yell at Danny for not pulling Dev in. That was a private thing and they wouldn't do it in front of anyone but me.

"We have to hurry." Nim used her sweater to wipe the blood

from the sword. She tossed it away when she was done and held Excalibur out for Daniel to retrieve. "The test has been passed. The king's blood has opened the veil and Merlin waits. I'm sorry for the violent nature of the test, Daniel, but it was necessary. There's no question now. You are the King of the Sword. Are you ready to meet your mentor?"

Daniel released Dev's wrist, licking the wound clean, and it quickly closed. He was on his feet and he helped Dev to his. Daniel patted his ruined T-shirt and sighed. He zipped up his leather jacket, covering the blood. He nodded to Dev and they each took an arm to escort me. It was how we had entered all state functions when we were in Faery. Daniel was signaling he wanted to continue the practice on this plane. "We're ready."

The demon held out his hand to stop us. "Please allow me to educate you in this. Your Highness, you should go first. It's tradition. This is a very important moment. It will be commented on and talked about. We must get it just right. The king enters and then the queen and then the rest of your retinue. You're at the center of this kingdom and we follow you."

Daniel actually threw back his head and laughed. "Stewart, you know nothing of my kingdom if you think I'm the center. I haven't been the center of my world for at least twenty years and I don't ever intend to be. As for tradition, well, it's time I made my own."

In between the two men I loved more than anything in the world, I made my way into the prison of Myrddin Emrys.

CHAPTER TWENTY-TWO

Though we had walked into the pocket world at dusk, the sun was full and high in the sky in the prison. It made the crystal castle in the distance sparkle and shine like a jewel in the middle of a fertile field. The world here was so still and calm it felt quite unreal as Daniel and Dev lead me through the tear in the fabric of space and time and into the small world Nim had created to house the wizard.

I glanced behind me and saw Neil entering just after Lee. It was odd to see another entire world peeking through the small doorway the veil made. The veil shimmered and closed as though it had never been there at all.

"It looks like it goes on forever." Neil put a hand over his eyes to block the sun as he gazed at the mountains to the north of the castle.

"That's an illusion," Nim explained. "It's actually quite small. It took an enormous amount of energy for me to form this world. I'm still not sure I've recovered from it entirely. I should have been able to easily handle the Order, but they got the jump on me."

"You were concentrating at the time," Stewart allowed. "That spell wasn't a simple one."

"Still," she said, frowning. "I remember how Arawn had to take me to the otherworld for several hundred years to recover even a part of my strength." The otherworld was the Welsh place of the gods and the dead. It was Arawn's kingdom.

"How is the wizard going to handle you showing up after all these years?" I asked as we walked toward the castle.

Nim sighed. "I probably should have told him what I needed to do, but he can be very unreasonable. The rest of us were selected for our duties. We knew the risks and the rewards and we chose to be here. Myrddin didn't have a choice. He was and always will be a wild card, so to speak. He straddles two worlds. He's both demon and human."

"His demonic nature will always be the dominant of the two," Stewart said, his voice all snooty and superior.

"I'm not so sure about that," Nim replied. "He was excellent with Arthur."

Stewart rolled his borrowed eyes. "Arthur failed in the end."

"He didn't," Nim argued. "He set up an entire system that stood for years. He kept this part of the world strong. It wasn't the wizard's fault that he let the personal stuff get to him."

Stewart turned back and his smile was slightly malicious. "But darling girl, the personal stuff, as you put it, is exactly where a demon would strike."

Dev's hand squeezed mine and I knew it was his way of telling me he wouldn't let Stewart hit us there ever again. Stewart was right. Something fundamental had changed in Dev since we lay in that tiny bed together and made a choice to move forward with our lives. A sense of calm had come over him. He was content with us and, for the first time, with himself.

"We just need the wizard to fix my heart," Daniel said. "I can take it from there."

Nim's violet eyes turned to Daniel. "Your Highness, you must listen to all the wizard has to say to you. He's wise and excellent at prophecy. He'll be able to guide you. I might have a difficult relationship with the man, but I can't criticize his work. If he chooses to mentor you, it's because you need him."

Daniel sighed as we moved closer to the castle. Though it seemed to be made of crystal, I couldn't see inside it. It protected its secrets.

"I will consider it," Daniel allowed, but I heard that stubborn edge to his voice. Myrddin would find Daniel a difficult pupil.

"He mentored me," Nim said as she contemplated her work. "I knew nothing of magic before I met the wizard."

"Then how did you trap him?" Dev asked.

Stewart laughed. "How does a woman ever trap a man? For all his power, the wizard is also a man with a man's desires. Nimue is a lovely woman. Even I can appreciate her on an aesthetic level. She got the wizard all hot and bothered and tricked him into her prison."

Nim stopped and crossed her arms over her chest. "That's not how it happened. Well, mostly not. He's a horny old goat. He used to try to get his hands on anything with breasts and then he wants me to believe that he loves me. After all the women he went through, I'm supposed to believe he thought differently of me. I wasn't buying it, not for a minute. He even tried to convince me he would be willing to share me with Arawn. He was just on the prowl. Like Arawn would ever agree to that. Besides, I needed him contained. I needed him locked away to wait for the new king. I couldn't allow my emotions to engage."

But it had been tempting. I could see that on Nim's face. She'd felt something for the wizard. It might not have been love, but something about all of this made her feel guilty. She pushed forward, but I could see the tension in her eyes. She was nervous about seeing him again after all these years. When we finally stood at the door, she had to take a deep breath before moving on.

Nim pushed the heavy doors open but a hand locked on my wrist, pulling me back.

"Not on your life, darlin'," Lee growled. He stood in front of Dev and Daniel. "I'll check it out. She isn't going anywhere until I make sure it's safe. Neil, wait with Zoey. Don't let her go in until I get back."

Daniel waited but his eyes were on the wolf as he walked by. "Why do they call me the king if everyone tells me what to do?" He nodded at Zack, who was eagerly waiting his go-ahead to follow his brother. "Go on then."

Zack ran to catch up.

"It's perfectly safe." Nim shook her head as though she didn't understand the fuss.

"Lee takes his job very seriously," Dev explained. "He really won't believe you until he's checked out the place for himself. Say, there aren't any cool traps that might kill him in there, are there?"

"Dev!" I said, batting his arm because he sounded like that would be a good thing.

"Well, my goddess, he is very bossy," Dev replied. "He thinks he's ultimate authority when it comes to you."

"You're jealous," I said, shocked. "You're jealous of Lee?"

Daniel shrugged. "I told you he was ridiculously possessive. And we're pretty much jealous of anyone who looks at you. I sometimes don't like how much time you spend with Neil."

Neil laughed heartily. "That's ridiculous. The two of you spend more time together than you do with Z. What do you want her to do, sit somewhere and wait for the two of you to get home and pay attention to her?"

"Yes," Dev replied, not sounding at all ashamed.

"Preferably she would wait naked," Daniel added.

"Nice." Dev's hand came out for a low-five.

I rolled my eyes, thankful Lee was already on his way back. "Don't expect that little fantasy to happen anytime soon."

Dev hugged me from behind and pulled me into his chest. He bent down and dropped a little kiss on my cheek before whispering in my ear. "I'll settle for barefoot and pregnant. Goddess, you're going to be so fucking gorgeous pregnant. You'll be so round and lovely. Daniel and I will have to take very good care of our sweet wife."

Daniel pulled me out of Dev's arms and kissed me himself. "He's insane. He really thinks pregnancy will make you all soft and sweet. I know better, baby. I'm getting out of your way for those nine months. I'm going to hunker down and try to survive."

I punched Daniel in the arm. I was sure he didn't even feel it but it seemed like the thing to do. "Jerk," I said affectionately.

I had to give the edge to Danny on this one, though. I doubted having two babies kick me from the inside, gaining fifty pounds, and having to go to the bathroom constantly was going to turn me into a sweet little woman.

Lee looked a bit disturbed as he walked back out. "I think it's fine. We're definitely alone but…"

Zack shook his head as he followed his brother. "That wizard dude looks gross, man. Damn, dude be old, if you know what I'm saying. I don't think he'll be trying to get your goodies anymore, Nim."

Nim smiled briefly. "It should be amusing to see how the wizard handles today's…youth."

I was allowed to walk through the double doors and inside the castle. It looked as though the building had been sleeping for a thousand years. There was almost no light coming through the walls. Though they appeared crystal-like from the outside, they kept the light out from the inside. Nim walked around, throwing open windows and revealing the high, arched ceilings and magnificent stonework on the floor. There was very little in the way of furniture but books were piled high in shelves and stacked on the floor. There was a thick coat of dust over everything. When the light hit the great room, I could see that plants had tried to make their way in but the lack of light made them sad-looking creatures.

"This just won't do." Dev shook his head as he walked around. He placed his palm to the side of what looked like a stone wall. In an instant, we were surrounded with life. Vines popped out and flowers bloomed, and great sprigs of holly and ivy were everywhere.

"Beautiful," Nim said with wonder, looking around at the roses suddenly blooming around all the doorways. The burst of color and life changed the gloomy building into a faery castle.

"Show off," Daniel complained under his breath, but I caught the wink he sent Dev's way.

"I sense the wizard." Stewart's eyes closed, rapture plain on his face. "He's close."

Nim walked to the back of the great room. She had found a torch and lit it. "He's in the room below. Come now, Daniel, Stewart. The rest of you may make yourself at home. I don't know how long this will take."

"Like I'm staying here." I moved toward the staircase that went down into the darkness. The wizard Merlin was sleeping in the floor below, and Daniel was about to wake him. I wasn't hanging out upstairs, pruning roses. I turned and waited for Daniel. I wasn't going to be left behind, but I knew the protocol. I was testing Daniel as it was. I certainly wasn't going to go anywhere without him.

Dev was right behind me. "I'm with my goddess. I have no intentions of allowing Daniel to have all of the fun."

"It could be dangerous, Your Highness," Nim pointed out to Daniel.

He shook his head. "I got no scene control, Nim. They'll just follow us anyway, and Z will probably find a way to make a dangerous situation into something truly insane."

"Well, at least the wolves can…" Nim began.

Lee elbowed his way past them, followed by Neil, who wasn't letting anyone leave him behind. Zack frowned and hung back. He watched Lee's and Neil's heads disappear down the spiral staircase and looked completely pitiful. Nim rolled her violet eyes and gave up the fight, following Neil down the dark stairs.

Daniel sighed. "Come on then, Zack. I'm not going to punish you for being the good one. I won't leave you up here all by yourself."

Zack scampered down the stairs like an eager puppy.

"You know you would miss all of us," I teased Daniel as he began down the stairs.

"No one ever lets me miss them," Daniel complained, but I could hear his affection. He loved his little crew even when we annoyed the hell out of him. Dev and I followed.

Nim and Lee were busy lighting torches as we entered the dungeons of the crystal castle. Down in the dungeon, even the air was heavy. There was a feeling of deep gloom in every aspect of my surroundings. It was a large room, but it somehow managed to feel cramped. I could hear the sound of rushing water. When there was enough light, I saw a large fountain in the back of the room. Upon really studying it, I found it was more like a small waterfall, and a man could probably stand beneath it and shower.

"He's not happy," Nim said under her breath.

"No, he is not," Stewart concurred.

"How do the two of you know?" Neil walked to where Stewart stood looking down.

I joined him and caught my breath at the sight of the desiccated body in a glass coffin. The wizard lay there, still dressed in his deep purple robes. The garment seemed to be made of velvet, but the wizard had shrunk inside his clothes. They were obviously made for a much larger man. They hung off the corpse-like wizard, sliding from his shoulders like they wanted to escape the confines of the coffin.

I had to agree with Neil. The wizard looked like he would never feel anything again. His face was a thin sheet of papery skin over bones, his eyes sunk deep into his skull. In the low light of the dungeon, he was an ashen gray color.

"This isn't the way I left this room." There was a scowl on Nim's face as she glanced around. "I left it in good shape. His own anger has made it so gloomy. Devinshea, could you please?"

My fertility god flicked his wrists negligently, and I heard a slithering sound. Rose vines from upstairs wound their way down. They snaked around the staircase and formed lovely patterns across the walls.

Nim took a deep breath as the place lost its musty scent. "Much more cheerful."

All at once the roses withered and died on the vine. Dev's eyes widened as he took in the scene. Flowers never died around Dev.

Nim walked up to the coffin and slapped it with the flat of her hand. "That was rude, Myrddin. He's only trying to help. Leave those roses alone this time or I swear to the goddess, I will let you rot in here."

Dev touched the vines and they came back to life. This time they stayed that way.

Daniel walked over to inspect the coffin. His eyes showed no emotion as he peered down at the wizard. Almost as though compelled to, Daniel reached down and touched the top of the glass. I took a startled step back as Merlin's hand shot up as though magnetically attracted to Daniel's.

"He knows you," Stewart said with a satisfied smile.

"I've put it off long enough," Nim confessed. "He's ready. Daniel, if you'll help me get this lid off."

With very little effort, Daniel lifted the lid and set it against the wall. He pulled Excalibur from its sheath and handed it to the Lady of the Lake, who motioned Stewart forward. There was such reverence in his blue eyes I thought he might weep.

He held his hand over the wizard's mouth and allowed Nim to

use the sword to draw a thin stream of blood from his forearm. The blood dripped onto the wizard's mouth, but he didn't move.

Nim frowned, staring down for a moment before trying again. She drew more of the demon's blood down onto the wizard's mouth.

"That should have worked," she said, frustration evident in her voice.

Daniel watched the proceedings with great curiosity. "You said the wizard required something of both the Heaven and the Hell plane to rouse him."

She nodded shortly. "Yes, given the circumstances of his birth, both are necessary."

"But Excalibur is just a tool here," Daniel mused. "It isn't something he can taste. You offer him blood from the demon but nothing so sweet from the angelic side. I would hold out for something better if I was him."

Nim thought about that for a moment. "I would need an angel for what you suggest, Daniel. I don't think I'm going to find an angel from the Heaven plane to help me wake Merlin Satanspawn."

Daniel chuckled. "No, I doubt you would, but then Stewart over there isn't exactly in his purest form. His blood is mixed in this form. If that would work then I don't see why a pure angel is required. I'm a vampire, Nim. Trust me. I know what Heaven tastes like."

Daniel took my arm and offered it to Nim. I sighed and prepared for the small pain of the sword across my flesh. It made sense that I be the one offering my blood. A companion was part angel. It was why we tasted so damn good. Nim squeezed my arm gently and let a fine line trickle down. It mixed with the demon's offering on the wizard's lips.

Slowly, so slowly, the slightest bit of a gray tongue peeked out and the blood disappeared into his mouth.

The wizard's eyes flew open and I felt Daniel's arms pulling me back. He shoved me toward Dev so he could lean forward once more. Devinshea's arms held me close, but we were both trying to take a look at the wizard.

His rheumy eyes stared up and around until they zeroed in on Daniel. He held a single hand up.

"I need the waters, Your Highness." The request came out

croaked and harsh.

"The fountain at the back of the room," Nim clarified. "It will restore him, but you'll have to get him there. He can't walk."

Daniel reached down and gingerly picked up the wizard's decayed body. It would weigh nothing in his hands, but he was very careful with him. He made sure he tucked the matchstick arms inside for fear they would dangle and potentially fall off. The last thing we needed was a one-armed wizard. Walking slowly, Daniel made his way to the fountain. Lee carried over an extra torch, illuminating the back of the dungeon.

"Shall I hold you under the water, teacher?" There was a certain kindness to Daniel's voice I didn't hear often when he spoke to strangers.

"Just set me down, child," came the cracked reply. "I'll do the rest. I've waited a very long time for you."

Daniel lowered the wizard's fragile body into the water, leaning over to make sure he didn't go under. I watched the scene, wondering when Daniel had last treated anyone but me or Dev with such care. The torches were all lit now, and I could see the wizard's face contort as he felt the water on his body. He lay in the small pool for a moment before finding the strength to get to his knees. Daniel rushed forward to lend him a hand, and Myrddin managed to get to his feet. I held my breath, hoping the man didn't just fall apart.

"I'm fine now, Daniel," Myrddin said, though no one had told him Daniel's name. "Help me under the falls and then step back."

Daniel helped him back under the fountain and then something weird happened. It was like the water washed away the age. Slowly but surely as the wizard stood under the falling water he became younger, stood taller. He loosened his robes and they fell away as his flesh became young and firm. He transformed from a desiccated corpse into a muscular man. I turned to look at Nim, but she didn't seem surprised at all. She walked over to the small dresser near the coffin and pulled out a rich, velvet robe.

When I glanced back, I had to admit Myrddin Emrys was pretty damn hot. He had dark wavy hair that he pushed back behind his ears. It reached the nape of his neck. His eyes were dark—from my vantage they appeared almost black—and his face was lovely but hard, as though carved from granite. The body was rock hard, too.

"Wow," Neil whispered beside me.

"Double wow," I said because I'd just gotten a good look at his package. A large hand came over my eyes. "Dev!"

"Like you would allow me to stand around and ogle naked women," he whispered in my ear. "Nim, would you hand him that robe, please? Our queen is getting an eyeful."

I heard Daniel's laugh but when Dev finally let me look again, the wizard had stepped out of the fountain. He was robed, and the rich red color of the velvet did wonderful things for his now-perfect skin.

Myrddin's black eyes took in the room, stopping briefly on each person as he made assessments with a single look. He stopped when he reached Nim, his face contorting. "Bitch goddess."

"Nice to see you again, Myrddin," she said. "It's been a while."

He shook his head. "At least a thousand years. You tricked me."

"I had a job to do," Nim replied softly. "You always knew that."

"I loved you," he said, but it was harsh and bitter—an old regret.

Nim simply sighed. "I doubt that. It doesn't matter anymore, magician. The King of the Sword has risen and you are needed again."

Myrddin's smile seemed genuine as he turned to face Daniel. He bowed from the waist in an old gesture of respect. "Daniel Donovan. You're a very interesting king. Nimue, he isn't human."

"He's a vampire," Nim replied.

Myrddin's eyes widened. "No. Show me."

Daniel allowed his fangs to pop out. He growled a little as he let Myrddin look his fill.

Myrddin clapped his hands together. "A vampire. How interesting. I don't suppose I need to teach this one how to fight."

"No," Nim said with a little laugh. "He could teach you a thing or two, Myrddin. He's a death machine."

"Yes, I can see that now. He's older than the last one."

"Times have changed, Great One," Stewart said. "In this time, the king is considered to be young. He's only twenty-eight in human years, and he only turned eight years ago."

Myrddin smiled, showing white, even teeth. "Come forward, little demon."

Stewart ran forward eagerly. "It's my greatest pleasure to meet you."

With one hand, Myrddin patted the demon's head as though he were a harmless pet. "You're going to be troublesome, aren't you?"

"Yes, I promise," Stewart agreed. "I'll bring great chaos."

"Well, I trust you to play your part." Myrddin turned back to Daniel. "I'll need a full briefing on this time and culture and the political climate. I suspect you do not have your crown as of yet."

"I'm working on it," Daniel replied.

Myrddin nodded shortly and turned his eyes to me. "Hello, bright one."

So he could see my shine. "Hello."

"You're his queen?"

"Yep."

He glanced back at Daniel. "She's quite beautiful. She must attract every vampire she meets."

"You have no idea," Daniel said with a sigh.

Myrddin glanced around the room. "These men are your knights?"

"Two of them are bodyguards." Daniel gestured to Lee and Neil. "They protect the queen. Her glow causes her no small amount of vampire attention. I've found the werewolves can be very persuasive in keeping unwanted men from my wife."

"Werewolves, interesting choice," the wizard said, studying Lee, who glared right back at him. Myrddin shook his head and turned toward Zack. "And this one?"

"That's my servant, Zachary Owens." Daniel introduced the wolf. "He's blood oathed to me and beyond reproach."

Myrddin seemed to like that idea. "Yes, that was an excellent idea. I'm beginning to see the definite advantage to your vampire state, Daniel. But tell me, who is the dark one? He looks Fae to me."

"I'm Devinshea Quinn," Dev said with a friendly smile. "You have a good eye. I'm the High Priest of the Unseelie."

"And who are you in regards to the king?" Myrddin said in a voice that told me he couldn't give a crap about a Fae priest.

"I'm Daniel's partner," Dev replied.

"Think of him as Daniel's advisor," Nim said, seeking a reference to make the wizard understand the relationship. "Of all the men, he's closest to the king."

"I thought so. He has that look about him," Myrddin said, his voice hard. His gaze stole past me and I knew I was about to get accused of something. "My first piece of advice to you, Daniel, is to execute the faery immediately. He will say he is your beloved friend and advisor, but it's all a ruse. He's fucking the queen behind your back. I can see the lust between them even as they stand there. Kill him now before he ruins everything because he can't keep his cock in his pants. The queen will just have to get over it."

I opened my mouth to protest but Dev was already stepping forward. "I do not fuck Zoey behind Daniel's back. I do it to his front. He would be upset if I tried sneaking around. He enjoys watching very much. Now, I will admit, often I fuck our queen behind her back. I find the position infinitely versatile."

"Dev," I hissed. "Too much information."

Dev looked gorgeously innocent as he leaned over and kissed my nose. "Darling, he did accuse me of adultery with my wife."

Daniel shook his head with a rueful sigh. "You'll have to excuse my partner. He's Fae and they love to talk about sex. He'll describe our last lovemaking session if you let him. Don't you dare, Dev. I'm not going to execute my partner, teacher. We share a life and our wife."

Myrddin's eyes flew to Nim. "I told you it was the way of the future."

"They're not the norm in this world," Nim corrected him. "And perhaps if you looked as good as you do now I would have considered taking your proposal to Arawn."

"You know I take the form that is needed," Myrddin said with a wave of his hand. "Well, I'm glad to know the queen, at least, is an open-minded lass. If the three of you can enjoy each other without jealousy then I will agree to the relationship."

"I'm so glad to hear that." No small amount of sarcasm flavored Daniel's voice.

Myrddin rubbed his hands together, an eager gleam in his eyes. "Now, Your Highness, how about I fix that heart of yours?"

CHAPTER TWENTY-THREE

"What's going on?" I asked, slightly freaked out by the events of the last hour. I stood by Neil, who'd kept a close eye on Myrddin and Nim.

"They keep arguing about something," Neil replied. "Nim doesn't think this is a good idea, but the hot wizard guy thinks we have to do it."

I turned around and found Daniel, who sat quietly apart from everyone. Dev had left the castle after Myrddin had told him which plants he needed. Dev would know where to look and if the plants weren't up to snuff, after a minute or two with a fertility god, they would be.

"Has anyone mentioned how he's going to do it?" I asked, hoping Neil's hearing was back at full speed.

Lee came up behind me quietly. "I heard something about a stasis chamber and the need for a balance."

"What's that supposed to mean?"

Lee shrugged. "I don't know, darlin', but I don't like any of it." He looked around the room, his eyes settling on Daniel. "I really don't like how damn quiet Donovan's gotten. He should go into this believing he'll come out. I don't think he does."

Daniel had been sitting in the corner ever since Nim and Myrddin began their never-ending argument over how to fix his heart. "Did he say something to you?"

Lee stared me straight in the eye because aside from keeping multiple murders from me, he never lied. "He wanted to make sure I knew how to get to the Unseelie *sithein*. If anything goes wrong, that's where he wants you. The minute I think something's up, I've been ordered to get you and Devinshea out of here and find a way to get to Scotland. I'm supposed to leave Daniel behind and not look back."

"Well, you might be able to handle me, but I doubt you can handle me and Devinshea," I huffed, pissed at the thought Daniel wouldn't allow us to help him. "The minute Dev knows Daniel is in serious trouble, he'll fight to get to him."

"I've been given permission to knock the both of you out if I have to," Lee said and I knew from the look in his eyes that he would do it. "You know I only take orders from you, but I'm with Daniel on this. Neil and I will get you where we need to go. I just wanted you to know."

"Neil won't do it."

"Yes, I will," Neil said quietly.

I whirled on him. "You don't have to obey Daniel, and you don't have to obey Lee."

"And I sure as hell don't have to obey you," Neil shot back. "I have to do what's right for my best friend in the world and her husbands. If it goes south here, we're cutting and running. This is the end game, Z. Daniel wins or he dies. Do you think he can even fight if there's no possibility of you getting out alive? I love you, Z, but damn, sometimes you can be his worst enemy."

"What's that supposed to mean?" My question came out as a shocked gasp. Neil had never turned on me, but that's what it felt like now.

Icy blue eyes regarded me. "It means that no one else around here will give you the swift kick in the pants you need. Lee is too loyal. Dev and Danny are too much in love, and Zack is too submissive. Maybe if Sarah was around she could have this conversation with you and then you wouldn't be so pissed with me, but she had to go get knocked up, so that leaves me."

I gave him the floor with a bitter frown. "Well, don't hold back, Neil. If I need a kick in the ass you should give it to me."

Neil's hands clenched at his sides. "He's over there waiting patiently to find out what horrific way they're going to use to pull a bomb off his heart, Zoey. He knows there's a giant possibility that he's going to die and you're going to be at the mercy of everything he's been fighting against, but are you over there working with him? No. You're standing here plotting against him just like you always do. You're so stubborn."

"I'm not working against him," I denied vehemently. "I'm trying to keep us together."

"But he needs to know if the worst happens, that you'll be all right," Neil insisted. "God, Dev understands, at least. When we were out there with the Order, do you think Dev wanted to leave Daniel? He didn't but he knew what Daniel really needed was to know that the people he loved were safe so he sucked it up. You think what you're doing is noble but, Z, it fucking kills him. How can he concentrate on anything if he's always worried about what you're doing? It will get him killed in the end and you aren't going to be able to live with that."

"I won't hide in a corner somewhere when I could help him," I said firmly, but some of what Neil was saying was finding little cracks in my armor. I didn't like the feeling one bit.

"I'm not telling you not to fight for him." Neil sighed, his anger spent. "I'm just asking you to be reasonable. Let him go into this surgery, or whatever the hell this is, believing you'll do what he needs you to do, even if you have to lie to him. Let him concentrate on surviving instead of seeing what will happen when he dies and you do something insane to try to avenge him. He would rather you were happy with Dev somewhere. It's all he wants. It's why he does everything he's done. It was all so you could be safe and happy. Give him this."

I was crying by the time Neil finished and feeling no small bit of shame. I never meant to fight Daniel. I meant to fight for him, for us. Neil stared at me intently, as if waiting for me to explode, but I wasn't mad at Neil. I was mad as hell at me. I'd always thought Daniel didn't trust me to be strong enough to sacrifice for him and he was right. I wasn't even willing to sacrifice this for him. He had all the responsibilities of a king, all the trouble and pain that went along with the weight of the world on his shoulders, but his own wife wouldn't sacrifice an inch of her pride for his peace of mind.

I leaned over and kissed Neil on the cheek before making my way to where Daniel sat patiently. He looked up and I saw the fear on his face before it gave way to a tired acceptance of what he thought was about to happen. He thought I was coming over to give him hell about what Lee had just told me. His jaw firmed and he got ready to play the bad guy because that was the position I put him in over and over again.

I sank down onto his lap and rested my head into the curve of his neck. He'd taken off both his jackets and his ruined T-shirt to let Myrddin take a look at his chest, and he was sitting around in jeans and his boots. I let my hands find his cool skin and my cheek press against the swell of his shoulder muscles.

"Z?" Daniel's hands curled around my waist, pulling me in close.

"I'm scared, Danny." If he was comforting me, helping me face my fear, he didn't have to dwell on his.

"Baby," he sighed into my ear. His hand cupped my cheek and he kissed me sweetly. "It's going to be all right."

"We don't know that." For the first time in a long time, I just let my fear hang out. Too often I shoved the fear down and let anger be my primary emotion but Neil was right. There wasn't a place for anger here.

"We have to believe it, Z," Daniel said firmly and I could sense a shift in him. He already seemed stronger, more confident. He always rose to the occasion when I needed him to. He'd never once let me down.

"Lee told me what you want us to do," I said quietly.

His whole body tensed beneath me. "Zoey…"

"I'm not fighting you, Danny," I said. "I just want you to be sure when you give the order. I'll go and I won't fight Lee or Neil. I promise. You just promise me that you won't give that order unless you're damn sure."

"Are you serious?"

"Yes, Danny." I couldn't blame him for being suspicious. I'd pulled some crazy stunts in my time. "I promise you, if things go to hell, I'll run as fast as Lee's legs will take us and I'll hide in the *sithein*. I'll understand that if there is any way for you to survive that you'll come for us. If you don't come for us…"

"Then I didn't survive and you can't come back, Z," Daniel finished for me.

"My dad…" I started because I couldn't stand the thought of my dad not knowing what happened to me. He would go looking and he would get in trouble.

"What do you think we talked about that night we called Stewart?" Daniel asked. "We talked about what we would do. He knows if I don't contact him that things have gone bad. Dev drew out a map to the *sithein*. He'll be welcome and so will Sarah and Felix, if they choose to come. I think they will because if I don't win and they have a girl…"

"Given Felix's DNA, she'll almost surely be a companion." A deep fear lodged in the pit of my stomach. Sarah was known in the vampire world. Someone would be watching. I couldn't stand the thought of her losing her baby girl to a vampire. I was glad that, according to Oliver Day, Felix's brother and my guardian angel, I was supposed to have twin boys. I didn't want to worry about my daughter being sold at auction. It struck me then that if Daniel didn't win, I really wouldn't be able to come home. I would live in a *sithein* and raise my family there. I would live and grow old and die there.

"Z," Daniel said and I could feel his heart ache. "I wish I'd never started this. I should have done what Marini wanted me to do. I should have taken you as my companion and been his *Nex Apparatus*. I could have hidden you from him. As long as I did what he wanted me to do, he would have left you alone."

"Danny, you can't think like that," I replied, trying to banish the pain I felt at never going home again. "He was never going to let you be. He would always have found a way to get a look at me, and once he did, his path would have been set. Don't look back. We just move forward."

"And we're having this morbid conversation because?" Dev asked, looking down at us. He carried a sack filled to the brim with all sorts of greenery.

"You know why, Dev," Daniel replied, hugging me tightly.

Dev's expression tightened. "You cannot go into this thinking you're going to die. You promised me you would be positive. Walking into this with a negative outlook is like asking for it to fail."

"I'm not negative," Daniel replied somewhat defensively. "I'm just realistic. There's a little bomb on my heart. It's not going to be easy."

Dev let the bag drop. "Have you considered that up until now, fate has given you everything you need to win this fight and for the most part all you've been required to do is accept it?"

"What are you talking about?" Daniel asked, his brows in a confused *V*.

Dev was ready with an explanation. "You needed a companion. Essentially Zoey turned you. She was your first real blood and she imprinted on you in a way that Marini couldn't overcome. You needed a patron, someone on the Council who could teach you how to blend in and behave so you didn't get caught immediately, and there was Marcus just waiting for you. You needed to be able to daywalk and suddenly I show up with the perfect magic to give you the strength. You needed an army and the Order of Galahad knelt down before you and pledged their loyalty. Now you need someone who can magically fix your heart and freaking Merlin wakes up at your command."

I was smiling when Dev finished his somewhat righteous speech. "He has a point, Danny."

"But what do you do?" Dev threw his hands up in the air in disgust. "You brood. You wait for the worst to happen. Just this once I want you to expect that the universe is going to take care of us as it always has."

"Because you never have doubts, Dev," Daniel challenged.

"Not in this, I don't," my faery prince shot back. "I believe with all of my being that Daniel Donovan will win the day. I believe you will be king and you will right the wrongs the Council has visited on the world. I know it deep down, and you can't convince me otherwise. I will promise you that if it comes to it, I'll take our wife and keep her safe, but it's an easy thing to swear because I know I won't have to."

Myrddin stood above, looking down on the three of us with great curiosity. His dark eyes were filled with anticipation. "Listen to your advisor, Your Highness. He's giving you sound advice. Perhaps he's not what I first thought. He'll make an excellent balance. It's obvious he cares deeply for you."

"And what is this balance you seek, wizard?" Bris's voice startled me, for the change was almost instantaneous.

Myrddin was surprised as well. His eyes narrowed as he studied my faery prince. "No one told me the Fae was an ascended god."

"Perhaps you did not need to know," Bris replied. "Now, tell me what you wish from my host and I will tell you if I'll permit it. He cares very deeply for Daniel and would do anything to see him and our goddess safe and happy. I won't allow you to use him to your own ends."

Myrddin leaned negligently against the wall, his lips curving into a secret little smile. "These are not my ends. I serve the king as I always have. There's only one way I know to fix the king's heart trouble. If you have another idea, I would be more than willing to listen. Are you a god of healing, Fae?"

Bris frowned. "I'm a fertility god."

Myrddin nodded, and I felt a sense of deep satisfaction from him. "Then, Fae, when I need someone to impregnate the queen, I assure you, I will think of you. Perhaps not first. She's very attractive and it's not as though the king can handle the task himself, but your name will be on the list."

Bris was suddenly in the wizard's space. I could see the barely controlled rage in his eyes. "She's mine. Wizard or no, if you so much as think of touching her it will be your heart in trouble. I will pluck it from your body and think nothing of the loss. She's my goddess and no other shall have her."

"Interesting," Myrddin murmured. He sent Daniel a pointed look. "I find it interesting that he uses the word mine instead of ours. The host would have said she is ours. She's your goddess? I assumed she was Daniel's companion first. I obviously have the timeline confused. If her loyalties are in question then perhaps the king should reconsider her place."

"You overstep your bounds, demon," Bris hissed, stepping forward.

I scrambled off Daniel's lap. Myrddin seemed entirely entertained by the fertility god's show of anger. He was grinning and there was a certain mad glee in his dark eyes. He would enjoy the chaos of a fight. He'd been waiting for it. I got between Bris and the wizard. I wasn't happy to see Stewart approach and take a place at the wizard's side.

He watched the dark man with a worshipful gaze. "I love to watch a master at his work."

"Please calm down." I tried to ignore the demon and focused my attention on Bris. The fertility god's power might seem soft, but I'd watched him take out an army of red caps without breaking a sweat. I didn't want to think about what he could do to the wizard if he lost control of his temper.

"You cannot trust this demonspawn, my goddess," Bris insisted, his face stubborn. He pointed at his rival as he accused him. "He's infamous. Daniel shouldn't be allowed to come under his influence. I won't allow him to use you."

Myrddin watched the fertility god and then turned to Daniel. "Is the fertility deity in charge, Your Highness?"

Stewart shook his head. "It would seem he thinks so."

Myrddin pursed his lips thoughtfully. "He seems to believe he owns your companion. Does he have authority over the queen? Is he the one I should look to in regards to her?"

He made the question sound so innocent, but I could see Daniel's face harden and his lips moved slightly. If you didn't know what to look for you would miss it, but I knew his fangs had popped out, a sure sign of his temper rising, and I didn't think he was getting pissed off at the wizard.

"She's my wife," Daniel all but snarled. He was emotional to start with. The last thing he needed was someone to challenge his rights to his companion. It was an instinct for a vampire, like waving a red flag at a bull. Daniel would charge. Myrddin knew exactly which buttons to push and seemed more than happy to push them.

"It seems to me this fertility god claims much which should be yours," Myrddin said quietly, as though merely concerned. "He takes over your advisor's body when the whim takes him. He claims rights to your companion. Perhaps you're a different kind of vampire. I thought you would be possessive of those whose bed and blood you shared. I commend you on your forward thinking, Your Highness. I will need to rethink things, though. I had not expected a submissive king. It gives me different challenges."

I felt Daniel's roar before I heard it. "I submit to no one. She is mine. He is mine. I will kill anyone who thinks to take them from me."

The chair Daniel had been sitting in sort of exploded when he brought his fist down.

"Myrddin, what are you trying to do?" Nim walked back in from the small kitchen. She'd been preparing some sort of concoction to aid in the wizard's plan to fix Daniel. Her violet eyes narrowed suspiciously as she took in the scene.

"I'm attempting to discover who is truly in charge in the king's household," Myrddin explained simply. "I thought it would be the king, but it appears his queen belongs to an ancient god."

"She is mine!" Daniel growled and he abruptly pulled me from Bris.

"Stop that!" I shouted at the wizard. "You're the one causing trouble. Bris was only trying to protect his host."

"Daniel," Myrddin said calmly. He ignored me and he sounded so much like the voice of reason. "The fertility god may seem helpful, but he will crowd you out. He'll attempt to take your place in the queen's heart. He'll say he's interested in his host, but it's all a ruse. He merely needs a proper body to get close to his goddess. His magic doesn't work without a proper goddess from which it can flow. That goddess would be either a fertility goddess or something close to it."

"What's close to it?" I asked, knowing I wouldn't like the answer.

Myrddin smiled. It was the kind of smile you use on a naïve child when you feel a little sorry for them. "A companion, my dear. You would be almost useless when it comes to magic on your own, but that glow would cause his magic to flow and flow. Did you think vampires are the only ones who could see it? Everyone wants to feed off you. Some just have different ways of doing it."

I felt my face fall as I turned to see if this was the truth. Bris frowned as he reached for my hands, his voice sweet and cajoling.

"Goddess, is this so surprising? What does it matter why I'm attracted to you? Devinshea's love for you is just as appealing as your glow. I've grown to love both you and Daniel."

Daniel jerked me away from him. "Don't touch her."

Bris's eyes widened. "Daniel, he's pushing you. He's trying to bring out your beast to sow discord between us. He realized he couldn't get rid of Devinshea. You're far too close, and so he's attempting to do the same thing by turning you against me. He wishes to be the only voice in your ear. He's threatened by me and my host. Don't allow him to shove a wedge between us. I've been nothing but loyal to you and he has not proven his worth. He's only proven the he's part demon and understands how to get his way."

"Bris, it might help if you let Dev come back." I needed Dev to come and smooth over this argument. "Let Dev come back so Daniel can be assured his precious blood is here and his."

"This is a mistake, my goddess. The demonspawn will cause trouble between the three of you. We'll speak on it later."

"Daniel," Dev said suddenly, his eyes normal again.

Daniel didn't have to say a word for Dev to know he was riding that volcanic anger of his.

"Don't you dare, Daniel." Dev walked straight up to the pissed-off vampire. I had watched him do this many times. He had no fear when it came to Daniel. "We made the decision together. We decided it would be best for all of us if I attempted to ascend. You knew that meant bringing a fertility deity into our lives and our bed. We did it to make me strong for the fight. You don't get to play the innocent, wounded party now that someone we've known for five minutes has passed judgment on our lives. Bris has done nothing but defend our wife and give up his corporeal being to save your life. If your jealousy and possessiveness are worth more to you than our friendship then you should tell me now. Am I your advisor, your partner, or is it this man?"

I watched the anger recede like a balloon deflating. Daniel put both hands on Dev's shoulders and looked him deeply in the eyes. "You know it's you. You've never steered me wrong, friend."

"And I never will." Dev leaned forward, getting close to Danny. "This is my life as well, Daniel. I have as much at stake in seeing this done well as you do."

"Are you done with this test?" I asked Myrddin and I could hear the shortness in my voice. I didn't like the way he'd just played with us.

Myrddin's big hand came over his chest as though he was hurt I would accuse him of something so heinous. "Your Highness, I was merely confused. You'll have to excuse me. It has been many years since I was in the company of other humans. Perhaps I've lost my tact. I have a job to do and I intend to do it well. I'm the king's loyal servant. I apologize profusely if I did or said anything that would cause you harm."

I doubted seriously that the wizard's sleep had caused him to lose a single step. He knew what he was doing and he'd enjoyed it. Stewart was smiling like he'd just enjoyed a really well-produced play and when I thought about it, he had. We'd merely been the unwillingly players.

"It's my fault, teacher," Daniel said. "I try very hard to keep my temper in check. It's always there under the surface. I apologize for letting it boil over."

I didn't like the way Daniel acted around Myrddin. Since that moment when Daniel had reached down to touch the glass coffin and the wizard had stirred, it seemed to me that Daniel and Myrddin had formed some strange connection. I knew my Daniel. He should be angry at the wizard for attempting to come between us, but he behaved in an almost deferential fashion, as a son might look to a father. I didn't like it one bit.

"No need, Daniel," Myrddin said with an affectionate smile. "You never need to apologize to me. I'm just grateful that Devinshea is so good at talking you down. You boys make a very good team."

Dev turned his eyes toward the wizard. "You should remember that in the future. We are always a team."

Myrddin clapped his hands together. "Now, it's time to put that team to work. Daniel, you'll need a balance to keep you alive during this piece of magic I intend to work."

"A balance?" Daniel asked.

Nim's soft voice answered. "Think of it as a machine to keep you alive. It's a form of life support."

"All right. Why Dev? Zack is my servant. He has my blood and he's very strong. This seems like the perfect job for him."

"I can do it," Zack piped up, sitting a little straighter in his chair. "Tell me what to do."

Myrddin considered it for a moment. "No, wolf. While I don't doubt your loyalties, I still think the faery will be a better balance. Were he not here I would certainly use you, but Devinshea is already Daniel's true balance and he's the perfect candidate. While you care for your master, Devinshea truly loves him in a way you cannot."

"What about me?" I asked. I loved Daniel.

"No," Dev and Daniel managed in perfect accord.

The wizard shook his head. "Your Highness, it's sweet that you would do this for your king, but I doubt you would survive the pain."

"I'm stronger than you think I am," I shot back. Daniel could handle it. I didn't doubt that, but Dev didn't like pain. He could be such a baby about a stubbed toe or a paper cut.

Dev whirled me around and I found myself being hauled to the far end of the room. When he thought we were far enough from prying ears, he turned on me.

"You may be stronger than everyone thinks, but you also may be pregnant," Dev said under his breath. "Even now the conception of our children may be occurring deep inside your body. Daniel and I would never risk you nor would we risk our possible children. Please do not fight us on this."

I was backed into a corner and had no choice but to numbly nod my head. "All right."

Dev pulled me into his arms, and his fingers tangled in my hair. "I love you, Zoey. It's going to be fine."

"It is," Daniel said, taking his place at Dev's side. "Dev and I will get through this. My heart will be healed. We have our army. Once our allies are in place, we'll take down Marini and then we'll go home and raise our kids. You'll see, Z. It's gonna be fine. Besides, did you think about the connection we have? It can't be you, baby. You won't work as life support for me. My body would sense your body's weakness and try to compensate."

That would be a disaster if it really worked that way. I wasn't so sure. The Fae healer had told me it only worked over long periods of time. If I was suddenly killed, Daniel wouldn't necessarily die. It was a long-term illness that would claim us both. Daniel's blood could keep Dev and me alive for a long while and we wouldn't age on the outside but inside, while it might be slower than a normal human, our organs would age. Old age would claim me in the end, and Daniel would go down with me.

"You trust this man to help us?" I wasn't sure I did and I was risking them both.

"I do, baby," Daniel promised. "I can't tell you why, but I know he's on my side. It's going to work out. You'll see."

I let them hold me for the longest time, but even when I shut my eyes I could see the wizard. He had plans for us. Daniel might survive the surgery, but I had no doubt that none of this was going to be easy.

CHAPTER TWENTY-FOUR

"What is this place?" I asked as we were shown to a small space off the great room on the ground floor. Nim had thrown open the doors and light spilled in, illuminating the odd knickknacks that populated the floor-to-ceiling bookshelves.

"It's a workshop." Nim was busy chopping and cooking the plants Dev had gathered. She stood at a wooden table looking perfectly competent. "I brought all of Myrddin's books and supplies from Camelot so they would be here for him. I guess we're going to have to figure out what to do with all of this stuff now that he'll be leaving the prison. I guess I should have all of it moved to the club. Dev owns the whole building. He can probably come up with the space."

I didn't necessarily think Myrddin would leave the prison. "Is that such a good idea, Nim? I mean, once we get Danny's heart problem figured out, shouldn't old Merlin there go back to his napping? We won't have much use for him. Danny doesn't need a teacher."

Nim's head fell back and her laughter echoed through the small room. When she finished, she tossed some herbs in a pot and lit a fire under it before pouring some water in. "Do you really believe Daniel is prepared to lead the entire supernatural world? Eight years ago,

Daniel Donovan was a college student getting ready for a life in mid-level corporate America. He only went to college because he needed a decent job to take care of his girlfriend and buy comic books. If twenty-one-year-old Daniel had his way, he would have made a living playing online games. He had no ambition and no drive beyond making you happy. You think he's ready to deal with the ramifications of changing the entire supernatural world?"

Put that way it did sound a little crazy, but we had an ace in our pocket. "Devinshea will help him. He understands politics and the other races listen to him." The Fae tended to be welcome wherever they went. Dev opened doors for Danny that he wouldn't have been able to knock on without him.

"But Devinshea is twenty-nine years old, Zoey. He's very young for a Fae." Nim turned slightly so she could see me. Her hands never stopped at their task. "He might have been able to get you here, but things aren't going to go as smoothly as you imagine. Do you think all the vampires are just going to fall in line? Do you think they'll follow the new king's dictates on things like slaves and companion auctions? Devinshea has never dealt with any of these things before. Besides, I have a feeling Dev will want to nest a little. You'll have to forgive me. I'm not trying to pry, but you two seem a little baby crazy."

I shrugged, not wanting to go into it. "Lots of people have a family and a career."

"The fact that you can think the analogy fits just shows me you have no idea how difficult this is going to be," Nim said with a shake of her head. "You're trying to change thousands of years of behavior and it won't go down without a fight. Myrddin has been here before. You and Dev should concentrate on making Daniel happy. Give him babies and a nice place to come home to. Let Myrddin do his job and make him a king."

"You know, I didn't expect that from you, Nim. Maybe it was too much to hope that you would follow the girl code but damn, I wasn't expecting a 'stay home and fuck Daniel because that's your job' lecture."

Nim frowned. "I didn't say that, Zoey."

"Oh, I think you did," I replied shortly. "I might not be an immortal with a high-profile gig, but you know Dev and I have done a damn fine job with Danny so far. We've gotten him to this point and we haven't needed you. If you think I intend to fade into the background and let Myrddin take over then you should think again. I don't know what Guinevere was really like, but she must have been pretty damn pathetic if she let Myrddin take over her marriage."

"Myrddin introduced her to Lancelot," Nim said with an odd smile.

"I'm sure he was thrilled when they got together."

Nim shrugged. "It must have made his job infinitely easier to not have to deal with the queen."

"I'm not Guinevere. I love Daniel, and I won't let some wizard take him from me. I love Dev and I won't let his contribution be shoved to the side. I kind of love me, too, and I won't let myself be marginalized because you immortal pricks haven't joined the feminist movement. So you and that wizard should get ready, because you haven't met a queen like me. Now I want you to tell me what the hell happened up there, Nim."

I couldn't get that fight out of my head. Myrddin had provoked the whole thing, but I didn't understand why Daniel had reacted the way he had. Danny had anger issues, but he usually had better control. I didn't like how easily Myrddin had pitted my men against each other.

"What do you mean?"

"I mean Danny was at Dev's throat."

She waved it off. "He was angry with Bris, not Devinshea."

I felt my eyes narrow. "Myrddin played him like a damn guitar."

Nim sighed and finally gave me her full attention. "How do I explain this? Myrddin and Daniel are connected in a way even I don't fully understand. It's always been this way between Myrddin and the king who wields the sword."

I didn't like the sound of that. "So he's doing some kind of mind control on Danny?"

"Nothing of the sort. He's simply very charismatic. Daniel has free will. I think you'll simply find Myrddin is very influential and there's nothing wrong with that. He knows more about power and ruling a kingdom than anyone walking the planes. He doesn't abuse the power."

She hadn't seen the whole fight. "I have to disagree with you on that one."

"Zoey, you might not always like his methods, but he does have to very quickly figure out the relationships within the group," Nim explained. "I fear the fact that Dev is an ascended god threw him for a loop. You'll see as time passes that Daniel will get used to having a mentor. After a while Arthur stopped taking Myrddin's counsel and that was when things went bad."

"I don't like a bit of this."

"It's necessary, Your Highness," Nim said in all seriousness. "I can promise you that if it comes to it, I will handle the situation. I truly will. I believe that once Myrddin settles down, you'll see that everything is fine."

"I'll handle the fucker if I have to."

Nim's smile was vibrant. "I don't doubt it. You're right. I think you will be an entirely different queen. You're going to give Myrddin hell, aren't you?"

"It depends on how he treats me and Dev and Danny," I replied.

"Then I shall have to treat you well, my queen." Myrddin entered the room, stopping to greet me with a small bow. "I find myself apologizing to everyone today. I just spent some time with Devinshea making certain he understood I was only attempting to feel out the relationship between Daniel and the god living inside him."

I seriously doubted that. "Yes, that's what you were doing. You weren't testing Daniel in any way."

I could see in Myrddin's eyes that he was taking my measure. "Your Highness, if I've offended you, I apologize. I need to understand this world. It seems to have changed so much since the last time I was a meaningful part of something. Women have a different place than they did before. I'm far behind the times, and I must ask you to make allowances."

"Z, come on, baby," Daniel said as he walked in behind Myrddin. "I really want the two of you to get along."

It took everything I had not to roll my eyes at Daniel's eager statement. He really did want us to get along and that bothered me. He didn't know this guy. My husband should have been much more wary. I had to hope that Nim was right and Daniel wouldn't always feel Myrddin's influence.

"Zoey, he comes from an entirely different time," Daniel explained. "You can't expect him to understand how a modern marriage works. He'll get used to treating you as a woman expects to be treated these days."

"Yes, we'll have to make sure the wizard properly integrates into modern times," Dev said, a set to his lips.

Daniel didn't seem to notice how stiff Dev seemed. "We've already made plans. Dev is going to make sure he has a proper place to stay and that will help him integrate into this time. There's no place quite like Ether to introduce Myrddin to the modern supernatural world."

"Bris didn't have any trouble." No matter what that wizard said, I still counted Bris as one of the good guys. He wasn't going to change my mind so easily.

The rest of the group crowded into the small room.

"Bris has all of Dev's memories to call upon," Daniel pointed out.

"I am alone in the world," Myrddin said and again I felt the need to stop my eyes from rolling.

I wanted to argue. I wanted to point out that maybe we should listen to Bris, despite the fact that he may have hidden certain key facts from me. I had to go by his actions and they were above reproach. He defended me at every opportunity. He'd given up his host to save Daniel. If he was just trying to get to me, it would have been easier to do if he just let Daniel die. I wouldn't have known he could help. I would have let him comfort me while I mourned. I would have drowned myself in his love and sympathy. He hurt his own cause by helping my husband. I had to believe he had our best interests at heart in this case as well. If he told me to think twice before trusting the wizard then I would. But it was obvious Daniel wasn't willing to listen to me now.

"I'm sure you'll find living in Dallas very amusing," I murmured.

The wizard's smile was infectious. "I'm looking forward to it. It sounds like a very interesting place, and I look forward to getting to know our little court. But first, we should fix your husband's heart trouble. Nimue, have you finished the purgative?"

"Everything is ready," she said, taking a deep breath. "I have all the before and after elixirs prepared. I also prepared the bed for Daniel and a recovery room, though he'll be much more comfortable if we get him back to civilization as soon as possible."

"Why? Daniel heals very quickly." The idea of Danny struggling physically startled me. It wasn't something I'd had to worry about since his turn. He'd never had so much as a cold. He'd been weak during my first pregnancy due to our connection, but other than that, anytime he was injured all he had required was blood to be back to fighting strength very quickly.

"This isn't a traditional surgery, Zoey. This is a whole lot of magic to deal with, and it's going to make Daniel very ill. He's going to be weak for a while," Nim explained, making my stomach churn. I didn't like to think about a weak Daniel.

"How long?" Daniel asked, his voice tight.

Myrddin waved off the worry. "You'll need a week or two to recover, Your Highness. A month at the most. That's all. When you do recover, your heart will be as strong as it ever was."

"We'll consider it a small vacation, Dan," Dev said reassuringly. He seemed to let go of the tension from before. "We'll move into the Order's headquarters where we'll be perfectly safe. Justin and the others will join us there. I talked to Justin before we came here and he's bringing along your emergency supply of blood so you can gorge on companion blood. That should quicken the process. We need time for our allies to gather anyway. It won't hold us back. It will give us time to figure out exactly how we should use our forces."

I saw Danny and Dev exchange a brief nod and knew what they were thinking. It would give them time to figure out if I was pregnant. If I was then I would be sitting out the last battle. I wouldn't argue with them. I didn't want to endanger our babies any more than they did. My reckless days were coming to an end.

"All right," Daniel agreed. "Where do you need us?"

"Daniel, if you would take your place on the table." Myrddin nodded toward the narrow but long table Nim had placed on the raised circle in the center of the room. I could see symbols painted on the circle and the matching ones on the ceiling. The circles were perfectly in line. "Unfortunately, Devinshea, I need you to take the purgative."

Dev sighed as Nim passed him the small metal cup. He took a sniff, his nose wrinkling. "I suppose it does what the name implies."

Nim nodded and handed him a bucket. "You're going to need it. There's a small room right over there, if you'd like some privacy."

He stopped in front of me, pulling me close. "Everything is going to be fine, Zoey. We'll fix Daniel's heart and then we'll figure out where to go from there."

His eyes met mine and I knew he wasn't going to allow the wizard to pull us apart. He would fight to keep Daniel. He kissed my forehead.

Dev already looked a little green as he walked into the room. I tried to follow because I could at least rub his back or put a cold rag on his neck, but he didn't want any help. When he came back after what seemed like the longest time, he was shaky and his skin had turned a pale white. He had discarded his shirt and shoes.

"I believe I have sufficiently purged," he stated quietly.

Nim handed him a second cup. "For strength."

"Because you've just taken all of mine," Dev replied sarcastically. He sniffed this one as well. "Do you make anything that tastes good, Nim?"

She thought about it for a moment. "I make a mean piña colada."

Dev growled but downed the entire drink. I reached up and held his hand. After a moment he seemed steadier. "I'm ready."

I was glad Dev was ready because I wasn't. I followed him, his hand squeezing mine as we made our way to the platform. I walked onto it with him. Daniel lay on his back, but he smiled up as I came into view.

"Hey, baby." Daniel took my other hand and placed it over his heart. "It's going to be fine, Z. I love you."

I leaned down and pressed my lips to his, fighting back tears the whole time. "It better be."

I got back up and kissed Dev while he made me the same promise.

"Your Highness, it's time," Myrddin said quietly and I could almost believe he cared about us.

He held his hand out to help me down. I touched them both one last time before allowing the wizard to lead me away.

Lee, Neil, and Zack were crowded together.

"Lee," I heard Dev say, "if anything goes wrong…"

"I know what to do, Dev," Lee replied.

"Even if it's both of us?"

"Especially if that happens," Lee promised. "She'll be fine. I'll make sure of it. We'll disappear and no one will ever find us."

Dev nodded and then Myrddin was staring at me. "I apologize, but this is too many people. Could we please bring it down to two? I understand that you need to be here and I'm willing to accommodate you."

"Zack will stay as well," I said, much to Neil and Lee's surprise. "You won't be able to get him away."

"No, you won't," Zack said stubbornly.

Of the three wolves, Zack was the only one who truly loved the men on that table. Lee tolerated them. Neil was their friend, but Zack had a true connection. I wasn't about to toss him out because Neil would be better comfort for me.

"Excellent," Myrddin said. "I was going to suggest the same thing."

I felt Lee press something cold into my hand. One of his semi-automatic pistols. I palmed it and liked the weight in my hand. I shoved it in the back of my jeans and pulled my shirt over it. He nodded as he left, and Neil made me promise to get him as soon as it was over.

Then there was nothing left to do except get to it. My stomach turned over as the wizard and Nim made their final preparations.

"Devinshea, you must keep your hands on Daniel," Myrddin instructed Dev, who immediately pressed his palms on Daniel's shoulders. "No matter what happens, you must stay in contact with the king. Do you understand?"

Dev kept his hands on Daniel's shoulders. "I understand. I won't fail."

"No matter what," Myrddin warned. "If you let go, even for a moment, he will die."

"I will not let go." Dev's green eyes met mine and made me a promise. He would never let go. He would die before he failed.

"Where do you want me?" Nim asked.

Myrddin pointed to the other side of the circle. "You're out of practice, Nimue. Are you sure you can handle this?"

Nim's violet eyes flared. "I can handle anything you throw at me, wizard. Don't forget who won the last fight we had."

"I will never forget that, Nimue," the wizard promised, his voice silky and smooth. "Then we begin."

Simultaneously, both Nim and Myrddin threw their arms out as though they could embrace the circles, and I felt a strange wave of energy roll across me. Zack was suddenly at my back, his hands coming up on my shoulders. They were there for comfort but also to pull me back at the first sign of any danger. With Lee gone, Zack would consider me his first priority, even above Daniel. My safety would be paramount in his master's mind, so Zack would make that his job. There was a loud hum and then a crackle in the air as a long tube of blue light seemed to advance from the bottom of the circle. It made its way slowly up toward the top, like water filling up a cylinder.

Myrddin was murmuring something, but I didn't recognize the language. It wasn't Latin. I suspected it was older than that. This was magic like I had never seen before. It filled the room and seemed to be searching for something. It flowed from the wizard and I could feel it move about like a living thing, seeking a place to strike. Zack pulled me back against his chest when I felt the tendrils brush against us. There was a tingle where it touched me, but it quickly realized I was not what it was looking for and moved on.

There was a crack and a pulse as that magic found what it wanted. It hit Nim with impressive force and I saw her stagger a bit on the impact. She breathed through what looked like no small amount of pain and her violet eyes went a deep purple as Myrddin's magic invaded her body. The blue tube of light shot up the rest of the way to the ceiling and there was a sucking sound, like it had sealed itself off.

I suddenly heard the sound of rival thuds. One was quicker than the other but both kept a steady beat.

"Excellent. The stasis chamber is well established. I believe

Nimue can hold it on her own." Myrddin turned to us, his eyes sparkling with excitement. He reminded me of a child with a new toy. He walked to the basin and washed his hands carefully, like a surgeon. When he returned, he carried a tray that he placed on a table next to the stasis chamber.

"So this stasis chamber will help Dev keep Daniel alive?" My voice was shaky because it was all happening so fast.

The wizard's head bent to his task while he answered me. "Yes, it takes the king and Devinshea out of this reality and into a more suitable one for the required surgery. It's a small slice of a more magical plane that I keep in touch with. It makes certain things possible that wouldn't be on this plane."

I didn't understand entirely, but I had visited several planes and knew there were many I couldn't name or even conceive of.

"Are we hearing their heartbeats?" Zack's hands were still on my shoulders, though I think they were more for comfort than anything else. Zack and I had fought and argued over the years, but we were family.

"Yes, wolf." Myrddin stood now and flexed his fingers. "It will tell me how much time I have. The king's is the slower beat. A vampire's heart beats much more slowly than a regular human, while the faery's beat is slightly faster. I need to monitor them closely so I know when to put the king's heart back in."

"What?" I couldn't have heard him correctly. He said he would have to put Danny's heart back in. That would necessitate him taking it out.

Rather than answering, he shoved his hand through the blue light of the stasis chamber and reached into Daniel's chest. Like his hand moved through thick mud, he had to shove just a little, but then he was wrist deep inside Daniel's chest and after a second's work, he pulled out his heart. It pumped in his hand.

The wizard's smile was triumphant as he held the heart up. "See, I told you it was simple."

CHAPTER TWENTY-FIVE

"Zoey, don't try anything," Zack whispered urgently into my ear.

"He pulled Daniel's heart out of his chest." My hand was on the gun Lee had left me.

"That would be my point," Zack explained. "Do you know how to get it back in?"

I hated it when Zack made sense. "Of course I don't know how to reattach a heart, but I know enough to know we shouldn't have let some freaky wizard pull Daniel's out. He's holding his heart, Zack."

Panic threatened to overwhelm me. I looked to where the wizard bent over his tray, his fingers working rapidly. He kept moving from the heart to the small set of tools he'd unrolled prior to ripping my husband's heart from his chest. He moved with a weird grace, his hands flowing effortlessly as he worked. Perhaps that should have given me some comfort, but I couldn't get over the sight of Daniel's heart pumping in the wizard's hand.

"It worked out in *Temple of Doom*, right?" Zack asked.

"No, Zack," I muttered back. "That dude died."

"Well, maybe he wasn't a vampire," Zack offered.

I sighed heavily and told myself I wouldn't yell at Zack. I was going to try to remain calm and not think about the fact that Daniel was lying on the table in front of us without a heart in his chest. I moved forward slightly and I could see Daniel plain as day. He laid on the table, his big body still. So very pale, but I could see his chest moving up and down with each purposeful breath. It was a forced motion, not free and easy like a normal breath would be. There was thought and effort attached to each one, and my eyes moved toward the man behind each lungful of air Daniel's body was taking. Dev's eyes were closed, his head down as he concentrated fully on bodily functions that should come naturally. I saw the fine sheen of perspiration that coated his body, and every now and then a tremble would start in his hands and move all throughout his limbs.

"Is it just me or is Dev's heart rate increasing?" Zack's brown eyes watched Dev carefully.

I listened and he was right. Every second that went by, Dev's heart beat just a little faster.

"Are you all right, Dev?" I asked quietly, not wanting to disrupt his concentration.

"He cannot hear you." Myrddin poked at the small silver device on the front of Daniel's heart, testing it. He used forceps and tried to pull it off but it was stubborn. "Once the monitor became audible, Devinshea and the king became locked in the chamber."

I walked up to the wizard, Zack following hard behind. I peered down at the heart, trying to think of it all as a surreal dream. It resembled a strange piece of meat, not that piece of my husband that held his love for me. It just pointed out to me that what we loved about others was something completely intangible. I loved Daniel's soul, but it needed a place to stay and it would be forcibly evicted if we didn't get his heart back in his body.

"Dev's heart rate is increasing," I pointed out.

The wizard stopped briefly. He listened, turning one ear up into the air and holding his body still. "Yes, you're right," he replied and then went back to poking and prodding.

Zack and I exchanged exasperated glances.

"Is that normal?" I asked, trying to keep the frustration out of my voice.

"I have no idea," Myrddin admitted.

"How can you say that?"

"Well, I've never actually done this before."

"Then what made you think that this was a good time to start?" He was experimenting with Daniel's life, and he'd pulled Dev into it as well.

"I decided it was a good idea because otherwise the king would die once your enemies get close enough to set off this little device." Myrddin had a small magnifying glass and he inspected the metallic implant closely. "This is actually quite ingenious. I'm very much looking forward to seeing what the humans have come up with. They're so sadly lacking in magical skills, but their ingenuity never fails to amaze me."

"I'm glad you're looking forward to technology but can we get back to the fact that you have Danny's heart in your hand and Dev's is speeding up rapidly?"

It was. I could hear the throb of Devinshea's heart picking up the pace.

"It's only to be expected," Myrddin replied simply. "His body is working double time. It was going to struggle, though the faery seems to be deteriorating faster than I expected. Perhaps Daniel's vampire body required a stronger balance. Oh well, if it gets worse, I'll need you to be ready to take the faery's place, wolf."

Zack breathed a big sigh of relief, and I knew that sitting on the sidelines was killing him. He would much rather be in that chamber with Daniel than standing out here having to watch and wait. "Why don't I just go in now? I don't mind. I think you'll find I'm strong enough for both my master and myself. Let Devinshea rest."

I was kind of all for that plan. I didn't like the way Dev was shaking. His skin was getting pale and I saw how his fingers had tightened, like he was worried about losing his hold on Daniel. Zack was stronger than Dev. He always had been. Zack might not be an alpha, but he was a predator, and when you combined that with a steady dose of vampire blood it made for one tough wolf.

"You'll get your chance, wolf," the wizard murmured.

"When?" I asked.

"When the faery's heart explodes, the wolf can jump in and take his place." The forceps were back in his hands. "Be quick though. The king will have very little time once the faery dies."

I staggered back and Zack had to catch me. The only thing that kept me from throwing myself bodily at that fucking wizard was the fact that Danny's heart was literally in his hands.

"I swear to everything I hold dear that if my husband dies in that chamber, I will find a way to kill you," I said between clenched teeth because I knew exactly what he'd done. "You let Dev go in there because you knew he wouldn't refuse to help Daniel. You knew he would do anything and everything you asked because he loves me and he loves Danny. You sent him in there knowing Zack was a better choice."

"And why would I do that, my queen?" He sounded merely interested, not shocked or insulted by my accusation. He poured a solution of something over Daniel's heart and grunted at the result.

I stepped forward. "You would do it to get rid of your rival. You know that Devinshea is Daniel's closest advisor. He'll be able to talk Daniel out of things you want him to do. You won't be able to control Dev."

The wizard chuckled. "I assure you, if I wish to control the faery, I will. It won't be hard. It's all about knowing what someone wants and needs and giving it to them. Those men in that chamber, they both want something. Daniel wants to know he's not alone. He's terrified that he's ill equipped for the job he must do. He looks to me as Arthur did. He can lean on me. Devinshea is looking for a father figure. Even with the fertility god inside him, he wants to prove he belongs. He wants so much to be a part of Daniel's inner circle. I can provide both with the attention they seek. Trust me. I will be invaluable to Daniel's knights. It isn't Devinshea who concerns me, Your Highness."

"You can't control Bris. Is that what the problem is?"

"There are many problems I have with an ancient deity having control over one so close to the king," Myrddin admitted. "Look at how he reacted to me. He gave me no chance, merely began spouting the worst tales of me. He has hidden his agenda to everyone. He allowed you to let yourself believe he was interested in your husband when the truth of the matter is, he was always after you. He wants you and he'll do what he has to do in order to get you. In the end he'll destroy Daniel and Devinshea to get what he wants." Myrddin shook his head and turned back to his task. "Or at least that's the way it seems to me. The fertility god will be troublesome, but I would never attempt to get at him through Devinshea."

"That's not the way it looks to me." Anger and fear warred inside me. That beat was getting louder. The strain on Dev's heart was obvious now. The rhythm was fast, and sometimes it would get erratic for a time before settling back into a quick but steady beat. He was failing and it would only get worse.

"Go, Zack, get Dev out," I said firmly. "Take his place and keep Daniel alive."

Zack was on the task immediately.

"I wouldn't do that if I were you," Myrddin said calmly.

Zack hit the wall of light that marked the boundary of the stasis chamber and was thrown back a good ten feet. He smashed against the wall on the opposite side and fell to the floor unconscious.

Myrddin shook his head ruefully as he glanced down at the wolf. "I told you. Now there is no one to take the faery's place if he fails. I'll have to work quickly." His dark eyes found me and they narrowed, and for the first time I believed fully this man had ties to Hell. "I suppose I could be content with Devinshea's condition if the god inside him were to cause no more trouble."

I was in a corner and now I didn't even have Zack to back me up. I was the only thing standing between Dev and his heart exploding. "And how am I supposed to convince him to let you have your way?"

"Like I said before, I've found it's only a question of discovering what a person wants and giving it to them. The fertility god wants a loving goddess. You won't find the task unpleasant, dear. I think you'll like serving the god. Bear him a few children, pass them off as the faery's, and make certain you spend plenty of alone time with the god. I'll let you know when I need Bris's attention focused elsewhere. I don't do this for my own good, but rather for Daniel's. He's my charge and my only focus. If you have objections to this plan then I can merely wait and hope Daniel survives without a balance. It's possible. He's strong."

There were angry tears pricking my eyes as I glared at the wizard. "You won't get away with this. I'll tell Danny exactly what you said."

"And I will deny that I meant it that way, dear." He lounged against the table looking altogether too comfortable. "I'll tell Daniel that I was merely speaking aloud, trying to work through some problems with the queen, who I have come to greatly respect. I need your counsel if I'm to understand. I don't know why the queen would take things so out of context, unless she is jealous and perhaps overly emotional. Can you think of anything that happened today that might make you overly emotional, dear?"

My heart stopped. They wouldn't. He couldn't know about that. Not even our closest friends knew what had happened earlier today. "Besides watching you rip my husband's heart out?"

He chuckled, the sound sickening to my ears. "No, dear, I'm talking about the three of you trying to make a babe. Given that the faery is a fertility god, I would say the odds are high. Conception happens very quickly when fertility magic is involved. It can be very draining for the female. I will point all of this out to Daniel when you make your accusations. The queen will need her rest, you know. We wouldn't want anything to upset her delicate condition. Don't look so surprised. Daniel already feels our connection. He wanted to share his news with me."

"Bastard," I snarled. He would use my condition and our babies to lock me out. He would convince Dev and Daniel that I needed to be protected, and it wouldn't take much. They already wanted me coddled and sheltered. I was running out of options. Zack was still out. I caught sight of Nim. "Nim will tell them what she heard."

The room reverberated with laughter as the wizard passed a hand in front of Nim's unseeing eyes. "Child, she lost consciousness when she took hold of the chamber." A strange, brooding look came over the wizard's face. "If I really wanted revenge I could just leave her here like this, her body forever in this state, unseeing, unhearing. It would be fitting." He turned back to me. "Do we have a deal, Your Highness? That heartbeat is getting faster and faster. There's not much time left."

The sound made my soul hurt. Dev's heart was straining to keep up with the demand and it was going to burst soon. His heart would fail and now there wasn't even Zack to save Daniel. It was everything I had feared it could be. I would lose them both.

"Tick tock, Queen Zoey. Time is running out," Myrddin said in a weird sing-song. "Lose them or save them. It's up to you."

"I'll do what you ask." I made my deal with the devil, but I was going to find a way out. I wasn't about to let this man have my husbands. I would go along for now but he'd made an enemy of me, and I promised myself I would be a formidable one. "Save them."

His smile was charming and he walked back over to the tray. "It would be my pleasure." He pulled the device off the heart and it exploded, sending liquefied silver everywhere. Myrddin squeezed the heart gently and silver poured out of the arteries. He doused it in a solution and within a minute pronounced it clean.

"That was all?" I hissed the question. "You knew what you were doing the whole time?"

He walked to the stasis chamber. "Of course, dear. I might not have performed the magic before but I knew what I was doing. There's very little magic I can't master quickly. I needed the extra time to spend with you. While I was working on Daniel's heart, I thought I'd work a little on your soul, Queen Zoey. I know who holds power and who doesn't. I think we'll make a good team. You'll see. We'll make Daniel a great king."

As Dev's heart reached a staccato crescendo, the wizard shoved his hand through the blue light and carefully pushed the heart back into Daniel's chest. His hand disappeared. I could see him moving and shifting until he was happy with the placement and he gently pulled his hand back out. The flesh closed as the wizard's hand retreated.

I stood there, completely helpless, watching Dev fail, hearing his heart getting ready to explode. There was nothing I could do except pray that it would be over soon, hope that the wizard would be satisfied with my promise and let Devinshea live through this. I bit my lip as the pounding of Dev's heart began to make one long sound, the beats so close together I could barely tell there was any time at all between them. I watched as his face tightened with the strain, and there were tears squeezing out of his eyes as he realized his time was almost up. He wouldn't be able to hold on much longer, and it would cost him everything.

Then just like that I heard the most beautiful of sounds. Slower, so much slower than Dev's, Daniel's heart began to beat. Dev's hands came off Daniel's shoulders and he slumped to the ground, every bit of energy he had utterly expended. His heartbeat tapered off rapidly but then it found a natural rhythm and though my faery prince didn't move, I could hear the glorious beat of those two hearts making a time and music of their own.

"You see, Your Highness," Myrddin said with a completely satisfied look on his face. "I always manage to do what I promise. You should remember that when dealing with me in the future. Your husbands are both alive and I suspect you will find them very grateful to me. Tell them what you wish, but I'll be able turn it to my advantage. Or you can keep your bargain with me and we can handle them together. I don't have to cut you out entirely. I would rather you were my partner in helping the king. He needs us both, you know."

I nodded numbly, all the while thinking that this time I was going to let Lee rip out his throat. I would wait until the time was right and I couldn't be accused of anything. I would come up with some scenario that made Lee seem entirely innocent, but my wolf was getting let off the leash. He'd been wanting to kill someone for me for the longest time, and it looked like Christmas was finally here. I'd held him back when he wanted to do in Declan Quinn, but I wasn't going to play around with Myrddin. The wizard made Dev's brother seem like a helpless infant. Lee would rip the wizard to shreds and I would be waiting with a hose to clean his fur and a big bag of beef jerky for a job well done. I smiled at the thought and was very pleased when the wizard seemed disturbed.

"Your Highness?"

I gave the wizard my biggest, wide-eyed stare. "I'll do what you think best, Myrddin."

That really made him uncomfortable. "Somehow I doubt that. Call your guard back in. We'll need help moving the king and Devinshea to the recovery room."

I called to Lee as I always did when I needed a strong arm, and in seconds he was at my side.

I sat in the middle of the two beds and waited. It had been several hours since the successful end of the operation, and Dev had woken briefly. He'd managed to choke down Nim's elixir and promptly slipped into a deep sleep, but not before I'd seen Bris's emerald green eyes staring up at me. I knew he'd been there lending his host every bit of strength he had. I'd leaned over and kissed him softly, whispering my thanks. The ancient god had looked satisfied and let his host's body get the rest it needed.

Daniel had been still as a corpse. He was in that deep, dark sleep most vampires suffered through every day. Daniel had both companion blood and Dev's magic to feed from. When he was well he slept more normally, like a human would. We were able to rouse him if needed and he would sometimes toss and turn in his sleep. Myrddin had explained it was just an effect of the deep healing his body was attempting to do. To prove to me Daniel was all right, he'd asked Zack to feed his master. Zack had been more than willing to donate. He'd been slightly sheepish at getting knocked on his ass by something as scary as blue light. He'd opened his wrist, and the sight of Daniel's mouth opening to get that blood mollified me. If he was feeding, he was healing.

Lee turned from his place at the window. Night had fallen and he was watching the half moon. I wondered if he was thinking about roaming. I knew it was always there in the back of his head to wander. How hard was it for my wolf to stay with me?

"When can I kill him?" Lee asked abruptly.

I'd filled Lee and Neil in the minute we were left alone. I'm not good at keeping things to myself. Lee had thought eviscerating the wizard was one of my more brilliant ideas and wanted to follow through at the earliest convenient time.

"When the time is right, Lee. We have to be patient and we have to be careful." I walked over to where he stood and Neil joined me. I kept my voice low. I didn't think Daniel would be listening in, but you never could tell.

"I don't like patience," the wolf admitted.

Neil crossed his arms. "We have to take a page out of the boys' playbook. They do a damn fine job of keeping things from our side of the family. They do it to protect us and stuff, I get that. We're assassinating Daniel's mentor for the same reason. If you think about it, Z, it really is an act of love."

"Not for me," Lee shot back. "It's an act of violence, and I'm looking forward to it. I hated that fucker from the first moment I saw him."

I decided not to point out that was kind of Lee's reaction to ninety-nine percent of the people he met. He couldn't help it. It was his nature. "We have to be very quiet about it. Danny is already under his spell or whatever you would call it. I don't want to put Dev in the middle of this so we'll leave him out. We can't mention it to Zack. As much as I trust Zack, he'll tell Danny. The only person we can trust with this is Bris."

Neil frowned.

"What?" I sighed because I knew that look. It was the one he got when I had a stupid idea and he didn't know quite how to tell me I was an idiot. It was a look he only got when the situation was serious because otherwise he had no trouble telling me how dumb I was.

"Zoey, you're walking a fine line here," Neil said. "You have to be careful with Bris. I know he looks like Dev, but he isn't Dev. He's a whole other person…deity thing and working with him behind Danny and Dev's back…"

"You don't have any problem with my working with you and Lee," I replied.

"We don't sleep with you, honey," Neil pointed out. "Think about it. Girl screws fertility god, all the while plotting the death of her husband's close advisor. It all sounds very noir. Those never end well, Z."

"I'm not cheating," I said firmly.

"As I said, fine line," Neil allowed. "If Myrddin has his way, you'll be having Bris's kids behind Dev's back…front…oh, I don't know. It's all very confusing."

"I won't be doing that at all," I threw back at Neil. If Daniel could run around telling people we'd just met then I could certainly tell the two people closest to me. "I'll be having Dev's baby."

"I'm sure one day…" Neil's voice tapered off. His eyes went wide. "Did you let Dev touch your bits without a glove?"

I couldn't help but smile, remembering just how good that had felt. "Yes, we did. We decided that we'd waited long enough so we're trying."

Lee put a hand on my shoulder. "Darlin', you don't try having a baby with a fertility god. You let him do his thing and then you're pregnant. If Dev did the deed then we have to consider you pregnant, Zoey."

"Lee, we just tried this afternoon. We don't know anything yet. His swimmers are probably still floating around in there looking for an egg to attack." Unless Myrddin was right and conception backed by fertility magic occurred faster than a normal pregnancy. My last pregnancy had symptoms very quickly. Before I even had a chance to pee on a stick, Daniel's body was taking over because I was so tired.

"No," Neil said, shaking his head. "He's got Olympic gold medalist sperm, Zoey. They're fast and they're damn accurate, and if they can't find an egg they'll just walk up to your ovaries and coax a few out. How many times have you had sex with Dev without a condom before?"

"Once." And I'd gotten pregnant. Of course it had been the night of Dev's ascension and there had been powerful magic involved. It was entirely possible that without such crazy fertility magic that it could take longer. Maybe.

"Case closed, so I'm with Lee on this one," Neil said, suddenly going into organization mode. "We'll need to work with the Order and get you everything you need."

I expected Neil would be planning a gorgeous maternity wardrobe and redoing the condo to allow for a tasteful nursery.

"We'll need a Pilates instructor and a new chef because I don't think Albert does healthy," Neil said. "We need to fight Dev and Daniel on this. Trust me, they'll be stuffing chocolates down your throat and giving you ice cream at two a.m. It's my job to make sure you can get back into those size eight dresses. You'll thank me in the end."

I punched him soundly.

"All the more reason for me to kill the bastard now, Zoey." Lee brought the conversation back around to his favorite subject. "If you let him, he'll use your baby against you. I won't let that happen."

"Won't let what happen, wolf?" Myrddin asked innocently as he walked in the room. "Is there a threat I should know about?"

Nim and Zack walked in behind the wizard. Zack had gone hunting while Nim had prowled around, looking for edible vegetables in the gardens. The kitchens were woefully understocked.

"There are many threats to my queen's welfare," Lee said, baring his teeth in a sure show of dominance. "Don't worry about it, though. I always take care of them, even when they seem to be friends."

Nim's eyes widened, as no one could mistake that threat. "Okay, so Zack found some rabbits for supper and I have managed to put together a nice salad. If you like we can all go downstairs for some food. We need to keep up our energy."

I glanced back at the beds where my husbands lay.

"They won't be awake for hours," Myrddin said.

"I don't know about hours, but someone said something about food," Dev said, his voice shaky.

I flew across the room and was in his arms before he could take a breath. I covered his face with "grateful he was alive" kisses.

Dev laughed but even that was a tired sound. "You're happy, my wife? I feared you wouldn't be over your fright. The experience was a bit more intense than any of us bargained for."

I kissed him firmly on the mouth. "I'm ecstatic you're alive."

"Daniel is fine?" His green eyes wandered until they saw our vampire laid out on the bed beside him.

Nodding, I reached out and held his hand. "The device is gone and his heart is fine. He hasn't woken up yet but he's taking blood. He just needs rest and so do you. You've been through a lot. I'll go downstairs and make you a plate and I'll feed you myself. Don't move, Dev."

He smiled lazily and leaned back against the headboard. "Well, my loving wife, with you as my nurse, I may never move again. I might be in desperate need of a sponge bath."

I smiled down at him. "I'll see what I can arrange."

I tucked him back in and turned to see the wizard looking warily from me to Lee. Smiling brightly, I walked past him and headed down to the kitchens. My husbands were alive. I could allow the wizard a little more life, but his days were numbered.

"Will you be joining us for dinner?" I asked him as we all started down the stairs.

"No," he replied. "I must think for a while. Now that the king is on the road to recovery, I believe things will happen very quickly. I have a feeling that big events are upon us, and I need to decide how to handle them."

"Shouldn't Daniel decide?" I wasn't able to stop the question from leaving my mouth.

"I must make sure he understands all the possible outcomes," Myrddin said mysteriously. "I have found that when playing chess, it's important to think many moves ahead. You must anticipate your opponent's next move and decide your strategy accordingly, even if that strategy requires some rather odd maneuvering. I will think on it. Good evening."

Somehow, I was pretty sure he wasn't really talking about chess.

CHAPTER TWENTY-SIX

It was forty-eight hours before Daniel was up and walking. I spent that whole time taking care of Dev, who was the biggest baby about having his heart reach critical mass and come minutes from exploding. He needed someone—that someone being me—to hold his hand. He was too tired to feed himself. He was scared at night and had nightmares and needed me to hold him while he slept. When he mentioned he was too tired to have sex but really needed it and a blow job might be helpful to Daniel because he fed off sexual energy, I just laughed at him.

After that he found the strength to pin me down and take full advantage of the fact that he didn't have to wear that little piece of dreaded latex. The funny thing was he was right. Daniel woke up about an hour later, his head throbbing and in desperate need of a fix. After a little play time with me—and he got the blow job I wasn't about to give Dev because his heart had actually come out of his body—he was ready to get out of bed. I had been eating like a horse, anything Nim cooked, because the last thing I needed was to get weak and have Danny's body try to take up the slack, so I was sure I wasn't dragging him down.

"Is that a good idea?" Dev asked as he walked in front of Daniel down the stairs toward the main floor of the crystal castle.

Daniel growled a little. "Dev, I've been in bed for days. I'm fine. I'm not going to get better if I don't get up and move around."

"Well, I felt terrible for days," Dev said, backing down the stairs. I'm not sure what he intended to do beyond be something Danny fell into if he lost his balance.

Danny's dimples came out. "That's 'cause you're a wimp, Dev."

I threw my hands up and moved passed them. "I don't think it helped that I was so freaked out I promised him anything. I fed the man for a day and a half and rubbed his feet because he said he couldn't feel them because the operation had screwed up his circulatory system."

Daniel held his hand up and Dev smacked it. "Nice, Dev," Daniel said. "I should have thought of that. All I managed to get was a blow job."

Dev shook his head. "I overplayed my hand and asked for oral too late into the game. She was tired from all my other requests."

"I'm peeing on a stick at the first given opportunity," I swore. "And after that, the two of you are waiting on me hand and foot for the next nine months."

"Z," Neil said from the bottom of the stairs. "You should hurry. Myrddin and Nim are screaming at each other."

"About what?" I hurried down because if Nim was going to turn Myrddin into a pretzel, then I wanted to see it.

"I don't know." Neil guided me toward the stairs to the dungeons. "You know how Myrddin's been doing all that prophecy stuff? Well, he thinks he knows what's going to happen and he won't tell Nim."

I could hear Nim yelling from the top of the stairs.

"You can't! You know we can't do that," Nim yelled, her voice hoarse. It was obvious they had been at it for a while. "He needs you. He needs a mentor now more than ever. You can't just leave him."

I wanted to jump up and down and throw a big old party at the thought of Myrddin leaving, but then I saw Daniel's face. He steeled himself and started down the stairs.

"Damn it, Dan," Dev cursed. "Be careful, please."

Daniel wasn't listening. He rushed toward the fight and Dev,

Neil, and I followed.

"What do you mean you're leaving?" Daniel asked, and I heard the little boy behind the question. It made me wonder what that single moment when Daniel had reached out and Myrddin answered had meant to my husband.

Myrddin's face was long as he turned to his pupil. "Daniel, you have to understand that things will play out as they will. I've spent the days since I fixed your heart in quiet contemplation. I have been musing on the way things must work and I've come to several conclusions."

"Like I don't need you?" Daniel asked and there was an accusation behind the question.

Myrddin sent him a sad smile. "You do not, Your Highness. Not just yet."

Daniel's jaw firmed, a sign of stubborn will. "How can you say that? I just had surgery and I have to go out to the biggest fight of my life. I need everyone I can gather on my side."

The wizard walked forward and placed his hands on Daniel's shoulders. They were almost the same height and Myrddin looked deeply into Daniel's eyes, seeming to find some connection there. "I know that it seems like that, my king, but this is merely the beginning. I have come to the conclusion that I must step back and allow you to claim the crown on your own. It's a mistake I made with Arthur that I don't intend to make with you."

Daniel moved away from him and began to pace the room. "How is it a mistake to get my crown? I thought that was the goal of all of this."

"I believe Myrddin is saying he needs to allow you to claim your crown on your own," Dev interjected. He looked back at me and it was easy to see Dev was perfectly fine with Myrddin leaving.

The wizard nodded. "That's exactly what I'm saying. Daniel, I don't want to take this step but I believe it's important. Part of Arthur's problem during his reign was the fact that some of his subjects believed I placed him on the throne and then controlled him. It was not the truth, but we couldn't get past the rumor with some."

"So you just let me hang?" Daniel asked.

"I don't know what you mean by that, Daniel," he replied,

obviously confused by the modern slang. "Please don't think that I want you to fail. I'm only doing this because I know you will succeed. You'll gain your crown and it won't be tainted by my presence. You'll be the king and no one can challenge you on it. When the time comes, and it will, I will return to you and be your good counselor."

"I don't give a damn what people think," Daniel challenged him. "I don't give a real damn about any of this. I just want to get it over so I can have my life back."

Sorrow dimmed Nim's natural light as she approached the vampire. "Daniel, I'm so sorry but whatever life you're talking about is gone. You will either be the King of all Vampire or you will die. If you die, Devinshea and Zoey won't be far behind. Once you're king, your life will be changed forever. You will never be the anonymous husband and father you wanted to be. You will never be left alone to live a quiet life. It's a sad truth about those with a grand destiny."

"I didn't ask for a grand destiny." Daniel argued, but he was caught and had been for a very long time. "I don't want it."

"Which is why you were chosen, Daniel," Myrddin said gravely. "Fame seekers and gold diggers are not given these great gifts for the simple fact that they would misuse them. But you were given great compensation for the job you must do. You were given your queen and your friend. Not many people get to spend a long lifetime with two people they love."

Daniel slumped into the nearest available chair, and I moved to his side, tucking my hand into his. Dev sat next to him. "And I am grateful for the love I've been given, but I don't see why I can't have someone to guide me through this. I don't know how to be a king. I was born in Newport, Rhode Island. I was raised in Dallas. There aren't a lot of kings there. My dad was a thief and my mom worked at a beauty salon washing people's hair. I don't how to do this."

Myrddin knelt at the king's knee. "You do, Your Highness. You know what to do deep down. You know what the world needs and you know how to achieve it. The rest of the stuff, the rituals and superficialities, Devinshea can teach you, but you were born to do this. I don't care where you were born or where you were raised, you were born a king and you will die one. No counselor can change that. Trust your queen. Trust your partner. Trust yourself. You will win the day and you will rule wisely. When you have true need of me, I'll come for you and then we can keep our acquaintance quiet. It doesn't need to taint your crown."

"I'm not ashamed of you, teacher," Daniel said with far too much emotion.

"And that makes me happy, Daniel," Myrddin replied. "You can't understand how that makes me feel. But Daniel, if you trust me, then you must trust me even when my wisdom runs counter to your own wants. You need to do this on your own. I swear I won't steer you wrong."

I felt Daniel squeeze my hand and he slowly let out a deep breath. "All right, teacher. I hope you're right."

"You're sure?" Nim asked, flustered by the turn of events.

"I am, Nim." Myrddin sounded tired of the argument. "I don't know how many times I have to say it. If you no longer believe in my magic then please feel free to find another tutor. I need to learn this plane as it is today. The king needs to claim his crown. It's not the end of his trouble, not even close. When he needs me, I'll find him."

Nim bowed her head in acquiescence. "All right, then. I will be your teacher in this. I know this world a little. I'll go with you and we'll learn what you need to learn."

"Nimue?" The word came out as a breathless question, and I could see the remnants of whatever feelings the wizard had once had spark back to life.

Nim flashed a brief smile. "I promise you nothing but companionship, Myrddin. I want to watch over you and make sure you cause no trouble. Devinshea, can you arrange to have the contents of the castle moved to a secure location? Now that the veil has been opened, any decent witch should be able to find it."

"I'll have it all moved to Ether," Dev promised. "Your rooms will be kept ready for you at any time and if you require money, I'll provide it."

"Are we leaving then?" Stewart walked into the room. He'd been conspicuously absent for the last two days. Zack had told me Stewart had acted as a focal point for the wizard's divination.

The wizard stood and regarded the demon with a certain affection. "It's time we all did our jobs, Nemcox. I'm sure there will be a reward awaiting you on the other side of this mess."

Stewart's smile was sure and slick. "I'm certain of it as well, My Lord."

Myrddin crossed over to a large table and picked up a box. "This is for you, Daniel. When I was exiled here, Nimue was kind enough to pack away certain important items she knew would be helpful to my next student. Among them are the thirteen treasures of Britain. They will be moved to this club of Devinshea's along with my other possessions, but you will need this one, I'm certain. This is the Mantle of Arthur and now it's yours."

Daniel let go of my hand and opened the box on his lap. He pulled out a long dark cloak. He looked at the wizard, confusion plain on his handsome face.

"Devinshea, if you will permit me?" Myrddin gestured for Dev to stand.

I started to protest because the last time the wizard experimented on my faery prince it had almost cost him his life, but before I could get a word out, he tossed the cloak over Dev's shoulder and everything from his neck down completely disappeared.

"Holy Harry Potter, it's an invisibility cloak," Daniel said with a look of wonder.

Myrddin shook his head. "I don't know this Potter boy, but he must be important. Your retinue references him often. Perhaps I shall seek him out. Anyway, it's indeed an invisibility cloak. Keep it close to you. You're still very weak and it may come in handy."

"Do I look like a dancing head?" Dev grinned as he moved around.

"Yes, it's creepy." I shuddered. We were on British soil, planning a coup. I didn't need to see my husband's head without his body. It was too close to what could happen if we got caught. "Take it off."

Dev drew the cloak off, but he was still smiling. "Halloween is going to be so much fun this year."

Daniel put the lid back on the box after Dev folded the cloak up. His lips turned down. "I should get back to the real world, then. Nim said I would heal better there."

"You will, Daniel," she said sagely. "It's your home plane. The energy of it will be more soothing to your body. You'll be feeling much more like yourself in a week or two. For now, you will go through periods of great weakness and you just have to get through them. No training for at least a week. Devinshea might need longer."

Dev shook his head. "I'm feeling much better. My body feels fine though when I attempted to use Bris's powers, they were a bit sluggish."

"The magic I used threw off his, I would think," Myrddin explained. "Can the fertility god take over?"

Dev's eyes bled to a full emerald green. "I am still here, wizard. If your thought was to get rid of me, you have failed."

Myrddin sighed. "Always thinking the worst of me. I merely wanted to make sure you could still come out. Devinshea says your powers are weak."

Bris nodded. "Yes, but I believe you're correct. The magic of the stasis chamber drained us both. We feel a bit better every day. We'll be in fighting form in a week or two. We need rest and sex."

Dev came back, giving me the most delicious grin. "Damn straight."

Daniel stood suddenly. "Right. We'll leave now. I need to get Z to the Order's HQ. I'm not the only one who needs to rest. She needs better than what we can provide her with here."

Myrddin shook Daniel's hand warmly. "I'll look forward to the time when you truly need me, Daniel. Get your crown. Take care of your queen. I'll see you before you know it."

"I'll look forward to the time as well," Daniel replied, obviously trying not to get choked up. He turned to Dev. "Let's go get the wolves ready. I want to leave as soon as possible. We'll get out of here and call the Order to come pick us up. Do you need a ride somewhere, teacher?"

"I think we'll figure something out, Daniel," Nim said. "We need a few more days here to get things ready and then we'll make our way. I'll go with you. I'd like to say good-bye to the wolves as well. Come along, Stewart."

Stewart followed eagerly but when I attempted to ascend the stairs, the wizard pulled me back.

"Your Highness, a word, please." His dark eyes took in every inch of me.

"What do you want?" I would prefer not to spend alone time with a dude I had a kill order on.

He let go of my arm and slumped into the chair Daniel had previously occupied. "I've spent the past days in divination. I've been attempting to see the future, but it all comes back to you, dear. Every single scenario comes back to you. Now why is that, my queen?"

"Maybe it's because I'm a nexus point." It was the only thing I could think that might answer his question.

The wizard threw back his head in rueful laughter. "Naturally. I was hoping you were some light-skirt I could distract with the fertility god but no, you have to be a nexus point. I'm leaving for a while because it has been made clear to me that this isn't my charge's fight."

"How can you say that? This is all about Daniel."

Myrddin pointed a finger my way. "No, this is all about you. I can lift Daniel's ego, but it means nothing. Daniel won't win this fight. It will be won or lost because of you, girl. You will either have the guts and the courage to look past your own grief or you will not. You must stay strong, my queen. You must not give in."

"Grief? Over what?" I asked, a chill running across my skin. Something bad was coming for me. For all of us. I could see it in his eyes. He'd seen my future and it wasn't good. "You have to tell me."

The wizard shook his head. "I do not envy you, my queen. I can say nothing further without angering people I don't wish to anger. They watch you, Queen Zoey. Heaven and Hell and everyone in between. If you survive, I'll see you again. I know we've started poorly, but I look forward to the day. Now go and play your part. In the end, it will be only you but you are never alone. Remember that."

"Please tell me what's going to happen." I didn't like to beg, but I would get on my knees if I had to.

The wizard put a hand on my shoulder. "The world is a balance, child. I cannot upset it without paying a price none of us wishes to pay. Even if I told you, the outcome wouldn't change. Some things are written. And some things that seem to be punishment are truly a reward for a job well done. You won't see it until much later." The wizard hissed and clutched his chest, his skin becoming pale. He looked up as though someone was speaking to him. "I understand. I will be quiet now." His eyes found mine again. "Don't hate me, my queen."

He took a long breath and then he was standing tall again, his face utterly blank. He would say no more to me.

I rushed up the stairs, eager to get back to Danny and Dev. I tried very hard not to think about what the wizard had told me.

Stewart seemed almost vibrant with happiness as we approached the veil. It was daylight and the pocket world seemed lit with radiance as we prepared to leave it. We hadn't come in with much and we were only leaving with one extra souvenir. Myrddin had made sure Zack had the Mantle of Arthur in his backpack. I found it odd that he'd been very specific. Zack must carry it. He'd instructed the wolf how to use it should his master have need.

Daniel sent the demon a brief smile. "Stewart, you know you're going to have to leave that host when we get to the Order's headquarters, right?"

Stewart pouted prettily. "But this meat is still so fresh. I haven't even torn it up yet. That seems a waste."

"I'm grateful, surprised even, that you've behaved yourself so well," Daniel explained. "I'll keep my promise. You'll have your seat on the Council."

"I look forward to it, Your Highness," Stewart said as he opened the veil.

I could see from my vantage point that it was night on the other side. Given Daniel's weakness, we decided it was best to travel at night until he was at full strength again.

Daniel walked through the veil first. Lee was at my back.

"Go on, Zoey. The faster we get out of here, the sooner we get home," Lee said in his western rumble. "Wherever that is now."

I followed Neil and Dev through the veil and when Lee made it through, I watched as it closed behind us, leaving Nim and Myrddin to themselves. I was relieved to be without the wizard but I had no doubt that he would return, probably at the most inappropriate time.

I heard Daniel sigh.

"Feel better?" I asked.

"Oddly, yes. Nim was right," Danny said, throwing his arm around me. "I feel more settled." He leaned over and kissed my hair. "Let's get you back to civilization. Dev, can you get a signal?"

Dev held his cell up and I wondered how he'd kept a charge for so long. He frowned in the darkness. "Not yet. I think once we make it back to the small town near the channel we should be able to make the call. It worked from there before. I just wrote a text to Sir Ronald. The minute we hit a signal it will send. He said he would keep a helicopter close by."

Daniel nodded and we made our way to town. I held Danny's hand and let him lead me. The night was a little cold, but I wasn't about to let that bother me. I looked forward to getting to the head-quarters and getting our household in order. I was eager to sleep in a proper bed again and have Albert pamper me the way he would once I told him about the babies. It had only been a few days, but I was starting to feel something. The smell of meat was beginning to make me sick. Myrddin had been right about the fertility magic. My babies were making themselves known faster than I could have imagined.

I pushed down my fear. I wouldn't have anything to grieve about this time. I wouldn't. I couldn't.

"Are you all right?" Dev took my other hand.

"I feel fine right now," I replied. "I just really want to get somewhere we can have a proper meal that has never seen the inside of Zack's teeth."

"Hey, I thought I did really well." Zack laughed.

Lee patted his brother on the shoulder. "You did, brother. Zoey's just picky."

"I'm with Z. Nim is a terrible cook," Neil complained as I saw the lights from the small town up ahead. "I want Albert back!"

I saw flashes of enchiladas and Albert's ridiculously decadent lasagna in Neil's eyes.

I stopped suddenly and realized it was Lee's hand that pulled me back. I felt myself let go of my husbands' hands and I was thrust behind my wolf's back.

"Zoey, when I tell you to run, you do it," Lee ordered.

I heard Daniel's claws pop out and then there was a strange sound. Something—things—rushed toward us at enormous speeds. One minute we were alone and the next we were completely surrounded by vampires.

"Get her out of here, Lee," Daniel said and even in the moonlight I could see him clutching his chest. The adrenaline was causing his heart stress.

"I don't think so, Mr. Donovan," a satisfied voice said as Louis Marini made his way toward us. "I think you'll find there is nowhere to go. I'll take my companion now."

CHAPTER TWENTY-SEVEN

Shaking violently, I stared at the vampires surrounding us. They were Louis's thugs. They did his dirty work so he could keep his hands clean. I recognized most of them but only knew Ivan's and Kevin's names. Ivan had gloves on and held a long silver sword in his hand. Kevin was aiming a pistol at Dev's head from across the circle.

Louis only had eyes for me.

"I'll never give her to you, Louis," Daniel spat. There was no reason to pretend now. Daniel allowed his full hatred to show. "You'll never have my queen."

"I wondered if you thought yourself a true king, Donovan. Did you think you could take me down and become the head of the Council?" Louis laughed before holding up the Blood Stone. It shone in the moonlight, a jewel stuffed and plump with powerful blood. "Do you know what this is, Your Highness?" The title was said with a distinct bitter bite of sarcasm. "This is the last king who defied me. You'll end up in one of these, too."

Louis held up the tip of the Blood Stone and shoved it into his palm. Again, as the first time, the stone flared as it sent power rushing through Louis's system and he seemed to swell with it. "By a full vote of the Council, Daniel Donovan, you have been declared a traitor and an outlaw. I challenge you to a duel for your life and your queen."

I heard a laugh and felt Stewart move beside me. He straightened his clothes and slicked back his hair. He walked past and I sincerely hoped he was about to do something horribly demonic to the head of the Council. A small bubble of hope rose in me. I had seen Stewart do some truly horrible things with a mere flick of his wrist. He could kill without breaking a sweat.

He did something terrible, all right. He walked straight up to Louis and shook his hand.

"My payment?" Stewart asked with a wicked look in his eyes.

"You may take the wolf," Louis offered.

My eyes flew to Neil, who backed up but found himself held captive by one of the vampires. Daniel started to move to protect Neil but another vampire suddenly had Dev in his grasp and there was a gun against his head.

"*Non*, Mr. Donovan," Louis said quickly. "I don't wish to separate the prince from his brain, but I will do it if necessary. Don't worry. I'm told the demon loves the little wolf. I doubt he will hurt him...too much."

Neil changed in an attempt to get away. His clothes ripped at the seams and suddenly there was a gorgeous white wolf struggling against his captor, but the vampire was old and strong. Even as Neil snarled and fought, trying to get a bite in, the vampire grabbed him by the neck and held him down.

Stewart held out his hand and another vampire gave him something. I heard Lee curse behind me as we both realized it was a silver collar and leash. Stewart sighed with pleasure as he gazed down at my best friend. "I told you I would have you, little puppy. I always get what I want. You're so beautiful. In either form, I find you lovely, and now you're all mine."

I bit back a cry as the demon forced the collar over his head and tightened it around his neck. I tried to pull away from Lee to stop this atrocity but he held me tightly against him.

"Don't, Zoey," Lee said quietly. I heard the strain in his voice. He wanted...needed to kill something but he couldn't. "They'll kill Dev and god only knows what they'll do to you, darlin'. They won't be gentle. They'll shoot you and just figure they can bring you back with their blood. You have to think of your baby now. We'll get out of here and I promise you, I'll find Neil. I'll track him if I have to go to the Hell plane to get him back."

I cried and felt Daniel's eyes on me. Lost, he was lost and agonized as he realized there wasn't anything he could do to save me. I was the only one who could help us now. I was the only one with anything Louis wanted beyond their deaths.

"Louis," I said, giving him as much of my vulnerability as I could. "Please. Please don't hurt Dev and please don't let that demon take my friend." I pulled away from Lee and let myself fall to my knees because when it came to my friends, my lovers, I had no pride. "I am begging you, Louis."

His dark head turned toward me and his eyes gleamed down. He liked me on my knees. He liked me begging. His big hand came down to touch my hair even as I heard Daniel snarl. "I don't want to hurt the prince, *chère*. If you like, we will bring him with us. I'm not a monster. I want to make you happy, companion."

I felt a bit of my power. He meant what he said. He wanted to make me happy. I would use it against him. "Then don't let a demon drag my friend off. I thought the demons had been told to stay out of this fight."

Louis shrugged negligently. "In this, I can do nothing. I made a deal with the demon. He gave you to me, and now I must let him take his prize. I'm sorry. Not even I can go back on a deal with a demon lord. It will be fine. Perhaps Lord Nemcox will come to visit and he can bring your friend."

"Absolutely," Stewart said as he started to drag Neil away. Neil struggled, trying to dig his paws into the ground. The silver in the collar was smoking as it bit into the flesh around his neck. Stewart pulled and Neil was losing the fight. "I would love to have a good relationship with the Council, Mr. Marini. I've always been fond of the little companion. I find her antics very amusing. And Zoey, don't think I'll be punished. We were told to stay out of the vampire king's way. This wasn't about him. I read the fine print, companion. It said nothing at all about making an exchange. You for my love. It's mere coincidence that the king happened to be here. Oops."

The little bastard. He thought he could skirt the language of

Lucifer's orders.

Stewart merely gave me a wink. "I'll bring my boy by as soon as I've brought him to heel."

Neil's head swung around and I heard him whimper as Stewart dragged him away. I let my eyes follow him and prayed to anything that would listen to make this all one long, horrible nightmare.

"Now, Ivan, if you would please prepare Mr. Donovan for transport," Marini said. "I want him in Paris this evening. We'll meet in the arena and I will legally kill the pretender. I'll take my companion with a full and properly witnessed ceremony. There will be no doubt at all about whom you belong to after this night, my Zoey."

There would be no begging for Daniel's life. I knew that wasn't negotiable with Louis. It wasn't even smart. The best case scenario here was Daniel getting away. I wouldn't get away. I would be in Marini's clutches and I didn't see a way around it. I needed to distance from Daniel in Louis's mind so I wasn't about to plead for my husband's life. But Daniel had to run. He couldn't fight in his condition.

My mind raced as Ivan approached my weakened husband. Adrenaline coursed through my blood because it was time for Daniel to make a move. When he got in reaching distance, Daniel's arm shot out and he threw Ivan to the ground with a vicious twist of the Russian vampire's neck. Daniel moved very quickly. Before anyone could react, Daniel was behind the man who held Dev and after separating them, he neatly took off the vampire's head with one swift move from Excalibur.

"Run, Dev," Daniel ordered.

Dev was on his feet and running for me, but Marini was behind him and he was now just as fast as Daniel. He caught my faery prince and tossed him aside like a child's toy. Dev hit the ground an impossible distance away and he stayed down. Just like Daniel, he wasn't anywhere close to full strength and he didn't have Bris to call on.

But Marini was at full strength, a king's strength. He stared at Daniel, a predator stalking his prey. Daniel was stark white in the moonlight, his energy obviously expended. Despite Daniel's efforts, the vampires still heavily outnumbered us. Marini approached Daniel, and Zack was at Danny's back.

"Come along, Daniel. This will all be over within a few hours," Marini promised.

Daniel stared at me, his face a mask of agony. I shook my head. He had to let me go. He had to live to fight another day. If he allowed them to take him to Paris, he was dead and everything crumbled.

"You'll let me take Dev?" I asked, hoping and praying Dev was still alive.

Louis turned. "Yes."

I tried my nonchalant shrug. "Then let's go, Louis. I'm tired and I need a bath. Please collect the prince and don't put me anywhere near the traitor. You have to know I didn't understand what Daniel was doing until a few days ago. He dragged me and Dev into this. We aren't disloyal, Louis."

I needed him to trust me and that meant I had to betray Daniel.

Daniel's eyes flared and he growled my way. He had a part to play. "You bitch. Do you remember what I promised would happen if you did this to me?"

I nodded through my tears. He hadn't promised me anything about this particular situation, but he had made me a promise. He would always come for me. Always. He would always love me no matter what happened. I would always be his.

Daniel was saying good-bye for now. He was going to run. He was honoring me by trusting me to survive, but he would come for me when he was strong enough.

"Take the traitor," Louis ordered.

There was a report of gunfire and Lee covered me quickly, taking us both to the ground. When he let me up, I could see that both Zack and Danny had been hit. Daniel was bleeding, his chest covered in it. Zack had fared better. Of course, he also hadn't recently had his heart ripped out of his chest.

"Zack, you get your master out of here," Lee ordered.

"But…" I heard in his voice he didn't want to leave his brother behind, but Daniel was still and unmoving as Marini reached down for him.

"Now, Zack," Lee ordered in best badass alpha voice.

Zack threw the Mantle of Arthur over his body as he covered his master. In a flash both disappeared.

"Où sont-ils partis?" Louis asked, searching the ground. He was enraged that his prey was getting away. *"Trouvez-les!"*

I didn't need a translator for that one. Every vampire in the area started looking for Daniel. Lee changed quickly and then his massive roar filled the night. He was giving Zack a chance to get Daniel out. He howled as every vampire turned to him, noting the new biggest threat against them.

I took the chance to run back and get to Dev. The ground beneath me seemed to shift as I ran through the grass to get close to him. I prayed Zack was getting Daniel as far away as possible. My heart stopped as I saw Dev's body on the ground. He lay face down in the grass. I hit my knees and touched his back, praying for the rise and fall of his chest. It was there and it was steady enough. Now I just needed to convince Lee to run and everything would be fine. Well, everything would be completely fucked, but Louis would be satisfied with me. He would be too busy trying to find Daniel, and Lee could slip away.

I leaned over and kissed my faery prince. He stirred and turned his face to look up at me. "Zoey?"

"It's all right, baby," I said soothingly. "Daniel got away. We're going to have to…"

"Go with Marini," Dev finished. He pushed himself up but it was a struggle. "Zoey…" I read the fear in his eyes. He knew what Marini would want.

"Don't you do anything that could get you killed. I already set the stage," I said as I stood up.

I heard the loud sound of a lot of guns going off at once, and my head turned to where I'd left Lee. I could only see what was happening in the shadows the moonlight cast on the ground. There was a great dark figure in the middle of smaller ones. The wolf fought so valiantly, but he was alone and there were so many vampires. They were taking their rage out on my wolf. Complete terror took over and I knew I had to get to him. I had to stop them before it was too late.

I started to run even as Dev yelled for me to stop. I ran as fast as I could because he was alone and he didn't want to be alone, not really.

He never had. It was a perverse kink of his nature that led him to solitude, but he wanted to be loved. He deserved to be loved.

I ran as fast as my legs would carry me because those gunshots wouldn't stop. The wolf howled and lashed out but the vampires didn't fight fair. They surrounded my wolf and shot at him from every angle. I watched in horror as his body twitched one way and then another, as though the hail of bullets wouldn't let him fall to the ground, wouldn't allow him respite from the pain.

"Arrêtez!" I heard Louis screaming as I ran straight for my wolf, not thinking about the fact that the vampires were still shooting.

Dev screamed his own warnings behind me, but I was only thinking about getting to Lee. The vampires ceased shooting and the night was quiet. I only stopped when I really looked at him. Then it took everything I had not to run from what they had done to my bodyguard, my protector, my friend.

His body was covered in blood. There wasn't an inch of him that hadn't taken some kind of damage. I moved forward and fell to my knees, trying to figure out which part of him to cover. I needed to stop the bleeding. It was happening far too fast, and it was coming from everywhere.

"Chère, it's too much," Louis said from above me. "The bullets were silver, every one of them."

I heard Dev struggling behind me, trying to get to us, but the vampires held him back.

"You may let the prince go," Louis said imperiously. "I think he will behave himself now."

"Oh, goddess," Dev breathed.

"Please, you can save him," I begged, holding onto the leg of Louis's pants. I beseeched him. "He needs blood."

The air beneath me spun as Lee's body changed.

"Won't work, darlin'," he said and even as he spoke he was spitting blood.

The damage had looked bad on his wolf body, but it was devastating to see it on his human form. Blood seeped from every hole, and they were everywhere. The poisonous metal had entered his bloodstream in so many places. His chest was a mottled mess.

"Please," I said, looking down at my wolf. He was pledged to me.

He was mine, and he was dying. "Please take the blood, Lee. I need you."

He smiled sadly. He was a realistic man. "They can't let me live, Zoey. I can't let them take you. If they brought me back, I'd just try to kill them all over again."

"No," I said through the tears that were running wildly down my cheeks. The world seemed so quiet now. It had been so loud before and now it seemed to narrow to just me and Lee. I knew Dev was there and the vampires looked on, but they didn't seem to matter much right now. I reached for Lee's hand, holding it. "You can just run. I'll be fine, Lee."

He coughed and it was a wet, ugly sound. "I could never run."

"You could be free." I was willing to promise him anything if he would live. "You could just run and you wouldn't have to look back. You always wanted to roam. You could roam. Zack is safe with Danny, and Dev will take care of me. You just run."

"Ah, darlin'," Lee said with a little smile. He managed to make his arm move and his free hand cupped my cheek lovingly. "I'd never leave you. I'd never leave Zack. I love you. I never loved anything but the two of you. It was enough, Zoey. It was enough."

"I love you," I cried, pulling his head into my lap. I cried shamelessly and smoothed back his curly hair.

"Devinshea," Lee growled but his voice was getting weaker and Dev had to lean in.

"Yes, Lee." Dev was quiet and solemn.

"You take care of her," the wolf said.

"I promise," Dev replied. "And Lee, thank you. For everything. We couldn't have asked for more."

In the dim light, I could see Lee fading, his energy, his life force waning. "Take care of Zack, Zoey."

I nodded and felt his chest heave as he tried to breathe. "I will. He's my brother now."

His chest rose and fell with a rattle. A great smile came across my wolf's face, as though he had seen something amazing. He stared past me and his voice was filled with wonder. "Now, that's something I didn't expect…"

The light went out of his brown eyes and Lee was gone.

307

I held him to me but there was nothing left and I could feel it. It was just a body in my hands. Whatever spark had been Lee was lost to me now.

"Prince, I need you to bring Zoey." Louis was talking but it seemed distant as I cried out my grief. "We must leave now. You'll be permitted to come with us if you promise to behave. If you step out of line I will be forced to kill you, and I don't think Zoey can handle any more grief today."

"I just want to be with her," Dev said. "You'll find me very helpful, I promise. I can help her transition if you let me."

"Bring her, then," Marini said. "You will be left alone in the boat until we reach France and then the new rules go into effect. You have until then to get her under control. This isn't how I wanted the evening to go. *Allons-y.*"

Dev pulled me up and I felt boneless as he hoisted me into his arms. He gathered me close and I could feel his shock at the events of the last few minutes. He rested my head on his shoulder and I glanced back.

Lee's body was still there. It wouldn't rise again. He wouldn't growl at me and tell me not to pet him. Neil was gone, dragged somewhere by a demon we never should have trusted in the first place. Daniel and Zack were on the run, and I didn't know how badly Danny was hurt. I hadn't even gotten to tell him good-bye.

Dev carried me onto the vampire's boat. As the boat pulled from the dock, I heard the thud of a helicopter in the distance. Dev's message had gotten to Sir Ronald, but it was far too late for any of us.

CHAPTER TWENTY-EIGHT

Dev held me tightly against him as we heard the lock click into place. There would be two guards on the door should I try to pick the lock. We'd been escorted to the boat and then forced to climb down a small ladder to get to the locked room that would be our quarters for the trip to France. We'd been told to expect that we wouldn't make our destination before morning and then we would be in lockdown while the vampires slept. There were several large human slaves willing to do their master's bidding, so Dev settled on the narrow cot and held me close.

I just cried for the longest time. I cried while we entered the boat and I cried while Louis explained to Dev that I was his to take care of for the night. We could stay together until we reached the Paris stronghold. After that, Louis would decide when and where and how we could be together. I cried when Louis locked the door behind him after destroying both of our cell phones so there was no way Daniel could track us. Dev held me, saying nothing beyond how sorry he was. I cried until I fell into a fitful sort of sleep in Dev's arms. When I woke up, Dev was still awake. He was staring into space, but I could see his mind was working.

"Can we?" I gestured to my mouth, silently asking him if it was all right to talk. I didn't know if the room was secure.

"No bugs," Dev said. "And the guard on the door changed about an hour ago. I think it's day, so no vampire ears."

"Do you think Danny's all right?" I asked, my voice hoarse.

Dev looked down, his eyes tender. "Yes, my wife, I believe he is. I believe that Zack got him away, and the Order will find them. They'll take him to headquarters and he will heal. When he's strong enough, he'll come for us."

"Neil?" I could still see him being dragged away. God, I might never be able to get the horror of the night out of my head.

"I don't know, Zoey," Dev answered, his forehead furrowing with worry. "He's very clever and he has skills Stewart doesn't even know about. He thinks Neil is just a pretty face. Neil can use that to his advantage. If anyone can get away, it's Neil."

He let a few moments go by as I knew we were both thinking about Lee, who hadn't gotten away. We'd left him there because there wasn't anything else we could do, but now I wondered if the Order had found his body. Had they taken his body so Zack could bury his brother? How was Zack feeling? Was he angry with me?

"Zoey?" Dev was treating me very delicately, but I could tell he wanted to talk. Dev would want a plan going in, and he wouldn't feel comfortable until we agreed on one.

"Yes, Dev." I tried to sound stronger than I felt.

"We need to talk about what's going to happen when we get to Paris." He held my hand in both of his and rubbed, trying to bring some feeling back into my body.

"I have to fuck Marini." I said it out loud because it was real and it was going to happen.

Dev's face fell, but he nodded slowly. "My goddess, I don't see a way around it. If I can think of anything, any way…"

I stopped him cold. "Stop thinking, Devinshea. I lost Lee today. I have no intention of losing you, too. We can't fight Marini. There's too many of them, and Marini is just as strong as Danny when he's on the Blood Stone. Fighting him gets me nothing but hurt. He's already proven that he'll hurt me to get what he wants. I can't have him knocking me around."

Dev's hand went down to my stomach, and he touched me gently. "Goddess, he could hurt our baby."

"Babies," I corrected him. "It's twins. Don't ask me how I know but I know. How is he going to react to me being pregnant?"

"He can never know, Zoey. We have to keep it a secret. Daniel will come for us. It might take him a few weeks, maybe a month, but no longer than that. You won't be showing even with twins. We can't tell anyone. Not even Chad."

"All right." I placed my hand over his. Chad would do his best to protect us while we were in Paris, but he was too unstable to be trusted with information like this. "I have to protect the babies and I have to get that Blood Stone back. How do I get Marini to trust me?"

I didn't like to even think about getting close to the bastard who'd killed Lee, but I had to think about Dev and Danny and our babies. Fighting Marini would just cost us all. If I was going to steal from him, it would be so much easier if he wasn't watching me suspiciously twenty-four hours a day.

"Louis, Zoey. We must call him Louis from now on," Dev corrected. "It's more intimate and we need for him to feel close to us. You know, we're going to have to play a part and it won't be pleasant. We need to get our stories straight, my wife, and we cannot deviate from it. The first and most important lie is this. We never really loved Daniel. He took you, forced you to be his companion. You loved him when he was a human but he changed when he turned. He was cruel at times and convinced you all other vampires were much, much worse than he was."

"They are," I pointed out.

"Of course, my wife, but we must get Louis into a position where he wants to convince you he isn't a vicious killer." Dev ran his fingers soothingly through my hair. "I will work on him. I know what he wants deep down."

"You know what he wants sexually."

Dev turned my head up to face him. "Don't think that doesn't matter. I can tell a lot about a person from their sexual needs. How they want to treat their partners and want to be treated says something about them, and not always what you think it does."

It was a serious subject for him. He'd told me once that when he had met me, he knew from the moment he met me how to seduce me. "So what does Louis want from us?"

I hated the fact that I had to use "us." Louis had made it plain he found my faery prince very appealing. I wouldn't be the only one dealing with Louis's advances.

Dev seemed to be relieved I broached that subject so he didn't need to. "He'll want us both, my goddess. I'm not looking forward to it but I can handle it and I can handle him. I'll convince him to take his more violent impulses out on me."

"Dev…"

"Shhh." He put a finger to my lips. "I can take a lot of damage. The vampire blood in my system will stay around for a long time. My body was built for sex of all kinds. I'll turn on my magic and I won't notice the pain. What Louis will want from you is softness. He'll want you to be Zoey, but he views himself as your savior. He wants you to want him. Don't overplay your hand, though. It must be convincing. Follow my lead. This is a game of sex and seduction. I know how to play."

"Or we could not play at all," Bris said, taking over suddenly. His deeply green eyes were practically begging me. "I'm sorry I could do nothing to save Lee. I'm still very weak, but in a few days I'll be back at my full strength. I can get you out of this situation, my goddess. When we get to Paris, I will call all things green to our side and we'll escape."

"You could get me back to the Order?" I asked even as I knew I would refuse him. I needed to stay close to Marini if I was going to get that stone. Daniel needed me to steal the stone back and take away Marini's advantage.

Bris sighed. "I don't think that's a good idea. I'll take you someplace safe." He placed his hand firmly on my belly. "The babies need safety now. There are two and they're male. I can protect them. I can ensure that they develop properly. Zoey, one of these boys is the fertility god that Faery has been waiting for. It's a second chance to have the child we lost."

"This baby is Devinshea's," I pointed out to the god.

"This baby is ours. This child is yours and mine and Dev and Daniel's, as the last one was. My goddess, I'm not trying to trick you. I love the children as I love you. I do not care who the children's biological parents are." He frowned suddenly and pulled away from me. "The wizard got to you as well."

312

I sat up and touched him again, pulling him into my arms this time. "No, My Lord. I still trust you. You have to forgive me. It's been a long day and it isn't over. I can't let you take me away. I have to steal that stone and I can't do it if I'm hiding with you. We need you, now more than ever. You can give Louis something he wants."

Bris nodded. "My magic."

"I know it seems wrong to use it in this way…"

He laughed briefly. "It isn't wrong to use everything I have at my command to aid my goddess and my host. I'll do everything I can to protect you and distract the vampire so you can do your job. But, my goddess, once we have the stone…"

"Oh, Bris, once we have the stone I give you full permission to get me the hell out of there any way you can," I assured him.

He pulled me close and we lay down on the small cot together. I let my head find his chest and listened to his heartbeat. The events of the day were a drag on my soul, and I felt so old in that moment.

"My goddess, I am so sorry about the wolf." Bris tugged my chin up. "He was a good man."

I nodded, feeling the tears well up again. "Bris, you know so much. Can you tell me something?"

"I can try."

"Where did he go?" I asked a child's question because it was the one I had wondered since the moment I felt Lee slip away from me. One moment he had been there and the next he was somewhere else.

Bris sighed deeply. "Zoey, I am a creature of the Earth plane. You may call me a god, but I'm not all-seeing. I think that's a question better asked of the Heaven plane, but I do know this. I've lived long enough to have met the same souls many times. Our journey does not end with death. We have many chances. Your wolf will get another chance and perhaps this time will be easier on him."

I rested my head again and hoped that wherever Lee was, he wasn't alone.

I was roused a long time later from a blissfully dreamless sleep when the door to our small prison opened. I looked up blearily, slightly confused at where I was. I felt Dev look up, raising his head. We were cuddled close together on the narrow cot, most of my body on top of Devinshea's.

Louis Marini walked into the small room, and it was illuminated only by the light outside in the hall. I wondered briefly where he'd slept but figured they probably had coffins in the hold for the vampires.

"Interesting." Marini stood over us, an imposing figure. He'd changed from his all black battle wear to more carefully chosen clothes. He wore black slacks and an olive sweater. The olive color did nice things for his skin, and I knew he had spent time getting himself ready for this meeting. Dev was right. He was more invested in us than he would be in simple possessions. "I rather expected to find the two of you in a more compromising position."

Dev's arms tightened around me. "That wasn't what she needed last night."

Louis nodded at Dev. "She was very upset by the death of her wolf. She cared for him?"

"I loved him," I corrected the vampire. "He was like a brother to me."

Louis's sensual mouth turned down, and I could see he was considering how to handle me. "I am sorry, then. He was right, though. I could not allow him to live. He was not a practical creature. He would have fought and fought until I had to put him down. The prince here is much more realistic. Now up, both of you. We've reached our destination and night has fallen."

I got up, trying not to look too hard at the vampire. Dev got up behind me and tried to put his arm around me.

"No," Louis said harshly. "If you want to touch my companion, you will ask permission."

Dev held his hands up. He took a step back from me, a bitter expression on his face. "I understand. You don't need to explain anything to me. Daniel warned us how it would be if we thought to run to you."

Louis's eyes flared with that last comment. Dev was playing his role and I did my best to look downcast as I nodded, agreeing with him. I stood by myself, allowing the cold to seep in and not trying to hide the shiver that ran across my skin. Marini had a lot to learn about taking care of a companion. We had been offered nothing to eat or drink and the cot was spare, with only one thin blanket that did nothing to fight the biting chill. I probably looked pathetic, but it might work to my advantage.

"What did Donovan say about me?" Louis asked, his dark brows meeting in consternation.

Dev frowned and shook his head. "We had a fight when we realized what he was doing. Neither Zoey nor I thought it was a good idea to try to take over the Council. Daniel hid his plans from us. When I discovered them, it was quite a fight. I threatened to take Zoey away and Daniel…I won't even go into what Daniel did to me. When I recovered, he explained the way it would be if we attempted to seek shelter with you. He said you would never allow us the freedoms he granted us. Daniel could be a brute but he allowed us to remain together, so we stayed and took his abuse."

Marini had the good sense to look confused. "I was under the impression Zoey loved Daniel."

"Zoey loves me," Dev said fervently, but even in this I could see his carefully planned actions. "She played the part of Daniel's faithful companion because he would have killed both of us if she hadn't."

"I offered to take her away," Marini replied, suspicion in his voice. "She has known for a long time I would take her from Donovan."

"I didn't believe you would accept me. I convinced her to stay. I thought you would take Zoey and kill me at the first opportunity. I'm still not sure you won't do it, but we didn't have much of a choice."

"Devinshea," I said suddenly and even to my own ears I sounded very weary. Marini was suspicious and I needed him to believe. I only knew one way to make a vampire trust me. He would be more easily swayed under the influence of my blood. "It's no use. Daniel was right. Vampires are all the same. Now, I can sense that Louis is very hungry. You didn't bring Rose?"

I had thrown him off with talk of food. I was sure he'd expected me to put this moment off as long as I could. "No."

"If you could leave us, Dev," I said. "I would rather do this privately."

Dev's face was haunted and I knew that was no act. "All right, Zoey." He turned to Louis. "I assume there are guards outside I can surrender myself to while you…"

Louis went and unlocked the door. He ushered Dev out and I heard him talking to someone. "Please take the prince to the galley. Order the slaves to prepare a meal for him and my companion. She'll join him shortly. David, he's a guest. I'll be angry if he is harmed."

I breathed a sigh of relief. Goal one was accomplished. He wouldn't hurt Dev. Now I had to make sure he didn't hurt me. The door closed and was locked again, and I was alone with my new "master."

"You wish to feed me, companion?" There was a bit of challenge in the question. He got into my space, looming over me.

"I've been shot at, watched my best friend carted off to the Hell plane, held my guard as he died in my arms. The man I love will never be allowed to touch me again without your permission. No, Louis, I don't want to feed you. I want to lie down and sleep and never wake up again. Please, if you're going to hurt me, just do it and get it over with. I have no intention of fighting you this time. I know it won't do me any good."

He actually pulled me into his arms as though I would find some comfort in the man who had done all the things I had mentioned before. I stood stiffly, waiting for him to strike.

"Zoey," he whispered. "I don't want to hurt you. I never wanted to hurt you. Come here. You're cold. I've been neglectful. Please forgive me." His hand ran the length of my back but stopped before going lower, as if he forced himself to not be too sexual. "Let me pull you in. Let me do this for you. I can make you feel good, warm, and safe." He was shorter than Daniel, but he still had to lean over to nuzzle my neck. He ran his nose all along my neck, sighing with pleasure. "We'll both feel so good, *chère. J'ai envie d'être avec vous.*"

I felt his magic drawing at me and, with a bitter push, let my guard down. It wouldn't do anyone any good to force him to savage me. If I gave in, he would be gentler and maybe not take so much. I relaxed against him as his strong magic washed over me. It was different from Daniel's. There was a dominance in this magic that was different from anything I'd experienced before. Louis pushed us toward the cot as his fangs grazed my skin and I felt his tongue there. He kissed my neck fervently as he lowered me down. Though I hated myself for it, that magic made me want his bite.

I sighed as he struck, his fangs piercing with a sweet pleasure and he groaned as my blood hit his mouth. Unwillingly, my hands wound into the dark curls of his hair and I let myself ride that drug. There was nothing of pain in this place. There was just a heavenly sense of contentment as he pulled strongly for a moment. As I had hoped, he didn't take nearly as much as last time. My submission gentled him, and I floated down as he let go and settled in against me, his tongue laving long licks of affection against my throat.

"J'ai besoin de vous," the vampire whispered.

I pulled my hands down and let them fall to my sides because he was pulling at my shirt now and if I was about to be raped, I might not fight him but I wasn't going to participate. His legs pushed mine apart and I could feel his erection nudging me. My eyes filled with tears. I'd never had sex with anyone but Dev or Daniel. My sex life might be considered kinky and wild, but I had never been touched by someone I didn't love, and I ached at the thought of losing this piece of me.

Marini sat up abruptly, his body shaking. He was heavily under the influence of my blood. Rose might be a companion, but I was betting from Louis's reaction that her blood didn't do the same thing for him. He looked drugged and happy and then slightly disturbed at the sight of me.

"Go," he said suddenly.

I sat up, not quite understanding.

"Join the prince." He rose and unlocked the door. "It's too soon. I won't have you think me a monster to take you while you weep underneath me. Go."

I walked out the door and a guard was there, taking my arm, leading me up to the galley where I would join Dev. Despite the fact that I'd given in to Louis, I found myself with a certain amount of power. Dev had been right. I could play him if I was careful. I hid a small, secret smile as I let my new guard lead me back to my husband.

317

CHAPTER TWENTY-NINE

My first look at the City of Lights was very brief. I'd been hustled from the boat onto a private train car that took us from the coast to Paris. Marini had found an oversized coat for me and I sat in my seat across from Dev looking like a pathetic waif. I watched the dark night pass by and couldn't help but wonder if Danny had woken up and if he was hungry. Justin was supposed to bring the reserve blood with him, but I couldn't be sure Justin had even made it to England yet. Daniel was alone and sick and probably terrified because he had no idea if we were alive or dead.

"You're still cold?" Louis asked me. I simply nodded and he moved closer, tentatively slipping his arm around my shoulders and pulling me to him. He knocked on the door and said a whole bunch of things in French to the vampire named David, who nodded and went off to do his master's bidding.

I was forced to sit quietly in Marini's arms but I caught Dev's satisfaction. A vampire's instincts are to protect a companion. A vampire wants to please a companion and a smart companion can use that to her advantage.

From the train we were settled into a limo for the brief ride through Paris. I couldn't muster any enthusiasm. I stared blankly out of the windows because all I could think of was Lee and Neil and Daniel.

"Is the temperature all right, Zoey?" Louis asked abruptly and I heard the fine line of annoyance in his voice. He was getting tired of my crying.

I wanted to slap the bastard. He'd killed someone close to me. He'd sent my best friend off with a demon and he was annoyed because I wasn't getting over it fast enough. I wanted to beat the shit out of him, but Dev's eyes were on me, begging me to play my part.

I gave the vampire a watery smile. "It's fine, thank you."

"Are you afraid, darling?" Dev leaned over to put his hand on my knee but then remembered himself and pulled back.

"Why would she be afraid?" Marini asked. "I've done everything I can to be gentle with her."

Dev sat back and let a little disgust show through. "You're taking her into a nest of vampires. She's been fought over by vampires for the last several years. Daniel has explained how it will be. You can't blame us for being afraid."

"Daniel never brought you to the Council," the vampire mused. "He kept you hidden away. I've wondered about that. He could easily have brought you with him when he visited. No one would have challenged him. So why would he hide you? Unless he was afraid you would be tempted by other vampires."

"Why would I be tempted by other vampires?" I didn't have to pretend my distaste. "I know what's going to happen when I walk into the catacombs. I'll be preyed upon by every vampire who can get his hands on me. I'll have to lock myself in somewhere so they can't get to me."

Marini gasped in obvious horror. "You believe I would allow my companion to be used by another vampire? You think I would allow others to frighten you and treat you poorly?"

"Daniel explained it all to us," Dev said, and he looked like he was steeling himself for something unpleasant. "He was the only one strong enough to protect us. Vampires are like animals around companions. They'll fight over her like dogs over a bone, and they won't care if she gets hurt in the process. Once they get a taste of me, it will be no different."

319

Louis sighed. "He kept you both so ignorant. A companion is cherished, Mr. Quinn. You have heard the term precious blood?"

I nodded. We had heard it many times. Dev and I, we were Daniel's precious blood. He held us higher than all others. It meant we fed him and loved him. We were his heart and soul, and it told other vampires that he would brook no disrespect to us.

"You'll be known as my precious blood, Zoey," Marini promised. "No one will touch you. You'll be honored. I know Donovan called you his queen, but I promise to treat you as one. You'll see. You'll be very safe and comfortable in my palace." The car came to a sudden halt. "We're here. Come, Prince Devinshea. Let me show you the depths of Daniel's deceptions. We'll talk further in my suite. Put these on. The catacombs can be hell on a pair of trousers." He passed Dev a pair of sturdy-looking rubber boots. They both pulled them over their shoes. My sneakers and jeans didn't require saving apparently.

Louis helped me from the car and I could hear and see the swell of people around me, but their eyes slid over us like we weren't there. They walked past on their way to the underground station. Dev was behind us as Louis pushed past the doors that led down to the catacombs. I would later learn that this was only one of several entrances. The catacombs were vast, a city underneath a city. I shivered despite the coat because even I could feel the death in this subterranean necropolis. Louis led us to a ladder that went straight down.

"I can't see anything," I said, my voice trembling because once the door behind us closed, we were enveloped in complete darkness.

"It's all right, Zoey." Marini's voice was smooth in the gloom. I felt his hand reach for mine. "I'll light a torch when reach the ground level. There are still tourists on this level, and I don't want them following us. I don't have time to take care of them tonight. Follow me. David, you will lead the prince."

I allowed the vampire to lead me. I carefully made my way down the ladder feeling each step was another step farther from Daniel. It seemed to take forever as I focused just on the next rung and not falling to my death. Finally I heard the sound of feet hitting water and then felt strong hands on my waist.

"I have you, companion." Marini pulled me off the ladder, securing me in his arms. "Put your hands around my neck. It's very dangerous down here."

I hooked my fingers together around the vampire's neck and held on. I listened as the rest of the party hit the water. Someone turned on a flashlight, and then I wished I'd been left in darkness.

All around me, everywhere the light touched, were bones. The very walls seemed to be made of them. They were stacked, coming up from the water we walked in to the ceiling above us. I gasped my shock and buried my head in the vampire's shoulder.

I felt Louis's deep chuckle as he tightened his arms around me. "My little companion is frightened, David."

"There is nothing to worry about," David assured me in heavily accented English. "My master will take care of any corpse that tries to get you."

I could feel the vampire's satisfaction in playing my protector. I didn't particularly want to take a good look around the catacombs. I briefly glanced over Louis's shoulder and I caught a flash of emerald green eyes taking in everything. Bris was memorizing the route, his ancient eyes seeing what Dev's could not. He would make note of the way out and any plants he could use to help us when we needed to flee. I relaxed slightly because I knew between Bris and Dev, I would be taken care of. I just needed to do my job.

"That's right, Zoey." Louis's voice filled the darkness with his pleasure at my misunderstood action. "Relax. I have you. I'll take care of you."

David moved forward as we stopped in front of a wall. He ran his hand down a crease and I heard a distinct click. There was a sliding sound and then a whole other world was revealed. Light flooded the passageway, and I had to blink for my eyes to adjust.

Louis walked through and we were at the top of a grand staircase. The sight of such opulence was surreal. We walked out of the tombs and into glorious civilization. The staircase was marble and lit beautifully by a hundred small sconces on the wall, each with a candle. It gave the entire place a gauzy, old-world feeling.

"Take the prince to my suite," Marini ordered. "I'll settle Zoey and join him there."

I wanted to touch Dev, but we were moving again and I studied the council stronghold with a small sense of wonder.

"You like it," Marini said, approving of the look on my face. He could have put me down, but he chose to walk down the stairs in his rubber boots though the rest of the party stopped to get rid of them.

I was honest. "It's beautiful."

I don't know exactly what I had expected. I supposed I thought it would be darker and more Gothic, but this was the inside of an airy palace.

"I loved Versailles," Marini explained as we passed people in the hall. There was a lot of life down here. There were humans, vampires, and I felt the stares of at least two companions as Louis carried me through the Council's stronghold. "This is my version. You'll find it quite luxurious and extremely well fortified. You'll be safe here, Zoey. Your every need will be met."

"L'avez-vous fait?" I heard and Louis spun on his heels.

"In English, Elof," Louis said. "She doesn't speak French yet. I'll hire a tutor tomorrow to begin her lessons. To answer your question, I only succeeded in part. I retrieved the lovely Zoey and the Prince has chosen to come with me as well."

The tall Norwegian's eyes narrowed suspiciously. "And Donovan?"

"I don't know. He had some sort of magic with him. I almost had my hands on him when he disappeared. I tried to use our fail-safe, but I can't say if it worked or not. I rather think he got away," Louis admitted bitterly. "I'll settle Zoey in and then I'll meet with you, Niles, and Niko. Marcus is still not here?"

I fought not to tense at the mention of Marcus's name. I didn't think it was a good idea for Marcus to come here at all. It would be better for him to stay with Daniel at the Order's compound.

Elof frowned. "He's mysteriously out of touch."

Now they switched back to French. So much for not being rude around me. Though I couldn't speak French, I was suspicious of what they were saying about Marcus. They spoke briefly and then parted ways, and I found myself being carried into a large suite of rooms.

A thin man opened the door for us and welcomed the head of the Council. He was an older gentleman with gray hair that had receded to the back of his head. He was dressed in the all black of a servant.

"Master Marini," he said in a low voice as he bowed deeply.

"Robert." Marini finally set me on my feet. He left the "t" off Robert. "This is Zoey. She is my companion. She speaks English. Please address her thusly." Marini sat on the couch in the living room of the large apartment and pulled the boots off.

Robert gasped slightly. "What about Rose?"

Louis stood again and waved off the question as unimportant. "She'll be sold or I'll give her away. I don't know. She no longer matters. Find her different quarters until I decide what to do with her." He turned back to me. "I'll meet with your Prince and we'll find a way for us to move forward, companion. Would you like that?"

I nodded because the alternative was me moving forward without Dev.

The vampire leaned down and I forced myself to accept his kiss. "You'll be allowed thirty minutes during the daytime to visit him tomorrow. A guard will come for you late in the afternoon. Once night falls, the three of us will discuss things. I look forward to teaching you about your new home, Zoey."

He turned, done with me, and walked out the door. I was left with Robert, who didn't like me much.

I stood there, not knowing what to do. I hadn't even been properly introduced to this man and I wasn't sure who he was. He seemed human and since he was a servant, he was probably a slave.

"I'm Zoey," I said, putting my hand out because it seemed the polite thing to do.

He stared at my hand dismissively. "I know who you are. You're Zoey Donovan. You will put my mistress out of her home."

"Now, now, Robert," I heard a familiar voice say. "This was never my home."

Rose walked into the living area. I don't know quite what I expected from Marini's companion. I'd only met her twice and she seemed like such a young little mouse. She was dressed in a silky shirt and nice slacks. The clothes she wore aged her by twenty years but they were of good quality. I wondered briefly if Robert had selected her wardrobe. There were tears in her eyes as she walked up to me. I prayed she wasn't going to beseech me not to take her lover. I would have no idea what to say.

"I am so, so sorry to see you here, Zoey," Rose said in her proper

British accent, quietly putting both her hands on my shoulders. "Please tell me they haven't killed your Daniel."

Rose's compassion cut through me like a knife, and I was completely caught off guard. Of all the things I expected to find in this place, kindness was the last. I looked at that little mouse whose place I would have to take and I burst into tears.

"Robert," Rose said quietly, "I think we could use a drink."

I managed to talk Rose down to a nice cup of tea. Robert seemed more kindly toward me as he poured the Earl Grey and offered me sugar, milk, and a box of tissues. I found myself telling the two of them everything that had happened with Marini. I left out anything personal about Daniel. I still had a part to play. I spoke of Lee and Neil, and Rose listened while Robert fussed over her.

"Then Daniel managed to get away," she said with what seemed like a relieved sigh.

I nodded, not wanting to give too much away. "I think so."

"But the prince is with you," Rose commented.

"Yes, he's with Marini right now." I took a small sip of tea and noted that it was getting very late. It was almost four. Even with my nocturnal lifestyle, I yawned. "I believe they're discussing how my life is going to work now. It would have been nice to sit in on that conversation."

Rose's eyes went wide. "No, Zoey, that isn't the way things work here. I'm afraid the vampires here are all very old."

"They're old fashioned," Robert added. "They don't think anything odd of a group of men planning a woman's life. You should be prepared because tomorrow the master will tell you how your life will be. You must nod and do as he says."

Rose agreed. "You should listen to Robert. He's been in Louis's service for many years. He knows how to survive. He has helped me all these years."

"How long have you been here, Rose?"

She had to think about it for a moment. "I was fourteen when they took me. I was walking to the store for my mum. I believe I am now twenty years old."

I was outraged for the young girl she had been. "He raped you when you were fourteen?"

Robert patted his charge's back. "No, she was lucky in that regard. The master's companion was getting older, but he was comfortable with her. He purchased Rose and she was allowed to be alone to mature until the previous companion died. Rose was seventeen when he married her."

"That's still horrible," I muttered.

"Well, we don't all get a vampire like Daniel," Rose said softly.

I wanted to talk about him. I wanted to tell her how lucky I was and how special Danny really was, but somewhere Dev was alone in a room full of old vampires, playing the part we had agreed upon. He was alone and vulnerable and I couldn't let him down because I was emotional.

"Daniel was like all the rest," I forced myself to say because while Robert and Rose seemed very supportive, I couldn't trust anyone down here except my husband.

Rose's brows rose. "I can hardly think that. I knew him. He was already here when I was brought over from England. The rest treated me like I wasn't even there but Daniel was kind. He gave me books to read. I always liked him very much."

"You weren't his companion," was all I could say.

"But he seemed to care so very much for you."

Robert's old eyes were wise as he stopped his charge. "Rose, dear, it occurs to me that if Mrs. Donovan is to survive this, it's probably best she plays to the master's desires. I'm certain the master doesn't want to hear of her great love for another vampire."

Rose laughed, a sweet youthful sound. "Of course. That's very silly of me. I don't suppose Louis would take very well to Zoey crying over Daniel. It makes me wonder why he allowed the Prince to come along."

She looked up to Robert for guidance, and I realized the older man acted much like a father to Rose.

"Vampires feed off sexual energy. I have told you this, little one," Robert explained academically. He turned to me. "Your prince is also a priest, correct?"

"Yes, he's a High Priest," I replied.

Robert nodded as though I had confirmed something he had suspected for a very long time. "The rumors are that the sexual energy given off by a faery priest is amazing. It could feed a hundred vampires, make them stronger and capable of doing things they could not when they haven't fed from the energy. I believe the master wishes to experiment. He believes the *Nex Apparatus* became stronger once he took the faery prince to his bed."

I sipped my tea and didn't comment on that. My mind was going in new and disturbing places. Daniel didn't begin to daywalk until the day after he, Dev, and I came together. The effect had been quick. The next day Daniel saw the sun for the first time in years. Dev's power had gotten supercharged since then. With Daniel feeding from Bris's energy, he no longer needed a daily dose. He walked during the day, free from the restrictions of a normal vampire. He still wasn't as comfortable as a natural daywalker like Marcus, but he would get there. Would a fertility ritual have the same effect on Louis Marini?

"Mrs. Donovan?" Robert asked and I had the feeling he had been attempting to get my attention for a bit.

"Yes," I said, pulled from my thoughts.

"It's late." Robert stood and lent me his hand to help me up from my chair. "I apologize for my earlier rudeness. My only excuse is my affection for Rose. I've been her servant since the day she walked into the catacombs. She's very dear to me as I have watched her grow. The knowledge that she will be someone else's responsibility soon was discomforting. I'll attempt to make your stay here comfortable, but I must go and find other rooms for Rose. It will be dawn soon and we must all be in our beds."

"Will Louis check?" I asked, suddenly not wanting to be alone in this strange place.

"No, probably not," the servant admitted.

"Then, please, stay," I asked. "I would rather not be alone."

Rose reached over and took my hand. "I'll stay with you. Come along and I'll show you our bedroom. Perhaps Louis will allow me to stay until he figures out what to do with me. I can show you things. I can help you. No one ever notices me so they don't bother to hide things from me. You'll be surprised at what I know."

"Do you know about the Blood Stone?"

Robert's wise eyes narrowed. "Yes, madam. We know of the stone. The vampires were very excited when it was recovered. It was when the master called to say he had the stone that they began to seriously talk about a war against the *Nex Apparatus*. They say it makes Marini a king."

"Temporarily." I looked down so they didn't see just how interested I was. "I'm merely curious."

"It's important to him," Robert said seriously. His mind seemed to be working overtime. "He would keep it close to him during the night."

Rose smiled, the act lighting up her face. "But not during the day. He would put it in the safe."

My eyes filled with tears because twenty-eight years of my life came into focus with one simple phrase. Everything I had suffered through had brought me to this place. The universe, god, fate, whatever you wanted to call it, had carefully moved me into this position and I knew what I had been born to do. I was a thief. I had sat at my father's knee and learned how to do one thing.

It wouldn't be strength or superpowers that won this war. It would be me and the sweet science my father had taught me.

"Rose, I'm going to need to know where that safe is."

CHAPTER THIRTY

"He put you in a jail cell?" I asked, shocked at the sight of Dev behind bars. I'd spent the day sleeping in a comfortable bed, but Dev had been tossed into a cell.

Dev shrugged and sat up, his eyes eating up the sight of me. "I've been in worse jails, lover. In my rankings of incarceration holding cells, this is really just below that little town in Montana I got arrested in. They served pie. It was damn fine pie."

I walked up to the cell and put my hands around the cold bars. "I don't want to know how many times you've been arrested, baby. It would shock me. It makes me think Neil is right about…"

I almost said our babies' bail fund but I caught myself. I couldn't say anything else because of the hulking werewolf who stood in the background. He was enormous, taller than Dev, and was at least two fifty, all of it pure muscle. He'd come to escort me down for my thirty minutes with my husband. He'd introduced himself as Trent, but I kind of thought of him as traitor. I wondered how a werewolf could work for a man like Marini, who was trying to subjugate his entire race. As I'd walked around the Council stronghold this afternoon, I'd seen that there were a lot of wolves and shifters who'd been lured with money to betray their brethren.

Dev had changed clothes and appeared oddly casual in sweats and a T-shirt that didn't quite fit. He'd managed to slick back his hair and even in a jail cell, found a way to make my heart race. The only problem was the look in his eyes.

"Are you all right?" I wondered how horrible his night had been.

Dev got up and walked to the bars of the cell. He put his hands over mine. "I'm fine. I survived the night, as did you, and that's all we can hope for. Now Trent, can you open this cell and allow me to hold my wife?"

"Damn it, Quinn, is this necessary?" The wolf growled back. "McKenzie will have my hide if I get caught. I've been undercover for six years. I'm not getting caught because you're horny." Trent's accent made me think he was probably a Red Sox fan.

Dev's eyes narrowed at the wolf and his mouth turned down. He was well and truly pissed off. He looked like he was about to start in on the much bigger guard when an idea struck him. "Sweetheart, why don't you tell Trent there to open this fucking cage of mine?"

I was beyond thrilled to discover he actually worked for John McKenzie, the alpha of the American wolf packs, but he still looked really mean. "I don't think he'll listen to me."

Dev's smile was arrogant, and I wondered what the hell had happened last night to put him in this mood. He was in full-on, fuck-with-authority mode. He was spoiling for a fight or something else. He needed to be in control and he could do it one of two ways. He could tempt the big were in to a fight or he could dominate me for a little while. I knew which way I would go.

"What are your orders, Trent?" Dev asked.

Trent's big, bulky shoulders slumped slightly. "You know what my orders are. I'm supposed to keep an eye out here. I report back to the Lieutenant and let him know what's going on. I've been working my way up for years, and I'm finally getting close to the Council members. When and if the time is right, I'll assassinate whoever I need to."

"Lieutenant?" I asked. "Is the army involved?"

Trent shot me a rueful grin. "Sorry, ma'am. I'm afraid once a Ranger always a Ranger. John McKenzie was my team leader when we were in the Army." His eyes softened. "I also knew your guard.

329

Owens was a good man. I was very, very sorry to hear about his death. Please know we'll avenge him when the time is right."

I nodded and Dev squeezed my hand. He stared at the ex-Ranger and got back to his point. We had very little time. "Now, tell me what your orders have been since last summer."

Last summer, we performed our ritual for the wolves. The babies had been born this spring. It was when Daniel had forged his alliance with the wolves.

Trent's jaw firmed to a stubborn line, but he answered. "I'm to aid the King of all Vampire in anything he might need."

"And?"

Trent growled a little. "And his queen."

I smiled but tried to keep it sweet. "I'm sorry, Trent. I'm going to need this door open."

And, because a good wolf always follows orders, Trent pulled out the key and opened the door. "Her Highness will have to shower and change clothes. Marini's senses might not be as good as a wolf, but they're damn fine. If he smells the Prince on you he'll kill me."

"I'll be careful," I promised, my hands itching to touch Dev's skin and remind myself that he was here and alive and with me.

Dev's mouth was on mine before Trent could quite get out of the way.

I heard his sigh even as Dev pulled me against his body. "You have exactly twenty minutes. I'll be right outside. If I knock, you two better separate."

I heard the door close and knew the wolf would stand right outside. He would hear everything and Dev wouldn't give a shit.

"Take off your clothes," Dev ordered, stepping back. His hands were shaking and his eyes haunted.

"What did he do to you, baby?" My stomach churned at the thought of what my green-eyed boy might have done to protect me. I'd been unwilling to give Marini what he wanted last night. Had he taken it out on Dev?

His smile was reckless and hid not a bit of his pain to me. "Nothing I can't handle, lover. Now take your clothes off. Do I have to ask you again?"

I didn't point out that he hadn't asked me at all. I pulled my clothes off because whatever had happened to put that look in his eyes had been bad, and this was the only way he knew to handle it. He'd been powerless last night, submissive to someone else's whims, and now he needed to get his control back. I was willing because he needed it and he would never, never hurt me.

Once I was naked and obviously willing, his stance relaxed slightly. The tightness in his eyes disappeared, replaced by hot anticipation. "I want you to step up to the bars of the cell, lean over, and hold them."

I did as he asked, holding the cold bars in my hands even as the rest of me warmed up at the thought of escaping everything for a few minutes. I didn't have to think about anything but pleasing my husband and letting him please me in return.

"Like this?" I leaned over and presented my backside in a wanton fashion that was sure to make his mouth water.

"That's right, sweetheart. Now spread those legs for me," Dev's smooth voice said behind me. His hands ran across my back and rear, caressing me like I was made of silk. "You're so fucking gorgeous, my goddess. I'll do anything for you."

"I love you," I said over my shoulder. I shivered as he palmed the cheeks of my rear.

He was still dressed, still perfectly in control, but I was quickly losing mine. I moved restlessly under the warmth of his hands.

"And I love you," Dev replied, leaning over to kiss the back of my neck. It brought the hard length of his erection firmly in contact with my backside. "You getting wet for me?"

I nodded breathlessly. His hands were tingling with magic. I worried a little about that. "Is this okay, baby? Won't the others be able to feel it?"

"I have control," Bris's deep voice intoned. "I'm still weak, but I can do this, my goddess. I have not needed to control the magic up until this point. I can focus it and control the flow. I can pour it into you and leave everyone else out."

"And why haven't you up to this point?" I asked because he'd always just let it run wild.

"Because it feels good to let it flow, and I didn't mind sharing it with those around us," the god replied. "We must be careful now.

Devinshea needs this. Last night was…"

"No big deal," Dev finished, wresting control back from the ancient god.

"Dev, what happened?"

"You are getting wet for me." He ignored the question. His fingers slid into my pussy from behind. He parted me and his thumb began to play with my clitoris. He pressed on that magic button and made little circles around it. "You're going be so tight on my cock. You're going to feel so fucking good."

He worked two fingers up high into me. I held onto the bars, needing them to stay standing. I pushed back on his fingers, my hips moving helplessly against him. "Your little pussy knows who the boss is, sweetheart. Oh, goddess, you're going to feel like heaven. Have I mentioned how much I like riding you bareback? I might just keep you pregnant for the rest of our lives so I never have to wear a condom again."

He stroked and rubbed and knew exactly where and how much pressure I needed. In a minute I was moaning, biting my lip to keep the noise to a minimum because I knew Trent was standing outside, and while the vampires might not be awake yet, there were plenty of people walking around the compound. It was the best I'd felt in what seemed like forever. I needed Dev. I needed him so badly. I was close, so close to falling over that sweet edge when Dev pulled his fingers out and away.

"Damn it, Dev," I hissed, looking up at him. His face was dark as he sucked the fingers into his mouth, licking off the taste of my arousal.

"You come with me, sweetheart, and not a moment before I'm ready," he said, not at all put off by my show of temper. I stood up, my whole body flushed with desire. I saw Dev take note of my very erect nipples. He frowned. "Did I give you permission to move, lover?"

I turned back to my previous position without further complaint. Something was riding him today, and he wasn't willing to share it with me yet. I gave him the only comfort I could. I gave him my compliance. There was the sound of his clothes hitting the floor and then he moved in behind me. I sighed in pleasure as his flesh met mine. Dev stroked his cock against my pussy, playing for a moment with no real penetration. He was content to tease me with the broad head of his penis rubbing against my clit.

"This is mine," he said, and I didn't think he was saying it to me. He was reminding himself. "This is fucking mine. No matter what he does, this is mine."

He thrust into me hard and gripped my hips to force me to move against him. I had to push against the cell bars to keep up with him. He wasn't gentle or sweet. He was hard and took what he needed, setting a brutal pace as he fucked into me. He slammed the full length of his cock in, only to pull out and start again. He hammered me from behind and I held on for dear life. He was teasing my sweet spot, knowing exactly what he was giving and withholding.

His torture seemed to go on forever but finally he was ready to let me fly. He reached around and thumbed my clit in perfect time to his thrusts. "Keep it quiet, lover. You know I love to make you scream but we have to be quiet."

I bit my lip as he hit that perfect spot and everything inside of me released. Pure pleasure sent all thoughts of the pain of the last few days fleeing. For a few seconds, all that mattered was him. I heard Dev grunt low behind me as he pushed deep one last time and I felt his come wash over me.

He threw a hand around my waist and pulled me into the cell and onto the low cot he'd slept on the night before. He tugged me down with him and covered my body with his, slanting his mouth over mine with soft kisses.

"I love you, Zoey," he whispered.

"I love you, baby," I gave back to him and wound my arms around him. "Tell me what happened, please."

His face went slightly blank and he pulled me against his chest. I was able to put my cheek against the warm flesh of his chest. "It was...unpleasant. Daniel is already at work."

I sat up suddenly, eager to hear anything at all about Danny. "What happened?"

"Marini owns several businesses in the US under a conglomerate," Dev explained as he toyed with my hair. "That conglomerate company is his main cash cow. Almost all of the Council's money flows through it. A long time ago Daniel and I decided that company would be the first domino to fall. I have contacts in the FBI and when the time was right, we were going to call them. The FBI raided their headquarters yesterday and froze all of their bank accounts."

The enormity of that hit me. "They froze his accounts?"

Dev nodded. "Marini isn't as smart as he thinks he is. Almost all of his cash was in those accounts. They can't do the same to Daniel. I've set up our cash in so many different places, under so many different names, they can't get it all. Daniel understands the whole of it so he will know where to go for cash if Marini attempts to hit us financially. This war will be fought on several fronts and Daniel and I intend to win on all of them."

"I bet he was pissed," I said, giving Dev an opening.

Dev pulled me back down so I couldn't see his face. "Yes, lover, he was angry. Elof and Niles were angry and Niko had to play along."

"Did they hit you?" I didn't ask the other question. I knew Marini was very attracted to Dev. He'd propositioned him on several occasions. I knew that being used in that fashion was one of Dev's worst nightmares. It had happened before and that single incident had a profound effect on his sexuality.

"Yes, sweetheart," Dev replied simply. "He beat me so badly I'm surprised I'm walking this afternoon. Daniel's blood kept me alive." He was quiet for a moment while I ran my fingers through his hair and kissed his cheek. "Dan can't let up. He can't stop. He has to apply as much pressure as he can. You have to give Marini everything he wants and that includes your body. Give him no reason whatsoever to hurt you. I'll take the punishment. I can handle it."

"I have Danny's blood, too." I didn't like the thought of Dev being forced to take all the pain.

Dev's hand found the center of my pelvis. "You also have our children deep inside your body. You have to let me do this. It's not only for you. It's for our family. Please just give him what he wants. Do you know how much it kills me to ask this of you?"

I hugged him tightly to me. "I know, baby. I'll do it. I'll do it for you and Danny and our babies. I promise." Maybe if Louis was happy with me he wouldn't take out his anger on Dev.

"He's going to come for us," Dev said with absolute certainty.

"Daniel will come for us when the time is right. He won't leave us here."

"He would never leave us here," I agreed. "It's killing him that we're here. You have to know that. He'll do anything he has to in order to get us back. But we have to live here and buy Danny some time. I found out where Louis's safe is."

"How did you find that out?"

"Rose," I replied. "She has a vested interest in fucking with Marini. She's seen him use the safe before. It's in his office behind a painting."

"I saw that painting yesterday," Dev mused. "It's behind his desk. The office is across from the bedroom in his apartment." His hands smoothed down my hair. "Perhaps we can convince him to let us sleep with him tonight and then in the morning we can slip out while he sleeps and you can take a look at the safe."

My gut clenched. "We'll sleep with him tonight?" I knew there would be no sleeping involved.

Dev sighed and hugged me tightly. "I promised we'll perform a ritual tonight for him."

"Is that such a good idea?" I asked. "When Daniel feeds off that magic he can daywalk. Do we really want Marini to be able to do that?"

Dev shoved a frustrated hand through his hair. "I don't see a way around it."

"Is there anything Bris can do?"

"I could withhold the magic," Bris said, his eyes changing so suddenly I found it shocking. Even the way his hands moved on my body felt different. "But I believe that would be potentially dangerous for my host. If Marini isn't getting something from Devinshea, then I believe he'll kill him just to prove a point to Daniel. He needs something from you, my goddess. He needs your blood. I need to give him a reason to keep my host alive."

The door opened suddenly, and I heard Trent's deep voice. This time he was damn serious and that tone brooked no disobedience. "Your Highness, I need you ready to leave in three minutes. Sunset is twenty minutes away and you have to shower and change before Marini is awake. The Prince must do the same."

"All right," I said, pushing myself up.

Dev was back and he pulled me close again. His mouth closed over mine and he kissed me deeply. "Try to remember that you're supposed to be relieved to be away from Daniel's plotting. You can be upset about Lee and Neil, but never show Marini that you miss Daniel. I'll see you in a while. Know that I will be with you. I can't stand the thought of his hands on you, but I'll be with you. I'll keep you safe."

I didn't say it to him because it would only have worried my husband, but I silently promised to protect him as well. I would do whatever I had to do to keep us together and whole until Daniel could come for us. I stood up and got dressed again. I was already thinking about how I could organize the job on the safe. I couldn't just rip off the door and run. I needed to crack the safe and beyond that, I needed to fool Marini into thinking everything was all right until Bris could lead us out. I wasn't sure how to do that but I would think on it.

Dev smiled from the small cot. "I love that look you get when you're working on a job."

I laughed softly as I attempted to smooth my hair back down. "I don't think I'll be working much from here on out. I think this might be my last job for a while."

Dev got up and stalked across the room. When he reached me, he dropped to his knees and hugged me to him, his face against my belly. "Would it be so bad, my wife? Daniel and I love to take care of you. You could only work when you really wanted to and only take jobs that interest you. I doubt this is the last time you work. You're too good and far too addicted to give it up completely."

I smiled down at him. "Besides, you think it's hot when I steal something."

"I do, indeed." He kissed my belly and then got up to press his lips to mine. "I'll see you later tonight. Go with Trent. You can trust him. I have to shower and, more than likely, change into even more inferior clothing. I wish they would have allowed me to pack for my incarceration. Jail cells are really hell on the grooming process."

Trent was in the room and he led me out, tugging me away. As long as I could, I kept my eyes on Dev because the sight of him was the only thing that kept me going.

CHAPTER THIRTY-ONE

Rose was waiting at the door to the suite as Trent hustled me down the hall. Trent looked suspicious of the companion but said nothing as she closed the door behind us, leaving Trent to stand guard outside.

"He didn't hurt you?" Rose asked.

"The guard? No." I wondered just how often Rose had been abused by the guards for her to immediately go to that question.

"Good." She pointed to the bathroom. "Robert thought you would need to shower after spending time with your husband. The shower's hot. Hurry. I'll take your clothes and Robert will wash them."

The hot shower felt good and I enjoyed feeling clean for the first time in days. Rose proved she didn't mind nudity as she was waiting with a towel when I turned off the water and exited the lovely, feminine shower. The glass enclosure had carved flowers all over it. Rose nudged me to sit in front of a vanity and began working a comb through my hair.

We were quiet for a moment as she worked. My hair was a mess but she was patient. I thought about Dev and Danny and she thought about…probably her very uncertain future.

"What's going to happen to you, Rose?" I asked quietly, looking at her in the mirror. She hadn't changed out of her pajamas yet. She wore an old-fashioned looking gown that somewhat swallowed her petite figure.

Her lips moved in a semblance of a smile. "I'll be sold again, I suppose. I didn't like that part."

I had seen the ritual auction of a companion once before and it had been completely humiliating. I didn't like to think about little Rose being put through that not once but twice. "How do you stay so calm?"

"You stay calm. How do you do it?"

I shifted uncomfortably because what I was thinking was a bit uncomplimentary, but I really wanted to know. "I have Dev and…"

Rose's smile was bright now. "Yes, of course. You have the men you love to bolster you. You think I don't have anyone I love?"

I felt like shit but she seemed amused. "I don't mean it like that. You were just very young when they took you and I find it hard to believe you've found someone in this hellhole."

"I found Robert," Rose said with a look that was wise far beyond her years. "I found a father, not a lover, but I have more than that, Zoey. I have faith. I believe that when the time is right I'll run and I won't look back."

So the little mouse had a backbone. "Yes, Rose, if you get that chance, you run for your life."

Rose sighed. "I dream about it, you know. I dream about walking into my old home and my mum's there and I'll tell her I'm sorry for taking so bloody long to get back from the store."

I laughed. "I think it would be a bit more emotional than that. Do you think she's still there?" It had been years.

"Yes, she's still there. It's the last place she saw me. She wouldn't leave. She'll stay there until I show up again or she dies. I want to go home, Zoey. I want to walk into that flat and find my mum waiting with a book in her hand. I want to tell her what she did for me. I want to thank her because all this time, all these years, I was never really apart from her. They could take me away and not let me see her, but they couldn't stop her from whispering in my ear. She told me she loved me. She told me that strength comes in many forms and the greatest is to face adversity and stay true to who you are. I'm still her daughter. No matter what happened. I am still Rose Beasley. I would let her know she never let me down."

"Rose, if you manage to get out…my father's name is Harry Wharton." I said, moved so deeply by her courage that I missed my own father sharply. "He lives in Dallas, Texas."

"I will call him if I can," she replied. "I'll let him know you love him. Now dry those tears. I expect the sun is down by now and our master will be here soon. I need to get your hair dry."

Rose went to work, pulling a brush through my hair as she worked it over with the dryer. I let her do the job as I mentally prepared myself for the coming evening. Daniel was alive. Dev was alive. I had to do everything I could to keep them that way. Rose brushed my hair and I let a sense of acceptance flow over me. Nothing mattered except doing my job. Once the job was done and Dev and I could run, then I would worry about the rest. Then I'd save Neil. Then I would avenge my wolf.

Myrddin had told me the only way I could win was to not give in to my grief.

"I would have expected the two of you not to get along," Marini said from the doorway of the bathroom.

I saw Rose's entire demeanor change the moment she knew Marini was in the room. She seemed to shrink in on herself.

I turned slightly to acknowledge the vampire's presence. "Why would you think that? Rose is very sweet. I like having someone to talk to."

Louis was dressed to kill in a dark designer suit. His black hair curled just at the nape of his neck and if he wasn't such an evil son of a bitch, he would have been quite handsome. "I would have assumed Rose would be angry that you're taking her place."

I managed to not laugh at him. It was truly a sign of my burgeoning self-control. "Louis, you're a practical man. Do you really believe you've treated her so well that she's in love with you?"

Louis leaned against the paneled wall and his lips quirked up in amusement. I suspected it had been a long while since any female spoke to him so saucily. It appeared he liked it, but I had to tread carefully so sauciness wasn't mistaken for disrespect. "I suppose not. I haven't been particularly kind to Rose. I admit I purchased her when she was far too young. She's not really to my taste."

Now it was time to treat him like a man, not just a vampire. If there's one thing I've learned about men it's that they appreciate a woman's sensuality. I smiled slightly and let my gaze find Rose. "I think your taste is wrong then, Louis."

His eyebrows shot up and he was suddenly very interested in what I had to say. "So she is to your taste?"

"I have wide and varied tastes." I let the words drip out like honey. I wanted Louis ready for sex, not violence, by the time my faery prince joined us. "I think Rose is quite lovely. She has a petite little body and perky breasts. I bet they have sweet little nipples."

The vampire's smile was sensual as he regarded the two of us. "I will admit her nipples are quite pretty but her breasts are too small."

"But small breasts are exquisitely sensitive." I was wandering off into truly unexplored territory here. I hadn't actually played around with small breasts, but I read that in a romance novel and those couldn't possibly be wrong. As for the sensuality of my words, I had to thank Devinshea for that lesson. He loved to talk sex. "I bet you could make her come just by sucking on them right."

Rose blushed all the way to her toes. She stared at me through the mirror and smiled as she ran the brush through my hair again.

Louis was fighting his arousal as he watched us. It was a vampire's instinct to be private with his companion, but I needed him to see that three could be fun.

"How was your prince this afternoon?" Louis asked, abruptly changing the subject. His change of course didn't alter the tent in his expensive trousers.

I had to flavor all of my answers with the truth. "He was in one piece, no thanks to you."

The vampire had the good sense to look slightly embarrassed. "I…was very angry about something Daniel has done. I will apologize this evening."

I nodded shortly, though an apology really didn't cover nearly beating someone to death.

"Tell me, *mon ange*," Louis began, his voice all dark seduction. "Did you kiss your faery prince this afternoon?"

No lies here. If I got hit I would just take it. Lying would only lead to other questions and the vampire wondering just how much I was covering up. "Yes, I did. Then that stupid wolf made me stop."

I pouted and sounded petulant even to my own ears. Louis's laugh boomed through the room. "I'll have a talk with Trent. I expected that you and the prince would be a bit naughty. You will have thirty minutes each day with him as long as your behavior is good. If you wish to kiss the prince, I'll allow it, but nothing more. Do you understand?"

I nodded and turned back to the mirror. "I don't like that wolf."

"Does the little companion not like her bodyguard?" Chad asked as he entered the room. I was grateful the bathroom was quite large as it was becoming full.

"I think she does not," Marini replied, smiling at the other vampire.

"He must be doing something right then." Chad had a dippy smile for his "master." He was wearing his customary leather and black. His hair was disheveled and he appeared even more insane than normal. His eyes softened as he gazed at me. "Your skin is so pretty."

"Do you think my companion is beautiful, Mr. Thomas?" Louis asked.

Chad sighed. "She's gorgeous. I want to trade places with her. It would be nice to be so pretty that everyone around you just wants to coddle you. All she has to do is spread her legs and show off that neck of hers and all the vampires come running. She doesn't have to do anything. They all just want to take care of her so she'll love them."

"You sound almost jealous," Louis noted.

"Then I'm not trying hard enough," Chad replied. "I'm entirely jealous of her. She gets everything handed to her. The prince treats her like she was made of gold. At least you'll challenge her, won't you, master? You'll show her who the boss is." Chad sneered at me, his face hard. "Your new master won't let you run wild. He'll beat the shit out of you if you step even an inch out of line, bitch. You won't be able to control him because he just wants your blood. He couldn't care less about the rest of you."

Rose had taken a step back and she put her little hand in mine to try to pull me with her.

Louis gripped Chad by the nape of his neck like a dog. Louis's claws were out and they dug into Chad's skin, drawing blood. "You will not speak to her like that. I have worked very hard to not frighten her and you come in spouting nonsense. Go."

Chad seemed to deflate, that violent rage going as quickly as it came. "I'm sorry," he said, seemingly surprised at himself. "I came in to tell you that you have a visitor in your suite."

Louis nodded. "Good, then all is ready. Go and do what I need you to do. You may go too, Rose. You'll find I've left money with Robert. He'll take you shopping. Zoey needs clothes."

Rose nodded but there was a little spark in her eyes as she left the room. Chad followed and I was happy he was gone, even if it left me alone to deal with Louis. At least I had some sort of a handle on how to deal with him. I took a deep breath and let myself look very vulnerable. Chad had given me the chance to be afraid of Louis again. Big hands cupped my shoulders.

"I left you a dress on the bed," Louis said quietly, his eyes filled with desire as he looked at me in the mirror. "I want you to wear it and come with me to my apartments."

I was very interested in the latter part of that statement. I wanted to get into his office.

"I will," I said quietly, turning my head to look up at him. His eyes were on my neck. "Are you hungry?"

Fangs shot out with a little snap. "I am. I am always hungry for you. Get up."

He sat me on the sink and with a flick of his fingers, my towel came undone. I forced myself not to cover my body. I felt his eyes trying to pull me in and gave over because there was nothing else to do.

An hour later I found myself dressed in an all-white silky sheath. It was tasteful but sexy. The bra he'd left for me was decadently lovely and just a tiny bit small. It shoved my breasts together but I didn't complain. I was barefoot because the sneakers I had come in didn't really go with the dress. Louis promised to rectify the situation as soon as possible. He'd dressed me himself, his fingers smoothing the silk over my skin, and then clasping a diamond collar around my neck. It was a gorgeous piece of jewelry that was far too much like a slave collar for my liking. The vampire had enjoyed dressing me and playing with my naked skin. He'd especially liked my navel ring but wanted a large diamond in the place of my emerald and sapphire. I don't know if he understood I'd chosen the stones to match Dev and Daniel's eyes, but he wanted the belly button ring to complement his collar.

I tried not to think about the fact that I couldn't say I'd only slept with my husbands now. Even though I wanted to cry and rage at the situation, I'd managed to get through it without throwing up on him.

I just wanted to see Dev again. I wanted him to hold me, to promise me he still loved me.

We stood outside the door to Louis's suite and he held my hand in his. "Zoey, you will remain quiet unless I give you permission to speak. Is that understood?"

I was a trophy and nothing more. I was all right with that. It would give me the opportunity to get the lay of the land.

"You will sit at my side and do everything I ask of you," he continued as he opened the door.

I followed him. His rooms were elegantly decorated. The first room was a sitting area with darkly paneled walls and tasteful art. I thought I recognized some of the painters, but I hadn't seen the paintings before. One resembled a Picasso but it wasn't one I was familiar with. It occurred to me it wouldn't be hard for a man like Louis to convince a painter to create a work just for him. He probably hadn't even paid for it.

"He's here," Niles said in his upper-crust British accent. He appeared slightly haggard, like his rest had been interrupted. I wondered what fresh trouble Danny was causing. Niles caught sight of me and he stared. "God, she's so fucking bright."

"Get used to her," Niko said from his place on the sofa. He wasn't haggard at all. The tall Greek was downright calm compared to Niles and the Norwegian Elof. "She's Louis's new pet. I think he'll keep her close to his side. Donovan is on the prowl. Louis wouldn't want to lose her."

"I have no intention of losing anything to that fucker," Louis growled.

"You mean anything else, don't you?" Elof asked. "He's already hit us where we'll feel it for decades. I can't get into any of my accounts and he blew up my safe house last night. I got word this evening."

"He's a busy man," Niles said. "My London home was raided by MI5. They found some very suspicious materials. Bomb-making materials. I can't bloody well go home but Louis is far too busy fucking Donovan's queen to take care of Donovan."

"How the hell is he everywhere at once?" Louis asked, his voice a low growl. He sank into a leather chair. I stood beside him because there wasn't room for me. "Zoey, sit."

Louis pointed at his feet. I thought of Dev in his cell and our babies in my womb and gracefully sank to the floor at his feet. His hand came out and nudged my head onto his lap. It forced me to hold onto his legs.

"There is only one group who has that kind of power and any interest at all in the supernatural underworld," I heard Elof say as my eyes wandered as much as my position allowed.

"Yes, the Order of Galahad," Niles replied.

Niko laughed. "Why would the Order have anything to do with Donovan? He's a vampire, not a demon. They try not to get involved in our politics."

They argued back and forth for a few moments, and I took the time to look at a door on the far wall. It was a dark wooden door with a lock on it, which I found odd because it was an interior room. I've learned over the years that locks in strange places are the equivalent to an *X* marking the spot where a thief can find treasure. I let my hand touch the rich carpet underneath me. I was sure it was Persian and old but more important, carpet tended to mask the sounds a thief made when she crept across a room to get to where she needed to go. I figured Louis's bedroom was behind the lovely French doors on the opposite side of the room to the office door. I would need to get from the bed to the office without light of any kind and making absolutely no sound.

"Zoey," Louis barked.

I brought my head up. "What?" I assumed barking my name

meant I was allowed to speak.

"Have you listened to a word I have said?" he asked, looking down at me.

"No."

The others laughed but Louis did not look amused. I would have to remember that he thought everything he said was important so I had to listen. It wouldn't be easy for me because I tended to go a little bit ADD whenever...well, whenever I was awake, to tell the truth. Danny and Dev thought it was a cute quirk, but Louis obviously found it annoying.

"I'm sorry," I offered with wide eyes.

"I asked you a question," he explained. "I asked if you knew of any reason why the Order of Galahad would choose to work with Donovan."

"I can tell you," a familiar voice said from the doorway. My heart stopped as Marcus walked into the room. I felt Louis tense.

"Mar..." I started to say.

"Not a word, Zoey. You will obey me or I'll take it out on the prince's hide," Louis said close to my ear. "Now go sit on the couch."

I did as he asked and felt Marcus's eyes on me the whole time I moved. He was dressed as the rest were in a dark, tailored suit. His silk tie was a vibrant blue and his shoes were none the worse for having come through the catacombs. He looked imminently competent, which was an illusion since the idiot had walked into the snake's den.

"Nice of you to join us, Marcus," Louis said smoothly, acknowledging the Council member. "We've missed you."

Marcus's smile didn't quite reach his eyes. "I was at my villa on Poveglia. It has no means of communication. I was quite surprised by the turn of events when I returned to Venice. I got here as soon as I could. When can I take Zoey home with me?"

Louis laughed at the question. "When you do the job you were contracted to do. I promised to give you the girl if you brought down Donovan. He's isn't down, Marcus. Far from it. He's taking his targets with ease. Now answer the question. Why is the Order working with Donovan?"

Marcus shrugged. "Because he has the sword."

Now everyone was talking at once and in several different languages. They all seemed extremely upset at the prospect of Daniel having Excalibur. Elof and Marcus got into a heated exchange, and I saw Louis stand and walk to the door. He opened it briefly, spoke to the guard outside, and then returned.

"Stop it," he exclaimed in English, which seemed to be the language of compromise. When they were all together they spoke English rather than their own languages. "Marcus, you are certain Donovan possesses the sword known as Excalibur?"

"I haven't seen him in weeks. I'm only certain that the Order of Galahad believes it."

"And they are now listening to Donovan?"

The Italian laughed at that. "They aren't listening to him, Louis. They're obeying his every order. They have proclaimed our *Nex Apparatus* to be the next King of the Sword and they will follow their liege."

Louis ran his hand across his face in a weary gesture. "That fucking demon should have told me."

So Stewart had very likely stayed true to the letter of law Lucifer had set down regarding Daniel and the Council. It disappointed me because I really would like to think about Stewart being punished by the big guy.

Louis paced the floor. "How did we not see this? Haven't we had a spy on Donovan since he left the Council? Nowhere in his reports did he mention that Donovan was doing anything like this."

"I believe you will discover that Michael House is no longer in Dallas," Marcus offered. "From the reports I've received, he recently joined his king in London. You'll find that many of your influential vampires are now at the Order's headquarters."

"I was a fool not to execute him the minute he set foot in the catacombs," Louis said under his breath.

"I believe I mentioned it at the time." Niles looked a little bit green.

I deeply enjoyed the rampaging fear that was running through the room at the thought of Daniel and his army. They didn't even know about the wolves, the alliance of shifters, or the Fae army that would soon be breathing down their necks.

"I know how we can convince Donovan to come out into the open," Marcus offered.

Louis's eyes were suspicious and I wanted to yell at Marcus to be careful. The door opened and Chad entered. His eyes were strangely bright, lit with something close to glee. He took his place near Marini but said nothing.

Marini refused to explain Chad's sudden appearance. "You were saying?"

Marcus was unsettled for a moment as he glanced at the magician but he quickly got back to his point. "We use the faery to lure out Donovan. We announce his impending execution in some place that Donovan can easily get to. When he shows up, we kill him."

Louis shook his head, obviously unsatisfied with that plan. "Or we could hit Donovan where he will hurt. I like your plan of using the faery prince. I believe Donovan truly does care for him. When we toss his dead body on the steps of the Order's headquarters, he'll know we mean business. Mr. Thomas, if you will do the honors."

Chad's eyes lit up like it was Christmas. "It would be my greatest pleasure."

"No," I yelled, not giving a shit I wasn't given permission. I launched myself bodily at Chad but Marcus got in the way. He pulled me into his arms and held me tightly as I started to scream at Marini.

"You promised me," I yelled from the cage of Marcus's arms. My whole body was flush with rage and fear and I was pretty sure they could hear my heart beating all the way in London. "He could have gotten away, but he came with me because you promised you wouldn't kill him."

"He probably shouldn't have believed me. Look, darling girl, once the traitor finds the faery's corpse, he'll know I'm serious. I'll offer up a trade. I'll let the Order take you in exchange for Donovan turning himself in." Louis came up to me and held my face in his hands. "You can't think I would really believe that crap about Donovan not loving the two of you. I watched him when he thought you were gone. He would have met the dawn if you had truly been lost to him. He'll exchange himself for you."

"Don't kill Dev," I begged, fighting to get away from Marcus. I couldn't let it happen.

Louis seemed satisfied to let Marcus deal with me. He walked away and grabbed something from behind the sofa. I watched as he stood back up and nodded and Niles and Elof jumped into action. They quickly grabbed Niko and I heard Marcus gasp.

"There will be a lot of killing today, sweet companion." Louis stood tall and showed off the stake in his hand. "I am not the complete fool everyone thinks I am. I believe it is time to end the reign of the academics."

Niko roared and tried to pull away from the other vampires, but they held him tight and Louis didn't hesitate. He marched straight up to the Greek who had walked the Earth plane for over two thousand years and with one single thrust brought his long life to an end. The vampire's face went blank as the stake entered his chest and then he turned to dust before my eyes.

I could hear Marcus breathing heavily, shocked at the quickness of Niko's exit from life.

Marcus slipped something into the palm of my hand. It was cold and felt like a small stone. I closed my fist around it just before Louis turned back to us, that stake still in his hand.

"Are you going to run, Marcus?" Louis asked, his fangs long. "I have to wonder why you showed up at all."

"I had to see her," Marcus said quietly.

"Marcus, that was suicide," I replied, horrified at the fact that he was willing to do it.

"No, *cara*, it was fate. You remember what the oracle said. You're the woman I would meet death for. It doesn't matter that you can't love me."

"Now that's just...repulsive," Louis said with a shudder. "Take him."

Elof and Niles shoved me aside and gripped Marcus as they had held the Greek before. They took his hands and held them as far apart as they would go. I saw the strain on Marcus's face as the stronger warriors were pulling him apart. His brain wasn't going to help him now. I looked down and caught a glimpse at what Marcus had shoved at me. It was a replica of the Blood Stone. I would be able to take the stone and switch it. I quickly shoved the fake Marcus had given up his life to get to me deep inside the bodice of my dress. It nestled between my breasts, my flesh covering it completely.

"I willingly give my life for my king and *mia regina*," Marcus said with conviction. "*Cara*, your king sends you greetings through me. He begs you to stay alive. He loves you with every fiber of his being and he will come for you."

Louis pulled me up and forced me into his embrace. "He can come but I'll kill her before I allow him to take her from me. You're pathetic, Marcus. You're still looking for that woman who'll bring you the death you crave. It isn't going to be my Zoey. I have no intention of killing you."

Marcus's eyes got wide as he thought of the implications of that statement. "I have betrayed you. I've been on Daniel's side since the beginning. I worked against all of you."

"Yes, you have," Louis admitted. "You also convinced the only woman I've ever loved to kill herself to further your own plots. So, Marcus, I will take this woman you love. I'll take her and you'll know that I have her beneath me while you rot in a coffin for all of eternity. You will lie there and know that I have purged the world of your line. The last academic. That's what you'll be when I'm done."

I cared for Marcus. I truly did, but I had another problem. Somewhere Chad was getting closer to Dev, and I wasn't sure he wouldn't do it. He seemed hopelessly insane and even if he wasn't, he'd proven in the past that he was all about the job. Daniel was his master and he'd been told to keep his cover intact. If that meant giving up Dev to do it, Chad just might. I started to crawl away, thinking if I could make it to the door I might have a chance at stopping Chad. I could find something to fight him with. I was perfectly willing in that moment to kill Chad if it meant saving Dev.

"No, Zoey," Marini said, hauling me up by one arm, "You're not going anywhere."

I struggled against him, crying in my frustration. "Let me go."

Marini sighed even as Elof and Niles started escorting a very shaky Marcus to the door. "Calm yourself, Zoey. It was a ruse to create a bit of panic. I've long suspected Marcus of perfidy. I put a spy in Niko's household as well. I knew the academics would betray me in the end. Mr. Thomas was a distraction. He won't kill the prince. I still intend to get a taste of that magic."

349

Marcus struggled against his captors. "You cannot allow this to happen, my queen. This will be disastrous for Daniel. You must not allow the prince to perform this ritual."

"She has no choice, Marcus," Marini said. "The prince will perform or I'll kill him and toss his body like garbage on Donovan's doorstep. Now, take him to the dungeons. The coffin is there and ready for its new occupant. I want Zoey's face to be the last thing you see, Marcus."

Marini dragged me along. Marcus, upon realizing there was absolutely nowhere to go, had chosen to walk with dignity toward his grave.

"Come, *mon ange*," Marini said as we headed down the stairs toward the same dungeons that held Dev's jail cell. "You'll feel better once you see that the prince is alive and well. You should be happy with my plans, darling girl. It means you'll be allowed sexual access to the prince. Perhaps I'll find I enjoy watching the two of you."

"Zoey, I'm begging you." Marcus was ahead of me, but he kept trying to turn, to plead his case. "Do not allow this to happen. You know what that magic did for Daniel. Don't allow Louis access to it. It will cost Daniel his existence."

But I didn't know what else to do. We were caught, Dev and I. If we didn't give Marini what he wanted he would kill Dev and that would leave me alone. I couldn't let that happen. Daniel wouldn't want it to happen.

As we walked toward the dungeons, I tried to come up with some plan that would work. I needed to talk to Dev, to Bris. Mostly I just needed to see him.

"Oh, god," I heard Marcus breathe as he entered the dungeon. "Oh, no."

That coffin must be really awful I thought as Marini guided me in, but then I realized that wasn't what he was upset about.

Dev's cell was open and Chad held Dev firmly in his arms, his fangs in my faery prince's neck, his throat working. He looked up and saw us and released Dev. His big body hit the floor and he didn't move.

"You wanted me to kill him, master," Chad said with a smile as blood dripped from his mouth. "It was a pleasure to obey."

Chapter Thirty-Two

I couldn't quite make my mind believe what I was seeing. Chad stood over Dev's body and he practically glowed with health. Somewhere deep in the still functioning parts of my brain I knew a vampire only did that when he gorged himself on blood. The room was silent as I stared down at Dev. His face was to me and his eyes were closed. He looked like he was sleeping.

Louis dropped my arm and I ran to help Dev up. It was obvious Chad had taken too much and I needed to get some blood in him. He was going to need a transfusion.

I hit my knees and put my hands on him. "He needs blood."

"Oh, *cara*," Marcus said, his voice quiet and deliberate. "He's blue. He is past needing blood."

I held his hand in mine. Marcus was right. His skin was a ghastly pale and he was cold to the touch.

"He needs a blanket," I heard myself saying. "He's cold."

It seemed wrong that he was cold because he was always, always so warm. His skin was almost hot sometimes and I complained on many occasions that sleeping with him was like sleeping next to a furnace, but he'd said I'd been stupid enough to marry him so I had to put up with his body heat. He would wrap himself around me when he slept. He didn't like to feel alone even when he was sleeping.

He needed blood. Why weren't they giving him blood?

"Mr. Thomas, what have you done?" I heard Marini ask harshly.

Why was he worried about that now? Dev needed blood and I didn't care that it would come from Marini.

"You have to give him blood, Louis," I implored quietly, my hand on Devinshea's chest, looking for his heartbeat. I couldn't find it. He was still under my hands. So still. There was nothing moving, no heart beating, no lungs filling with air.

I felt Chad moving behind me. "He doesn't need blood, Zoey. He needs a coffin. I took all the blood. He tasted so good. He was like heaven."

Louis pulled him roughly away from us and tossed him to the far side of the room. "I swear if you weren't so fucking important to my plans I would kill you where you stand. You insane idiot. Do you have any idea what you've done?"

"Louis," I shouted because we were running out of time. I could barely see him through my tears. "Stop talking. He needs blood. Save him."

"Zoey, he's dead," Marini said sharply. "I'm sorry, but there is nothing I can do. He has no blood left. There is nothing for the vampire blood to work on. If I gave him blood at this point he would come back as a revenant and I would be forced to kill him again."

My hands started to shake as reality set in. Dev was beyond cold and he wasn't moving at all. His face, so full of life, was passive now with nothing left to animate him.

It wasn't true. It couldn't happen. I'd made love with him a few hours before so he couldn't be dead now. I sat there with my hands on that face I loved so much. He would wake up. Daniel's blood would work and he would wake up and tell me he loved me. He would make me baby him for weeks after this, and I wouldn't complain. I would give him everything he asked for. I would give him that sponge bath he'd wanted. I would wait on him hand and foot.

"Don't go," I heard myself saying. I saw a tear hit his face and slide down his cheek and off his strong jaw. It took a moment to realize I was the one crying. "Don't go. Please. Please don't leave me." I hunched over because he was heavy and I couldn't pull him up, so I leaned down to wrap myself around him. "I love you. I love you. Don't go."

I have no idea how long they let me sit there, pleading with whoever would listen to give him back to me. We'd gotten so close to what we'd dreamed of, a family and a home for the three of us. He couldn't be dead when I had his babies inside me. He couldn't be gone. I had led him to this. I'd walked into his club when I had no right to and begged him to love me when he shouldn't have. He would be alive right now if I'd just stayed away from him. I would have given anything in that moment to take back that one decision.

I would have given up everything to know he was alive somewhere even without me. My green-eyed boy. How would I ever live without him?

"*Cara*, you have to let him go," Marcus said.

"I can't." I held onto Dev. I sobbed against his chest because the look in Marcus's eyes told me this was really happening. He was really gone and I had no idea where he was. I sobbed, my body heaving grief that felt like it would never end.

"Marcus, please help her." I heard Marini say.

Marcus pulled me up, using his strength to drag me away from my husband's body. "It's over, *cara*. I'm so sorry but it's over."

Rage poured over me as I caught sight of that bastard Chad, who Daniel had trusted. He sat against the stone of the wall. He stared at Dev's body, and I couldn't tell if he was still with us. He didn't move or say a thing, simply stared straight at my husband's body. Obviously nothing mattered but whatever was going on in that fucked up brain of his and I couldn't stop what came out of my mouth next.

"He's a traitor," I screamed, pointing at the man who had killed Dev. I couldn't stand the thought that he would walk the night filled with Dev's blood. I wanted him dead in that instant and I didn't care who it hurt. Marcus's hands tightened on my body, but I didn't heed his warning. I charged on recklessly, thinking only of my husband's body cold on the ground. "Daniel turned him himself. He's been a spy the whole time. Kill him."

Marini looked at me and I could see he didn't believe me. "You are unwell, Zoey. I'm sorry about the prince. I truly am, but Mr. Thomas is far too crazy to be a spy. It's the nature of his class. Even if

Daniel planted him, he long ago passed any effectiveness."

Chad's laugh sent shivers down my spine. "Yes, Daniel Donovan killed me. He shoved a knife through my heart and there was blood but the faery's blood took its place. He lives in me now, Zoey. I have him now. You can still talk to him. Daniel killed me in your backyard and there were wolves that night. I fell in love that night when I died and now I have two people inside my body."

Marini shook his head sadly. "You see, he's insane. I would kill him to make you happy but I need his talents. They're still useful to me. Perhaps after the battle with Daniel I'll execute him to please you, but Mr. Thomas has just managed to take away my secret weapon, and now I'm going to be reliant on him."

I fought Marcus now and Chad was back to his weird concentration, every bit of his focus on the dead body in front of him. Marcus let up and I fell back down to Dev. They were going to take him away. They would take his body and toss it on the steps of the Order's headquarters, and that would be how Daniel found him. That would be how Daniel found out Devinshea was dead.

I felt Marcus pulling me up again and I gazed one last time on my faery prince's face. "You wait for me. You promised. You wait for me."

A great tide of grief overwhelmed me and I cried out again. I couldn't leave him there. I couldn't leave him lying on the cold floor.

"Marcus, please," Marini implored the man he would soon place in a coffin.

"Zoey," I heard Marcus's voice, but it seemed to come from deep inside my brain. It was soft and seductive and it took over. "Sleep."

The world and all its horror winked from existence.

I woke up in the grotto, surrounded by the sights and smells of home. There were always flowers blooming in the grotto. During the day, roses bloomed along the walls and at night, on the balcony, the flower beds came alive with evening primrose. I closed my eyes and could almost hear Albert walking through the kitchens, getting dinner ready. Dev would sit with me and his hand would brush mine as we ate dinner with Neil and oftentimes Lee. My wolf would wander up just in time for whatever Albert had prepared and look surprised to be asked to stay for dinner. He would always ask for seconds and thirds, and by the time dessert rolled around, I would be teasing him about being a walking-talking garbage disposal.

I was almost able to believe, but then I remembered and knew where I really was.

"Not here, Marcus." I knew he could hear me. "I can't be here yet."

The scene changed abruptly around me. One minute I was at home and the next I was staring at a crowded square filled with tourists and more pigeons than I could ever remember seeing in one place. I was under an awning and I could smell dark, rich coffee. The day was bright, but I stood in the shadows and felt no desire to be in the light.

"Is this better, *cara*?" Marcus asked, walking to my side. He stared out over the courtyard.

"I've never been here before so I won't be expecting Dev to show up at any minute," I said, my voice sounding very flat. I felt flat and dry.

"I'm so sorry, *cara*," Marcus said with genuine sadness in his eyes. "I know you loved him."

"Well, at least he can't upset Daniel's plans now." I couldn't forget how Marcus had begged me not to let Dev perform his ritual. If Marini hadn't felt the need to trick Marcus, Dev and I would be getting ready for that ritual. We would be nervous and worried and together.

Marcus turned me to him. "That's not fair, Zoey. I didn't kill Devinshea. I would never have done that. You also cannot blame Daniel. He'll be devastated."

"I don't blame you," I said hollowly. "I don't blame Daniel."

Marcus's eyes softened. "Zoey, *cara*, you can't blame yourself."

But I could. I could blame myself and I would until the day I died and found out if my prince had managed to wait for me.

"Please, you have to stay strong," Marcus said. "You're not

alone. Daniel needs you."

I shook my head. "I don't see what I'll do for Daniel now." It would be infinitely harder to get the stone without Dev. I needed a lookout or I would get caught and the stone gone from me forever. If I gave Marini too much trouble, he might decide to send Daniel another present and I would be seeing Dev again soon.

"You can do this, Zoey," Marcus said. "We're all relying on you. Daniel is close to being ready to raid the catacombs. He needs you to take the Blood Stone out of play."

I turned to look at Marcus for the first time. "You've seen Danny?"

"I have," Marcus replied. "He is resolute, but he's sick at heart, Zoey. It took all of us to convince him not to trade his life for yours. He wanted to walk into the catacombs by himself to face Marini."

"He can't do that," I said, horrified at the thought.

"I made him realize that it would only get him killed and you would still be at Marini's mercy. He must follow the plans, but it's killing him."

"How is Zack?" I asked, worried about the young wolf.

Marcus sighed heavily. "He wanted me to tell you something, Zoey. He made me promise if I got a chance that I would speak to you."

I took a shaky breath and prayed I would survive the next couple of minutes. Zack had to be angry with me. I'd gotten his brother killed. I shouldn't have left him when I ran to check on Dev. I should have shielded the wolf. I deserved whatever vitriol Zack wanted to throw my way. I nodded and indicated I was ready to listen.

"Zack told me to let you know that his brother died doing his job. He would have been proud to die in such a fashion, protecting someone he loved deeply," Marcus related Zack's words to me. "He wanted to thank you for making Lee's last years his happiest. He was happier and more settled in the last several years than he'd been his whole life. Zack wants you to know that when the time comes, he will be at Daniel's side and he will come for you. He will come for you because you're his family now."

I fell into Marcus's chest and sobbed against him. I had lost so much in Lee and Dev and I had to go on. I had to stand up and do the job because I wasn't alone. Daniel was depending on me. Zack needed me. I had to live and fight because I had to get out of this prison and find Neil. I wanted to lie down and fade like the Fae did. I wanted to be still and wait for death to take me, but I was full of life that wouldn't get a chance if I didn't find a way to fight. It seemed so unfair that I wasn't allowed to wallow in my grief, to let it swallow me up until it was all that was left of me, but I couldn't. I had to fight for Danny and Zack and Neil, but most of all for the babies inside me that were all I had left of Devinshea.

Marcus allowed me to cry for the longest time. He stroked my hair and said nothing at all, just let the tourists in the square walk past us. They ignored us since they only existed in Marcus's mind. We were alone.

I sniffed and probably looked like hell but it didn't matter. "Where are you, Marcus? I mean in the real world."

"I'm in a silver coffin wrapped in silver chains deep in the dungeons, *cara*," Marcus replied simply. "It's nothing to concern yourself with. When Daniel makes his push, he will find me and release me."

"How long have I been out? Where am I?"

"You are in your rooms. You were moved to your bed and now I believe they have a werewolf watching over you. It's been roughly a day and a half, I believe. Time is odd when you're in a coffin, but I believe you will find it's day."

"Is the werewolf's name Trent?"

Marcus smiled slightly. "Is that one of McKenzie's plants? I was told he had a few spies in the Council headquarters, but I don't know their names."

"I complained bitterly about him," I said. "I think it made Louis believe he was the perfect guard for me."

"I believe Trent is the name Louis used." The Italian straightened up. His face was resolute. "It's time, *cara*. You must wake up and do what you need to do. I will be here with you when you sleep. Know that I am thinking of you, *cara*."

I woke up on the bed Rose and I had shared the night I entered the catacombs. I was still in the shift I'd worn the night Dev died.

I sat straight up in bed and the grief washed over me as fresh and sharp as the minute I realized he was gone. I slapped my hand over my mouth when I realized I was going to throw up. I tossed back the covers and ran to the bathroom, barely noticing that Trent had opened the door upon hearing me wake up.

I slammed the bathroom door behind me and barely made it to the toilet before what little I had in my stomach came heaving up. I sat there on the cold floor completely miserable, my body shaking with grief and sickness. When I finished, I laid my head down on the cool marble.

"Zoey," I heard Trent's Boston accent through the door. "Are you all right? Should I get a doctor?"

"I'm fine," I lied, pushing myself up. I felt something move against my chest and I reached down.

I pulled out the fake Blood Stone and was grateful no one thought to undress me. I held it up to the light. It would pass inspection, but not if Louis studied it closely. It didn't have the same shine as the original but I just needed it to hold the Blood Stone's place for long enough to let me get away. I needed a place to hide the fake Marcus had given up his freedom to get to me.

I forced myself up and opened one of the cabinets, looking for a place to hide it. There was a big box of tampons. I doubted any man—human, werewolf, or vampire—would think to look for something there. I put the fake in and covered it up. I rose and caught sight of myself in the mirror.

The face that stared back was a shock. I was older, weary. This was the face of a widow.

I shoved my grief as far down into my soul as I could. I had a job to do. I had living people who needed me. This was what Myrddin meant. I had to push aside my pain and do the job. I had to live because if I didn't then Dev had died in vain and Lee's sacrifice meant nothing.

I memorized the face in the mirror and I was ready to go to work.

CHAPTER THIRTY-THREE

I ate every bit of the eggs and bacon Trent brought me thirty minutes later. I ignored the coffee but downed the orange juice and forced myself to finish off two buttery croissants and a bowl of fruit. While my soul might not be interested in food, the two boys growing in my belly were insistent on it. I was famished and my fingers just kept on putting food in my mouth.

Trent watched closely. I was sure I was an odd sight. My face was puffy and my eyes red. I'd gotten back into the jeans and T-shirt I'd worn the night I was kidnapped because I saw no evidence Rose had been successful in her mission of buying me clothes. In fact, I saw no evidence of Rose or Robert at all. Had she been sold while I was sleeping?

"Where is Rose?"

The Boston wolf leaned forward and kept his voice low. "Are you feeling up for this, Your Highness? A lot has happened since..."

"Since my husband was murdered," I finished for him. I steeled myself because I was going to have to be tough. I couldn't give in to the urge to wail every time I thought of Devinshea. I had to hold it together until I was in Daniel's arms again. When that happened, I could grieve and cry all I wanted and Daniel would grieve with me.

"Yes, ma'am," Trent replied carefully. "A lot has happened since then, and I don't think you're going to like some of it."

"I don't like anything that happened in the last several days,

Trent," I said bitterly. "Is Daniel alive?"

"Yes. Yes, ma'am," Trent replied quickly. "Your husband is alive. I'm sorry. I didn't mean to scare you like that. The king is alive and well and giving the Council hell."

Something inside me released and I realized I was just waiting for someone to tell me Danny was dead. I had to keep faith. I nodded and poured another glass of orange juice. Despite sleeping for a day and a half, I found myself exhausted. I hoped it was the aftereffects of Marcus's magic and not another symptom of my pregnancy. "Tell me everything."

"Almost all of Marini's strong supporters are now in the catacombs," the wolf told me. "Donovan started picking them off one by one, neat, clean executions. Now they're all hiding here, plotting what to do next. There are plenty of vampires who are staying neutral and the king has stated as long as they offer no aid to the Council, he won't touch them. The rest of them are with Daniel in London. As far as I can tell, every living academic has either gone into hiding or they're in the Order's headquarters. Marini is pissed. He's sworn to kill them all."

"And Rose?"

"Rose is missing," Trent replied, holding his hands up to let me know it was a mystery. "She and her manservant left to go shopping in the city. Marini couldn't afford to give her a full escort. The vampire sent with her lost track of her. He searched all night but couldn't find her. Marini thinks Donovan snagged her in retaliation for him taking you."

So Rose had gotten her chance and she'd taken it. I smiled, thinking of Rose running. She would run straight for her mother and she wouldn't look back and she'd managed to save Robert in the process. She would feel the sun on her face again and know her mother's arms around her. She would get her life back, and I was so grateful for that.

"That's marvelous," I murmured. "How's Marini taking all of this?"

"He's this close to losing control," Trent said, holding his thumb and forefinger very close together. "He's been violent and cruel. I worry he's going to take it out on you."

"I think you'll find a companion has many talents," I said enigmatically. I would have to sooth the vampire and I hated the prospect, but I couldn't have his beast loose. I swallowed twice before I got the next question out. "Has Daniel...does he know about...Dev?"

Trent frowned. "I think so. I haven't heard, but I can't communicate every day. This is the part I don't think you'll like. Marini sent the magician and two other vampires to deliver the prince's body to the Order's headquarters last night. Only Thomas came back. He said they were ambushed and only he got away. I don't know why, but I think he was lying about something."

"Naturally he survives." I hated Chad with everything I had. Before all of this was done, I was going to kill that vampire. I knew Neil would be upset but I wouldn't let Chad get his hands on my best friend after what he'd done to Dev. I would protect Neil by avenging my husband. "How long do I have before sundown?"

Trent checked his watch. "Fifteen minutes. If you're all right, I need to get down to the dungeons and check something out. This morning a couple of the guards found a wolf prowling the sewers. He won't leave his wolf form, and they couldn't chase him away. It was like he was tracking someone and wouldn't give it up. I think he's sick but I need to figure out if he's a friendly before Marini up and kills him. Maybe I can get him out."

My hands started shaking. "Is he white?"

"I think so," Trent said.

I was running for the door before Trent could get up.

"Neil?"

My voice was hushed in the gloom of the dungeon. I forced myself to go in. I was pretty sure that my every nightmare would take place in this dark prison from now on. The first thing I saw when I entered the dungeons was Dev, that big body of his hitting the floor with a resounding thud. He wouldn't get up again. I hated the fact that when I closed my eyes and thought of my husband, this was the image I got.

I shook the thoughts from my brain and rejoined reality. A white wolf lay on the stone floor of the same cell where my husband had died. He was so still, his fur matted and drab, and I feared I was too late again.

"You know this wolf?" Trent was careful now because there was a shifter watching us.

I nodded. "He's my friend. He was tracking me. I have no idea how he managed to get all the way here, but I'm sure he was looking for me."

"Marini will be thrilled to find out he got close enough to sniff out his companion," the shifter muttered. I was almost certain he would shift into a large snake. There was something about the eyes even in human form that reminded me of the cold dead eyes of a snake.

"I need to get in there with him." I forced myself to concentrate on Neil and not the predators that surrounded me.

"No," the men said in perfect harmony.

"Please," I begged. "He isn't dangerous."

"I'm not taking that chance," the shifter said. "The master is going to be pissed enough we let him get anywhere close to us. The last thing I need is him knowing I let his companion into a cell with an unknown wolf."

Neil's white head struggled as he tried to look around for me.

"I'm here, sweetie," I said through the cell bars. I moved to the cell and shoved my hands through. I was able to get close and Neil whimpered as he finally caught my scent and realized it wasn't a trail but the destination. His clear blue eyes turned and found mine, and I cried as he crawled toward me. "It's all right, Neil. I'm here. It's going to be okay."

I didn't know why he wouldn't change, but I didn't care. He often stayed in wolf form when he felt vulnerable. I just let my fingers run through the soft fur of his back. He crawled close and turned over to offer me his belly, a sure sign he needed comfort. I rubbed him and murmured reassuring words to him.

That was how Louis found us some time later.

"I see you woke up," the vampire said, staring down at me as I kneeled by the cage. Even with some distance between us, I could feel his rage. "And you found a friend."

I kept my expression as soft as I could. Louis's beast was dangerously close to the surface. Daniel's plans were working. Marini was losing control and he was more prone to make mistakes when he panicked. Unfortunately, he was also more likely to beat the shit out of me. I had to avoid that at all costs. "You remember Neil."

He should since he was the one who had given Stewart permission to cart him off to the Hell plane.

"I remember the wolf," Louis said with not a whit of concern in his voice. "He was given to the demon as payment for the demon's betrayal. He looks worse for the wear."

"I need to get him out of there and take a look at him," I said quietly. "He needs food and water."

The vampire's dark eyes were calculating. "I think not. The faery's body didn't seem to move Donovan much. He killed another two of my vampires while you slept and he stole Rose. I was going to use her as payment to a loyal subject. Now I have to come up with something else. This one was his servant. Perhaps his death will mean something to the king."

"He won't care," I lied quickly. "He and Neil haven't worked together for a very long time. Neil turned his back on Danny and Danny won't forgive him. He only lets Neil stay around because he's my pet."

Louis laughed, a nasty sound. "Of course. So I get to be the bad guy once more. It seems to be the role you have me cast in. You blame me for the prince's death and now it seems I am cruel even to your little pets. I don't think I can win with you, companion. Perhaps it's time I cut my losses."

Some big part of me panicked at that thought. He could do it, and I had always known he could. He could decide I was far too much trouble and slit my throat and toss me on Daniel's doorstep, but I doubted he would do it himself. He would let one of the guards do it because no vampire would waste what I could give them. Then again, the sun had only been down for a few minutes. He must have run to find me so quickly. I had to gamble that he was trying to get the upper hand.

Pushing down the bile that threatened to rise at the thought of what I was about to do, I stood. Neil whimpered at my feet and it was a sad, pathetic little sound. I glanced down and I could have sworn that wolf winked at me. He knew what I had to do and he would play his part, too.

I walked up to Louis and got close enough so I knew he could smell me, hear my heart beating in my chest, see the pulse quickening at my throat. My voice was slow and the words honeyed. "If you're going to kill me, Louis, please make it quick. I would prefer not to suffer. I haven't done anything to you but give you my blood, my body. I think I deserve a quick death."

I stood there as he watched me like a hawk watches a fluffy bunny right before she becomes dinner. His eyes told me he wasn't thinking about how to kill me anymore. "If I allow the wolf to live, what do I get, companion?"

"Louis, you don't have to negotiate with me," I replied, my voice soft. "I'm already yours."

Louis looked around and realized the two guards were listening to everything we said.

"Out," he barked and the shifter and Trent walked away, closing the door behind them. I knew in that instant that I had him. If he didn't want to look weak in front of his employees, then he wasn't really thinking about killing me.

The vampire walked around me and toward the cage where Neil lay. He regarded the wolf seriously. "He doesn't look like he's doing well."

"Yes," I explained. "He isn't on vampire blood and he wasn't the strongest wolf to begin with. As you can see, whatever Stewart did to him has weakened him further. Oh, Louis, he isn't a threat to anyone."

He stared for a moment and seemed to come to a decision. "If I allow him to join you in your rooms, you would vouch for his good conduct?"

Neil's tail started thumping and I nodded my head vigorously. "I promise. He'll be good. I'll be good. I've lost so much. Please, just let me have this one thing."

The vampire's hands found my shoulders and he held me carefully. He glared down at me, the full extent of his will my way. "No more grieving, Zoey. I'm sick of tears. You'll do your job. You will warm my bed and you will do it willingly. You just laid beneath me the last time. I found it unsatisfying. I want your passion. I want what you gave to Daniel."

He wanted me to make passionate love to him when my husband probably hadn't even been buried yet. I knew Daniel wouldn't send his body back to the *sithein*. Dev belonged on the Earth plane, where he'd been happiest. He belonged with us. We would be the ones who would truly mourn him. We deserved to keep his body close. Daniel would send him back to Dallas where we could see where he was buried, where I could take our children to visit.

"Zoey," Marini's voice startled me out of my thoughts. "I said no more tears."

I felt the wetness on my face and brushed it off my cheeks. "I'm sorry."

"The pain is still fresh," Louis conceded, and his eyes were softer now. He crowded me and his hands found my waist. He pulled me close and one hand reached up to tip my chin toward him. "Give me what I need, companion. I'll be good to you. I'll make you forget."

He could never make me forget my faery prince. He could never take his or Daniel's place, but I went up on my toes and placed a tentative kiss on his lips, pretending all along that they were Danny's.

Louis swept me up into his arms and he carried me out of the dungeons. He instructed the shifter to feed my wolf and settle him into my rooms comfortably. He practically ran the rest of the way to his apartments. Several vampires tried to stop and ask him seemingly important questions about the war going on all around us, but Louis was horny and didn't seem to care that his world was falling apart. I was satisfied with the annoyed looks I caught on the vampires' faces as Louis brushed them off. It was another way I could screw with him.

When he finally got me back to his rooms, he tossed me lightly on the bed and was on top of me before I could breathe. He spread my legs and used one hand to hook my knees around his waist. I was still dressed, but I knew that wouldn't last long.

"Do you have any idea what you do to me?" Louis asked, nuzzling my neck. I felt the wet warmth of his tongue there. "When you put your arms around me, I am enveloped by your light, *mon ange*."

I did what he wanted and wrapped my arms around him. I tightened my legs around his waist, feeling the hardness there grinding against me like he couldn't wait to get inside.

"Please bite me," I begged, thinking all the while that I should get an Oscar for my performance. Even to my own ears, I was breathless with anticipation. "Take me, Louis. Take me away from everything for a little while."

His magic filled the room. He slammed it into me and I was overwhelmed by it. I closed my eyes and let it flow over me, let it take me to that place only a vampire can take you to, but in my mind's eye it wasn't Louis who found my neck and bit down. It was Daniel I shared my body and my blood with. It was Daniel's sandy hair I sank my fingers into as he groaned against me. It was Daniel, my love, my friend, my husband, who took my mind off my grief.

I think I went a little crazy that first full night in Louis's bed because I really saw Danny. He was there with me, whispering to me. He loved me. He would forgive me for anything I had to do as long as I was alive at the end of it. When the vampire released the vein in my neck, it was Daniel's blue eyes that smiled down at me, happy and eager to get to the next part. It was Daniel's hands that undressed me and his strong body that moved against mine. It was his blood I took into my body and his voice that urged me on.

A long while later Louis pulled me against his satiated body and I knew my blood was working inside him. His hands moved over my skin like he couldn't quite stop himself from stroking me.

"Je t'aime, mon ange." He sighed as he kissed my forehead.

There was a loud knock on the door. It wasn't the first time, but Louis had completely ignored it before. Now he was irritated. He gently disentangled himself from me.

"I will tell them to go away, my sweet companion. It's our wedding night. I'm sorry we didn't have a properly observed ceremony, but there isn't time. The least I should expect is to be left alone to enjoy my wedding night," he grumbled as he got out of bed and wrapped a robe around his body.

I felt sick again at the thought of it. According to the laws of the vampire world, I really was Zoey Marini now. Daniel was an outlaw, declared by the full Council, so I was fair game. Louis had performed the ritual. He had taken my blood and I had taken his. We were married legally. It would be a short marriage because I was already planning a really permanent divorce from husband number three.

Louis was frowning when he returned. "I have to go, Zoey."

I forced myself to pout. "You're leaving me?"

He sighed and knelt by the bed, taking both my hands in his. He brought them to his lips and kissed them fervently. "Forgive me, darling girl. Niles and Elof are very insistent. They're being entirely unreasonable about interrupting our wedding night."

They were being entirely pissed about Louis screwing around in the middle of a war. I had to stop myself from smiling, but I was delighted at the chaos I'd created. I wondered how much more I could cause.

"Can I go with you?" I had just taken a full dose of his blood. It should have made me more pliable, more willing to do as he wanted and to want to be near him. It had been explained to me that this was part of the bonding process, but I was somehow different. I enjoyed taking Danny's blood but it never made me his slave. Louis's didn't touch me either, but he didn't know that.

"I don't know if that is a good idea, Zoey."

"You don't want me anymore?"

"How can you ask that?" Louis quickly moved in to allay my fears. "Believe me, if I could I would stay in that bed with you and never again allow you out of it. We're bonded now, Zoey. I told you it would be this way. You feel it now. I can see it."

I forced my lips to smile. "Can I wait here for you?"

Louis stood up and started to dress. He seemed to come to a decision. "No. You may come with me. You're my wife now. They will accept you. You must behave though."

I sat up on my knees, completely heedless of my nudity. It was a lesson Dev had taught me. "I promise. I just…would rather be with you."

The man who'd effectively murdered my husband finished dressing and leaned over to kiss me. "I knew you would once we were properly bonded. You'll see, Zoey. You'll like your new life."

He looked around but seemed unhappy with my clothes. They were definitely worse for the wear.

"I don't guess I'll much look like your wife in jeans and a T-shirt," I said, happy with the embarrassment in my voice. I'd just had a brilliant idea, but I was going to need to go about it slowly. I didn't want him suspicious.

He hauled me up and wrapped his robe around me. It was very masculine and it swallowed me, but I knew he would like me dressed in something of his. "You look perfect. Come along."

Louis led me through the sitting area, and my heart raced as he walked straight to the office door. I was going to get a good look at the scene of my future crime.

Niles and Elof stood up as Louis entered the room.

"Finally," Niles said in that upper-crust accent of his. "We've been waiting for hours...what the hell is she doing here?"

Louis's eyes narrowed. "Do you have a problem with my companion, Niles?" The question was an obvious trap.

"No, Louis," Niles replied, but I could see he was lying.

Louis sat down in the big wing chair behind his imposing desk and I began to sink to my knees beside him as he'd had me do before. It would be hard for me to see anything but the front of the desk and Louis's lap, but I needed him to trust me. The vampire made it easy on me. He pulled me up and indicated that he wanted me in his lap. I gave him an intimate smile and curled against him.

"Do you really think it's appropriate to have her in here?" Elof asked, obviously exasperated as he reseated himself.

I was going to have to think about changing my name to Yoko. I was really giving this little band of Louis's hell. I cuddled against Louis, and he practically purred at the close contact.

"She isn't going to cause trouble," Louis said sharply, his hand tightening like they might try to take me away from him. If I played my cards just right, I might be able to start a fight. "We just performed the ceremony, Elof. The two of you interrupted our bonding time."

"Well, excuse us, Louis," Niles said bitterly. "I don't think Donovan is going to stop his campaign against us because you need a honeymoon with his companion."

Now Louis was growling. "She's mine. Do you question my right to my companion?"

Elof rolled his eyes. "Of course not. Give it up, Niles. He's going to be unreasonable. You know how it is when you get that first real night with one of them. Can you imagine what she tastes like?"

"Yes, I certainly can," the Brit replied. "Which is why he shouldn't have taken her as his companion when we're in the middle of a bloody war and we're losing."

Then they were off and arguing about everything under the sun. Niles wanted to go after Daniel hard and immediately. Elof wanted to start waging a more guerilla-like approach to the war, and Louis was waiting to see if his demon contacts would come through. I heard them talking about the possibility of dealing with the Hell plane. It sent off alarm bells in my head. Thus far, the demons had stayed out of our skirmishes. That could go poorly for us, but I forced myself to remain in full-on sexy kitty mode. I rested against Marini's shoulder and pretended to doze as they argued on and decided to at least talk to the demons. They would call one tomorrow night once their witch was prepared.

I let my eyes drift around the room. It was very masculine, like the rest of Louis's apartments. It was stuck in the sixteenth century or somewhere close to it. Everything was dark wood and rich fabrics. There was his large, neatly appointed desk with everything in its place. There was a computer, but I was surprised to see it wasn't a sleek laptop like Dev and Danny preferred. It was a solid-looking machine, but it couldn't be easily moved. Dev never employed anything that couldn't be moved or destroyed fully and at a moment's notice, but then Dev was thorough...I took a deep breath. I had to keep my mind from going there. I had to focus. I couldn't think about Dev. I couldn't indulge in grief or memory.

The computer helped me. I thought long and hard about how that little piece of technology could be the opening I needed.

It seemed to take hours before they were willing to break up. I heard Louis curse as he realized dawn wasn't far away. Niles and Elof left the room but not before Niles looked down at me and shook his head. He was suspicious. I would have to be careful around the Brit.

"I don't think they like me, Louis," I said, sounding very insecure.

"They're just jealous of me." The door closed and Louis was pulling off my robe, his hands finding my breasts. "I have such a beautiful, bright companion. They can't stand the thought that they will never possess one such as you." His breathing was heavy, and I knew he was going to take me on top of the desk. His lips roamed across my neck.

"You don't think they will...try to steal me?"

Louis's head came up, and I saw the beginning of sweet, sweet paranoia in that brain of his. "They wouldn't dare."

I bit my lip and threw my arms around his neck. "You'll keep me safe."

"I promise, Zoey. I'll keep you safe from them."

Just before dawn, Louis led me back to the bedroom. He kissed my hand, turning the palm over to rub against his cheek affectionately. "Trent will take you back to your rooms, darling girl. Your little wolf should be there by now."

"Thank you for that." I picked up my sadly worn jeans and T-shirt. "I guess I'll have to clean them again. May I keep the robe until they're clean?"

Louis had promised to give me the things I needed. Under the influence of my blood, he would really want to keep his promise to me. "I'm sorry about the state of your wardrobe, Zoey. I know you're used to better than this. I intended for Rose to purchase nice clothes for you but...perhaps one of the other companions has something you could borrow. I know Elof's companion is already here."

I'd seen her. She was beautiful and cold and way skinnier than me. I sank down on the bed and did something that would have annoyed Danny to no end. "I can't, Louis. The other companions... I'm too fat to fit into their clothes." I sniffled slightly.

This would be the time when Daniel yelled at me for insulting myself. He'd long ago stopped listening to me when I did things like bitch about my weight. He wouldn't let anyone insult me and that included me. Louis simply knelt down beside me. "*Non, non, mon ange. Tu es pour moi la plus belle.* You are beautiful. Did I not prove how much I love your body tonight?"

"I know. It's just the other women. They can be mean."

"Then you must have your beautiful clothes," he replied,

clucking. "But Zoey, I can't send you out into the city. Donovan is watching."

I thought for a moment, even though I knew exactly what I was going to say next. I bit my bottom lip like I was thinking really hard. I finally smiled as if I'd come up with the best idea ever. "I could order them off the Internet."

He sighed and I knew I had him. "Zoey, I will know if you have tried anything."

I smiled brightly and threw my arms around his neck. "I promise, Louis. I'll just play around in the good websites. Neiman's and Nordstrom and Harrod's! I think Mark Jacobs has a new collection coming out. Neil can help me. He knows what looks good on me. Oh, I'm so excited. Can I start this afternoon?"

He pulled away slightly. "Perhaps you should wait until I'm awake."

"Oh, so you want to spend your time with me picking out clothes?" I asked, giggling like a fucking idiot. "I think you'd rather take them off me, Louis. If Niles and Elof let us have any time at all."

His face darkened. "I am still their master, Zoey. They will obey me. Fine. But if I find you've done anything you shouldn't…"

"Are you going to spank me, Louis?" I asked with a little smile. "I warn you, I might like it."

"God, Zoey, you're going to drive me crazy. I've never met anyone like you. Go. It's almost dawn and I need to get to my resting place. Don't ask me where it is. It's better you don't know." He released me and walked over to his dresser. He pulled out two things, a Visa and a set of keys. "If you look in the top drawer of my desk, you'll find the address of a hotel in the city where I keep a suite. Have your packages sent there and I will send someone to collect them. Zoey, don't break me, darling. We're in the middle of a war."

"I promise nothing," I said with a smile. I kissed the bastard and walked to the door where Trent would be waiting.

"I'll see you soon, *mon ange*," Louis said and the poor man looked love-sick.

I left his bedroom with the keys to Daniel's salvation firmly in my hands.

CHAPTER THIRTY-FOUR

Neil was pacing the floor wearing nothing but a pair of sweat pants and an overly large T-shirt when I slipped into the room. It took him a minute to realize I was with him, and I used that moment to study my best friend. He seemed...older, slightly harder. I couldn't have explained it if I had to, but I knew Neil was different.

When he turned his eyes to me I saw that he'd been crying. "Is it true?"

I didn't pretend to not know what he was talking about. I knew he'd heard everything Marini had said to me, including the fact that I blamed him for Dev's death. I felt the tears that were always there, just on the edge of my eyes, begin to seep out. "Yes."

Neil's mouth dropped open and he held his head in his hands. "Why? Why would Marini kill Dev? What the hell does he get out of it? Oh, god, how can Dev be dead?"

"I can't quite believe it either." I did what I did when I thought about Dev now. I breathed. I lived. My heart felt like it would stop, but I made sure it kept beating. It had seemed a distant reality while I was working, and that was what I thought of spending time with Marini, but it all rushed back in now. "I keep expecting to run into him as I walk down a hallway. He'll grab my ass and pull me into an alcove to have his way with me."

Neil slumped down onto the sofa. There was a plate of food on the table but he hadn't eaten much of it. If I hadn't already known something was wrong, that would have been a huge clue. "I knew the minute I figured out you were down here that Lee was dead. He wouldn't have let them take you. He would have fought to the death to keep you out of here, and he wouldn't have retreated, even though it probably was the smartest play. I knew when I caught your scent here that they'd killed him but…I thought Marini would want to keep Dev around."

"He did." I hesitated because I knew the next few minutes would be some of the worst minutes of my best friend's life, and now I was very unsure I wanted to be the one to tell him. "It was a stupid ruse to trap Marcus. He's in a silver-draped coffin god knows where."

"So how did Dev die? Was it an accident?"

"It wasn't an accident. He was murdered." I couldn't quite make myself form the words that would shatter his world but he was a smart boy. He knew there was only one name I wouldn't just toss out there as truth.

"No," he said resolutely. "No. It wasn't Chad. He wouldn't do that, Zoey. I know he seems crazy but he's harmless. I know him."

"I watched him do it, Neil." I had to tell him the truth. I couldn't risk Neil trusting Chad. Who knew when Chad might decide he needed another person in that body of his? "He drained Dev and then he tossed his body on Danny's doorstep. I watched it happen."

"I don't believe it," Neil said firmly.

I was tired and I'd had to spend hours making love to my worst enemy and pretending to enjoy it. I wasn't about to argue. "Believe what you want, Neil. If you hurry maybe you can find your lover before dawn takes him. He can tell you all about how good Dev tasted."

I walked into my bedroom and placed the keys and the credit card on the dresser and made my way into the bathroom. I needed a steaming hot shower. I needed to wash his hands off of my skin and feel vaguely clean again. I entered the shower with a certain bitterness I hadn't expected to feel this morning. All night, while Marini had used my body, I consoled myself with the fact that Neil would be waiting for me and I would find comfort with him. Now I wished he'd found Daniel instead of me. I wasn't going to listen to him argue that his lover was innocent. I still had a picture of Chad inside my head, standing over Dev's lifeless body with his precious blood dripping from his fangs. If Neil chose Chad then I would be done with him.

I scrubbed my skin with a vicious purpose. I knew I was being hard on Neil. I had no idea what he'd been through but grief is so selfish. I wasn't thinking of Neil that night. I was thinking of myself and how Neil had let me down. It wasn't fair and even in my grief I realized that, but I couldn't quite make myself care. I was focused on one thing and one thing only—getting into that office and getting the combination to that safe.

I went over the whole thing in my head and felt pretty good about the plan by the time I shut off the shower and realized I had absolutely nothing to change into. I wrapped a towel around myself and just stood there for a moment feeling completely numb. Neil's belief in Chad had thrown me for a loop, and now I only cared about finishing the job so I could get to Daniel. Danny would believe me. Danny would understand.

"How about we agree to disagree?" Neil asked from the doorway. His eyes were red from crying.

"This isn't an argument over what television show to watch, Neil," I heard myself saying. I felt hollowed out, like someone had opened me up and scooped out all the important parts. "Your lover killed my husband."

Neil's voice was quiet, cautious. "If he did, then he did it to save you or Daniel."

"Not good enough," I spat back, getting really angry with him. He hadn't been there, hadn't seen it. Did he think I just made it up for fun? "He enjoyed it, Neil. He liked killing Dev. He's wanted him forever. Sorry, but your murdering boyfriend wanted to cheat on you and when he couldn't have Dev, he killed him instead."

Neil shook his head. "Z, everything you say about it just reaffirms my belief that he was acting. He loves me. He wouldn't cheat on me. I know that deep in my soul. We're missing something."

I pushed past him to get out of the bathroom. "I didn't miss any-thing. I saw every second of it in vivid, vibrant color. Look, I'm tired,

Neil. I fucked Marini all night. I want to sleep. I don't want to hold your hand because you don't like the fact that your precious boyfriend is a lunatic killer. Just stay out of my way until I can get the job done and get us out of here."

I managed to get to the bed and I sat down feeling absolutely nothing. It was kind of nice to be so very, very numb. After the turmoil of the past few days, it felt damn good to shove Neil away. I didn't have to care about him. Caring about him would just hurt and I'd been hurt way too much. I didn't have to care about anything. I could just curl up in a little cocoon where no one could hurt me anymore. I would do the job and have the babies, but I didn't have to let them touch me. I owed Dev their lives. They were all that was left of him, but did I have to love them? Maybe my love had died with their father. I could build up my armor and I would be safe.

Then I heard him. He was trying to cover it up. I knew what I would find if I went back into that bathroom. He would be on the floor, his head buried in his hands, sobbing his grief away and trying to be quiet about it.

Those hated tears started up again. I didn't want to give a damn about his pain. I didn't want to love him or anyone at all. Shoving him away had felt good. It had felt empowering. Hearing him cry made me feel vulnerable because I was already on my feet, learning that my heart didn't give a shit what my head wanted. My heart would love and love and love. It didn't matter how many times it shattered to a thousand pieces. It was going to love, and there was nothing I could do to change it.

When I walked into the bathroom he was there, sitting on the floor looking as hopeless as I felt. I sank down beside him and wordlessly wrapped my arms around him, asking for forgiveness and giving it in return. We would agree to disagree, but there was no question I needed him and he needed me.

After the longest time we found our way to the big bed and Neil lay down beside me. I turned the lights out and his hand found mine. We were quiet for a moment.

"Zoey," I heard Neil's voice through the darkness. "Are we going to survive this?"

I gave him the only answer I could. "I don't know."

I pulled aside the framed picture that covered the safe anchored to the wall even as Neil found the website for Nordstrom.

"Why do they bother carrying the crappy shoes?" Neil asked, selecting the premier designer collection.

I touched the metal of the safe, letting it play against my skin. "We should be happy they do. Up until a couple of years ago we bought all our shoes from discount stores, and only when they had the buy-one get-one-half-off deal."

"I don't remember that ever happening," Neil said. "That espadrille is heavenly. What kind of shoes do we need down here? Do you think your foot will stay a seven and a half or will the babies fatten up your feet, too?"

"Neil, hopefully we're not going to be around to actually wear these clothes. They're a smoke screen to detract from what we're really doing, which is cracking this bad girl."

Neil turned in Marini's chair, looking at the safe. "Is it a one or a two?"

I rotated the combination lock. "Luckily, this beauty is a two." Combination safes come in two varieties known as ones or twos. The 1s are infinitely harder to crack because their combinations can accept up to six numbers. The 1s have more wheels in the lock mechanism. The type 2 combination is the type that would typically be found in a home or small office where someone just wanted to deter the average criminal. I wasn't average.

"His security is shit, Z." Neil turned back to the computer and ordered the aforementioned Valentino espadrilles. "I would have expected better."

I spun the knob, listening for the sweet sound of wheels tumbling. "He's the most powerful vampire in the world. Well, he thinks so. Who's going to steal from him?"

"You," Neil replied.

"Yeah, but only out of necessity. The catacombs themselves are a safety measure. Now, hush. I need to figure out how many wheels this baby has." It was an older model safe and I'd already tried the obvious. I'd searched the desk for the combination and made sure Louis hadn't left the safe in a day-lock mode where I would only need to know the last number of the combination. No such luck.

"Zoey," Neil said suddenly.

I turned from my work. "Yes?"

"How long was I gone?"

I thought it an odd question, but time worked differently on the Hell plane. It was the first time he'd mentioned his time away. I had asked briefly last night, but he hadn't wanted to talk about it. "It's been five days since Marini took us."

"No," Neil said. "That's impossible. I know I was gone longer."

I got down from the chair I was standing on. "Sweetie, how did you get away from Stewart?"

Neil was quiet, and I thought he was going to go back to his shopping for a moment. Then I heard his answer. "I don't know."

"How can you not know?"

I watched his curly blond hair shake and there was something about it that made me pause. I was looking at him very closely, and something was off about my BFF.

"I woke up in a field, Z. I don't know how I got there or where I was before. The last thing I remember was Stewart putting that collar over my head and leading me away, then I woke up naked in a field outside of Paris. The only thing I knew was someone had put a sock in my hand. It was one of yours and I followed the scent to the catacombs. Someone wanted me to find you."

But I was still looking at his hair. I walked over and ran my fingers through it.

"That feels nice," he said, leaning back.

Neil's hair is practically platinum, but I could see some very subtle differences. There was gray in there and a lot of it. There was gray that hadn't been there before.

"Look at me," I ordered him.

He turned to face me. "What is it?"

There they were—fine lines around his eyes. I'd never seen them before. "You were gone for more than five days, Neil. Is there anything else odd?"

He hesitated but then lifted the T-shirt Trent had given him that was a million sizes too big for his body. I gasped in shock at what I saw.

"How is that staying on your body?"

An elaborate tattoo covered the left side of Neil's chest. Werewolves loved piercings and body art, but the sad fact was unless the piercing was silver, the body would heal around it and the minute the wolf changed forms, the piercing was usually lost. Tats were even worse. The body reverted to its original form after the change. The ink wouldn't last through a change. I'd heard wolf after wolf bemoan that little fact. It was worse for the female. Her hair color reverted to natural following a change, so L'Oréal didn't last long on a she-wolf. She tended to get used to pesky grays.

"I don't know." Neil lowered the shirt again. "I woke up in human form and it was there. I figured it was a little demonic 'property of' sign so I changed as fast as I could, but it won't go away."

"And you don't remember anything?"

He growled. "No, I don't remember anything."

I shrugged. "I was just checking. Danny tries to hide stuff so I don't get worried."

"When was the last time I tried that on you, Z? I'm not your husband," Neil pointed out. "I'm much more important than that. I'm your gay husband. If I'm freaked you better be freaked, too."

"Well, I'm pretty damned freaked, Neil."

"Good." He smiled slightly and pulled a granola bar out of his pocket. "Here. I stole some from the kitchens when I got our breakfast this afternoon. I'll steal some crackers tomorrow. You might need them to deal with your morning sickness."

Neil had held my hair when I woke up just after noon, heaving up everything I had.

"The boys don't seem too fond of me waking up." Once that initial queasiness was done, they seemed ready to eat anything and everything I could get my hands on. I opened the granola bar, inhaled it, and Neil handed me another. "What happened to worrying about my spectacular figure?"

"You're beautiful no matter what your size, Z," Neil said. "I love you. I don't know what I'd do without you. Just have healthy babies."

I nodded because if I'd said anything at that moment I would have cried again. After a moment, I got back to the job at hand and Neil sighed over the new Gucci collection.

Thus the next few weeks of our life was set.

I spent the nights with Marini, allowing him free and liberal access to my body. Every time he touched me it felt like I was giving up a piece of my soul, but I did it. I did it for Dev, for Daniel, for the babies in my womb. I choked my way through every encounter. I hated him more than I ever hated anything in my life, even Chad. Chad had been able to kill Dev because of Louis. My feelings didn't matter during that time. I cuddled up to him and pretended I couldn't get enough of him. No one questioned my devotion. It seemed this was the normal pattern between vampire and companion.

More vampires came to the catacombs. Two new Council members were rapidly elected to fill Marcus's and Niko's seats. Two warriors. Adam Brooks and Rodrigo Vargas were old European vampires who seemed thrilled to be in on the action. They did what Louis told them to do. When Louis attended his war council, I sat at his side listening for any news of Daniel. The vampires had contacted the demons but working with demons was a slow, careful process. They were still banging out their contracts and it looked like it would be a while before Louis could expect help from that quarter. The tension seemed to make him short with the other Council members.

Neil and I became fixtures in the catacombs. Once it was obvious I was behaving properly, I was given a great deal of freedom. As long as my "guard" went with us, I was allowed to walk around freely. We only came across Chad once. I stopped in my tracks and Trent moved in front of me. Chad stared through Neil like he didn't matter but smiled at me.

"You should watch out for that one, Trent," Chad said as he moved past us. "She could get into serious trouble."

I turned to watch him walk away, and I caught the slightest brush of his fingers against Neil's. It was subtle. If I wasn't watching closely, I would have missed it. I couldn't see his face. He was looking the other way, but the action had an air of tenderness I couldn't mistake.

While I slept, Marcus and I walked the streets of Venice. I don't know what my dreams would have been like had Marcus not come to me each time I slept, but it was peaceful to walk along the canals with him. I visited the Piazza San Marco and the huge basilica. We dined at his favorite restaurant in the Cannaregio section of the city. I was surprised to find out Marcus had a favorite restaurant.

"I love food, *cara*," Marcus had told me as he ordered lobster *alsace*.

I learned that was spaghetti and lobster. It was delicious. "But you don't eat."

He grinned, the smile making him look young and carefree. "But my companions do. I might not be the strongest of vampires, as evidenced by my current predicament, but there are definite advantages to being an academic. My powers are mental and sensory. When I have a deep connection with a companion or even a human lover, I can sometimes taste through them. It's how I know that this dish is exquisite and how I can pass on the experience to you."

Then we were off. I tried just about everything Marcus could remember loving. I decided gelato was better than ice cream, but I preferred American pizza, much to his dismay.

My days were spent in Louis's office, listening carefully for that sweet little click that came when the pins were in the right position. Of course, if it was as easy as that I would know the combination almost immediately, but it's not. That click just told me a range of numbers. After first discerning the contact points and the number of wheels in the safe, I knew where to "park" the wheels before I started slowly moving the dial, waiting to hear that click. I used a piece of paper and pen to graph my results. After days of listening carefully, I had six possible combinations. Neil made fun of my carefully plotted numbers on my handmade graph when he could just tear that sucker open, but in this case we needed subtlety. I didn't intend to steal the stone the first chance I got. I had to time it just right. Once I had the combination, Trent was going to risk communicating with his outside contact. The contact would let Danny know I was ready to go. I just needed a day to exchange the stones and then Daniel could do his worst. Louis would be panicked when he heard Daniel was raiding the catacombs, and he wouldn't pay attention to the stone until he was ready to use it. It would be too late then, and Daniel would have the upper hand. If he discovered my deception too soon, I was worried he would run and regroup and potentially give us hell for the rest of our lives.

I came up with a different excuse each night why Neil and I needed to use the computer. We shopped for a few days because I obviously deserved a completely redone bedroom and I needed an awful lot of clothes. After that, we enjoyed playing games and watching American TV over the Internet. As Louis had never caught me doing anything wrong with the computer, he allowed it, all along stating he would install one in my rooms as soon as possible. I made sure Neil and I were sitting in front of the computer laughing at some comedy or OMGing over some ridiculous soap. The minute Louis entered, we sweetly broke up for the night and I acted thrilled to see my master.

Every moment of the day Dev was in the back of my mind, his memory constantly pulling me back to grief. I wondered if there would be a moment of my life that I wouldn't miss him, that some piece of me wouldn't be waiting to see him again.

I did end up getting those clothes we ordered, and I was already sucking in to get my pants closed. It was a daunting prospect that I was already gaining weight even with my morning throw-up sessions, but three weeks into my stay with Marini I began to see my belly starting to gently curve. I was barely a month along and my boys were making themselves known. The changes were subtle, but I worried if I had to be down here much longer, Louis was going to notice.

I had my final six combinations shoved in the pocket of my slightly too-tight Rag and Bone jeans as Neil sighed and sat back in Louis's big chair. "Is that it?"

"I think so. What time is it?" I asked, wondering if I could try them out now and figure out which one worked.

"Just after sunset," Neil replied. "Sorry, Z, but it's show time."

Not two minutes later Louis walked in. He smiled down at us. He was becoming fond of Neil, who had been true to his word and caused no trouble. "I like knowing exactly where you will be, Zoey." He helped me up and kissed me lightly. "I find I like this routine of ours. Perhaps I should think about moving you into these rooms with me. It seems silly that you should have to walk to your own rooms each morning when you would rather be here."

It would make it easier. I hugged him and nodded. "Neil could sleep with me in the big bed."

He smiled down indulgently. "Yes, *chère*, I'm accustomed to your little pet now. You can stop worrying. I know he has no designs on your person."

"Now that's where you're wrong, sir," Neil said. "I have lots of designs on Zoey's person. If you think she could dress herself, you're wrong. She needs me to look her best."

"She always looks beautiful, so I will thank you for that," Louis murmured.

Neil walked up and kissed my cheek. "Night, Z. See you in the morning."

The door closed behind Neil and Louis was on me immediately. He sat down in the chair Neil had vacated and his lips met mine in a ravenous kiss.

"I dream of you all day," he whispered.

He was starting to play with my neck when there was a long knock on the door.

"Go away," Louis growled.

"It's important," Niles said, opening the door anyway.

Louis's eyes narrowed. "It had better be."

The Brit frowned. "Well, I'm sure as it concerns your companion, you might be vaguely interested."

Now Louis was paying attention and so was I. I jumped off his lap and waited for Niles to tell me what was going on.

"Is it Donovan?" Marini asked, his voice tense. Everyone was waiting for Daniel to make his push. The weapons had come out of the armory and everyone walked around armed to the teeth.

"No," Niles said. "It's much stranger than that. I can't tell if it's a good thing or a bad thing. The Queen of the Seelie is at our gates, requesting entrance."

Louis went paler than normal and he spewed a litany of curses in his native language. He took my hand in his, squeezing tight. "She can't have Zoey."

Niles rolled his eyes. "I don't think she's here because she loves

Zoey. I went down and talked to her and heard that son of hers cursing Zoey's name. The heir doesn't like your girl."

Now I felt really sick. Declan was here. The last words I'd exchanged with my brother-in-law hadn't been pleasant ones. He'd warned me that there would be hell to pay if anything happened to his brother. Grief pulsed through me. How was I going to face Declan? How could I face Miria?

"I should warn you," Niles was saying. "I was taken by surprise. The heir looks just like his brother. It's eerie. Of course, once he opens his mouth, the differences are vast."

Marini turned to me. "What do you think they want?"

I shrugged. "I guess they want to know how Devinshea died."

"No." An evil little smile lit Niles's face, unsettling me. "The queen told me she knew why her son died. He died because he followed her. The queen blames Donovan and your companion for her son's death."

I gasped because I really hadn't expected that of my mother-in-law, but then this had been her greatest fear. She'd been terrified of losing her youngest son since the moment she learned he was mortal. She had to be devastated. It must be worse knowing how they had parted.

"I won't give her to them," Marini said again. I wondered how long it would take him to start worrying about fighting a war on two fronts. He needed the Seelies to stay out of the fight.

Niles laughed, a wholly nasty sound. "They don't want your bitch, Louis. They want the babies in her belly."

Chapter Thirty-Five

There was a loud cracking sound and I hit the ground as I took the full brunt of Louis's slap across my face. The shock of it hit me and then the pain. I tasted blood and my hands shook.

"Tell me it isn't true," Louis barked, pulling me up by my hair.

I hurried to get up so he didn't pull it all out. So much for loving me. I braced for the next blow.

"Fuck," Louis cursed as he dropped me so abruptly I fell back down.

Niles leaned against the doorframe with a smile on his face, enjoying the show. "Louis, as much as I love that little bitch getting her comeuppance, you really should think before you beat the fetuses from her body."

I backed up, primal instinct taking over, and I covered my belly. It wouldn't help if Louis wanted to kill me, but I had to try something. I had to do anything to protect my babies. I'd failed to protect their father. I had to save them.

"How could you?" Louis loomed over me, growling.

I put my head down and curled into a tight ball. I couldn't lose my babies.

Niles sighed. "Louis, you're an idiot when it comes to her. Think for two seconds. Those children might keep the Seelies out of this war or it might bring them to our side. The prince was a fertility god, the last of his kind. If little Zoey there has his spawn in her womb, that's a bloody big bargaining chip."

I huddled against the wall, hoping Niles's words got through to Louis. I was also wondering how the hell Miria knew I was pregnant. Had Bris somehow found a new host and informed the Seelies? I'd wondered where the fertility god had gone when Dev died. I had so missed his warmth.

There was no warmth at all as Louis hauled me up again, though this time he took his pleasure by nearly pulling my arm out of socket. "Tell the Queen she and her son will be allowed in with one guard apiece. I will assure their safety and we can discuss this mess we're in."

Niles nodded and smiled at me as he left.

"How could you lie to me?" Louis growled the question as he twisted my arm. I wondered if he planned to break it.

"I didn't lie," I replied through the pain. "I'm not sure if I'm pregnant."

"*Menteuse.*" He pushed me away and sat down in his chair. His claws were out and now I felt the blood where he'd dug them into my skin. "You have another man's seed growing in your belly and you do not see the betrayal."

I tried not to whimper as I rotated my arm. It still worked. Mostly. "It happened before you took me. You know Dev died before we were married. How can you blame me? He was my husband. Of course I slept with him."

Louis brought his big fists down on the desk. It cracked and he seemed satisfied with the destruction. "Get out of here, Zoey. Go and change your clothes and clean the blood from your body. You have ten minutes to be ready. You will be at my side when I greet the Queen. Understand this, my companion, you belong to me so whatever is in your belly is mine to do with as I please. If I decide giving those babes to the Queen when they're born is to my advantage, then that is what you'll do."

I fled the room to do what he asked and prayed I could survive seeing Declan Quinn again.

"You have to stay here," I told Neil when Trent came for me ten minutes later.

Neil shook his head. "After what he did to you, you expect me to leave you alone with him?"

"You don't have a choice. I'll take care of her." Trent was grim and had been since he'd heard the news. My pregnancy made his job ten times harder. "Look, Zoey has the combination to the safe, right?"

I nodded. I was sure it was one of the six numbers I had hidden in the bathroom with the fake stone.

"Tomorrow we take the stone and we run," Trent said. "We do it during the day and I just kill anyone who gets in the way. We can't wait for Donovan any longer."

It wasn't the best solution, but I had to think about my sons. They had to come before anything else, so I nodded.

"How does Miria know about the babies?" Neil asked. "She said babies, right? Not baby. How does she know you're having twins?"

Trent held the door open for me. I glanced back at Neil. "I don't know."

He looked like he wanted to say something, but when he opened his mouth he merely wished me luck and told me he would be waiting for me.

Trent cursed under his breath the whole time he walked me to the great hall. My pregnancy put him in a really bad mood. He'd been pissed when he'd seen the blood covering my arms and dotted on my face. The wounds had healed quickly, but there was no mistaking I'd gotten my ass kicked. Any questions I had about the blood bond being the same for all vampires had been answered forever. Daniel could be out of his mind angry and he wouldn't hit me. Daniel Donovan loved me and it had nothing to do with blood.

The great hall was filled to capacity by the time I got there. It looked like every vampire in the catacombs had come to see the Queen and her heir. Louis had changed his clothes. I was sure I'd been rude enough to bleed on him during his assault on my person. His stance was arrogant and angry as he motioned me over.

"You say nothing, do you understand?" he said harshly, pulling me to his side. "You are to speak only when spoken to and you obey my every command. When this is over we'll have a long discussion about the future, my companion."

Then the golden doors that led from the catacombs opened and I got my first glance at Miria, Queen of the Seelie. She was dressed in contemporary clothes for the first time in our acquaintance. Despite her five hundred plus years she appeared to be in her mid-twenties. Her golden red hair brushed her waist, hanging in a perfect waterfall. She wore a fashionable business suit that draped her slender figure. She moved down the grand staircase with a grace and elegance that befitted her royal status. I stared at her for a moment, putting off the time when I had to see Declan.

Tears sprung to my eyes and it took everything I had to remain upright. He looked just like Devinshea. He was in a tailored suit just like the ones Dev favored. Had favored. With his hair pulled back, I could almost believe Devinshea was walking toward me until I saw the cold arrogance in his emerald eyes. He sought me out immediately, and I knew beyond a shadow of a doubt he'd come for revenge.

Padric walked behind his lover, the queen. He was the head of the guards so it made perfect sense that he was with them, but I didn't recognize the other guard. He was short for a Fae but obviously fierce, with dark hair and brown eyes. He walked behind Declan, so he was obviously the heir's dedicated guard. Both he and Padric carried long swords on their backs that seemed incongruous with the suits they wore.

"I bring you greetings, Mr. Marini, from the Seelie Fae to the Vampire Council," Miria said formally. She hadn't looked at me yet. She kept her regal gaze on the vampire beside me. Declan had no such desire. He openly stared at me, and I caught his glance going to my belly.

"We're surprised to see you, Queen Miria." Louis's voice betrayed none of his earlier panic. He was smooth and calm. "You so rarely leave the *sithein*."

"Well, as my youngest son has so recently proven, the Earth plane can be very dangerous for the Fae," she said.

"I was very sorry to learn of your son's death," Louis said and I wondered just what Miria had heard. "I was actually quite fond of the prince."

"I bet you were." Declan eyed the vampire with overt distaste.

"Declan," Miria warned.

"Well, let's not mince words, Mother. My brother liked vampires. He was addicted to the pleasure of their bite. I loved my brother, Mr. Marini, but I have no illusions about him. He was a pervert, a slave to his own sick desires." Declan nodded toward me. "His obsession with that woman led to his death."

"Has the vampire who killed him been punished?" Miria asked as though she was merely inquiring about the weather. I had expected to see more grief, more emotion, but she seemed to be in full-on royal mode where nothing could touch her.

"Of course, Your Majesty," Louis lied smoothly. "I executed the vampire myself."

I wanted to shout, but I held my tongue because I wasn't sure Louis wouldn't kill me right there and I wasn't sure Declan wouldn't help.

"Good," Miria said, seemingly satisfied. She glanced my way. "Upon hearing of Devinshea's death, I performed some magic to attempt to speak with his spirit. He told me some interesting news. Are you pregnant, girl?"

I averted my eyes because I couldn't meet her judgmental ones. She'd talked to him? I wanted so badly to hear his voice just one more time.

"Answer the queen," Louis ordered.

"I don't know," I lied. "It's too early."

Miria sighed. "It might be too early for an inexperienced human, but I assure you, we can tell."

"I can tell from here, mother," Declan said with a vulgar leer. "Her breasts are huge. They look even more luscious than the last time I saw her."

Louis growled at the prince.

Declan rolled his green eyes. "Vampires. I suppose you 'claim' her now?"

Louis put an arm around me. "She's my companion."

"Well, I hate the bitch, but you can't blame me for noticing her tits," Declan said negligently. "They're gorgeous. Really, it would be rude not to notice."

"Please excuse my son," Miria said irritably. "He never has had a moment's worth of manners. You understand the implications for my people if she is carrying Devinshea's children?"

Louis played it cool. "I understand your interest in passing on the prince's unique DNA."

"We would be very interested in acquiring the children, Mr. Marini," Miria said, cutting past the bullshit. "I think we might be able to come to an agreement if the girl proves to be pregnant and you would allow her to carry the children to term."

"It would not be my first choice," Louis admitted. He would prefer to end the pregnancy and any evidence of another man's possession of me.

Miria's green eyes turned calculating. "I understand you are at war, Mr. Marini."

Louis's lips tightened as he answered the queen. "You understand correctly. I will take care of the pretender, of course."

Miria stared at Marini. "He seems to be giving you some trouble. I might be able to help you but I would need a reason."

The subtext sat there, plain to anyone with ears. Louis could have the Seelie on his side. Or he could fight against them. It was his choice. Of course, it was really no choice at all.

How much worse could it get? Would the Unseelie honor their word to their dead priest's partner? Or would Daniel find himself without any Fae allies at all? Would Miria send warriors to kill my husband? Would Declan attempt to do the deed himself?

Louis sighed. "Why don't we retire to a more suitable setting for our negotiations? I would have the full Council sit in with us."

"I agree. We can talk, but I want proof that the girl is carrying my son's children." Miria held her hand out, indicating the Fae beside Declan. "This is Callum. He is training to be a healer. He is also a guard, but I assure you he can discern if the girl is pregnant or not. Allow him to examine her while we talk alliances."

Louis looked like he wanted to disagree, but he needed that alliance and he was a practical man. After a long moment, he nodded. "Trent, escort the Fae healer back to my companion's rooms. He may examine her there. Stay with her and make sure she comes to no harm."

He wouldn't allow anyone else to hurt me. He claimed that pleasure all for himself.

Trent nodded and began to escort me out. Over my shoulder, I heard Miria speak.

"Declan, go with the healer and bring me news," Miria said.

Declan was suddenly at my side. He spoke quietly. "I've been wanting to get you alone for a while, Zoey."

The walk back to my apartments was one of the longest of my life. I was crying openly by the time we reached the hallway that contained my rooms. Looking at Declan hurt. It was an actual physical ache in my body. His jaw had relaxed and the arrogance in him had softened, leaving me looking at my husband. He looked so much like Dev it was hard not to believe it was him walking beside me. I wanted to reach out and grab his hand and hold it against my stomach, urging him to feel our babies growing inside.

I hadn't really said good-bye to him. It was over so quickly I hadn't properly had a chance to really process the fact that my husband was gone. I needed something from Declan and he would probably make me feel like a fool for asking, but I was going to try. He'd cared for me once.

I was hustled into the front room of my apartments and when I heard the door slam behind me, I turned to face my brother-in-law.

"Zoey," he said, but I heard Dev's voice.

"Don't," I started, unable to stop the tears from flowing. "Just let me talk for a minute and then I'll submit to any test you want me to take. I have done you service, Prince Declan, and asked nothing in return, but now I need something from you. I need ten minutes. Just ten minutes where you pretend to be him. Ten minutes, Declan. I need you to hold me and pretend. I didn't get to say good-bye."

The blood left Declan's face, his skin turning pale. He turned and I saw he looked at Chad, who must have joined us at some point. I hadn't noticed or I would have protested. I was about to launch myself bodily at the vampire, but Declan's words stopped me.

"You didn't tell her." It wasn't a question. It was an accusation.

"I made a call," Chad said, sounding saner than I had heard him my entire time in the catacombs. "You don't understand what it's like in here, Dev. If she'd given us away he'd kill us all. She almost fucked it up as it was. She announced plainly to Marini that I was a spy. Luckily, my insane act provided me with some cover. It was a good illusion. It certainly fooled Marcus."

"I'm going to kill Marcus when Zack finds that coffin of his. He's supposed to know things like this. Shouldn't he have been able to see through the illusion?"

Neil was standing beside me suddenly, holding me up. "It's all right, Zoey. Guys, I think she's going to pass out."

"Oh, my sweet goddess," Dev's voice said from Declan's body. He lifted me up. "I am so sorry. I had no idea they wouldn't tell you. I would never have left you knowing you thought I was dead." He looked back at Chad. "Daniel will be furious."

"Daniel isn't the one stuck in here." Chad relaxed a little as his gaze found Neil. "Neil knew."

"No, I didn't," Neil replied. "I just had faith in you, baby."

Chad's eyes were full of tears he wouldn't shed. "Tell me this means it's almost over, Dev. I want to go home."

"But Chad killed you." I stared at my husband, wondering if I'd gone completely insane.

"Did I, Your Highness?" Chad asked.

"Sweetheart," Dev said, sitting us down on the sofa. "It was an illusion. Once he realized how Marini intended to use my magic, he made the call to get me out of here. He knocked me out and when I woke up Daniel was staring down at me. I am so sorry. I didn't want to leave you, but they decided it was too dangerous to leave me here."

"I couldn't risk it," Chad explained. "I know what that magic did for my master. I couldn't risk Marini allowing every vampire in the catacombs to feed from it. They would all be able to daywalk. They would have been stronger, faster. I couldn't let that happen. I'm sorry it hurt Zoey, but her grief sold it."

"You had no right to use her like that."

"Do you have any idea how complex an illusion that was?" Chad asked, his voice low but full of indignation. "It's one thing to hide a couple of people, to make something disappear. It's another thing entirely to craft an illusion so real you can touch it, smell it and taste it. I had to concentrate. Zoey's grief gave me the chance to do it. If she hadn't distracted Marini with her tears, I would have failed and then we would all have been dead."

"You could have told her afterward," Dev complained.

"A—she wouldn't let me near her afterward, and B—I couldn't risk Marini figuring out she was lying," Chad argued.

The healer, Callum, walked up to Neil. He threw his arms around him and enveloped him in a brotherly hug. When he spoke, his voice was familiar. "I would love to hang around for the rest of this little drama, but I got a job to do. Neil, it's so freaking good to see you, man. Saves me a trip to the Hell plane to retrieve you." He turned to me. His eyes were soft and sympathetic when he looked at me. "It's good to see you too, Zoey. We'll talk later. I have to go let Marcus out so Dev can kill him." He walked to the door and turned around. "And, Zoey, this counts. That's like five to nothing now, sister."

He slipped out. "Was that Zack?" I heard myself ask but the sound seemed a little distant.

"Yes, sweetheart," Dev replied. "He's wearing a glamour, obviously. I didn't have to. I just had Bris grow my hair. I'll cut it again as soon as I can. I know it bothers your dad. He's in London, you know. Someone called him and told him what's been going on. He's been giving everyone hell."

"It's a trick." Tears started because this was beyond cruel. Chad was playing games with me again. I didn't know what I had done to Chad to make him hate me. Maybe he was jealous of my relationship with Neil. He always thought we were too close.

"Zoey," Dev said, shaking me lightly. "My goddess, it isn't a trick. I'm so sorry to have put you through this, but it was necessary. How can I make you believe me? Do you remember the first time you met my brother? He kissed you and that was how you knew it wasn't me. Kiss me, my goddess. Kiss me."

He leaned down and pressed his lips to mine and my whole world came back to me. I felt his unique magic tingle across my skin and knew beyond a shadow of a doubt that my faery prince was back. I cried, but it was joyful now and I opened my lips under his, allowing our passion to flare.

"You see," I heard Trent saying as Dev hugged me tightly to his body and stood up. "This is why I work alone. You're all crazy, you know that, right?"

"Perhaps," Dev said. "My mother and Padric will keep Marini and the Council occupied for the night. I'll spend some time with my goddess until Zack returns. If you wouldn't mind watching the door?"

Trent nodded. "I suppose this means Donovan is moving soon."

"Tomorrow night," Dev said. "I'll fill you in before I leave."

Trent stopped Dev as he opened the door to the bedroom. I saw that Neil and Chad were embracing. I was still a bit angry with the vampire. It was going to take a while to get over it.

"You tell Donovan he either moves tomorrow night or we leave the next day with him or without him," the big wolf said. "Marini beat the shit out of her tonight. We might be able to keep him off her the rest of the night but not much more. I'm worried he'll kill her, vampire blood or no."

Dev's face hardened. "Daniel and I will take care of him tomorrow. You just worry about her." He slammed the door behind us and we were alone.

He laid me gently down on the bed and ran his hands across me, checking for injuries.

"I'm fine, Dev." I loved how his name fell from my lips. He was alive and here with me.

"I'm going to kill him, my wife," Dev promised.

"I know, baby."

Bris came out and laid his hands directly over my womb. I felt a spark of heat and held my breath, waiting for his pronouncement. He smiled down at me. "Hello, my goddess. You're a beautiful sight to behold. The children are doing well. The boys are strong."

"I made sure he didn't hit my stomach."

Dev climbed onto the bed with me, his eyes wide with horror. "If I never hear you say those words again, it will be too soon. Do you know how much it has killed us to leave you here? Daniel...Daniel is a different person. He is beside himself with guilt."

"Tell him I'm fine and I love him." I touched his face, reassuring myself that this was real. If it was a dream, I didn't want to wake up. I would just sleep forever. "Tell him when I thought you were gone, the only thing I held on to was him. He was here with me. And if you might skip over the parts where I had to do gross stuff and got my ass kicked, it might help him not feel so guilty."

"He's not a fool, lover." Dev's hands made quick work of the buttons on my blouse. "He knows what you've gone through. He'll make it right. Do you have the stone?"

"I have the combination. I'll switch the stones in the morning." I pushed at his jacket, eager to get my hands on his skin. "You know, you really do a mean Declan."

He kissed me and made a place for himself between my legs as he shoved the jacket off. "Well, it's not hard. You just have to look exceedingly arrogant and have no filter whatsoever. The key to pulling off my brother is to just say every vulgar thing that comes to mind. It isn't hard around you. I think very vulgar thoughts."

"Who's playing the role of your mom?" I asked, wondering who they got to wear that glamour.

"It really is my mother, sweetheart," Dev replied, looking down on me, his shirt and jacket off. I could feel his heartbeat. "She wanted to help. Declan is back in London, waiting with the rest. He'll be with us during the battle. The Seelies will stand with us."

"You reconciled with them for me? What did you have to promise?"

A wistful smile lit his face. "It wasn't hard. Once they knew Bris had reintegrated, they were eager for me to be their priest again. I promised I would spend a week out of each year in the Seelie *sithein*. I can set the fields to rights and perform fertility rituals. It's the same as my contract with the Unseelie. Don't worry, Zoey. I don't mind doing it. It was the only way we could think of to get me in to see you and find out if you had the stone. We also decided it was a good bet that dangling the hopes of an alliance with my mother would keep Marini off you for a while."

I doubted he would leave me alone for any length of time, but I didn't argue with my husband. "You're talking to Declan again?"

"Well, I'm only using four letter words when speaking to him, but considering the fact that before I was using vulgar gestures, I believe he counts it as progress," Dev explained with a grin. "Now, my goddess, our time is limited. I have to report news of your fertile state to my mother soon but before I go, I have a package to deliver."

I laughed from deep in my soul because I knew just what package he wanted to give me.

"And I have to do it twice," he continued with a sweetly decadent look on his face. "I promised I would deliver Daniel's love to you as well."

I threw my arms around him, ready to receive all the love they had to give me.

Hours later, Dev looked deeply into my eyes and I knew it was killing him to leave me.

"Mother will keep the negotiations open until tomorrow night," Dev explained. "These things take time and Marini knows that, but he also knows that there will be no alliance without the safety of our children secured. Despite what Trent thinks, I believe he needs the alliance enough that he will leave you be."

"I'll try to stay out of his way as much as possible. I'll change the stones tomorrow. He won't know the difference until it's too late." I hugged Dev's broad chest, not wanting to be separated even one more night. "Is Danny well? Has he recovered? He must have gone through all the reserve blood supply. Has he gotten over the withdrawal yet?"

I couldn't stand the thought of Daniel coming in at less than full strength. He hadn't had companion blood. It could make a difference.

Dev shook his head. "He's fine, Zoey. His heart is healed and he's been taking regular companion blood thanks to your little present."

"My present?"

"Yes, Rose. We were shocked when she called Daniel's cell phone and told us to pick her up. She said you had sent her to feed Daniel while you were gone," Dev explained.

I bet she was also the one who had called my father down on my husbands' heads. I would thank her for that the next time I saw her. I would never think of her as a mouse again. "I'm glad that worked out."

"We need to go, Dev," Zack said. "Marcus is out and he's in pretty pitiful shape. He needs blood in a bad way."

Dev kissed me, a promise of things to come. "I love you, Zoey. Always and forever."

I nodded, my throat choked with emotion as I watched him leave.

"Are you feeling all right, Your Highness?" Trent asked, looking me over seriously. He'd seen me cry a whole lot in our brief acquaintance.

"I'm fine. Amazing, actually," I said to the burly wolf. He was a rough-looking customer to be so very concerned about a small female. I'd discovered the softest hearts were sometimes found in the roughest bodies. I missed Lee so much. "And it's Zoey, please."

Trent nodded and I finally got a real smile out of him. "All right then, Zoey."

Neil walked back in the room and he threw his arms happily around me. "It's going to be over tomorrow, Z. I can't wait. I want to go home so bad."

"Hey, it ain't done yet." Trent didn't seem like a guy who counted his chickens early. "We gotta switch those stones and we gotta do it so Marini isn't suspicious. If he thinks he's been tricked, he'll run and then we'll never hear the end of him."

"Well, I doubt he'll be giving me the keys to his office tonight," I said, being realistic. I would be lucky if he didn't show up to beat the crap out of me again. "So I'm going to need a couple of things from you, Trent."

The three of us put our heads together and worked out a plan. I went to bed but barely slept because I knew by that time tomorrow, it would all be over.

CHAPTER THIRTY-SIX

My hands worked quickly against the lock on the door to Louis's apartments. It was early in the afternoon so only the human slaves were up and about doing their work. There would be a contingent of supernatural guards, but they were mostly stationed at the perimeters of the complex, waiting for Daniel to try something.

As I held my improvised pick and tension wrench, I wished I had tried to find Louis Marini's daytime resting place. It would have been a satisfying end to our relationship to shove a stake through his sleeping body and sweep up his ashes to give to Daniel as a trophy.

"What's taking so long, Z?" Neil's gaze went to Trent, who was keeping watch on the hallway.

I pulled my hands away. They were cramping and this was work that required an enormous amount of dexterity. Had I known I was going to be kidnapped, I would most certainly have brought my own set of picks. As it was, Trent had procured a heavy wire hanger Neil had bent and worked over to make a decent tension wrench. I used a nail file to blunt the tip of a large safety pin to improvise a pick. They were inferior tools and I was slightly out of practice.

"Do you want to try it?" I asked Neil, irritated. I was doing my best, damn it.

"No, I want you to hurry," Neil replied, just as irritated with me.

We were all on edge, the joy of last night turning into the anxiety of being so close to the exit. If something was going to go wrong, now would be the time for it to happen.

I used the thumb of my right hand to knead my left palm. After the cramp stopped, I forced myself to try again. I gently scraped the pins of the lock.

"That's it," Neil said. He looked up at me. "I heard a click."

It was a very quiet little lock. I let Neil move in close as I held the pin in place and turned the cylinder. Neil indicated the clicks and before I knew it, the doorknob turned in my hands.

"We're in," Neil called quietly to Trent, who joined us.

"What the hell kind of queen knows how to pick a lock?" the wolf asked as we entered Louis's empty apartments.

"The same kind who knows how to crack a safe," I replied.

Trent walked to the door of the office. "Okay, then, let's see you get through this one."

I laughed quietly. I had no intention of picking the lock to the office. I walked straight into the bedroom and opened the dresser drawer. Sure enough, arrogance and habit were a thief's best friends.

"Want to charge some purchases to a soon-to-be dead guy?" I asked Neil, pulling out the numerous credit cards Louis had stashed in the drawer.

Neil went through the pile, shaking his head. "He has like four different aliases."

I shrugged as I palmed the key to the office. "Did you think the bastard was legit? If he'd had long enough, I'm sure he planned to take me back to Dallas and have me sign over all of Dev's assets to him. Vampires are almost all cons of some sort."

I came out, smiling at Trent. "See, key. A good thief never breaks in when she could just waltz through like she owns the place."

Trent closed the door behind us and watched through curious eyes as I pulled back the painting. I turned the dial and asked Trent the question I'd been longing to ask since I saw Dev pull him aside the night before. "So did you get a job offer last night?"

The big wolf blushed slightly. "Yeah."

I turned the wheel to the left and the right, trying out the first combination. "What did he offer you?"

"He said once the king took over, he would need someone to head security for you and the children." Trent went on to announce the high six figures Dev had offered along with free room and board.

Neil shook his head. "I would hold out for more. You don't understand how much trouble Dev's sons are going to be."

I moved on to combination number two. "You would probably have to liaise with the police a lot. I should warn you about that. Dev and Declan got into a shitload of trouble during their youth. Dev could write a Zagat's ratings system for jails across the Earth plane." No luck. I reset the wheel and started dialing number three. "It would mean moving to Dallas. If you have a pack you're close to, you should feel free to turn him down. I know how important family is to wolves."

Trent shook his head. "Nah, that's why I joined the Army. I needed to get away. I...had a mate. She died. I don't particularly want to go back to Boston. I was thinking about heading to Colorado after this was done and joining McKenzie's pack, but there's a bunch of competition out there. I don't know. I'm thinking about it."

Three was my lucky number. The safe swung open and I sighed in satisfaction. "Well, just so you know, I expect that it will be a boring job. I intend to be very dull for a long time. I just want to be at home and raise my little hoodlums. Your most exciting job would probably be escorting the boys and me to 'mommy and me' classes."

"Where the boys will aggressively pursue all the little girls and make their parents terribly uncomfortable," Neil added.

I tried not to think about that. I peered into the safe. "Wow."

"Wow?" Neil climbed onto the chair next to me. "Wow. That's a lot of cash."

The thief in me really wanted to pull out that cash. It must have been at least a hundred grand. It was Louis's war chest. I wondered if Niles and Elof knew their boss had all that cash at his disposal when they were struggling.

"We'll come back for it later," I promised. "Three-way split."

"Are you serious?" Trent asked.

If he was going to hang around, he should get used to how things worked. "Hey, you were a good lookout. On this crew we split the take evenly. Remember that in the future."

He smiled, and it softened his face, making him look younger. "I'll remember that, Your Highness."

I pulled out the Blood Stone. "Hello. It's nice to see you again."

Neil retrieved the fake out of his pocket and replaced it carefully, having noted the way the original had been sitting. "I think that's right." He looked longingly at the cash. "Good-bye, lots of little Benjamins. Soon you'll have a new home. I'm going to take such good care of you."

I sighed because Neil would spend that cash as fast as we made it. It was his nature. "Let's get out of here. I need to get back and look like someone who didn't just crack a safe."

Closing the door, I reset the dial and pushed the painting back into place. I glanced around the room and was satisfied that we hadn't left a trace. I stashed the stone in the front pocket of my jeans. Daniel was coming. I only had to wait another few hours or so and my husband would be here. Both of them.

Trent pulled me down, putting his mouth to my ear so he could whisper. "Shh. Someone's in the outer room."

"Oh, god," I replied softly. "I left the light on. It should have been off. Louis would never have left it on. Who is it?"

Trent breathed deeply and he and Neil looked at each other. "Shifter," they said at the same time.

My heart seized because that meant one thing and one thing only. If that was a shifter, he knew we were here. He would be able to smell us.

The door to the office opened and the shifter who worked in the dungeons stood looking at us with a smile on his narrow face. He was lanky to the point of skinny and his eyes were little black beads. "Trent, I always suspected you were a plant. Guess we get to see who's stronger now."

I felt Trent sigh against me as he moved me back. "Easy job, huh?"

I let the wolf put himself between me and whatever that shifter was going to turn into. "I did say the easy part came when we got back to Dallas."

"You stay back, okay?"

"Aye, aye, captain." I didn't have a weapon of any kind and I doubted the three days I lasted at kickboxing class were really going to come in handy now.

Trent used his strong legs to kick the other man back into the living area. It was a much bigger space, but the shifter was already changing. His clothes ripped around him and the air was heavy. Trent's change was quick. Though he started after the shifter, his massive gray wolf was charging by the time the other guy took his form. I'd been wrong about the snake. He was a huge, gross-looking lizard thing. He looked primeval, with dead, black eyes and a slithering tongue.

I was actually a little grateful for the lizard. Normally I'm of the firm belief that shifters should really only shift into other mammals. It makes sense to me. Humans are mammals, so I expect something warm blooded to try to kill me when I have to face down a shifter. When they turn into snakes or lizards or birds, it tends to freak me out. Not a one of them has ever turned into a giant frog, which I might find kind of funny. I have yet to see a giant spider. I think insects and arachnids are too hard. I think I'd just run from a huge spider. But while the lizard made my stomach churn, it also didn't make a ton of noise. A lion or panther would have roared and brought everyone down on our heads.

"Is that supposed to be a komodo dragon?" I asked, looking back at Neil. I would warn Trent not to let it bite him because their mouths were icky. I'd seen that in a documentary once. When I got a good look at Neil, I took a shocked step back.

His eyes were red and it seemed a little like he was caught in an in-between stage of his change. His features were distinctly wolf like, but his face still had human form. He was Neil…and he wasn't.

"Sweetie, are you okay?" I was slightly horrified by what he was becoming. I didn't leave him. Something instinctive inside told me to hold my ground. Running might get whatever was inhabiting Neil to chase me, and I didn't want that to happen. I didn't want him thinking I was prey.

"I'm fine, Zoey," Neil replied, his voice deeper than normal.

"No, I don't think so," I breathed back, all the while listening to the brawl going on right in front of us.

Trent was fighting quietly and methodically. He was excep-tionally well trained and it showed as he went straight for the lizard's underbelly, trying to turn him over so he could use his claws on the soft flesh there. The lizard managed to get one of Trent's legs into his gross and probably full of all kinds of bacteria mouth, and I heard Trent groan as the lizard bit down.

When I glanced back at Neil, I noticed something strange. Under the white fabric of the polo he was wearing, I could see the odd tattoo on his body had started to glow. I reached out to touch it and when I did, my fingers singed even as the fabric started to burn.

"Oww," I hissed, pulling my hand back.

"Both?" Neil was staring at the fight ahead of him, but there was nothing of my friend in those red eyes.

"I don't understand."

His eyes narrowed and finally found mine. "Where is my master?"

I didn't like the sound of that. I thought quickly. Neil was a wolf and I had to hope that whatever was riding him now still had contact with that essential part of his being.

"I am your master," I said, making my voice as firm as possible. It was the tone I used when I wanted someone to obey me.

"Both?" He gestured toward the room and indicated the com-batants.

My blood chilled as I realized what he was asking, and I wondered what the hell Stewart had done to my friend. Neil wanted permission to kill them both. I doubted a lecture from me about world peace and passive resistance would be taken well. He might question my status as his master. "Just the lizard thing. The wolf is a friend and must not be harmed."

He nodded and then he disappeared. I didn't know if he moved so fast I couldn't see him or if he did something wicked cool like teleport, but one minute he was beside me and the next he was straddling the lizard, his clawed hands around its neck. Trent seemed surprised by the sudden entrance of another person in the fight and he backed off.

There was a horrible crunch and then the lizard's neck bent at a weird angle and the body just stopped. It fell to the floor, deflating quickly. When I looked back up to Neil, he seemed confused to be standing there.

"Z?"

I rushed over as Trent was changing back into his human form.

"Neil, are you all right?" It was a stupid question to ask but the only one my lips seemed capable of forming.

"How did I get here?" He dropped the lizard's head and stared down at his hands. "I was talking to you and then…then I was standing over this thing."

"Good thing, too," Trent said. "That damn lizard had a hold on my leg and he wasn't giving up. I hate lizards. Give me a freaking panther any day. I'm gonna see if Marini has anything I can wear in those closets. Me walking around naked with a lizard corpse might draw attention. We need to clean up here."

While Trent took his naked self off to find clothes, I held Neil's shaking hand. "Stewart did something to you. That tattoo glowed and burned my fingers. Take a look at your shirt."

The fabric was burned in the shape of the tattoo. He shook his head. "Why didn't I hurt Trent?"

"I told you not to," I replied. "Look, we've been down here for weeks and this is the first time it's happened, right?"

Neil took a deep breath and nodded. "I've been fine the whole time, Z. After waking up in the field, I've been normal except for the weird ink on my chest."

"Then we have to assume that whatever is happening only happens when you feel really, really threatened."

"Or when I think you're threatened," Neil added.

"So we just stay calm and keep the adrenaline down, and when we get out of here we'll figure it out." I set about righting the living room. The fight had knocked down some lamps. I wasn't sure I could save the couch, but I managed to get it back into position. It would pass a cursory inspection.

"Man, I had heard you were kind of weak in the physical department," Trent said as he walked out of the bedroom dressed in slacks and a button-down. He quickly went about picking up the remnants of his former clothes. Even though the end game was at hand, we didn't want to tip Marini off that we'd been here. "But there was nothing weak about that performance. That was pretty damn awesome if you ask me."

Neil looked at me while Trent started to pick up the corpse, and I knew this was a secret we would keep between us.

"Well," I said brightly, "I suppose when you're a vampire king everyone looks a little weak."

"I guess so," Trent answered, picking up the corpse. "I'm gonna take this and shove it in the catacombs. Why don't you head back to your room and I'll meet you there? We can wait for Donovan's signal together. He better hurry his shit up, though. I don't want to have to get through another night here."

Neil and I carefully relocked the doors after taking inventory of the apartments and erasing all evidence that we had been there. The walk back to our rooms was a quiet one.

"Z?"

"Yeah?"

"I don't think I'm going to be able to stay calm for the fight," he said.

I was worried about that, too. There was no way that thing wouldn't come out when we took on two hundred vampires, their supernatural servants, and everything else they could throw at us. It had worked to our advantage in this case, but I worried what would happen in the chaos of a battlefield. I couldn't risk that Neil would harm our allies.

"I don't want to hurt someone I care about. I couldn't handle it."

"I'll figure something out," I promised.

Two hours later, we'd been waylaid by the cooks, who were freaked out about having to prepare a meal for her Royal Highness Queen Miria and a party of Fae. I could have told them I didn't think that dinner was going to happen, but I played my part and discussed the dietary preferences of the Faery contingent. I was tired and it was almost dark as Neil, Trent, and I made our way back to my rooms. My edge of anxiety was verging now on full-blown panic as I knew the time when Danny would make his push was coming at us with the speed of a steamroller.

"Neil, why don't you come with me?" Trent asked. "I got some weapons in my room. We need to move them in here so when the time comes we're not caught off guard."

Neil checked his watch. "We better hurry. Sunset is only fifteen minutes away. I don't want her alone after that."

"Agreed," the wolf said. "We'll do it in ten."

I entered my rooms alone and thought about how I couldn't wait to get one of those weapons in my hand. I hated feeling completely vulnerable, and it would be good to have even a little piece of metal to put between me and Marini. As I closed the door behind me, I wondered if I shouldn't have gone with Trent and Neil because the minute the door shut, I felt a hand around my waist, pulling me up against a hard masculine body that seemed very glad to see me. Before I could scream, the other hand slapped across my mouth.

"You don't want to do that, Your Highness."

CHAPTER THIRTY-SEVEN

"**Y**ou idiot," I hissed once Danny let me go so I could turn around and properly kick his ass. "What the hell are you doing here? Don't you know it's almost dark?"

His dimpled grin was one of the most beautiful sights I'd ever seen, and I threw myself into his arms despite my irritation that he seemed to be in his enemy's stronghold with no backup.

"I'm well aware of the time, Z," he said with his slow Texas drawl. His voice covered me like a well-loved blanket. He held me so tightly I thought I might crack. "It's long past time for me to come and get you out of this hellhole."

"I missed you, too," I whispered into his chest.

"You have no idea how much I missed you, baby." Emotion choked his voice. He kissed my forehead and made his way down to my lips. "I love you so much, Z. Do you have any idea how proud I am of you?"

"He…" I couldn't quite say the words, but he knew what I meant.

Danny cradled my head in the palms of his hands. "You're my wife. I don't care what he did. I don't care what rituals he performed or what you were forced to say yes to. You belong to me and Dev. You picked us. He can claim you all he likes, but you're mine."

I nodded through my happy tears. "I love you, Danny. You were the only thing that got me through. I saw you when he…did what he did."

I felt him shaking as he squeezed me tight again. "You'll never have to go through that again, baby. I promise. I'm going to kill him and he won't ever hurt you again. Dev said the babies are all right, but I want to hear it from you."

"They're fine," I assured him. "We're fine."

He brought his forehead to mine, resting our skin against one another. "I was so worried. When we found Lee's body I wanted to die. I thought Marini was going to kill Dev. I thought he was going to kill you. I wouldn't have survived that."

"He didn't." I ran my fingers through his thick, sandy hair. "We're both fine. I'm so sorry about Lee. I should have done something."

"You couldn't do anything," Danny said, shaking me lightly. "You cannot blame yourself. I've spent weeks getting Zack to realize it wasn't his fault. It wasn't your fault either. It was Marini's fault. We make sure he never hurts us again and Lee would be happy with that. Okay?"

I nodded. I let myself just hold him for another minute. Then it was time to get to the aforementioned, much deserved ass-kicking. I slapped at his T-shirt-covered chest. As far as I could tell, he wasn't even carrying a weapon. "You're such an idiot. How can you just waltz into the Council's stronghold alone and expect to be alive at the end of it all?" I looked around suspiciously. "Did Declan lend you that invisible guard of his?"

Danny smiled at the thought and chose to toss his big body onto the sofa, pulling me down with him. "No, baby. I don't think he lends them out. He's been a pain in my ass ever since Dev brought him back. And his wife is a shrew, let me tell you. She's fine when he's not in the room but, boy, the minute he walks in the whip begins. He looks a little beaten down. I think it's funny." He tugged me into his lap and sighed as he nuzzled my neck. "You smell so good, baby."

"Well, I'm glad I smell good for what will probably be my funeral," I replied sarcastically. "Chima is not the only one who can be a shrew at times. Danny, this is serious."

"I know," he whispered against my neck. "This is very serious. Rose is fine. She kept the shakes away, but I need you. I crave you."

"We don't have time for that," I said, squirming in his very firm grip. "The sun is down by now and Marini will be looking for me. Miria and Dev kept him occupied last night, but the minute he's up he'll come looking for me."

"I know." Danny kissed my neck, not letting me up. "Don't worry about it. I won't let him hurt you."

"I'm not that worried about him hurting me right now. On the other hand, he might have a few things to say to you."

Daniel chuckled against my neck and it made my skin tingle. "Bring him on. I have a few differences to iron out with him, too."

I huffed because he wasn't letting go of his prize. He put his hand low on my belly where the babies were growing and let it rest there. I sighed but wasn't about to let the sweet action soften my resolve. I wanted my babies to have both their dads alive and well. "He might show up alone, but he won't stay that way for long. He'll bring down his entire army on your head. There are at least two hundred vampires here, Daniel."

"Two hundred and five," he corrected simply. His lips pressed sweet little kisses across the sensitive skin of my neck. "There are also roughly a hundred weres, shifters, and witches down here."

I tried not to shake at the thought of that number. It would be Danny against everyone. How did he expect to win? Well, he wasn't totally alone. "I'm sure Trent and Neil and I will be fine against an army of hundreds of supernatural creatures."

"Nah," Daniel said, unconcerned. "Chad already detoured Trent and Neil. We don't have to worry about them."

I felt a burst of hysterical laughter bubble up. "That's great. That's two more corpses they won't have to worry about identifying. Why couldn't you have at least brought Dev as a backup? Or better yet, Zack?"

"Well," Daniel started to explain his actions, but he seemed to get distracted by the back of my neck. "I didn't bring Dev along because he already got alone time with you. I heard all about it in vivid detail. He got to spend last night with you and he got to spend a couple of days before that. I want equal time."

"Yes, those days before Chad convinced me he drained Dev and I was a widow were really thrilling for the both of us."

Daniel groaned. "I'm sorry about that. I didn't know. I thought Chad would tell you what we were doing. But I did hear something about a little incident in a jail cell."

"He doesn't have any discretion at all, does he?"

"Not an ounce. He said it was hot. He claims to have made very creative use of the space," Danny said and I felt his grin against my skin. "So you can see, I obviously deserve a little alone time with my gorgeous wife."

"And how did you get here?" I asked suddenly because the question popped into my head. I was so happy/pissed off to see Daniel that the fact that he was daywalking hadn't occurred to me. "Shouldn't you be just waking up?"

A very interesting thought struck me. Daniel could daywalk when he fed from the sex magic Dev gave off. It was easy for Danny to feed because he was usually in bed with us when Dev started up his mojo, but I hadn't been around for almost an entire month. Daniel should be back to sleeping in the day unless… "Have you boys been playing some games while the wife was away? There better be video or I'll be very unhappy."

Daniel's whole body shook with laughter. "There's no video, baby. Bris can do that thing where he focuses the magic and kind of pumps it straight into my body through his hands."

"Pretty nice, huh?" I'd seen Bris do it once before. Bris's version of supercharged magic came out as one long orgasm.

Daniel's hands came up to fondle my breasts. He sighed. "It was pretty awesome, and it's kept me strong for days."

I leaned back because Danny wasn't going to let me up so I might as well enjoy his attentions. "So no playing around at all?"

"I'm not going to lie to you," Danny said quietly. "I was damn glad to see him and we've been terrified. The truth of the matter is I'm used to sleeping with the two of you. It was hard to sleep by myself so when Dev came back, we shared a room. It made it easier for us to run through all the horrible scenarios of what was happening to you here. It made it easier for us to comfort each other."

I so wanted to watch that. "Just so you know, you're going to need to comfort Dev again."

Danny chuckled. "I suspect we'll do just about anything you want us to, baby. We get out of here and we're going to be your slaves. Anything you want, I'm going to make it happen."

"I'll hold you to that," I replied, happy that they had each other. "I wasn't alone, either. I had Neil."

"I'll need to hear that story soon, Z," Daniel said, turning my head toward him. He kissed me, our lips playing softly across each other. "I was glad to hear he got away. I'm sitting Neil out of this one. Trent will join us, but Neil is going to hunker down in a room with some of our more vulnerable allies and hide until it's all over. I don't know how much his time on the Hell plane took out of him, and he isn't on vamp blood. I don't want to risk losing him."

That was fine with me. I didn't want to risk losing him either.

"You're sitting out, too." Daniel's blue eyes were serious and his mouth turned down like he expected a fight out of me.

I had done my part. I didn't need to wield a sword. "Absolutely, Danny. Just tell me where I should sit and I'll do it."

Daniel let out a relieved breath. "Marcus will come for you when it starts. He's going to try to get you off the battlefield, but if he can't he'll hand you off to Padric and a phalanx of Fae guards. You do what Padric tells you to."

"In this instance, I will," I promised, but I didn't want him thinking he'd gained the upper hand. "Why am I going to be on the battlefield in the first place? Wouldn't it be easier to just ship me back to London?"

I felt him tense and then he was on his feet, setting me lightly on the ground. "It's going to be all right, Z. You just follow my lead and everything's going to be okay."

Daniel walked into the bedroom and quietly shut the door behind him. The look in his eyes as he closed the door promised he would defend me if he needed to.

The outer door swung open and Louis entered. He scowled at me for a moment before taking a deep breath and plunging in.

"I'm not going to apologize for last night, Zoey," he said, folding his arms across his chest as he regarded me with dark eyes. "You can't be surprised I was upset by your pregnancy. I don't believe you when you say you didn't know. I think you've known all along and that makes me suspicious."

My heart was pounding. I kept expecting Marini to walk to the door and open it and proceed to call everyone in the catacombs down on Danny's head. I tried to play it cool and reason with the vampire. "I find it hard to believe you could hold something against me that happened before I became your companion."

"Do you realize what this means for us, Zoey? Do you understand the insane demands the prince's relatives are making?"

No, but I was curious. I knew that after Dev had left me he'd joined his mother and Padric in the Council room where the negotiations had run all night long. Dev wanted to make sure Marini didn't get another chance to beat the crap out of me. I wondered what kind of insane demands "Declan" had made last night. "I'm sure my brother-in-law was difficult, to say the least."

Louis turned the prettiest shade of red. "He's a complete imbecile. I don't see how anyone thinks he'll ever be fit to rule a kingdom. He wants me to promise I won't feed off you for the next eight months. I will never agree to do such a thing."

Wow, that had probably been some kind of argument. I was sure Dev had enjoyed watching Louis flip out at the very thought of having a companion he wasn't allowed to feed from. The process wouldn't hurt the babies because the normal amount of blood a vampire needs on a daily basis was very little. It was even easier with Daniel because he fed from Dev as well, but Marini was a greedy bastard. It was a valid point with him. "Do you have to meet with them again tonight?"

He ran a hand across his face and looked like a man who needed a vacation. I was hoping to give him a permanent one. "Yes, the Queen will be here soon. If I didn't need this alliance so badly I would kick them all out and take care of this little problem myself. The thought of you...giving birth makes me ill. Don't get attached to those brats because the minute they leave your womb I'm letting the Queen have them. You won't be raising another man's children in my home."

"I won't fight you on that point, Louis," I shot back at him, really sick at the thought of him having any say over my children's lives. "I would much rather Miria raised them than they had anything whatso-ever to do with you."

I heard Louis grunt and knew I'd made a mistake. His hand raised and just when I braced myself for impact, I felt a brush of wind. Daniel had moved faster than the eye could track and caught Louis's hand before it met my cheek. Marini's eyes widened as he realized who was standing in front of him. Slowly, but with power, Daniel crushed the hand that would have hit me.

"You don't touch her ever again," Daniel growled.

He shoved Marini back with one hand and the vampire hit the wall. His crushed hand was already healing, and he pulled out his little black box and quickly pushed that button that should have ended Daniel's life. He looked confused for a moment but then tried again.

"Sorry, Marini," Daniel said, taking my hand. "I decided the old ticker needed an upgrade. You won't be able to kill me that way. I'll make this easy on you. I'll take my wife and my babies and get the hell out of your house."

Then we were running down the hall even as Louis shouted for help.

Danny ran through the hallways with unerring accuracy. Though he hadn't been here in the last couple of years, he still knew the place like the back of his hand. "I told you it would be okay, baby."

"Okay?" I heard myself asking even as I started to breathe hard. I wasn't used to running quite so fast. I struggled to keep up, but I knew why Danny wasn't carrying me. He wanted to act as a shield in case the bullets started flying. "Are you insane? Now they know you're here."

"Precisely," he said maddeningly. "Quite the plan, huh?"

He pulled me around the corner and glanced back. Sure enough, we had a tail.

I could barely breathe, I was so afraid. "I swear if we get out of this alive I'm going to kill you. This is the stupidest, most irrational, idiotic plan you've ever come up with."

He smiled down at me and then swept me into his arms. "I learned from the best, Z. I think they're all behind us now and they're herding us."

From behind, I could hear various languages being shouted

about, and over it all I heard Marini's yell.

"Get that bastard into the arena," Marini ordered.

"That doesn't sound good." I intertwined my hands around Daniel's neck.

"When did you become such a pessimist?" He turned sharply down another corridor and I heard the first shots firing from behind us. "Aren't you the girl who jumped off the top of a building once on the off chance that I could fly?"

It had been years before, right after I'd met Dev, right before Danny and I got back together. I had nowhere to go. Stewart had been chasing us and I had one crazy idea, one last attempt to save the man I loved. I'd jumped off the building and Danny had come after me.

Sometimes I think that single leap was the real beginning of my life.

We were in a long, narrow corridor, and I could hear the slap of feet against the floors like a herd of predators chasing after us. There was nowhere to go but through the huge, ornate ceiling-to-floor doors at the end of the hallway.

"You could fly so I was right to jump." I wondered if those doors might be the last things either of us saw.

Daniel's eyes were sheened with tears as he stared down at me. "I only flew a couple of times before that day. It seemed wrong, like it was the final proof that I was a complete freak. Then it saved your life and it seemed like a wonderful thing to do. I fly for you, baby." He kissed me and started toward those doors. "They're coming. This is it. You stay close and when all hell breaks loose, go with Marcus. He'll take you to Neil and the three of you just hunker down and survive. I'll come for you when it's finished."

"Marcus is in there?"

Daniel grinned. "He will be."

With one foot, Daniel made the enormous wooden doors swing open, and I found myself on the sandy floor of the arena. Daniel walked straight to the center of the large space. It looked like the set of a gladiator film, but then it was probably more accurate than a Hollywood film because some of these men remembered the time.

Daniel set me on my feet and I immediately sank a little. The floor was covered in sand. The whole place appeared ancient, with the only concession to modern times being the lighting. It was brightly lit so no one would miss a moment of the death and pain this place was known for. This was the place where vampires fought duels to the death, usually over companions. It was the setting for the Council's formal executions and their entertainments. It was a training space for young vampires.

It was also the place Daniel had first proven himself to be a king.

"There is no place to go, Donovan," Marini's voice said behind us.

He stalked into the arena, followed by his men. Niles and Elof took their places next to the head of the Council and the other vampires filed in behind them. They blocked what seemed to be the only exit from the arena.

Daniel turned and faced down his enemy. He squeezed my hand and I got very close to his side. There were so many of them. They poured into the arena, all of Marini's vampires, claws out and fangs long. They were ready to tear apart Daniel and they would do it with sheer numbers.

"I find it ironic that this should be the location of your final stand, Mr. Donovan," Louis said and I saw him reach into his pocket. He was playing with the stone, making sure it was there and ready for him to use. "How many vampires did you kill here before we finally stopped you?"

He referred to an act of torture inflicted on newly-turned vampires. As part of their training, they were tossed into the arena and forced to fight older, stronger vampires. In the end, the baby vamp was beaten to within an inch of his life and told to be grateful he'd been spared. It hadn't worked that way for Daniel.

"Twelve," Danny said with confidence. I knew he remembered that day well. It haunted his nightmares. "And you didn't stop me, Marini. You simply stopped sending them in for me to kill."

"Well, I think this time your experience will be different," Marini said, and he stared at me with possessive rage. I knew in that moment that if he could get his hands on me he would choke the life out of me. I had the feeling that if he couldn't have me, he didn't want anyone to. "There are more than twelve of us this time, though you are alone again."

"No, he isn't," a strong voice came from the stands. All eyes moved to the stone seats that rose high into the air, giving any audience an excellent view of the carnage. My breath caught as Dev gracefully leapt over the railing. He had a sword in his hand and he carried it toward us.

Marini laughed, the sound echoing through the large space. "Yes, Prince Declan, I can see how you're going to be such a help to Daniel. I'm surprised you're here, but then I'm sure he promised you something amazing that he'll never be able to deliver. You should have made your alliance with me. We'll see what you can do for Daniel. You can, perhaps, shield him for the two or three seconds it takes for us to rip your body in two."

Dev was dressed for his war. The Order had given him a full uniform of fatigues and combat boots. He made it look damn sexy. There was a P90 slung along his back and god only knew how many weapons hidden on his person. "I have no intention of getting ripped in two, Louis. You had your chance to kill me the night you beat the shit out of me. I won't give you a second opportunity."

Now the head of the Council's dark eyes went wide. "No. I don't believe it."

Dev handed Excalibur to Daniel and took his place at my side. He leaned down and brushed my lips with his.

"Well, you should," another familiar voice said and Declan Quinn leapt over the railing on the opposite side from where Dev had come. He was in his traditional tunic and soft suede pants. His bow was in his hand and his quiver on his back. I knew his arrows would be tipped with silver, each one a flying stake. "He is obviously not me. I am much more attractive."

"News of the Prince's death might have been exaggerated, old friend," Marcus said with a smile as he joined Declan. "Perhaps if you stand down now, Donovan will be merciful."

"No, he won't," Dev proclaimed with a huge smile.

"Now, Devinshea," Daniel started, "I'll allow anyone who wishes to not fight to leave the arena now, and as long as they follow the new government's laws, there will be no repercussions. But that doesn't apply to you, Marini."

"We're going to kill you," Dev promised. "You hurt her and

415

you'll pay for it. No mercy for you."

Marini bared his sharp teeth. "I'll be sure to remember that when I have you beneath my fangs, Prince Devinshea. Know this, both of you, I will have my companion and I will dispense of her after we've gotten rid of you. No silver coffin for you, Marcus. This time you get the death you've always longed for. I'll pit my army against the five of you any day."

The five of us stood together, facing down over two hundred vampires and another hundred weres, shifters, and witches. It was a daunting prospect, and I sincerely hoped that the Order was going to charge in any moment.

"Do you know what this is, Louis?" Daniel asked, his voice a calm presence. He held Excalibur reverently in his hands.

"I know what you want me to think it is," the other vampire replied. He'd pulled the stone out and had it in his hands.

Daniel smiled. "Oh, it's the real thing. This is Excalibur, wielded last by King Arthur. I am the King of the Sword because I carry it. I am the King of all Vampire by right of my birth. Do you think I don't have an army?"

Louis plunged on recklessly. "If this is your army, I think the sword should find a new owner."

"You should pay more attention to your wolves, Louis." Marcus gestured to the wolves who were close to the door. They had been kept at the back of the vampires. They were twitching and looking at a place behind us. "They know what you don't."

"And what is that, Marcus?" Marini spat the question.

"That we are not alone," Daniel replied. "Mr. Thomas, you may release the illusion."

There was a great shout as the back side of the arena was suddenly filled with hundreds of people, all chanting and raising the roof now that they could come out of hiding.

Daniel was right. We weren't alone. Not even close.

Chapter Thirty-Eight

The minute Chad released his hold on the illusion, two wolves ran forward, one brown and one gray. Zack took his place beside Daniel and the big gray wolf leapt in front of me.

Dev looked down at the gray wolf and smiled. "I'll take that as a yes," he said to Trent, who thumped his tail and got damn serious about growling at Marini.

Marini started to take a step back, but I watched as he forced himself to hold his ground. If he ran, his whole army would devolve into chaos. They would break ranks and run for the streets. Marini stood tall. "Impressive, but my vampires still outnumber yours and mine are older, stronger."

I wasn't so sure about that. I looked back at the army now marching to Daniel's back. I recognized Henri Jacobs and Hugo Wells, but there were many others I'd met when Daniel held his meetings explaining his positions. These vampires had chosen to follow Daniel. Many were younger, like Michael House, and they followed Daniel because they held a more democratic world view. I saw the vampires Daniel had turned. There were five of them and they stood behind Chad. Justin, in particular, seemed eager to finally get to the fight he'd been preparing for his entire vampiric life.

But we didn't just have vampires and unlike Louis's army, the werewolves, led by John McKenzie, weren't relegated to the back. We had a hundred wolves, the strongest of the American packs. They were all in wolf form and when they howled, it shook the rafters. Fighting beside the wolves were shifters of all kinds. Daniel and Dev had made sure they knew everyone was welcome at the table. Marini had been systematically assassinating the strong leaders of the shifters, and the ones left were ready for revenge.

King Angus stood beside Padric and Herne the Hunter, who'd brought Shuck and Barghest to the party. The hell hounds' tails were thumping with impatience to get to the fight. The Seelie and the Unseelie stood together now, and if Marini had known what a miracle that was he might have turned tail and ran.

There was a distant boom, and I noticed the satisfied look on Dev's face.

"Do you know what that is, Marini?" Dev asked.

Marini swallowed once but didn't answer.

"That's the Order of Galahad," Daniel explained. "My knights just breeched your perimeter. If you run now, they will have taken up defensive positions. They'll kill anyone who attempts to flee the catacombs. I gave you your chance."

"Then let me give you yours, Daniel." Marini held up his little fake stone and, even if I wanted to, I couldn't muster a lick of sympathy for him. "This makes me a king. I might lose this war but I will take you down with me, Daniel. I'll kill you and your partner and before I am done, I'll take my companion with me. You forget I have a secret weapon."

Daniel laughed but there was a bit of sympathy in it. "Oh, Louis. She isn't your companion. She never was. She's my wife and you forgot something, too. My wife is a hell of a thief." Daniel smiled over at me. "You got it, baby?"

I pulled the real Blood Stone out of my pocket and I held it up, letting Marini get a good look. I gave him my best "gotcha" grin. "Thanks for giving me so much access to the safe. It was a pleasure to steal from you, but as for the rest of it...I was faking."

Dev snorted beside me and I tossed the stone to Daniel even as Louis shoved the fake into his palm, trying desperately to get it to work. When it wouldn't, he tossed it aside and pulled a gun. "I will end you, Donovan, if it's the last thing I do."

"She's yours, Marcus," Daniel said quickly and I felt myself being shoved toward the vampire.

Daniel raised his sword and I felt the army at our backs twitch as they waited for that sword to lead them. Dev's gun was suddenly off his back and in his hands. Daniel's face was tense as he brought the sword forward, and with a roar, the battle began.

Marcus pulled me back as the world became one huge, noisy battlefield. I stumbled a little as we started for the exit. "Why does Danny have to go in first? Shouldn't the king be behind everyone? Shouldn't he be directing the action?"

I heard Marcus chuckle against my ear. "Daniel is a warrior king, Zoey. He leads his army, not the other way around."

"I can't see him anymore." I tried to get a single glimpse of him amid the throng of people fighting now. Both sides had met in the middle and they were fighting with a ferocity that stunned me.

The heavy doors closed. They slammed shut and it didn't seem like a natural occurrence.

"Is that a good thing?" I asked, following Marcus closely.

"We weren't going out that way, Zoey." Marcus raised his voice so I could hear him over the sounds of metal against metal and the reports of gunfire. Those sounds I could handle. It was the wet sounds that were making me sick. A body makes some horrible sounds when it's torn apart or someone shoves a claw through the soft portions of it. The groans and moans of pain and death made me wish I could be anywhere but here. "Zoey, get your head down."

I ducked as something, a knife, I think, flew past my head. "Which way are we going?"

Marcus seemed slightly annoyed with my questions, or maybe it was the arrow that almost took his patrician nose off. "Damn Fae. Why can't they join the modern age?" He pointed to a small door on the other side of the arena. "It leads to a series of tunnels. We can get back into the residential section from there."

"Is that where Neil is?"

"Yes, *cara*," Marcus replied, picking up the pace. "He's waiting for you. I found him surprisingly willing to stay out of the fight."

Marcus maneuvered me to the side of the arena. We clung to the walls, and suddenly he pushed me down into a crouch. I shrank against the cold stone as Marcus took a couple of shots at a vampire coming our way. I looked out over Marcus's broad shoulders and saw that it was David. He was bigger than Marcus and a warrior to boot. Marcus shot him four times and the big vamp just kept coming. His fangs were huge and his claws out. There was blood pouring from his burly chest, but that wouldn't matter if he managed to get his hands on me. My blood would heal him quite nicely, and I could see by the look in his eyes that he had certainly thought of that.

Marcus cursed and pushed me back, covering my body with his. He tossed the gun aside and pulled a silver knife. He would try to impale the vampire on it but I didn't think it was such a great idea to let that vampire get close. One small piece of silver seemed like very little defense against the super-strong warrior.

Just as David's claws came forward, there was a long howl and David's big body was knocked aside as a huge gray wolf leapt on him. His teeth were embedded in the vampire's neck before David had a chance to react. Blood coated the wolf's fur as Trent refused to give up his hold. He was savage and he used his sharp teeth to work on the vampire's flesh. David struggled but he'd lost a lot of blood to Marcus's bullets and his limbs moved limply as Trent applied all the pressure of his strong jaws to his prey. There was a loud crack as Trent finally broke the vampire's neck and proceeded to chew his way through to the other side. I'd never seen a wolf behead a vampire using only his teeth, but Trent seemed to think of it as old hat. I wondered what kind of training sessions John McKenzie conducted.

David turned to ash in front of me. All that was left was his bloody clothes, a wicked-looking semiautomatic pistol, and a silver dagger with the hilt wrapped in leather so he could hold it. I wondered why he hadn't used the weapons, but then I had seen the blood lust in his eyes. Sometimes when the blood was thick in the air, vampires went a little crazy. David's only thought had been to get to me. It gave me the chills. Trent used his nose to shove the weapons toward us. Marcus leaned down to pick up the pistol but Trent growled a warning.

"I think he wants me armed," I said to Marcus and I picked up the gun. I flicked the safety off and palmed the knife, too.

Trent growled at Marcus again and then gave me the same treatment.

"I know, I know," I said. "We'll stay out of trouble." He gave me another light growl and then a bark. I used my pointy finger on him because we needed to settle who was boss here and now. "Don't you use that tone with me. I speak wolf. We'll be fine. Go. Kill something else."

Trent barked and it sounded like he was amused. Then he was off, his gray coat lost in the fray. Marcus slipped his hand into mine and started walking, clinging to the sidelines. I let my eyes roam as my feet followed Marcus. I tried to see where Daniel and Dev fought. I caught the briefest glimpse of Devinshea. He was plowing through a group of shifters with his P90. I watched as his brother covered him and he pulled a grenade out of the pockets on his flak jacket. He dislodged the pin and lobbed it deep into enemy territory. There was an enormous explosion and my faery prince looked thrilled with the destruction.

Daniel was in the thick of everything. I could barely see him for the throng of people fighting around him. I saw Excalibur moving, but Daniel was a bit of a blur. I noted that the sand around him was already soaked in blood. Daniel would be wading through it soon.

I felt a little sick at the death all around me. Everywhere I looked a fresh horror was being played out. War, no matter the righteousness of it, was simply a terrible thing to be caught in. I averted my eyes from a group of Unseelie goblins who were pulling apart a vampire. I thought it might be Niles. As much as I had hated that Brit, I wouldn't have wished quite so awful a fate on him.

"Are you all right?" Marcus asked.

I was pretty sure I'd gone pale at the thought of the people I loved being in that mess of chaos and death. My hand went to my stomach. I really didn't want my babies stuck out here. I suddenly thought of something I hadn't before.

"They can all see me, can't they?" I asked as we crouched down to avoid another volley of gunfire. Marcus covered my head with his torso.

"Yes, *cara*," he said. "I'm afraid you still glow for all of the vampires. I don't think any of us quite considered the implications when we began."

The implications were huge. These were vampires caught up in blood lust. Many of them had lost a large portion of their blood volume. They were dying and I was a bright bag of sweet, sweet healing just walking around for the taking. Daniel loved me dearly, but when he was close to death I feared his beast because the instinct was to live and I was a vampire's best shot. My bright glow made me stand out. It was a big neon sign saying "get it here."

Marcus's dark eyes searched the crowd and I knew he was terrified that those vampires would be coming for me. "I need to get you out of here. There are a couple of places where we might be able to slip away."

A pair of fighting vampires landed on the ground next to us. They were locked in mortal combat, their claws at each other's throats. I recognized Henri Jacobs. He was married to a friend of mine and had helped Marcus save Dev's life a while back. He was losing his fight. He was beneath a big vampire I knew from my time in the catacombs, one of Louis's thugs. His fangs were out and his claws were making a mottled mess of Henri's throat. The smaller vampire tried to kick his opponent off, but he couldn't get a really good position. Henri Jacobs was seconds away from leaving his wife a widow. I really couldn't stand the thought of that.

I moved from behind Marcus and put the muzzle of my gun against the bigger vampire's head and, with no remorse at all, I pulled the trigger. The bullet was silver and the vampire's brain couldn't handle it. At such close range, I had blown away a large enough portion of his brain that it worked as a decapitation. The vampire seemed to swell briefly and then he turned to dust and covered Henri's body.

Marcus growled and pulled me back, cursing in Italian.

"Thanks," Henri said, jumping up and dusting off his former opponent from his clothes. He stared at me for a moment, his fangs long in his mouth. He turned away from me. "Marcus, you have to get her out of here. I heard Marini telling his men to get her and bring her to him. He's being a coward. He won't stop and face the king. He keeps moving just out of range, killing weaker fighters but not letting Daniel get near him. He thinks he can get out of this if he can lay his hands on the queen."

"I am trying," Marcus replied.

"Well, try harder," Henri said. "I don't think Marini will let her live."

"Why aren't they fleeing into the catacombs?" I asked as Henri leapt back into the fray and Marcus continued his careful maneuvering toward his destination somewhere at the back of the arena. At least we were behind our own lines now. "Doesn't it make sense for them to get those doors open and move this fight into the residential parts?"

They could employ more of a guerilla mentality.

Marcus pointed toward the top of the arena. "They've tried to get the doors open but I'm afraid Daniel's witch is very strong."

She was hidden behind a group of Fae warriors, but I could see Sarah Day standing far away from the battle. She didn't have to be close to be effective. She held her hands out and was concentrating on the door. She was dressed for protection, her torso covered in Kevlar and a helmet on her head. Her husband, Felix, stood at her side, watching the battle with a worried look on his face. I was sure he thought about the baby Sarah was carrying. She was five months pregnant and the bulge in her belly was barely visible under the protective Kevlar. Beside her stood my father's girlfriend, Christine. Her mouth was moving and I knew she was chanting quietly, lending strength to Sarah's spells. Christine might not be the greatest witch in the world, but she was good at adding power to a spell.

"Daniel couldn't keep her away," Marcus said. "She showed up in London with your father and Felix. She promised to stay out of the line of fire and to follow the orders of Declan's guards.

"Is that my dad?" Tears filled my eyes. My dad was here.

"Yes, *cara*, he wouldn't stay away either."

My father was watching the action. His eyes were following Danny and Dev, watching to make sure they were all right. He stood behind his Fae guards and I knew it was killing him that I was down here.

"I need to take you to Neil," Marcus said. "The vampires won't care about your father and they probably don't even realize what Sarah is doing, but they will notice you."

I nodded, wishing I could climb the stairs and join my father, but

I was one big walking target and I didn't want to bring the war to them. Sarah was being incredibly effective. There was so much chaos that no one really noticed they had an audience and if they did they would have to look very closely to see the small, pregnant female who was blocking their exit. I was satisfied Sarah and the rest were as safe as they could possibly be here.

We were closing in on the opening in the sides of the arena Marcus had pointed out earlier. I breathed a small sigh of relief. We were close.

Marcus gave me a nod and then broke for the opening that lay roughly a hundred feet ahead. I started to follow but my poor human feet sank into the sand, making running very difficult. My sneakers felt like the ground was sucking at them and I fell behind. Marcus cursed as he came back and hauled me up into his arms.

He ran the last hundred feet, his long legs eating the distance in a way mine never could. The sand didn't bother him. He powered through and then we were inside the shelter of the archway. Marcus set me down and I turned to see the battlefield. Daniel was looking for someone, probably Marini. He was covered in blood, but it didn't seem to be his. The combatants around him gave him a wide berth, some actually running when they realized he was near.

Devinshea had a deep cut across his face but it was healing even as I watched. He had a long silver knife in his hand and he shoved it into Elof's back as the vampire tried to flee Daniel. He must have shoved the knife in the proper place because Elof exploded. Vampires sometimes do that. I nearly laughed at the shocked look on Dev's face as he got coated with vampire guts. I said almost. It was really too horrifying to laugh at.

Marcus took my hand. "Come, *cara*."

"But it looks like the fight is winding down." There were a lot fewer people fighting than there were before, replaced with a whole bunch of piles of ash.

"Yes, it is and this is when the vampires on the other side will get really desperate," Marcus pointed out. "I need to get you somewhere I can easily defend you."

I peered into the darkened space where Marcus wanted to take me. It looked like a gaping hole to nowhere. The light stopped about ten feet in and I could tell from the slope I was on that it went down. Going down a long dark hole held very little appeal.

Then I saw them. At least three vampires, when they weren't fighting, were moving their heads around, working in tandem to find something or someone. I shrank back against my protector. They were almost certainly looking for me.

"Let's go," I whispered to Marcus, hoping we could move before they caught sight of us.

Marcus blended into the shadows as he led the way. As we moved down the slope, I noticed my feet getting wet. I could hear them sloshing in water that was getting deeper. The battle seemed like a different world now as I could only hear muffled sounds coming from the arena. I clung tightly to Marcus's hand.

"What is this place?" I asked, my voice sounding tiny in the darkness.

"It's the sewer that runs under the arena," Marcus replied.

I wished he hadn't told me that. "Ewww."

"It's abandoned, Zoey. It's no longer in use but it remains here and it floods sometimes when the rain in the city above is very heavy."

"Is it dangerous?"

"It isn't deep and we don't have far to go." Marcus stopped and his hand briefly left mine. I heard him fumbling with something and a squeak, like a rusty hinge being forced open. Lights above my head flickered on. Then they flickered off.

"Sorry," the vampire apologized as the lights went off and on at random times. "It isn't the most reliable electric system."

I nodded and he started to lead the way again. I kind of wished I'd been left in the dark. The flickering of the lights made everything seem unreal, like we were in some stop motion film. Marcus moved and then the lights went out and when they came on again he was in an entirely different place without the sense that he had walked there.

"Come along," Marcus urged me. "Two turns and there is a hidden passage that leads to the residence. It will take us directly into the room where Neil is. Louis and I designed it ourselves for just such an occasion."

"Yes, we did, and we designed more than one way in and out if you remember," a dark voice said and as the lights flickered back on, I saw the hulking form of the one man I really didn't want to see down here. He had a gun in his hand. "It was one of your more brilliant plans, old friend."

"Zoey," I heard Marcus say. "I am so sorry. Run."

Then Marini shot his old friend. I felt Marcus fall beside me and went down on my knees to try to help him back up, but Marini stood over us now. He shot into Marcus's torso another three times, the Italian's body bucking with each shot.

"You lose, Marcus." Louis stared down on the man who had been his friend for almost two thousand years. His hand shot out and grabbed my left wrist, hauling me up. "You always were weak. I only made you a member of my Council because you were wise, but now you have proven that's not true. How could you back that fledgling over me?"

Marcus struggled to speak. "That fledgling is right. Our time of dominion over the world is long past. We must change or die."

"Well, let me make the choice for you, Marcus." The final gunshot exploded and echoed through the sewers.

Marcus's head fell back and I saw his body only briefly as I was pulled along.

"I loved you," the vampire said, his voice filled with rage.

"No, you didn't." I tried to think of any way to get out of his grasp. I held onto the knife in my right hand. He hadn't noticed it.

"Don't you question me, Zoey," he snarled.

As the lights flickered off and on, I could see plainly that Louis hadn't come out of the fight unruffled. His clothes were ruined. They were ripped and bloodied, and I saw the wounds he had that weren't healing. It was a sure sign that he was low on blood. My body chilled at the thought. Marini took too much when he wasn't injured. He would almost certainly drain me once he got to a safe place.

"I gave you everything." He was continuing his diatribe on where our relationship had gone awry. "I treated you like a queen."

"Yes, I especially loved the part where you beat the shit out of me."

We turned a corner and I couldn't see Marcus anymore. He needed blood. Louis had just left him to die down here in the sewers like a rat. I really couldn't stand the thought of it.

"You need discipline," Louis spat. "That was where I went wrong. I won't indulge you this time, companion. This time our marriage will be on a proper footing. You will serve me. You will submit to me."

I pulled back, nearly wrenching my arm in the process. I shouted, hoping, praying anyone would hear me. "Daniel!"

I got to meet the back of Louis's hand for my trouble. I barely managed to hold onto the knife as I tumbled into the water. I tasted blood in my mouth.

The vampire stood over me. "Don't you ever say his name again, Zoey. You will never speak of him."

I was willing to do anything to delay the inevitable. He seemed to want to go through some weird therapy session and all I could think was the longer we talked, the more time Daniel had to figure out something was wrong.

"What are you planning on doing with me, Louis?" I didn't bother to get up. The knife was still in my hand but he would surely see it if I brought it out of the water now.

Marini's dark eyes gleamed in the low, flickering light. "I plan on keeping you. You're mine. I won't let Donovan have you."

"He'll come after me," I pointed out. "He won't ever stop looking for me and neither will Devinshea. You'll have an entire army after you if you take me."

That seemed to actually penetrate his brain. "He'll search for me anyway."

"How will he know you didn't die in the battle?" I asked and immediately saw my mistake.

The vampire's fangs were long. "Well, darling girl, I assume he will know when you tell him."

I doubted promising him I would keep my mouth shut would work. He could hardly believe me.

Reaching down, Louis placed his palm against my cheek. His eyes were slightly wild. "I might be going down, my Zoey, but I will not go alone."

He leaned in to brush his lips to mine and I thrust up with everything I had. I pushed the silver knife up into his chest with as much accuracy as I could muster. I went for the heart and heard Louis groan. He looked down at the silver sticking out of his torso. It had to be very close to his heart. His skin turned pale, ashen.

He managed to stand, but didn't try to take the blade out. I think he knew it was inevitable, but he had one last trick up his sleeve. He raised his pistol. I got to my feet as quick as I could and began to back away.

"As I said, my precious blood," Marini intoned, "I won't go alone."

I felt the bullets enter my body—two in my chest and one low in my gut. I felt the blood begin to flow even as Louis Marini turned to dust before my eyes. I stumbled and couldn't quite get my legs to work. I placed my hands over the wound in my gut and tried to stop the bleeding. I didn't like how low it was, almost to my pelvis. I couldn't help but think about the babies growing there.

I stumbled through the water, almost making it back to where Marcus had been left and then my legs gave out completely. Up ahead I could almost see the light from the arena where Daniel and Dev still fought. I hit my knees as a wave of nausea overcame me.

Vaguely, as though from a great distance, I heard someone calling my name, but it seemed so far away as to be inconsequential. My face hit the water and I couldn't breathe, couldn't make myself turn over to get a breath. The world was dark and cold and it didn't seem to matter anymore.

I woke up in the grotto, the light warm on my skin, and I seemed nice and whole and unharmed.

"Hello, Zoey," Oliver Day said with a big grin on his face. "Nice job."

I could only think of one thing to say given my current predicament.

"Shit."

CHAPTER THIRTY-NINE

"Is that any kind of language to use around your guardian angel?" Oliver asked with a sarcastic grin.

I looked up at the angel, who seemed happier than I'd ever seen him, and scowled. "Seriously? I go through all of that, suffer through being Marini's companion and fighting everything under the sun to reach this grand destiny of uniting the supernatural world and what do I get for it? I'm dead. Let me tell you something, Oliver, as rewards go, that sucks."

"I told you she'd be unhappy," a soft feminine voice said.

I sat up from the couch I'd been lying on. It was the same couch where Danny, Dev, and I sat and watched movies and fooled around. I wouldn't be doing that anymore. "Well, look, the gang's all here," I said with a bite. Then I realized Felicity could answer a question for me. "Is Dev all right?"

Felicity smiled. The angel was a stunningly beautiful blonde. Oliver was her masculine counterpart. "He's fine, though it wasn't easy. He's very reckless. I had to work hard to keep him alive."

"Daniel is fine, as well," a third voice said. I looked around and saw another male. The way I understood it, angels worked in threes. Oliver represented judgment and justice, Felicity love and devotion, and this one must be Jude, who had taken Felix's place. He would represent faith.

"They won't be once they find my body," I muttered, thinking about how it would affect them both. They would have lost me and the babies. I wasn't sure they could handle that.

Oliver rolled his blue eyes. He seemed very disappointed I wasn't excited by the turn of events. I was bringing down his little victory party. "Come on, Zoey. This isn't time for gloomy predictions. We won. You did it. Don't you feel an enormous sense of accomplishment?"

"No." I stood up and looked at the three of them. They were dressed like suburban yuppies going to a garden party. Everything about them was perfect. "I feel pissed off that I'm dead."

"Well, I'm thrilled," Oliver admitted. "Do you have any idea how many bets you just won me? I'm the man right now. Any assignment I want is mine for the taking. There isn't an angel on the Heaven plane who isn't thinking that Oliver Day is hot shit."

Felicity shook her blonde head with an amused grin. "I wasn't thinking that. Were you, Jude?"

"Not at all," Jude replied.

"Well, you should be," Oliver said, not letting his siblings bring him down. "I just pulled off something spectacular and all I had in my arsenal to work with was one obnoxious girl."

I frowned, looking at Felicity. "You would think the man did everything himself. I did take part, you know."

"You'll have to forgive my brother," she said as Oliver went into a fist pumping dance. "This really was a long shot. No one thought he could pull it off. You were his secret weapon, though he'll never admit it. He's actually quite fond of you. He won't admit that, either."

I turned and stared out the window. The balcony door was open and I saw the little bistro table where Albert served Dev and I our coffee when we woke up. We would sit out on the balcony in our robes with Danny and discuss what we needed to do that day. I wouldn't do that ever again.

My eyes filled with tears and I thought about the promise I had made Dev that day not so long ago. I needed to find a way to wait for them. "What happens next?"

Oliver stopped his happy dance and regarded me seriously for the first time. "Well, Daniel begins the new Council. He takes his place on the throne, but he shares power with those around him. It's going to be a time of change for the whole supernatural world. It's very exciting."

I was sure it would be an exciting time but that wasn't what I meant. "What happens with me?"

Oliver's handsome face became very serious and he caught his siblings' eyes. They took a moment and I knew they were having some sort of internal discussion, probably an argument over how much to tell the little human. I just stood. There wasn't an exit sign or something that pointed the way back to my body. I was stuck and there wasn't a damn thing I could do about it.

They finally came to some sort of consensus.

"What happens next is up to you, Zoey," Felicity said.

I perked up because I hadn't been expecting that. "What do you mean?"

Oliver crossed his arms. "Well, we discussed it and we agree with you. It doesn't seem particularly fair, given your unique nature, that you not be given a choice. Up until this point our whole endeavor has been dependent on the choices you made. You affected everyone around you with your decisions, and it seems wrong somehow to take that away from you at the end. It wasn't like you wanted that vampire to shoot you a whole bunch of times and end up dying in a cesspool."

"It wouldn't have been my first choice, no." I didn't like to think of my ignominious death. Somehow I expected it to be cleaner.

Jude took over. "It occurs to us that your death would probably bring the other side an enormous amount of satisfaction. There are events coming up in the future that you would probably play an important part in if you survived."

I didn't have a whole bunch of fans on the Hell plane but I also knew that the Heaven plane tended to follow the rules to the letter.

Felicity read my mind. "We're merely bending the rules, Zoey."

Oliver laughed. "Oh, don't be so understated, Felicity. We're breaking the rules here, but they don't play fair so why should we?"

"Tweaking is a more accurate term, brother," Jude argued.

"Just freaking tell me what you mean." They would argue semantics forever if I didn't interrupt.

"Fine," Oliver replied. "Let us say we're taking a page from the other team's playbook. Even now, Neil has discovered your body and taken it to Daniel. He's attempting to revive you. Technically, you're dead."

I nodded. I was here so I got that. "And not technically?"

Felicity walked around the couch and put her arm around my shoulder. "Vampire blood can do amazing things, Zoey. Who's to say he can't bring you back? Who's to say it wasn't the vampire blood that brought you back rather than us?"

"We're betting no one asks," Jude said.

"Besides," Oliver admitted with a grin. "If it's not supposed to work then the big boss will stop us. We'll get a stern lecture and be sent on our way. Despite what you humans think, he's not big into punishment."

My hopes were starting to soar. I was willing to go back into that broken body if it meant being with Danny and Dev again. "Okay, let's get on with it."

Oliver held up a hand. "Not so fast, Zoey. I said you have to make a choice. The Heaven plane is a nice place. It's safe and you'll never feel alone or have a moment's worry again. When you join us, you'll know everything. All those question you have will be answered. There's peace and serenity and knowledge here. It isn't something to be taken lightly."

"If you go back," Felicity began, "you will face more adversity and I can't promise that it will all go well."

"I'm willing to take that chance." I bit my lip because I wasn't sure I wanted the answer to my next question. That bullet had been awfully close to my pelvis. "Are my babies all right or did I lose them?"

Jude's blue eyes were sympathetic. "That's up to you, Zoey. The vampire blood will work on the fetus that was slightly injured, but there could be implications for the future."

"What?" I heard the panic in my voice.

"I can't tell you the specifics," he said. "You either accept the child or you don't."

There was no hesitation in me. "I'll take him." I didn't care if he had struggles. I would be there and so would Danny and Dev. We would help him. We would get through it as a family.

"He might be a handful," Felicity said thoughtfully. "That one is a recycled soul. They come with some baggage, but I doubt you'll mind. He was very insistent on having you as his mother. If you go back, your path will be set and so will your sons' paths."

Oliver gestured to the kitchen. "Perhaps you should talk to someone who's been here before you make your decision."

"Hello, darlin'," a low voice said.

My eyes filled with happy tears. "Lee!" I rushed to my wolf and threw my arms around him. I kissed his cheek, so overjoyed to know he was here. "I am so…"

"Don't," he growled. He pushed me back so I could see his stubborn face. "Don't you say you're sorry. I did what I did to save you. I wouldn't take it back for the world. My little pack is fine and that's all I could have hoped for."

I ran my hands across his face, assuring myself he was here and he was real. His skin was rough against my hand. He didn't bother to shave even in Heaven. His wardrobe hadn't improved either. He was still in jeans and a slightly rumpled T-shirt. I found it wholly endearing. "So how is Heaven treating you?"

He chuckled, his chest moving with his laughter. "The beer's pretty good and boy do they know how to make a burger. It's a nice place, but I think you won't be staying, will you?"

My heart ached at the thought of leaving him again, but I had other obligations, including those babies of mine. "No, I have to go back."

He grinned. The smile on his face was freer than any emotion I'd seen on him before. He looked young and carefree. That piece of Lee that always seemed to be somewhere else was gone now. He was here, completely, and happy to be. The Heaven plane had done wonders for my wolf. "We were kind of hoping you would say that."

Now I realized Lee wasn't the only newcomer. There another man standing in the doorway of the kitchen, and I would have guessed from the pushed back chairs that they had been sitting at the table together. There was a deck of playing cards on the countertop.

"I've been trying to teach him how to play Hold'em," Lee said with a shake of his head. He glanced back at the other male with great affection. "He's complete crap. He can't bluff to save his life."

I stared at the young man, who appeared to be seventeen or so. His lanky body had yet to fill out. He had gorgeous silky black hair and emerald green eyes. The expression on his face was so sweet as he watched me.

He was the spitting image of my husband.

"Is that—?" I couldn't quite finish the question because I was pretty sure who he was.

Lee smiled and this time his eyes were watery. "He's your son. He isn't allowed to talk to you, but he wants to. He's brand new so I've spent my time here filling him in. I've told him all about you and Daniel and Dev. The angels are only letting me talk to you because they want you to make an informed decision. It could get rough in a couple of years. You've earned your peace, Zoey. If you want to rest, we'll understand."

I shook my head as I stared at the dark-haired boy and memorized every inch of that face I wouldn't see again until he was grown. I felt a deep connection open between us and I hoped he felt my love for him. He was my son, the boy I'd lost and mourned and never stopped hoping for. "I don't want to rest. I want all of it. I want the good and crappy and everything in between. I want my life. If it gets rough, then I'll have to be tough, won't I?"

Lee hugged me again. "You are. You'll get through all of it. We'll get through all of it." He said that last bit with an emphasis on the "we."

I pulled back as the implications hit me. I was having twins. I had two boys. "Recycled soul?"

Lee's face lit up. "I was given a choice, too. I know where I want to be. I would promise to be a very good kid, but we both know that would be a lie. I'll probably be hell on wheels."

My hands shook and I held him so tightly, I thought I might never let go, and I was gloriously happy that I wouldn't have to. He would be mine again, but this time I would be the one to protect him. He would get everything I had.

"Zoey," Oliver said solemnly from behind me. "Time to make your decision."

I kissed Lee's cheek again and thought about the fact that the next time I kissed him would be about eight months from now. I waved at the man who would be with him when the time came. His grin looked so much like his dad's my heart seized. He was going to break some hearts that one.

"I'm ready to go back," I announced.

"I knew you would." Oliver put his hands on my shoulders and his blue eyes were solemn. "It is an honor to watch over you, Zoey. I know I can be a jerk sometimes but know that I'll continue to do my best to keep you safe. Just remember, whatever happens, you're never alone."

"Thank you," I said gratefully. "So how exactly do I get home?"

Felicity gestured to the balcony. "Do what you do best, Zoey. Take a leap of faith."

I laughed. I had promised myself I would never jump off a perfectly good building again, but that was one promise I was going to break. I glanced back at Lee and his brother watching me.

"I love you. See you soon, Mom," Lee said, his arm around his brother's shoulder.

I nodded at my sons, too filled with emotion to speak. Then I turned and ran, my heart pumping with joy. I leapt over the balcony and I was free.

When the pain came I took every instant of it because it meant I was back. I opened my eyes to see the bright lights of the arena all around me.

"Oh goddess, Daniel, it's working," I heard Dev say, his voice hoarse. His hands were on mine and I felt him squeezing. "Give her more. She's coming back. She's coming back."

I swallowed and tried not to gag because my mouth was already full of blood. I breathed deeply through my nose, ignoring the pain in my chest. The blood slid down my throat and immediately went to work.

Daniel wasn't waiting. He shoved his wrist against my mouth for what was probably the hundredth time. I could tell from the relief in his face that he'd been opening his wrist for a while. He was pale and I knew that he would have sat there until he was empty trying to bring me back. I reached up and touch his cheek.

He brought his forehead down to touch mine. "Don't you leave me, Z. Don't you dare leave me."

He'd been crying and I could see Dev was emotional as well. His face was stark and his eyes were red. I drank for a moment, letting the blood heal me and the child Marini had injured. After a minute, I pushed Daniel's arm away.

"Are you sure?" he asked, perfectly willing to give me more though I could see he was low.

"Yes, baby, I'm fine." I let him help me sit up. I was still wicked tired. Dying will do that to you, so I leaned against his chest. Dev was right there, folding his arms around my waist and laying his head on my shoulder. We sat together in the sand for a moment.

"She's all right?" I heard Neil ask.

"Thanks to you," Daniel said, and I heard the gratitude in his voice. He looked down as he stroked my hair. "Neil heard you screaming. He punched through the hidden door and tracked you down."

"You were face down in the water, Z." Neil's voice was shaky as he spoke. "I had to get you to Daniel. It was hard, but I stayed me."

I knew what he was talking about, but the others glossed over his last statement. The blood and adrenaline had almost brought out that strange new side of him, but he'd kept it together for my sake. He'd saved my life. I mouthed the words "thank you" and "I love you."

My father put a grateful arm around Neil and thanked him himself.

"Marcus." I'd been forced to leave him. I couldn't stand the thought that he was a pile of ash somewhere in those sewers.

"Is feeling better, *cara*." He stepped into view and I was happy to see him. He was pale and his hands shook slightly, but he was walking around. "Neil took note of my almost-corpse and sent Hugo and Henri back to find me. They revived me in no time at all. I'm very old. I can take a lot of damage. I heard everything Louis did while I lay there, Zoey. I was so sorry I could not help you."

Daniel hugged me tightly, thinking about what could have happened. "You did everything we could have asked for, Marcus." He looked over my head at Dev. "The babies?"

"They're fine," I tried to assure Danny but Bris was already laying hands on me. His warmth filled me. I hadn't known just how cold I was.

"Our goddess is correct," Bris said. "The babies are fine. But something has changed. I can't put my finger on it, but one of them has been slightly altered. They're no longer completely identical. I don't think it's anything to worry about. They're strong and active."

I would take that. I happened to know my boys were more than fine.

My wounds had healed, and Dev laid his head down over my stomach. "We almost lost you."

I let my hands find his hair and thought of how much our sons would look like him. "I'm not going anywhere, baby." I glanced up at Neil, who was surrounded by my dad, Christine, Sarah, and Felix. Zack moved in to get close to the action. I had a story for that wolf. "But I think I'll need that bail fund."

Chapter Forty

Eight months later

"Just a little bit more, my goddess," Dev said, holding my hand.

I stared at my husband. He looked close to perfect while I was a disgusting, sweaty mess. "You think it's just a little bit more, Dev? You really think so? Well, if it's so fucking easy, Dev, then I'd like to see you do it, you son of a bitch."

I ground out my words as another contraction hit and I pushed as hard as I could. The other thing I did was squeeze Dev's hand until I thought it would break.

"See, you are doing so well, my sweet little goddess." Dev grimaced and winced as he let me squeeze his hand. He'd managed to keep that soft, encouraging tone for all ten hours of my labor, even when I screamed obscenities at him and promised he would never touch me again.

"You should stop talking now, Dev," Sarah said with a knowing smile. She was sitting on a stool at the end of the bed where I was giving birth to twins. Sarah had served as my midwife/confidante for the duration of my pregnancy. I was willing to listen to her. Felix and their sweet little Mia were in another room of the condo with our entire strange family waiting for news.

"I'm supposed to coach her," Dev insisted.

"You were supposed to get me drugs when they would have worked, asshole," I snarled at him.

"I told you to get her an epidural," Daniel said from the back of the room. I forgave him for not standing too close. The blood would get to him.

"She said she didn't want one," Dev replied. "She didn't want to go to the hospital. She told me to deny her one because she wanted the birth to be natural."

"And you were stupid enough to believe her, Your Grace." The Fae healer who was overseeing the birth laughed. Miria had sent the woman herself. So far she'd merely watched over and approved of everything Sarah had done. She was also heartily amused at the way I was giving Dev hell.

I groaned as another horrible wave hit me and I bore down.

"It's too late now." Sarah clapped her gloved hands together. "Here we go. Zoey, you're crowning. I see the first one's head."

"Oh, god," Daniel moaned, putting his hands over his eyes. "That just sounds horrible."

"You shut up," I yelled at him. "You might be smarter than him to stay out of my range but I can get you later, vampire."

Then I was done talking. Grunting, crying, and screaming were my preferred mode of communication for the next few minutes. I pushed harder than I ever had in my life. I held on to Dev and, despite my words from earlier, I was so grateful to have him grasping my hand.

"He's out," Sarah said happily. "Oh, Z, he's so beautiful."

She quickly cut the cord. She passed my first son to the Fae healer, who cleaned and wrapped him carefully and handed him to Dev. He seemed shocked to be holding a small bundle of life in his hands.

"Congratulations, Your Grace," she said.

Suddenly the blood wasn't so daunting to Daniel and he moved in to take Dev's place because I wasn't done.

"Don't kill me, Z," he said, his voice breathless.

"No promises." I squeezed him every bit as hard as I had Dev.

Our second son was born two minutes after the first. The healer cleaned off the second boy carefully and gave him to Daniel, who took him with shaking hands. He and Dev shared a glance as they moved in close to me.

"We have babies," Daniel said as though he was trying to make it real in his head. "Which one is which? Didn't Bris say they weren't identical? They look pretty alike to me."

I held my shaky arms out and took the first boy from Dev. I smoothed back the downy bit of fluff covering his little head and he opened his eyes for the first time. I knew exactly who he was.

"Hello, Lee," I said as he fastened his chocolate eyes on me. The brand new baby yawned as though the birthing process had been a tiring one. Then he opened his mouth and let loose with a yell.

"I think he's hungry," Sarah said with a smile.

"Then that one is definitely Lee," Dev agreed.

I pulled down my gown, exposing a breast. I was prepared for breastfeeding to be hard, but this baby was a natural. He latched on and sighed as he started to suck. I cuddled him to me and he was safe and warm. I had told my husbands of the brief time I spent on the Heaven plane. They had been very interested, but I think they thought I'd had an odd dream. They'd been fine with me naming one of our sons Lee, however.

"Well, Rhys has my eyes," Dev said, proudly looking down at the baby in Daniel's arms.

"Let's hope he has my intelligence," Daniel said with a goofy grin. He was fascinated with the child he held in his big hands. "Then he'll know to stay out of his mama's way when she's yelling like that."

"I wasn't that bad," I said because the yelling seemed like it had happened to another person. Now there was just peace and a great sense of relief. They were here.

"You threatened to cut off my balls with a pair of rusty scissors at one point," Dev said. He looked at Daniel. "Let me hold Rhys. I haven't gotten to hold him yet."

Daniel held him carefully to move him to Dev's arms. "Hey, watch it. You've got to support the head."

Dev held Rhys close to his body and gave Daniel a dirty look. "I'm a fertility god, Daniel. I think I know how to hold a baby."

"No," Danny replied smugly. "You know how to make 'em. You practically slept through our childcare class."

It had been an interesting couple of days. We were the only ones there as a threesome. We had coyly refused to answer questions and, much to the boys' dismay, the consensus had been that I was a surrogate for their infertile love. I had not corrected that impression.

"Stop fighting," Sarah said. "Now, go. Show off the baby who isn't nursing. Zoey needs to rest."

Dev looked down at me. "Thank you, my goddess. Our sons are beautiful." He kissed me soundly and I had no desire to let a pair of rusty scissors get anywhere close to him now. "I have to go inform my brother that I have two sons to his one."

Danny leaned over and kissed me as well. His hand covered Lee's tiny head as he fell asleep. "I love you, Z. I...god, baby, it's so much more than I could have hoped for."

I nodded and we watched our son sleep.

I woke up many hours later to find myself alone in bed. I smiled and was very grateful for the swift recovery Daniel's blood offered me. Though I had only given birth hours before, I felt marvelous. My eyes adjusted to the dimness in the room, and I noticed that the light in the nursery we'd built was on.

When I opened the door, I saw Zack sitting in a rocking chair holding a baby. He looked up at me and he was crying unashamedly.

"I didn't believe you," he said.

The baby squirmed, already trying to get out of his swaddling.

I had told Zack about seeing Lee in Heaven. He'd hugged me and told me how nice that was. Now he had to believe. I put a hand on his shoulder.

"Zoey, this is my brother," he said, emotion choking his voice. "He smells like Lee. How is that possible?"

"Heaven works in mysterious ways," I replied, letting the baby grab my finger. He was already so strong.

Zack sniffled before laughing and running a gentle hand over the baby's head. He leaned over and kissed him. "Well hello, Lee. Hello again, my brother. You had it rough before, but it's going to be different this time. You won't ever feel alone. I'm going to be your Uncle Zack, and I promise to help you with all the crazy stuff you and your brother will come up with." He passed the baby to me. "And that's your mom. You couldn't ask for better than her, Lee." Zack gave me a quick hug. "I'll see you in the morning, Zoey. Trent wants to go over the new protocols we'll use with the kids."

"Night, Zack," I said, sitting down in the rocker. I rocked gently and heard Rhys making sweet little baby sounds in his crib. I thought about everything that had happened since that day in the arena.

Daniel was the formally acknowledged King of all Vampire. He had spent months forming the new Council and while the politics still gave him a horrible headache, his chief advisor actually enjoyed all the intrigue. Dev was a master politician and since the war, he'd been enjoying the acceptance of those in Daniel's circle. He'd reconciled with his brother, who was a frequent visitor, along with his mother.

Sarah and Felix moved back to Dallas and Felix was finishing his degree in counseling. They had moved into our building with their daughter, Mia. Sarah's hair was a sunny yellow and it matched her perpetual mood now.

Marcus was the elected representative of Vampire. He held the seat and was discovering he enjoyed the political side of a true government. I still caught him looking wistful at times. I could only hope he would find that woman who could make him complete.

Neil and Chad moved in together one floor down from us. Since he'd pushed the beast down to save my life, Neil had reported no further incidents, but I was nervous. He didn't want to investigate further, preferring to enjoy his new, settled life with his lover and I hesitated to disturb his peace. I worried that we would have to deal with it eventually. These problems didn't just disappear.

The door opened and Danny and Dev walked in.

"There you are," Daniel said with a dimpled smile.

Dev went over and picked up his sleeping son and settled into the rocking chair beside me. Daniel sank into his and the three of us rocked, passing the babies between us. We sat like that, peacefully watching the light grow in the sky.

As for me, I learned a lot over the last few years. I learned to really accept the love that is given to me. I have learned to accept myself for who I am. I've realized that I have many names and many titles.

I am the Queen of All Vampire and in Fae society they call me Your Grace, but those fancy things don't hold a candle to my favorite titles. I am my father's daughter. I am Daniel and Dev's wife. I am Lee and Rhys's mom.

Because I am all of these things, I am the one thing I never thought I could be—happy.

Zoey, Daniel, Dev and the whole crew will return in a series featuring a brand-new heroine with ties to them they can't imagine. Join me for Ripper: Hunter: A Thieves Series, now available.

Ripper
Hunter, Book 1
A Thieves Novel
By Lexi Blake
Now available.

Kelsey Atwood is a private detective with a problem. She came from a family of hunters, growing up on the wrong side of the supernatural world. Tracking down bail jumpers and deadbeat dads may not make her a lot of friends, but it's a lot safer than the life she turned her back on. She was hoping to escape from the nightmares of her past, but her latest case has brought them right back to her door.

A young woman has gone missing, and she didn't go willingly. When Kelsey discovers that the girl is actually a shifter, she knows she should drop the case and walk away. But this shifter was a sweet kid, and she's in serious trouble. More females are missing and the evidence points to a legendary killer. Bodies are piling up, and her case is becoming center stage for a conflict that could shatter the fragile peace between wolves and vampires.

As the hunt intensifies, she finds herself trapped between two men—Gray, a magnetic half-demon lawman, and the ancient vampire Marcus Vorenus. Both men call to her, but when a shocking secret about Kelsey's family is revealed, it could ruin them all. To stop the killer, she will have to embrace the truth about who—and what—she truly is.

$$\sim\!\!\infty\!\!\sim$$

"They make a beautiful family," a voice said from the doorway. He was backlit from the blue light coming from the club and I only saw his silhouette.

I turned quickly, hoping he wouldn't catch me crying. I wiped away the obnoxious evidence of my self-pity. "Yes, they're lovely."

One minute he was behind me and the next he was right in front of me. His hand cupped my jaw, his thumb gently rubbing across my

445

cheek, sweeping away the tear caught there. I should have backed away, but I was too surprised to move. Vampires are fast.

"Did Devinshea make you cry?" the vampire asked with a melodic accent. Italian, I realized as I recognized the man from last night. "He can be rude though not usually with a woman. Should I talk to him?"

"Marcus Vorenus." It came out as a breathy revelation.

In the dim light of the office, I saw a smile break over the vampire's face. It tugged his lips up and caused his dark eyes to crinkle appealingly. It took him from a gorgeous work of art to something far more dangerous. He was just a handsome, approachable man when he smiled.

"You're the girl from the club." He sounded like he was happy to have found me again.

"I am." I had to wonder if I would be crying if I'd followed through on my initial instinct and taken Marcus up on his invitation that night. I probably wouldn't be standing here crying over Grayson Sloane.

He stepped back and dropped his hand. He seemed a bit wary now. "You came to look for me?"

"No." I wished a little I could lie to him. "I'm a private investigator. I'm here on a...murder case. Mr. Quinn just kind of became my new client. He said I needed an escort so I suppose he picked you. And I wasn't stalking you or anything. I was staking the place out and you just happened to be there."

He looked amused as he leaned back against the desk. "An investigator? Very interesting. You must be a good investigator since you already know my name. Why don't you tell me yours?"

"Kelsey Atwood." I wondered if someone was laughing at me. I'd just gotten dumped by one guy out of my league. Now I was standing alone in a room with another too beautiful man, and I was determined not to make an idiot of myself over this one.

"Kelsey. An interesting name for an interesting girl," the vampire said. "It used to be a surname. Old English, I believe."

"I have no idea. I think my mom just liked the sound of it. Are you really two thousand years old?" He looked like he was maybe thirty-five.

His head moved ever so slightly, an aristocratic gesture in the negative. "Not quite. If you include the twenty-two years I walked the plane as a human, I have one thousand nine hundred and seventy-four years."

I stared at him, thinking about what that meant.

"Tell me, Kelsey." His mouth turned down as he stared back at me. "Give me the first thought you had when I told you just how old I am."

He seemed really interested, so I gave him my honest answer. "I thought that was a lot of time for regrets."

He was in my space again. "Almost all humans have a different reaction. They say how much I must have seen and how amazing it must be to never have to die."

"I guess it says something about me." I wished I'd given him a less than honest answer, but it was me and I didn't see a reason to hide it. "I think about what you must have lost along the way. I don't think I'd want to be immortal."

He didn't touch me. I knew all I had to do was ask and he would. "Do you belong to the demon, little Kelsey?"

"No," I said quietly. "He doesn't want me now."

"But you want him."

All I had to do was say no and I knew the vampire would offer himself to me. We had a strange connection, Marcus Vorenus and I, and if I hadn't met Gray when I did I would have been all over him. But I had met Gray and even though he'd walked out on me, it seemed too soon to consider anyone else. "Yes," I said and I heard the longing in my own voice.

"He is a fool." The vampire backed up. His face was once again pleasant, but without the emotion that previously lit it. This was Marcus as he wanted the world to see him—cool and regal, distant. "But then aren't we all? I thought, for a moment, that Devinshea was doing me a favor. I thought, perhaps, I was reading too much into our situation. I see he's still playing a game with me."

The vampire sounded bitter, and I hated the fact that I'd made him feel that way. "I'm sorry. I wasn't trying…"

"It isn't your fault, dear girl. You must be careful around the fertility god. He always knows what he is doing when he puts two people in an intimate situation. He knew I would be attracted to you. He knew you're precisely the type of female to catch my attention. He also knew you're involved with another man. It's his way of telling me it is time to go home, that there is nothing here for me."

A wave of disappointment rolled over me. I'd been looking forward to his company, but I didn't want to hurt him further. He seemed sad enough as it was, as though the world had turned on him. I didn't want to add to his troubles. "I'll ask Mr. Quinn for another escort. I'm sorry to have taken up your time. I'll just wait here for him. I'm sure he'll be back."

I sat down again in the chair where I'd talked to Quinn and tried to hold myself with as much dignity as I could muster. I prayed the next vampire he sent me was obnoxious and unattractive.

Marcus kneeled at my side. "I'm sorry, Kelsey. I shouldn't have tried to drag you into my troubles with Devinshea and Daniel. My only excuse is that I've been thinking of you ever since I saw you last night. I'm a bit tired of wanting women I cannot have."

Now I was the slightly bitter one. "Well, Vorenus, then stick by my side. I can assure you after you spend a little time with me, you'll change your mind. They all do after I pull a gun on them or yell too much. And this," I gestured to the dress and shoes, "ain't me. This is someone else's magic. I'm a jeans and T-shirts kind of girl, and I don't do relationships well, obviously. I drink too much, cuss too much, and can be very unpleasant to be around. I think you'll discover your heart is perfectly safe around me if you give me the chance to annoy you."

Marcus's eyes closed and a rueful smile took over his lips. "He knows me so well." He sighed and opened his eyes, holding out his hand for me. "Let us forget this portion of the evening and begin again. I am Marcus Vorenus, your escort. Consider me your knight and your guide. So, tell me, Kelsey, how may aid you? I am entirely at your service."

Author's Note

I'm often asked by generous readers how they can help get the word out about a book they enjoyed. There are so many ways to help an author you like. Leave a review. If your e-reader allows you to lend a book to a friend, please share it. Go to Goodreads and connect with others. Recommend the books you love because stories are meant to be shared. Thank you so much for reading this book and for supporting all the authors you love!

About Lexi Blake

New York Times bestselling author Lexi Blake lives in North Texas with her husband and three kids. Since starting her publishing journey in 2010, she's sold over three million copies of her books. She began writing at a young age, concentrating on plays and journalism. It wasn't until she started writing romance that she found success. She likes to find humor in the strangest places and believes in happy endings.

Connect with Lexi online:

Facebook: Lexi Blake
Twitter: authorlexiblake
Website: www.LexiBlake.net
Instagram: www.instagram.com